PLAYING WITH FIRE

JAYNE DAVIS

Verbena
Books

Manuscript development: Antonia Maguire

Copyediting & proofreading: Sue Davison

Cover design: Spiffing Covers & P Johnson

ACKNOWLEDGEMENTS

Thanks to my critique partners on Scribophile for comments and suggestions, particularly Alex, Adam, David, Daphne, Jean, Jim, Thomas, and Violetta.

Thanks also to Beta readers Tina, Cilla, Dawn, Doris, Helen, Kristen, Leigh, Mary, Sue, and Wendy.

MAPS

FRANCE AND SOUTHERN ENGLAND

Some places in France and southern England mentioned in the text. Fictional places are underlined.

PLACES IN THE MEDITERRANEAN

CHAPTER 1

rance, 5th February, 1793

"We will stop here," the Comtesse de Calvac declared. She sat back against the velvet squabs, straightening her redingote and tucking her hands into her fur muff as the coach jolted round a corner.

Phoebe, sitting across from her aunt, twisted round to look out of the window. A fine drizzle misted the flat landscape and the bare trees. She could just make out an inn ahead, with houses lining the road either side of it.

Phoebe curled her fingers, nails digging into her palms. "It's still daylight, Aunt," she said, keeping her voice calm. "We could get beyond the next town before we need to stop. We only travelled thirty miles yesterday." Now France had declared war on Britain, they needed to reach the coast as quickly as they could and find a boat to take them to England.

"Oh, don't be silly, Phoebe," Cousin Hélène said. "I'm hungry, and I'm tired of being bumped and jolted."

"We are stopping," the comtesse repeated. "See to it, Anson."

The steward lolled at the other end of the rearward facing seat, his eyes closed, lines of strain on his face even in sleep. Phoebe leaned over and shook his shoulder.

"Anson!" The comtesse's voice was shrill. The steward awoke with a start.

"I want a rest from this infernal jolting," the comtesse said. "See to it."

"But Aunt," Phoebe tried again, "if we stop now, the journey to the coast will take even longer. It isn't safe." The innkeeper last night had taken too close an interest in their papers for her peace of mind. Only the sight of extra coins had distracted him from scrutinising their travel documents.

"Don't argue with me, Phoebe. I've had enough of you and your opinions these last few days. Remember your place."

"But Madame—" Anson began.

"We are stopping!"

The steward's shoulders sagged. He took up the stick from the seat next to him and banged it on the roof of the coach. As he pulled the glass down to call to the driver, an icy blast of air made Phoebe shiver. By the time he had refastened the window, the vehicle was pulling into the inn yard.

Anson picked up the small strong-box resting near his feet and climbed out of the coach. Phoebe clutched her cloak around her and followed him into the building. As they entered the taproom, the innkeeper came out from behind the bar and Anson asked for rooms in his halting French.

"*Combien de chambres?*" the innkeeper asked impatiently.

Anson glanced at Phoebe and shrugged.

"A room for three," Phoebe said in French. She didn't want to share a room with her aunt and cousin, but it was the safest option. She asked for a separate room for Anson and a bed somewhere for her aunt's maid. Masson and Dubois, the driver and guard, would sleep over the stables.

The innkeeper sniffed at Phoebe's shabby gown and cloak before leading the way upstairs. The large double bed took up over half the floor in the room he showed them, leaving little space for the truckle bed that Phoebe would be forced to use.

"Is this the best room you have?" she asked.

The man shrugged. "Take it or leave it. The servants can sleep in the attic rooms."

"We'll take it," she said, her heart sinking. Her aunt would not like it. It would be Phoebe's fault, or Anson's. It usually was.

They went back downstairs to find the comtesse inspecting the dingy hallway with downturned mouth. The maid, Jeanne, trailed in, her face pinched with cold from travelling outside. She carried the comtesse's jewel box and Hélène's book.

"Jeanne, see that those men take the trunks to the correct room," the comtesse said, "and make sure there's a fire." She had, at least, remembered to speak French. The maid bobbed a curtsey and followed Anson up the stairs.

"Send chocolate to the parlour," the comtesse ordered. The innkeeper nodded and retreated.

"Oh, yes, Mama, that will be lovely," Hélène said. "I'm glad we stopped. The jolting in the coach was horrid."

Despite the fire, the air in the parlour was chilly. The comtesse crossed the room, deposited her muff on a table, and held her hands out to the flames, shielding what warmth there was from everyone else. Phoebe frowned as she took in the four oak tables with chairs, and two benches by the fire. She had assumed this was a private room, but it looked as though it might be the main dining room. Her aunt would not be happy if the inn was too small to have another room downstairs.

"If we had outriders, they could have made sure everything was ready for us," the comtesse complained. "It was much more comfortable when we came over from England last month. I am not used to travelling like this. Monsieur de Calvac will have something to say to Anson about this when we get to London."

"*Tante*, it is not wise to draw attention to ourselves," Phoebe said, as she had many times before. And with as little expectation of being heeded.

"Nonsense! Why do you always think you know best, Phoebe? It is not a pleasant characteristic. No wonder you are still unwed at twenty."

Phoebe kept her expression blank. After four years of living with her aunt, it was getting a little easier to ignore the constant disparaging remarks. She took the comtesse's cloak when it was held out to her, draping it over the back of a nearby chair.

Her aunt sat down at a table close to the fire, smoothing her skirts. "Sit here, Hélène. Make sure you are not sitting in a draught—you do not want to catch cold. A red nose is *not* attractive, and we don't want anything to impede you making a splendid match this year."

"Yes, Mama." Hélène draped her cloak over the back of another chair. "I hope the dinner will be better tonight." She wrinkled her nose. "It was not very nice yesterday."

Phoebe had enjoyed the roasted capon the previous evening, but perhaps Hélène was bemoaning the lack of pastries and fruit. No doubt the absent outriders would have chosen a larger inn.

Half an hour later the room was pleasantly warm, the hot chocolate had arrived and been drunk, and the other two had gone upstairs to change. Phoebe moved closer to the fire, although the chill within her was due to apprehension.

Travelling alone, as her uncle had instructed, Anson would have retrieved the estate papers he'd been sent for and been safely back in England by now. Instead, while the comte was away from London on business, her aunt had insisted on accompanying the steward. Hélène had wanted to see her old home at Calvac again, and Phoebe had been brought along too—to help Anson translate, she suspected. Her aunt had said she wanted to retrieve some jewellery that had been left at Calvac when they all moved to England over a year ago, but Phoebe wasn't sure she believed her. Her uncle would not be pleased to find all three of them absent when he returned to London.

Tension behind her eyes signalled an impending headache, and she massaged her temples. If she was lucky, it would take Jeanne at least an hour to help the comtesse change and re-powder her hair, and then assist Hélène. Phoebe couldn't understand why her aunt thought it so important to put on an evening gown to dine in a roadside inn with no-one to see except her steward. Besides, it seemed particularly ill-advised to flaunt wealth in these revolutionary times.

Phoebe leaned her head against the rear of the chair and closed her eyes, but she could not relax. The knot of tension in her middle was still there, as it had been for the last fortnight.

The news of the king's execution had reached them shortly after they'd crossed the Channel, when they were only two days into their journey to Calvac. Protests from both Phoebe and Anson against continuing the journey had fallen on deaf ears. The comtesse had insisted she was an English aristocrat by birth, and their travel papers were in order, so they would continue. Only when word reached Calvac that Britain and France were at war were they able to persuade the comtesse that they should return to England as soon as possible.

The coach was a worry, too, emphasising the wealth within. Her aunt had decided to use the coach kept at the château rather than hiring one. Phoebe had persuaded Anson to get the crest on the doors painted out, to much complaint from her aunt, but Anson's apology and explanation that the paint could not be removed had finally silenced her.

The gentle crackling from the fire soothed Phoebe's aching head, almost drowning out the muffled noise from the taproom beyond the closed door. Dozing, she started as something touched her ankle, then smiled at the sight of a black cat curling up by the fire.

Phoebe pulled her sketchbook out of the pockets she wore beneath her gown and made a quick drawing, using short strokes of her pencil to give it texture. Then, longing for the happiness and security of the home she'd had to leave four years ago, she tried to draw what she could remember of Beech House. She added her father setting off in his gig to see a patient, and her mother cutting flowers in the garden.

Her uncle had shown no sign of resenting the need to support his wife's sixteen-year-old niece after Phoebe's parents died, but he left her to her aunt's supervision. The comtesse thought that her niece should be grateful to be living in luxury with her titled relatives. Phoebe would have traded it all for the chance to turn the clock back, to have her parents still alive.

Turning the pages, she paused at the watercolours of Caribbean islands she'd painted based on the descriptions in Joe's letters, wondering if her images looked anything like the real places her brother mentioned. She wasn't likely to get the chance to see for herself.

The next drawings were of Georges, Hélène's young brother, gawping at spears and shrunken heads in the museum on a trip with his governess. Miss Bryant was a friend, and Phoebe enjoyed accompanying the two of them to see the sights in London.

She smiled at the caricature of her aunt on the packet boat crossing the Channel, her face tinted a pale green. The remaining sketches were scenes of the countryside near Calvac, done to distract herself from worries about their safety.

Putting the sketchbook away, she closed her eyes until she heard her aunt's voice in the hallway—finding fault as usual. If she went upstairs to freshen up now, she might get another half hour of peace before dinner.

CHAPTER 2

*L*ights glimmered in the distance, and Alex sighed with relief as an inn sign came into view. It had been dark for an hour, and the earlier drizzle had turned to sleet. The tired horses clattered over the cobbled yard to the stables, and Alex dismounted stiffly. Although bone-weary, he volunteered to get the horses stabled while Hugo de Brevare enquired about rooms.

A pile of hay in the stable loft would be fine, he thought, as he unsaddled the animals and rubbed them down with a cloth thrown to him by a stable boy. Anywhere would do, as long as he could lie down and rest. Various parts of his anatomy were reminding him that he hadn't ridden for months, let alone on such a sorry, jolting nag. He muttered a curse at himself as he stretched stiff muscles. Why in heaven's name had he allowed Brevare to buy the horses?

The activity was encouraging the blood to move in his hands and feet, helped by the comforting, if pungent, warmth coming off the horses. He threw his sodden greatcoat over a wooden partition, resisting the impulse to finger the lining again.

The place seemed in good repair. Several other horses were munching hay or dozing, and a coach stood in the yard. The light from the stable lanterns showed a deeply padded interior.

"Who does that belong to?" he asked the stable boy.

The lad shrugged, not looking away from the horse he was brushing. "Don't know. Their money's as good as anyone else's."

Alex raised an eyebrow—it wasn't the best of times to flaunt wealth across the countryside. When he'd finished with the horses, he crossed the yard to the inn. The taproom was warm, but crowded and noisy with voices. Brevare had a mug of ale waiting for him, having already downed most of his own.

"We've got a room each," Brevare said. "In the attics, and tiny, but they'll do."

Alex didn't mind; having a separate room would let him lock the door, and perhaps he might sleep instead of wondering what Brevare really wanted and what he might do. A few mouthfuls of ale revived him a little, and he glanced around, eyeing half a dozen new customers crowding into the room.

He attracted the attention of one of the serving women. "Busy tonight?" he asked, taking care to keep his accent close to the local one.

"Yes," the woman grimaced. "Apothecary's getting married." She pointed at a middle-aged man in the corner, better dressed than the rest. "He's treating all his customers on his last night of freedom. If you want a meal, citoyen, you'd best have it soon."

Alex drank more ale, wincing at a loud burst of laughter and the beginnings of an out-of-tune song. "Is there somewhere quieter? We'll have today's ordinary."

"Through there," the woman said, tilting her head to a door on the other side of the room. "I'll get it sent in."

The dining room was across a dim, stone-flagged passageway. Alex and Brevare entered behind two young serving women carrying platters of meat, cheese and pastries, and a bowl of stew. Alex's stomach rumbled as he breathed the rich smell of beef and vegetables. The two men put their bags on the floor by the door and draped their wet greatcoats over chairs.

The serving women went over to the table nearest the fire and began to transfer the dishes. An older woman gave sharp instructions about where to place them and how to move the chairs. Her hair was heavily powdered, dressed high on her head, and her embroidered gown had rather too much lace and too many knots of ribbon for dining in a wayside inn such as this. The carriage in the yard must belong to her. She appeared to be in her late thirties, but it was difficult to tell in the dim light. Her face, still almost unlined, would have been attractive without the downward droop of her lips that gave her a discontented expression.

A younger woman sat beside her, eyeing the dishes as they were set out. One corner of Alex's mouth turned up in appreciation. She had unpowdered golden hair, dressed loosely to frame her delicate heart-shaped face, and her pale blue gown curved nicely round a generous bosom. A daughter, from the facial resemblance.

Beyond the beauty, an older man in plain black sat next to another young woman in a shabby gown. All Alex could make out of this woman was a roundish face and a wide mouth, with some red curls escaping from beneath a simple cap, their colour clashing horribly with the orange of her gown. These two must be servants, allowed to eat with their mistress and her daughter, but kept at a proper distance.

Crossing to an empty table, Alex pulled a chair out and sat with his back to the wall. Brevare stood staring at the golden-haired woman until Alex leaned over, nudging his elbow. Brevare looked down at Alex and took his seat.

Once the table was finally arranged to the older woman's satisfaction, she sat down and dismissed the waiting women. The golden-haired beauty whispered something to her; the older woman looked in their direction, her brows drawing together.

"This is a private parlour," she said, her French oddly accented and her tone as sharp as her expression.

"It is the only parlour, *citoyenne*," Alex said. "Where else do you suggest we eat?"

"That is not my concern." She glared at them before turning back to the meal and transferring several slices of meat from a serving dish to her plate. The golden-haired one nudged her arm, and the older woman looked around again, her eyes widening as she saw that the two men had not moved.

"I am the Comtesse de Calvac," she announced. "Have some respect for your betters and leave us!"

"It is not wise—" The low voice came from the redhead, addressing the comtesse.

"I insist you leave the room." The comtesse's voice was louder and, if possible, more shrill than before.

Alex took a mouthful of ale, not stirring from his slouched position. He and Brevare were trying not to draw attention to themselves, but these aristos were not the people they needed to avoid. Another burst of raucous laughter from the taproom reminded him that this was still the best place to eat.

"How dare you defy me?" the comtesse demanded, getting to her feet.

"Surely you have heard, *citoyenne?*" Alex put deliberate insolence into his voice. "The abolition is nearly three years old. There are no more titles in France, and you are the comtesse of nothing at all."

The comtesse flushed an unbecoming red and tilted her head so she appeared to be looking down her nose. "I demand—"

"You do not own this inn." Alex cut across her words. "Nor have you paid for this parlour."

At that moment a serving woman entered with the meal Alex had ordered, setting the dishes out on their table.

"Ignore her and eat," Brevare said, picking up his fork.

The comtesse watched them, her lips set in a thin line. She turned her gaze away when Alex's eyes met hers, helping herself to more meat with jerky stabs of her fork.

Alex pulled his chair round to face his meal. The stew was hot, tasty, and filling, dispelling the last of the chill in his bones. After the long ride, both he and Brevare had second helpings, followed by a plate of cheese.

When he'd eaten his fill, Alex leaned back in his chair and studied the other table. The comtesse and her golden-haired daughter were playing cards. The redhead bent over a book on the table in front of her—drawing, perhaps. The older man's head rested on the back of his chair, his eyes closed and lines of fatigue clearly visible on his face.

"Brandy?" Brevare asked.

Alex shrugged. "If you want some." The sounds of a drunken song reached them from the taproom. "It might be some time before someone comes." He helped himself to more cheese.

Brevare stood, muttering a curse under his breath, then left the room.

The comtesse looked up as the door closed behind Brevare. "As you have finished your repast, surely you will allow us some privacy now?"

Her words were conciliatory, but her expression held the same disdain as before.

"This is not your inn, *citoyenne*. You do not have authority here," Alex said calmly, wanting only to sit in peace. His attic room would be cold and possibly damp.

"Please leave us. I am not used to using common dining rooms."

"New experiences keep life interesting, do they not?" he said, as if making polite conversation. There was a muffled sound from one of the comtesse's party. Alex glanced at the others at the table, but could not tell who had laughed.

The comtesse stiffened her back and threw down the cards she was holding. "I am the Comtesse de Calvac, whatever the upstart government of this country says, but I am also—"

"Aunt!" This time the interruption was sharp and loud, from the redhead. "Please—we should retire."

"Mama? Can we leave this room?" The soft voice of the golden-haired beauty had more effect, and the comtesse stood up.

"Very well." Moving round the table, she caught the arm of the woman in orange and pulled her to her feet. "I will not be told what to do by you. You should be seeing to my comfort, not forever scribbling in that book!" She snatched it up and threw it into the fire.

11

Alex saw a fleeting expression of dismay cross the younger woman's face before it became a blank mask. The comtesse kept a firm hold of her arm and swept her towards the door. The man in black moved to the fire, but was stopped by a hissed command from the comtesse, and reluctantly followed the rest of the party out of the room.

Alex got up and used the poker to push the book away from the edge of the fire. The cover had become somewhat scorched at the edges, but the comtesse's aim had been as poor as her manners. He dusted it off and was about to set it on the table when curiosity drove him to open it.

It was full of drawings, ranging from images of flowers and birds, intricate in detail and colouring, to sketches of trees, houses, and landscapes. Caricatures of the comtesse and her daughter almost made him laugh aloud—it was just as well the comtesse had attempted to burn the sketchbook, rather than confiscating it and finding those.

Mixed in with the realistic drawings and caricatures were what surely must be imagined scenes of ships on stormy seas, tropical islands, and mountains. The redhead was a dreamer, perhaps? A letter fell out as he turned the pages but, although curious, he tucked it back without opening it. Perusing her sketches without her leave had already been a violation of her privacy. He put the book into his pocket.

Brevare returned with a bottle and two glasses, glancing at the now-empty table by the fire. "I wonder what they're doing here," he said. "The comtesse is a harridan, but the daughter... she reminds..." He shook his head and poured a generous amount of brandy into both glasses, biting his lip.

"They are courting danger," Alex replied flatly, picking up his glass. "Flaunting their wealth and announcing their nobility." It was lucky for all of them that only he and Brevare had heard the comtesse.

They sat in silence for a while, Brevare staring morosely into the fire and Alex wondering what Brevare was thinking about. Finally, with the level of brandy in the bottle considerably lower than before, Brevare stood.

"I'm going to see if that serving wench fancies a bit of company." He picked up the bottle and took it with him.

There was more than one serving maid, but all Alex wanted now was a good night's sleep, so he headed upstairs to his room.

CHAPTER 3

he next morning, Phoebe woke well before dawn. She washed using the now-icy water left in the jug, then dressed and crept out of the room without waking her aunt or cousin. Downstairs, Anson was already in the taproom, attempting to make the innkeeper understand the comtesse's requirements. Jeanne had finished her breakfast, so Phoebe asked her to take coffee and rolls up to her aunt and cousin and get the two women dressed.

"I've asked for the coach to be ready in an hour," Anson said, keeping his voice low. "Could you check they understand? And do you think we should ask for some food to take with us, instead of stopping for lunch?"

"That would be wise, yes," Phoebe agreed, not looking forward to another day of trying to persuade her aunt to behave with more circumspection. She made the request to the innkeeper, who nodded and went off to the kitchen.

In the parlour, the two men from the previous evening ate at the same table, the smell of their coffee and rolls making her stomach rumble. Phoebe sighed as she saw the fire already blazing—she had hoped to rise early enough to see if any of her book had survived the flames. There was no sign of it, even in the ashes. Although she hadn't really expected to find it, she still felt a stab of disappointment. She was sorry to have lost the sketches, but more importantly, her latest letter from Joe had been tucked between the pages. She had read it so many times she knew most of it by heart, but as well as enjoying his descriptions of the distant lands he'd visited, handling the letter made her feel closer to the only immediate family she had left. Taking a deep breath, she resolved not to let the comtesse see she was upset by its loss.

Their breakfast arrived, and she sat down with Anson to eat, surreptitiously glancing at the other occupied table. Last night she'd been too worried about the comtesse's lack of discretion to pay much attention to the men. In the thin morning light, with no distractions, she had a better view. The taller one had blond hair tied back neatly, and features that resembled a Greek statue, with a firm chin and blue eyes. A tired Greek statue, going by the lines beside his mouth.

The other—the one who had upset the comtesse—had a stockier build, with a square, rugged face, brown hair, and brown eyes beneath straight brows. He slouched in his chair, looking into his cup of coffee, his eyelids drooping. Tired, she wondered, or worried? Perhaps both.

They were dressed for riding, their coats and breeches bearing splashes of mud and dirt. She turned her gaze to the fire as the second man looked up and spoke to his companion. Their voices carried in the quiet room as they discussed finding an inn for a midday meal and to rest their horses. From the corner of her eye she saw them stand and reach for their greatcoats. The blond one left the parlour, but the other approached Phoebe.

"*Citoyenne*," he said, with none of the derision he'd put into that term when addressing her aunt the previous evening. He placed something on the table and made a small bow. "I wish you a good journey."

He smiled, nodded at Anson, then turned on his heel and followed his companion before Phoebe could say anything. She looked down. Her sketchbook lay in front of her, barely singed.

"Best not to let Madame see that," Anson said, his lips curving up.

"Indeed." Phoebe smiled as she flicked through the pages, checking that Joe's letter was still safely inside before putting it in her pocket. All of a sudden, the day did not seem quite so bad.

"We need to get further today," she said. "We must try not to stop so early. Do you think…?"

"What?" Anson prompted when Phoebe didn't continue.

"Do you think Masson could be persuaded to take orders from you only? You will be the one giving him his pay, after all."

"I'll try," Anson said doubtfully. "It's not Masson, really. *I* would have to ignore her instructions. Still, I would rather be alive at the end of this." He squared his shoulders and reached across the table to pat her hand. "I'll see what I can do. I am as keen as you to be safely back in England. We should be able to reach Tours today, if we don't stop."

"Should we stay out of the city?" Phoebe asked. "In fact, the smaller the village, the better."

Anson nodded his agreement, and they finished their meal in silence, Phoebe wondering if Anson felt the same miserable knot of tension in his stomach as she did.

They were making good progress, Alex thought with some satisfaction. Even his aching rear didn't bother him as much as it had the day before. It wasn't raining, the wind was behind them, and the road, although potholed, was not too muddy.

His horse started to limp.

"*Merde!*"

He dismounted and inspected the animal. It had lost a front shoe.

"Ride it anyway," Brevare suggested.

Alex glanced at the stony surface of the road, then up at Brevare. "Won't do it any good. We passed an inn not long ago. I should be able to hire a horse there."

Brevare frowned. "We should press on," he said. "It can't be far to the next one." He eyed the puddles in the road. "I'll ride on, shall I? I can come back with another horse." He kicked his mount into motion and rode off without waiting for Alex to answer.

Alex swore again. Not only was there *definitely* an inn a mile or so behind them, but he'd be able to buy something to eat there as well. Now Brevare had gone on, it would waste more time if he went back than if he remained here. It was too cold to stand and wait, so he set off along the road, the horse limping behind him.

The countryside here was sparsely populated, the hedges standing stark and bare beneath still-grey skies. The gloom was relieved only by occasional clumps of snowdrops along the verge and pockets of pale slush from yesterday's sleet.

Damn Brevare. Had he deliberately chosen the option that would waste the most time? It seemed that way, but Alex couldn't work out why he would do so. Brevare's story that he'd been sent to recall Alex wasn't true; Brevare hadn't used the code word, and Alex was due to return within a week or so in any case. But apart from that, Brevare had done nothing suspicious other than seeming a little too helpful when offering to carry Alex's bag when they arrived at each inn.

As he trudged on, he regretted agreeing to travel with Brevare at all, but at the time he'd thought it was safer to keep his eye on the man. He regretted his boots, comfortable enough for riding or for walking around town, but not made for long distances along rutted roads. And he regretted the winter spent in inns, coffee houses and offices; the lack of exercise meant he now had sore legs as well as blistered feet and the aches and pains caused by spending several days in the saddle.

In an effort to divert his mind, he contemplated the redhead with the orange dress. He'd taken her for a servant at first, until she called the comtesse her aunt. A poor relation, then, but an interesting one, judging by the mixture of drawings he'd looked at last night.

A cart passed. Alex asked about a lift, but the man was only going his way for less than a mile. Several coaches trundled past in the opposite direction, one spraying him with water as its wheel dipped into a puddle. Alex cursed, and limped on.

~

Phoebe sat in the parlour for well over an hour before Hélène and her aunt came downstairs, and it was mid-morning by the time Masson and Dubois had the luggage loaded onto the coach roof and everyone was settled inside. As before, the comtesse and Hélène took the forward-facing seats, with Phoebe and Anson facing backwards and the basket of food filling the space between them.

As the coach jolted into motion, Hélène took a bundle of fashion plates from a little bag, fanning them out and selecting one. "What about this, Mama?" she said, holding out a drawing of a walking dress in pastel yellow.

Phoebe tried not to listen as Hélène and the comtesse discussed ribbons and trimmings, necklines and lace. Colours, too—the comtesse pointing out that any gowns that did not suit Hélène could be passed on to Phoebe. Yet more clothing that clashed with her hair and made her skin look pasty. Visits to mantua-makers and shops would start in earnest when they returned to London. Recalling numerous such appointments last autumn, Phoebe wondered how many gowns Hélène needed.

She was not looking forward to the coming season. The comte had insisted she would be attending balls and other functions with Hélène, in spite of her aunt's protests. The life her cousin was destined for—a brilliant match, her time filled with social calls, balls and gossip—held no attractions for Phoebe. A loving marriage, as her parents' had been, was more important than a title or wealth. If she could also have a useful role, as her mother had in supporting her father's work, so much the better.

Going to society events would introduce her to a lot of young men, she supposed, and perhaps one of them would have some interests beyond the usual gambling and drinking. Picking up the novel she'd borrowed from Hélène, she tried to put these thoughts out of her mind.

They made good time during the remainder of the morning, and Phoebe persuaded her aunt and cousin of the unsuitability of a small inn not long after midday, when they stopped to eat from the basket and rest the horses. She lost interest in the book, distracted by her cousin's constant prattle and the jolting of the carriage, so she stared at the passing hedges and trees instead, idly wondering about the destinations or the business of the people in carts and carriages going the other way.

It was still early afternoon when she saw a man leading a horse. Both were moving slowly, both were limping. As the coach rattled past, she recognised the man who had rescued her sketchbook, weariness evident in his face.

She had no idea who he was, but he had been kind. Amusement returned at the memory of the way he had stood up to her aunt, and she pursed her lips against a smile. But that meant there was no point suggesting that the coach could stop and offer him a ride on the roof. Leaning back in her seat, she recalled a flash of talk that morning, that the two were planning on stopping at an inn for lunch. Perhaps there *was* some way she could repay his kindness. She sat upright and clutched her stomach.

"Is something wrong, Miss Deane?" Anson said in concern. "Are you unwell?"

Phoebe nodded, turning the corners of her mouth down. "Perhaps something I ate disagreed with me." She heaved realistically, putting one hand over her mouth. Anson banged on the roof with his stick and called to Masson to stop. Phoebe gave one more heave for effect, then picked up the lunch basket and climbed onto the rutted road, walking around the back of the coach until she was out of sight of its windows. There was not much left in the basket, and she hoped her aunt and cousin would be too self-absorbed to question why she had taken it with her.

The comtesse was tapping her foot impatiently when she returned. She wiped her mouth with her handkerchief.

"Sorry, Aunt. I feel better now. I was—"

"Spare us the details, for goodness' sake! Anson, tell them to drive on!"

. . .

Phoebe and Anson had agreed that they should not halt before evening, but as they passed through the narrow streets of a village, the comtesse insisted they stop.

"It is too early, Aunt," Phoebe protested. "We could get much furth—"

"I'm cold. I want something hot to eat, and more hot bricks."

Beside the comtesse, Hélène murmured a word of agreement.

Anson exchanged a quick glance with Phoebe. "Madame, we—"

"Anson, see to it!"

With an audible sigh, the steward banged on the roof of the coach, and let the glass down to shout an instruction to the driver.

The Auberge du Cygne was much bigger than last night's inn, a three storey building surrounding a stable yard bustling with activity. Phoebe and the steward picked their way between men unloading barrels from a cart and entered the inn. In the passageway, Phoebe stopped a serving woman with a loaded tray and asked for a private parlour.

"It's being used," the woman said. "Eat in there." She jerked her head towards a door, then pushed past them.

Phoebe and Anson exchanged another wordless glance and went to investigate. The taproom was loud with talk and the rattle of cutlery on plates. Tables were set close together, with barely room to squeeze between them, and most were in use. Anson sat at the largest of the unoccupied tables to keep their place, and Phoebe squared her shoulders and went back to the coach.

The comtesse wasn't pleased, but sat down at the table to await service, her mouth pursed. Although there were several serving women bustling around, no-one came to take their order. Phoebe whiled away the time watching customers come and go, trying to ignore her aunt's tapping foot. A man eating in one corner looked remarkably like the blond traveller from the last inn, a plump couple argued nearby, and a thin man slurping his stew at the next table kept turning his gaze on their party, his eyes narrowed. He wore a short wig, a messily tied neckcloth and a stained brown jacket.

Phoebe looked away, thankful that her aunt had so far said nothing, even though her expression was becoming more and more pinched. The comtesse's glare switched between her and Anson.

"I'll… I'll go and make sure Dubois has arranged a change of horses," Anson said, pushing his chair back.

Craven. But Phoebe couldn't blame him. Nothing was ever her aunt's fault, after all.

The blond man got up to leave; it *was* one of the travellers she'd seen at breakfast. The comtesse's gaze followed him, then turned back to the table he'd vacated. The corners of her mouth curved down further. A new customer had taken the traveller's place, and a serving woman was talking to him.

The comtesse stood, her chair screeching against the floor. "I demand service, now!"

"Aunt!" Phoebe put a hand out, only to receive a stinging slap on her arm. The knot in her stomach intensified.

"I am the Comtesse du Calvac, and I will *not* be ignored!"

The hubbub in the room quieted.

"No comtesses in France now, *citoyenne.*" The words came from the thin man at the next table, a malicious smile on his face.

The comtesse glared at him, ignoring the innkeeper making his way to them through the crowded room.

"I am also the daughter of an English milord, and—"

"Aunt, please—"

"Mama—" Hélène's voice was faint, her eyes wide.

"—I demand—"

"English spies!" the thin man exclaimed, wiping gravy from his chin as he got to his feet. The remaining talk in the room stopped, all eyes turning their way.

That statement had shocked the comtesse into silence. Too late.

"Mama, *please* sit down."

To Phoebe's surprise, her aunt did.

"Spies, Perrault?" the innkeeper asked, his expression dubious. "Announcing themselves to anyone with ears?"

"You should lock them up, Jean," Perrault said. The cold gleam in his eyes made Phoebe's skin crawl.

"Where do you suggest they go?" the innkeeper asked sourly.

Phoebe watched him stop to talk to someone a couple of tables away, and caught sight of Anson in the doorway. From his expression, he'd been there long enough to witness the comtesse's outburst. Catching his eye, she jerked her head to one side. He left without drawing attention to himself.

Around her, customers were murmuring about spies, traitors, and aristos, the murmurs turning into louder demands for someone to do something.

The innkeeper turned back. "You have no authority to arrest them, Perrault, but I will set Sarchet to guard them while you get the magistrate."

Perrault looked at his half-eaten dinner.

"Take it or leave it. If you put your dinner above national security, that's your choice." The innkeeper stamped off, irritably elbowing a customer out of his way. Perrault scowled, muttering something under his breath as he pushed his plate away and stalked out of the room.

"Aunt, let us leave now, before that man returns."

The comtesse made no move.

Phoebe stood and leaned over the table towards the comtesse. "Aunt, they will—"

"Sit down, *citoyenne*." The innkeeper had returned. A large, unshaven man stood beside him, a blunderbuss cradled in one arm. Phoebe almost gagged on the smell of garlic and sweat surrounding him as she sank back into her chair.

"Sarchet, they're not to move," the innkeeper instructed. Sarchet grunted and sat down. The other customers gradually resumed eating, drinking, and talking.

There was nothing they could do but wait.

CHAPTER 4

*A*lex had been walking for over an hour when he heard another vehicle approaching from behind. Turning to wave it down, he recognised the coach he'd seen at the previous night's inn. His arm dropped as the coach rattled by; there was no chance of help from that quarter. He caught a glimpse of a white cap and a pale face at a window before the coach rounded a bend in the road.

He trudged onwards, going over everything Brevare had said since he arrived the week before. He was so lost in thought he almost didn't notice the flash of colour on a fallen branch beside the road. A piece of red cloth, a napkin, tied up in a bundle. It was dry and clean, so could not have been there long.

Curious, he undid it and found bread, a lump of cheese, and a bottle of ale. A paper fluttered to the ground. He almost laughed out loud when he saw what was on it. The sketch comprised only a few lines, but it clearly showed a coach with a horse tied on behind and someone riding on the roof. This was in a bubble coming from a woman in a cap. The other figure, unmistakably the comtesse, was saying *non* and pointing up the road.

He folded the paper carefully and put it in his pocket, then sat on a nearby stone. He drank the ale to slake his thirst, and ate the bread and cheese. His legs still ached, but he felt more cheerful, and it wasn't only because he had eaten. He took his boots off, not without a struggle, and rubbed his feet for a few minutes before forcing them back into the boots.

There was more to the shabby *citoyenne* than met the eye, he thought as he started walking. Much more. A pity they would not meet again.

Half an hour later, the wind changed direction, blowing spatters of rain into his face. His cheerful mood was disappearing rapidly when he saw a horseman approaching, leading another animal. Brevare, at last.

Alex muttered a brief thanks as he swung into the saddle of the spare horse, still annoyed with Brevare for rushing off earlier. They set off, limited by the speed of the horse Alex was now leading, but at least he was riding instead of walking. They came to an inn twenty minutes later.

Twenty minutes each way, Alex thought. Less, really, as Brevare could have ridden faster. Perhaps another twenty to hire the spare horse. Brevare had been gone nearly two hours—what had he been doing? He'd think about that when he'd had a proper meal.

"Here, you must know where to take them," Alex said to Brevare, handing over the reins of both horses. "I'll get something to eat before we go on."

Brevare went off with the horses, and Alex headed for the main door. A coach at the edge of the yard caught his eye—the Calvacs again. It wasn't the sight of the coach itself that made him stop, but the older man who he had last seen in the parlour that morning. He stood behind the coach, clutching a box and peering nervously around the end of the vehicle towards the inn.

Was the party in trouble? He wouldn't be surprised, after seeing the comtesse's behaviour last night. What had happened?

There was no need to get involved, he thought, slowing down to get a better look at the older man. Getting his information to England was his priority. The redhead had only repaid him for saving her sketchbook, after all.

She *had* helped, though. She'd gone out of her way to leave him some food, and must have deceived her aunt to do so. There was the daughter, too—he doubted the golden-haired beauty was responsible for whatever trouble they were in.

He should at least find out *why* their manservant stood there looking afraid. He moved towards the coach, ignoring that little internal voice that said that he would come to regret this.

~

"How long are they going to keep us here?" Hélène's voice trembled on the edge of tears as she asked the question for the third time.

"This is outrageous," the comtesse said. "I have never been treated like this in all my life. I will not stand for it any longer!"

The comtesse stood up, but Sarchet waved his blunderbuss and she subsided. He was a man of few words.

Cringing as her aunt's exclamation drew attention to them once more, Phoebe resisted the temptation to bury her head in her hands. She needed to stay calm. "We have only been waiting for half an hour," she said, glad to hear her voice didn't convey her fear. "I'm sure the magistrate will sort this all out when he arrives. Aunt, please try not to antagonise these men any further."

The comtesse scowled, but said nothing more. Hélène stared at the table—she, at least, apparently had the sense to be worried about their situation. Savoury smells drifted from other tables, but the serving women didn't seem inclined to attend to people who might soon be under arrest.

They waited another twenty minutes before Perrault reappeared.

"The magistrate is away," he said to the innkeeper, loudly enough to be heard by most of the people present.

"We can go, then." The comtesse started to rise, but Sarchet raised the blunderbuss a few inches and she sank back into her chair.

"Certainly not," Perrault said. "You will have to wait until he returns."

"Don't be ridiculous," the comtesse said. "We cannot stay here for days waiting for some local magistrate!"

"Why not?" Perrault looked at the innkeeper. "You have a room free?"

The innkeeper nodded. "If they can pay," he said. "I'm not guarding them, though. We're short of help as it is."

"I refuse to pay to be imprisoned here." The comtesse's voice was getting louder and shriller. "Where is—?" The blunderbuss moved, and she stopped talking.

"Mama." Hélène's voice was almost a wail. "Mama, what will happen to us?"

"We should ask the citoyen to arrange our room," Phoebe said. "We are all tired—"

Phoebe broke off as she noticed the comtesse's open-mouthed stare, and turned her head to follow her aunt's gaze. Two men stood in the doorway. When she had seen them at breakfast, they had not been wearing tricolour cockades on their hats, or holding pistols.

"What exactly is going on here?" The cold, commanding tone matched the menacing lines of strain on the brown-haired man's face, and silenced everyone in the room. He had looked friendly this morning when he returned her sketchbook. He was not friendly now. His expression showed the kind of controlled fury that was far more dangerous than red-faced anger.

He looked directly at Perrault. "You have probably ruined our plans."

Perrault's face reddened. "Who are you?" he demanded. "What right—?"

Sarchet turned his blunderbuss towards the men.

"My name is Alexandre Leon," the brown-haired man said, pointing his pistol towards Sarchet. "I suggest your friend keeps his weapon away from me."

The man with Leon raised his own gun. Phoebe glanced around; if shots were fired, someone would certainly get hurt in this crowded room. She slid down a little in her chair, her heart racing.

"Sarchet," Perrault said to the guard, and the man pointed the blunderbuss at the comtesse again.

"Why have you detained these people?" Leon asked.

"They are aristos," Perrault said. "And English! You *do* know we are at war with England?"

"Naturally." Leon raised one eyebrow. "But, as yet, being English is not a crime."

"So we can go." The comtesse stood up. Phoebe couldn't decide if she was being brave or stupid.

"Sit down and shut your mouth," Leon said to the comtesse, waving his pistol in her direction. Her aunt subsided once more. Leon's gaze swept over Hélène, now sobbing into a handkerchief, and stopped briefly at Phoebe. He gave no sign of recognition as he returned his attention to Perrault.

"By what authority have you detained these people?" Leon asked again, more forcefully this time.

"Out of a citizen's duty," Perrault said. "I *told* you why. What business is it of yours, anyway?"

"We work for the Committee of General Security." Leon indicated the three women. "They are suspected of carrying information to the enemies of France."

Phoebe kept her expression neutral with an effort. If that were true, why hadn't he said something yesterday?

"I knew it!" Perrault crowed. "Didn't I say they were spies?"

"We are not spies!"

Leon shrugged, his glance at the comtesse dismissive. "You would naturally say that. Now be quiet or I will have you removed." He paused, pulling a red cloth from his pocket to wipe his face.

That was the napkin she had left by the road that afternoon. A tiny nugget of hope began to form inside her. Her gaze lifted to Leon's eyes, but he was once more looking at Perrault. Everyone else was avidly watching the unfolding drama.

"Why do you think they are spies?" Leon asked Perrault.

Perrault hesitated, suddenly appearing less sure of himself. "They are English. And you are not from the Tours committee," he added, sounding more confident. "I would recognise you."

"We are from Grenoble," Leon said.

"Then you have no jurisdiction here." Perrault's triumphant smile made Phoebe's skin crawl.

"What is all this?" the comtesse asked. "We are not—" She closed her mouth when Leon's pistol once more pointed in her direction.

"Why not let her speak?" Perrault asked, his expression pinched with suspicion.

"You have been speaking to her for some time. Has she said anything useful?"

Perrault had to shake his head. "But what has the Committee in Grenoble got to do with these aristos?"

"We have been following them for days," Leon said.

Phoebe glanced at Perrault; was he going to accept the explanation? Her nails dug into her palms and she forced her hands to unclench. For whatever reason, Leon *was* attempting to get them out of this situation.

"We should discuss this without those two," Leon said, pointing at the comtesse and Hélène. "They will be questioned in detail later."

Phoebe shivered, despite her increasing conviction that Leon was not their enemy.

"This servant can answer any questions about their journey." Leon gestured towards Phoebe.

Whatever Leon was doing, they probably had a better chance with him than with Perrault—provided that her aunt did not upset his story. Phoebe leaned over and put her head next to Hélène's.

"Now would be a good time to swoon," she breathed, hoping that Hélène could hear her. "Or they may kill us." She half believed it herself.

Hélène gave a little wail and slumped down in her chair.

The comtesse turned her gaze to her daughter. "Hélène, what—?"

"Brevare, get them into a bedchamber and lock them in." Leon spoke over the comtesse's voice. "Innkeeper, a room. You—Sarchet is it? Go with them and guard the door once they're locked in."

Such was the authority in his voice that the three men obeyed without question. Brevare walked around the table and picked up Hélène, carrying her easily in his arms as the innkeeper led the way up the stairs. Sarchet took the comtesse's arm, taking no notice of her protests, and dragged her after them. The lace on the sleeve of her gown caught on a rough part of the door frame and tore loudly as Sarchet pulled her through, but he did not stop.

Alex waited until the sound of the comtesse's voice died away, then sat down, gesturing to Perrault to take the other vacated chair. Some of his tension dissipated as he took in the assessing gaze from the redhead. She seemed to have quick wits—and had helped him get the comtesse out of the way. Now he just had to get rid of this interfering busybody.

"Where are their other servants?" Alex asked.

Perrault looked blank.

"They weren't driving their own coach, were they?"

Perrault's mouth opened and closed a couple of times. "I don't know, *citoyen*. What does it matter?"

"I wish to question them," Alex said. His hastily concocted story sounded thin to him, but he was relying on intimidation. Few people wished to cross agents of the Committee of General Security. "You have let the servants escape and ruined our whole plan."

Alex caught a movement out of the corner of his eye. Brevare and the innkeeper had returned, and both took up a position by the door. Good. He hadn't explained to Brevare what he was doing—he hadn't really known himself. He'd just told Brevare to back him up but, from what he'd seen so far, the redhead was likely to be a better conspirator than Brevare.

"The older one said she was the *ci-devant* Comtesse de Calvac," the innkeeper said, shaking his head. He drew closer to their table. "I've heard of Calvac; it's less than three days from here. It's nowhere near Grenoble."

"True, but—"

29

"*Citoyenne*, your name?" Perrault cut him off, turning to the redhead. He looked at Alex with a challenge on his face. "If you are speaking the truth, then she can confirm your story."

Perrault returned his gaze to the woman, his eyes narrowing as he inspected her face, then her gown. "That is a rather fine garment for a servant," he added, suspicion deepening on his face.

"I am Phoebe Deane," the redhead said, her voice wobbling a little. "This gown was her daughter's." She pulled at one of her curls. "Would someone with hair like mine choose an *orange* gown?"

One of the watching serving girls giggled. "She's right, she'd be stupid to—"

"Enough!" Perrault snarled. He turned back to Miss Deane. "Where have you come from?"

She raised her chin. "Why should I answer your questions?"

Truly defiant, Alex wondered, or making time to think? "Tell the truth," he said. "If you give us the information we need, we may release you." He smiled, hoping his expression looked encouraging. "What loyalty do you owe your mistress, anyway?"

"He is correct, *citoyen*," she said to Perrault, pointing at the innkeeper. "Calvac is only two days' drive from here."

Perrault smiled.

"But it is not their only château," Miss Deane went on. "We have been at the Château Sarlande. It is between Grenoble and Lyon."

Perrault's face fell, and Alex felt his shoulders relax slightly.

"And where are you going?" Perrault asked.

"England. We are to find a boat at Calais. Madame is afraid of the revolutionaries."

A pity the woman hadn't been *more* afraid, Alex thought, anger rising. This redhead before him would surely have had more sense than to be in France at such a time if the decision had been hers to make.

"Is she really English, as she said?"

"Yes. She is the daughter of an English viscount. She married the Comte de Calvac."

"And the *ci-devant* comte?" Perrault almost spat the words.

CHAPTER 5

*T*he carriage lurched and rocked along the road, moving at a faster pace than Masson had achieved. Phoebe sat in the middle of the seat, crushed between Hélène and her aunt. Today she was facing forwards, but she preferred the rear-facing corner she had occupied for the two previous days. Alexandre Leon reclined there, his square face stern and expressionless, his brown eyes cold. Perrault occupied the other corner. Sarchet was driving, with Brevare on the box beside him.

Phoebe leaned her head back, enjoying the unaccustomed peace. They had put several hours' drive between them and Perrault's village yesterday afternoon, not stopping until long after dark. Once in the coach, Leon had answered her aunt's initial strident remarks by stating that she could either travel inside without talking, or she could sit on the box with the driver. Her protest had been met with an icy and contemptuous stare, and she had relapsed into a stiff silence. Perrault's attempt to discuss the political situation had received a similar response.

Last night's inn had been smaller and dirtier than the one where the comtesse had caused such a disastrous scene. They had been locked in a bedroom overnight, together with a simple meal of cold chicken, bread, and cheese. Phoebe winced at the recollection of her aunt's complaints: the food, the lack of respect, disloyal maids—Jeanne—who ran away at the first sign of trouble, and ungrateful nieces who were less than competent when standing in for a lady's maid.

Her aunt had also been angry with Anson for deserting them, but Phoebe managed to impress on her that the steward's freedom was a good thing. Phoebe's small trunk with the false bottom, containing most of the money they had with them, was safely strapped to the coach roof. When she'd checked it, some money was missing, but she guessed Anson had taken what he needed to get to England.

Perhaps he could find someone to help them?

She'd let her aunt think that Anson had absconded with nearly all the money, hoping that it would stop her demanding that Phoebe produce coin for bribes or better service.

Observing the men sitting opposite, she'd noticed Perrault's almost constant attention on them. His gaze was piercing, as if he were looking through her clothing, and she resisted the impulse to wriggle in discomfort, glad that Sarchet was outside with Brevare. On occasion, she caught Leon watching them, too, his face always impassive. But most of the time he leant on the squabs, his hat tipped over his eyes, legs stretched out. Phoebe tried to concentrate on her novel, looking up now and then when her aunt shifted position and found Leon's legs in the way. Phoebe could have sworn his lips twitched slightly, even though he was supposedly asleep.

They stopped in the early afternoon for another change of horses, and Leon ordered some bread rolls and cheese brought to the carriage. Phoebe felt too nervous to eat, and her aunt and cousin barely picked at their food. At Phoebe's polite request, Leon escorted the three of them to a parlour where a maid joined them with a chamber pot. She dismissed the idea of asking the maid to help them—the woman could do nothing alone, and who else would assist them?

Last night the comtesse had said, repeatedly, that it was all a mistake and the ambassador in Paris would sort everything out, as if saying it enough times would make it true. Hélène seemed to believe her, but Phoebe did not. Did England still *have* an ambassador now they were at war? And even if he were there, how could he really help?

She settled back in the seat when they set off, picking up her novel to try to take her mind off their troubles. The lowering sun shone through the coach window as she turned the pages, but the adventures of Lucinda in *The Pirate's Cavern* seemed no more likely now than they had yesterday. She read only a few pages before setting the book aside.

She felt for Joe's letter in her pocket, extracting it without letting her aunt see the sketchbook. Reading his descriptions of the Caribbean islands and shipboard life, she tried to imagine she was there instead of in this jolting coach. For a few moments she had a warm, salty wind in her hair, smelled exotic spices, and enjoyed the idea of deciding her own fate.

A particularly deep pothole brought her back to reality, and the worry caused by Joe's last, hastily scrawled, paragraph. His ship had been lost, but he was safe. There was no more than that—no indication as to whether it had been an accident or due to enemy action. It could be another year or more before Joe was able get leave and return to England. Until then, she'd have to make do with his letters, hoping his next one gave her more details. With a wry twist of her lips, she thought she would at last have something interesting to write to him if they all came out of this journey safely.

Tucking the letter back into her sketchbook, she looked up to find Leon watching her. His expression continued to give nothing away, but his gaze did not make her as uncomfortable as Perrault's inspection did. When he saw her eyes on him, he turned his attention back to the passing countryside.

How long would it take them to get to Paris? Two days, perhaps, so they could be there tomorrow. A shaft of sunlight was shining on the back of the coach above her aunt's head—that would mean they were heading west. But surely Paris was to the north-east? Not that the roads were straight, but that did seem odd. Perhaps her knowledge of the geography of France wasn't as accurate as she thought.

Leon refused to have all their boxes brought in when they stopped for the evening, so Phoebe pointed out the few they really needed, and Sarchet was sent to carry them upstairs. Their room was cold, with an empty grate, a bed, and a single chair. Tonight the thought of sleeping on a truckle bed didn't concern her—they were still alive, and possibly *not* being taken to Paris. What the future held, she wasn't sure, but it seemed a little brighter now.

Phoebe went to open her own trunk, but she paused as her aunt spoke.

"I have never been treated so in all my days! Being forbidden to speak in my own coach—just wait until I talk to the ambassador. *That man* will pay for this insolence."

"It is your own fault, Aunt!" Phoebe said, at the end of her patience. "Perrault would never have caused trouble if you had kept quiet yesterday. They have nothing against us, but that has not stopped other people being accused and condemned."

Her aunt glared back, high spots of colour in her cheeks. "How *dare* you tell me what to do? You should be grateful Monsieur le Comte took you in, and show more respect for your betters."

Phoebe clenched her jaw against a retort.

"Mama, we should get ready for dinner," Hélène said hesitantly. "Why don't you change your gown, and I will tidy your hair for you."

"Very well, my dear. I'm glad I have someone who respects me."

Phoebe flashed a grateful smile at Hélène and turned back to her trunk. She lifted her clothing out, then the false bottom. The bags of money were still there. She felt the weight of them, and put one into her pocket. It would bump against her legs, but if the trunk was stolen, searched, or left behind, they would still have a little money with them.

"Aunt," she began cautiously. "It might be wise to carry your jewels on your person. Our trunks will not be looked after as—"

"Yes, yes, Phoebe. There is no need to explain as if I were an imbecile."

For once, the comtesse did as Phoebe suggested, borrowing one of Hélène's pockets and tying it on between her petticoat and gown. Phoebe, busy tidying her hair, thought she saw a packet of letters go into the pocket as well, but when she tried to get a better look, her aunt had turned away.

The comtesse did not speak to her again until they were all ready for dinner. *"That man* seems to have decided you are a servant," she said, holding out the blue gown she had been wearing. "So you can mend this lace." She didn't wait for an answer, but tossed the gown at Phoebe and swept over to the door, banging on it and demanding to be let out.

Phoebe sighed, bundled up the gown, and opened her trunk to take out the housewife containing her needles and thread. It would give her something to do in the parlour after dinner.

A key scraped in the door and Sarchet entered without knocking. "Downstairs," he grunted, and gestured with his hand. The comtesse swept out ahead of Hélène, her nose in the air. Phoebe followed, uneasily aware of Sarchet's gaze sweeping over her as she passed him. They were ushered into a dining room, warm from the fire blazing in the hearth. The only people present were Leon and Brevare, sitting at a table near the door.

"I'm glad you realise what is due to my station, young man," the comtesse said.

Leon inclined his head. "It is generous of you to pay for all of us," he said, waving them into the room.

Phoebe suppressed a chuckle. It was no laughing matter, but she couldn't help being amused.

"I will do no such thing."

"You can eat in the taproom, then."

The comtesse opened her mouth, clearly about to protest further, but stopped as Perrault and Sarchet entered the room with tankards of ale and sat down at another table.

"What are they doing here?"

"We will all be eating in here."

The comtesse glared at Leon, then looked around the room. She finally took a seat at the table closest to the fire, gesturing for Hélène to join her. Phoebe guessed that the warmth had outweighed her aunt's desire to maintain her status.

Leon must have already ordered food, for it was only a few minutes before a couple of serving women entered with laden trays. They all ate in silence, except for some, thankfully quiet, remarks from the comtesse about the lack of choice.

The ragout was of lamb and vegetables, tender and smelling of rosemary. Phoebe ate slowly; although it was tasty, she was still too worried to enjoy it. Leon and Brevare ate mechanically, both appearing tired and preoccupied.

Alex took a draught of ale, studying the other occupants of the room. Brevare seemed taken with the comtesse's daughter, although his gaze seemed to be looking through her rather than at her much of the time.

The redhead looked away whenever Alex's eyes met hers. He studied her through half-closed eyes as she ate. The colour of the ill-fitting gown made her pale skin look sallow, and he wondered what she'd look like dressed properly, and without that enveloping cap. Appearance aside, she was quick witted and capable of controlling her emotions. His story yesterday afternoon hadn't been very convincing; without her corroboration, he almost certainly wouldn't have succeeded. He would have found himself under suspicion, wasting his efforts of the last few months and endangering all his contacts.

Perrault and Sarchet, at the far side of the room, slurped noisily as they wolfed down their bowls of stew. Sarchet left when the two had finished eating, returning with more ale. Sarchet's gaze, too, was on Hélène; he stared at her while Perrault talked to him in a voice too low for his words to carry.

What was Perrault saying? He would have to get rid of the pair of them in the next couple of days, but an inn parlour with the three women present was not the place for a confrontation. The pistols in the pockets of his greatcoat, thrown over the back of a nearby chair, were there as a precaution only.

A serving woman cleared the plates, and Alex watched as Miss Deane moved her chair closer to the candles on the mantelpiece. She took a needle, scissors, and thread from her housewife, and began to mend lace on a blue gown.

He was roused from his deliberations by the sound of wood scraping on the stone flags as Sarchet stood up. He dragged his chair to the women's table and sat down next to Hélène.

"Pretty hair," he said, winding one golden curl around a grubby finger.

Hélène jerked away. "Mama!"

CHAPTER 6

*A*lex swore under his breath. He should have anticipated that a man like Sarchet would try to take advantage. Had Perrault goaded him? At the edge of his vision, he registered Miss Deane putting down the gown she was working on and sitting forward in her chair, alert.

"Get your filthy hands off her," the comtesse cried, slapping at Sarchet. He paid no attention.

Brevare got to his feet, and Alex muttered another curse as he put out a hand to restrain him. "Good revolutionaries do not spring to the defence of aristos," he said in a low voice, turning options over in his mind. "Let me try something first."

Brevare's hands curled into fists, tension further evident in his clenched jaw, but he resumed his seat.

"Perrault," Alex called out. "Call him off."

"Why?" Perrault stood up and came over to Alex's table, looking down at him with a sneer. "Why, *citoyen*? Does it matter what happens to the little bitch?"

"We are taking them for questioning. They are not yet officially guilty of anything." He glanced over at the women. Sarchet had taken his hand off Hélène. She leaned against the comtesse, her face ashen, tears running down her cheeks. Miss Deane watched from her place by the fire; she had a set look about her lips, but her expression was otherwise under control.

"Too good for Sarchet, is she?" Perrault said. "Because she is an aristo?"

"Any woman is too good for Sarchet," Alex retorted, but the insult appeared to go right over Sarchet's head. He wondered if he was about to make matters worse, but he would have to do something tomorrow, anyway. Perrault's greed could be the key.

"Actually, Perrault, I've been thinking about a change of plan. It will be to the advantage of all of us. Sit down. Brevare, get more ale. Sarchet, go with him."

Used to taking orders, Sarchet half rose from his chair before he realised what he was doing, then looked at Perrault. On receiving a nod Sarchet followed Brevare out of the room.

"They stay in here." Perrault pointed at the women.

Alex shrugged. Getting the women safely locked up in a bedroom would have been the best way out, but he hadn't expected it to be easy.

"Your plan?" Perrault asked.

"You remember what she said yesterday?" Alex asked, jerking a thumb in Miss Deane's direction. "The woman is too stupid to be any danger to France—"

The comtesse's gasp carried across the room.

"See?" Alex said. "She cannot hide what she is feeling—how could she be a spy?"

"What about the daughter?" Perrault asked.

"Swooning." Alex tilted his head towards Hélène. "Look at her! Good spy material there, you think? And the other is only a servant. She knows nothing."

"So why are—?"

They were interrupted by Brevare and Sarchet returning with the drinks. Alex gestured for them to sit.

"Why are we wasting our time taking them to Paris, citoyen?" Perrault asked. "We could have kept them until our magistrate came back. In fact, why were you following them at all?"

41

Brevare glanced at Alex.

"I was misinformed," Alex said. "I will deal with my informants later—they have wasted far too much of my time. For now, I have an idea to compensate all of us for the trouble these women have caused." He pointed at the comtesse; the woman was scowling, one hand clenched on the table, but not looking as if she were about to say anything.

"She's rich," Alex said. "Her husband will pay to get her back. We should go to the coast instead of Paris, and send word to England for a ransom."

An avaricious gleam appeared in Perrault's eyes, followed by doubt. "Would anyone really pay for *her*?"

"He will pay for them all," Alex said. "If he doesn't, we will make it known in England that the *ci-devant* Comte de Calvac deliberately sacrificed his family to the revolutionaries."

Beside him, Brevare nodded. "He will do his duty by them. The aristos' sense of honour will not let him refuse."

Perrault folded his arms, shaking his head.

"I've met many of their type." Alex injected a suitable note of disdain in his voice. "They think their *honour* is more important than anything else."

"How will we share out the ransom?" Perrault asked, poorly hidden greed returning to his face.

"Half for me and my friend, half for you and Sarchet." He turned to Brevare. "Does that suit you?"

Brevare's gaze was back on the terrified Hélène, and he did not answer. Exasperated at the man's lack of attention, Alex kicked him under the table.

"Er, yes, that suits me."

"Good." Alex leaned close to Perrault, keeping his voice low. "I'm sure you can divide your share appropriately," he said. "You are taking much of the responsibility, after all."

Perrault looked thoughtful for a few moments. "Very well," he said at last. "We head for the coast tomorrow. How long will it take us to get to Calais?"

"Somewhere like Caen would be better. It is closer, and less likely to be watched by the authorities."

A fleeting doubt crossed Perrault's face.

"We are doing nothing wrong, *citoyen*," Alex reassured him. "But anyone who stops us would want a cut for themselves."

Perrault's face cleared, and Alex relaxed a little.

"We won't get a ransom for damaged goods, though," he added, addressing Sarchet as well as Perrault. "So you must keep your hands off the women."

Phoebe sat watching the four men, her throat tight with anxiety as Leon talked with Perrault. She'd heard the discussion about ransoms, but what were they saying now? Perrault's changing expressions indicated that Leon might be succeeding in what he was trying to do, but she had no idea what that was. Sarchet, meanwhile, alternated between staring at Hélène and at Phoebe, a frown gathering on his face.

"Not her, though," Sarchet said loudly, pointing at Phoebe, his eyes fixed below her neck. "No aristo will pay good money for a servant."

He stood and headed around the table towards her, his mouth twisting into a leer. She had no doubt what he was planning, and her gaze darted to the table as she leapt to her feet, swinging her chair into his path. She grabbed her scissors and took a step back.

Sarchet strode forward, snatching the chair and throwing it behind him. He reached for her arm and she swung the scissors, feeling the tips catch in his flesh. Sarchet jumped back, one hand clutching the other, his mouth open in shock.

"*Merde!* The bitch stabbed me!"

He was already striding forward as he swore, his arm swinging. The blow to the side of her head knocked Phoebe sideways, one hip striking the edge of the table, her foot catching and sending her to the floor with her head ringing.

He loomed over her, and she scrabbled backwards across the floor.

She sucked in a sharp breath as his hand closed on her cap, then rolled free, using an empty chair to pull herself to her feet.

"*Salope!*" Sarchet was advancing on her again when he suddenly froze, a metallic click loud in the sudden silence. He spun away from her, and Phoebe saw Leon behind him with a pistol pointing at Sarchet's face.

"Leave her alone."

Sarchet reluctantly moved a few steps away. Phoebe put a hand to her head—her face was smarting from Sarchet's blow, and her hair had come loose from its pins and was trailing down her back.

In a tableau of frozen shock, the comtesse and Hélène stared at Sarchet, open-mouthed and ashen-faced. Brevare and Perrault hadn't moved from their own table.

Phoebe moved back as far as she could, leaning on a table as her knees threatened to buckle beneath her. Her breath still came fast— the immediate danger was past, but what would happen now?

Thankful that Miss Deane, at least, had not been paralysed by fear, Alex swiftly ran through his options. Admitting that Miss Deane was no servant wasn't one of them. His whole story would unravel, and they would draw even more unwanted attention than they were getting at present.

"Ransom?" The comtesse's voice, although quiet, carried clearly.

"Papa will pay for Phoebe, won't he, Mama?" Hélène said, her voice wavering.

The comtesse looked at Miss Deane. "She called me stupid."

Good grief, he hadn't thought the woman could be so vile.

"But Mama, Phoebe is—"

"A beloved servant?" Alex interjected. "He'll pay."

The two women gaped at him.

"Brevare, get these women to their room and lock them in." He glanced at the comtesse. "Move!"

Miss Deane started to move towards the door, the other two rousing themselves to follow.

"Not her," Sarchet repeated, grabbing Miss Deane's arm hard enough to make her wince.

Damn. At least getting two of them out of the way was a start.

"Brevare!"

Brevare finally stirred into motion, and escorted the other women out.

"The comte will pay," Alex stated again. "It would be against his honour."

"You cannot guarantee that, *citoyen*," Perrault said. His eyes darted towards Miss Deane and then back to Alex. "Nice hair," he added, running his tongue over his lower lip. "Explain to me why a good revolutionary like Sarchet here should not have the pleasure of this English servant?"

"Why should he? What has he done other than drive a coach for a day?"

"Want her for yourself, do you?" Perrault suggested slyly.

That had possibilities. "Why not? I could enjoy taming that one." Alex allowed a smile to cross his face.

Sarchet, still gripping Miss Deane's arm, started to play with her tumbling red locks, the way he had with Hélène's hair earlier. "It was my idea," he said. "You can take your turn." He pulled her towards the door, her efforts to twist out of his grip futile.

Alex put his pistol on the table. "No-one is going to take *turns*," he stated, controlling his rising anger. He grabbed the collar of Sarchet's coat and pulled.

Sarchet let go of Miss Deane and Alex staggered backwards, his grip still firm on Sarchet's coat. He came up against the table; his pistol fell to the floor and the powder exploded, sending the ball into the ceiling.

The door crashed open, revealing the innkeeper armed with a shotgun, backed up by two very large men. Brevare stood in the passageway beyond, biting his lip and making no move to enter the room. There would be no help from that quarter.

"Outside," the innkeeper said, in a voice that brooked no argument. "I don't care if you want to kill each other, but you will not damage my property." He glared at them. "Or have you finished fighting?"

"These two have unfinished business," Perrault said, taking Miss Deane's arm himself and pushing Sarchet towards the door.

Not the conclusion he'd hoped for, but it might serve. He picked up his coat and shoved the pistol back into a pocket. "Don't let Perrault go off with her," he hissed at Brevare as the innkeeper ushered them towards a rear entrance.

Phoebe struggled as Perrault pulled her along the corridor. Although shorter and lighter than Sarchet, his grip was just as tight.

The cobbled yard behind the inn was lit only by light spilling from a couple of windows. Crates and barrels lined the rear wall of the inn; darker shadows looming against the sky must be stables and other outbuildings enclosing the space.

Perrault pulled her aside as a sudden rush of people erupted from the door and spread out into the yard. Most held tankards of ale, a few carried lanterns. Voices rose in the crowd: arguments that the large peasant had the size and reach, the better dressed one would be faster; shouted odds and wagers.

Perrault let go of her arm and Phoebe shrank back against the wall as he disappeared into the press of spectators. Leon was one of the last men out, stopping near the door to drape his outer garments over a nearby barrel.

Alex caught a glimpse of Miss Deane as he laid his waistcoat on a barrel. Where the hell was Brevare? Hands grasped his shirt sleeves, pulling him forward through a gap in the crowd, and he put her from his mind.

Concentrate on Sarchet.

The hands thrust him forward, and he stepped smartly to one side as the men beside him retreated.

Sarchet's fist whistled past his ear.

So much for a fair fight. He dodged sideways again and planted a fist in the bigger man's midriff.

Sarchet swung at him. Alex moved back, swaying out of reach. The crowd pressed in as he circled warily, watching for an opportunity. Speed and agility were his advantages, but only if he were given the space to use them.

Phoebe couldn't see what was happening, but shouts of encouragement or dismay from the crowd told her that the fight had started. She eyed the barrel where Leon had left his coat. He must have had his pistol in a pocket of his greatcoat, and pistols were often carried in pairs.

No-one was watching her. She felt through the pile of clothing until she came across a heavy, solid lump, running her hand over the cloth until she found the pocket flap. The same acrid smell that had filled the parlour a few minutes ago told her this was the pistol that had been fired.

A cheer spurred her on. It was a fight, not a boxing match, and wouldn't last long. She found another pocket and tugged on the pistol inside. It was caught on something. Cloth tore as she pulled harder.

All attention was still on the fight. She risked holding the garment up to catch more light, and untangled the pistol from the folds of cloth. Something pale fell to the ground as she pulled the gun free—a little packet. Phoebe picked it up and put it, along with the pistol, in one of the pockets beneath her skirts.

Moving away from the barrel, her skirts caught on something and she almost fell over a collection of rakes and other tools leaning against the wall. She regained her balance, and turned to see what was happening in the middle of the yard.

Alex cursed as he felt the cool of rain on his skin. The cobbles were already slippery; rain would make them worse. He dipped and twisted to avoid a wild swing from Sarchet. Jabbing an elbow sideways, he connected with the man's face. Sarchet stepped closer, blood running from his nose.

Ducking, Alex struck upwards, his fist slamming into Sarchet's chin. The bigger man staggered backwards, arms flailing, and sprawled on the ground, panting for breath.

Cheers and catcalls from the spectators goaded Sarchet into movement. Alex heard glass breaking as the man regained his feet.

Sarchet held a broken bottle.

That changed the stakes.

Alex retreated, the spectators giving way behind him. Sarchet charged with swinging bottle; Alex threw up an arm to block. A sharp bite of pain was followed by warmth and he dropped to one knee. A jagged edge of the bottle had caught his arm, but he had no time to see how badly he was cut.

A long pole moved through the edge of his vision. Alex reached out and grabbed it, swinging it round in front of him, jabbing the end at Sarchet as he rose to his feet. He only noticed it was a pitchfork when Sarchet screamed in agony, one of the tines sticking into his shoulder.

"Give up!" Alex yelled.

The pitchfork was long enough to keep the jagged glass from his face, but Sarchet still thrust the bottle towards him. Alex twisted the pitchfork, and Sarchet collapsed, his voice hoarse as he yelled for someone, anyone, to get the thing out of him.

CHAPTER 7

*P*hoebe shrank against the wall as the spectators headed back to the taproom. She couldn't be sure, but she thought the agonised cry had been Sarchet, not Leon. She swallowed hard. That was the outcome she'd wanted, although given his comment about taming her, Leon might be only the lesser of two evils.

"There you are, *citoyenne*."

Perrault. He held a lamp in one hand, its light showing his gaze moving from her mouth to her bosom.

The least of three evils?

"Upstairs, *citoyenne*, ready for the victor." He reached out, fingers digging into her arm as his hand closed around it. She tried to pull away, but he only tightened his grip as he pulled her into the inn and up the stairs.

The hidden pistol bumped uncomfortably against her legs, but she had no idea how she could use it. He pushed her into a room, set the lamp on a table beside the bed, then turned and shut the door.

"Sit down," he said, indicating the straight-backed chair near the fireplace.

Phoebe didn't move. She had more chance of trying to dodge him if she stayed on her feet.

Perrault's lips thinned, but he did not press the point. "So, tell me again where you have come from."

As far as she could, she repeated the story about the journey from the fictitious château, elaborating on the inns they'd supposedly stayed at, inventing incidents on the road—anything to keep him off her until Leon arrived.

Perrault paced in front of her—two paces one way, and two the other. When her recital finally ended, he nodded.

"Very well. Perhaps you are what you say. A pretty bit like you..." He took a step closer, putting a hand out to touch her hair. Phoebe stepped back, her heart racing and a sick feeling settling in her stomach as she jerked her head sideways. She had no scissors this time.

"Don't be coy, *citoyenne*." He moved forward. "Leon didn't look to be in a fit state to enjoy his prize."

Her back was almost against the wall. She recalled Joe's instructions, and curled her fingers into a fist, thumb on the outside.

"I wouldn't want you to be lonely." Perrault's gaze dropped to her bosom.

Her fist shot out, shock running up her arm as the blow landed in the middle of his face. She hadn't hit him hard, but Perrault was taken by surprise; his hand flew up to his nose as he stepped backwards.

Between the legs, Joe had told her. She lifted her skirts and kicked. She wasn't sure she'd aimed well enough, but Perrault doubled over and staggered away.

"*Putain!*" He collapsed onto the edge of the bed.

Phoebe put her hand through the slit in her skirt, but before she could pull the pistol from her pocket, Perrault had drawn his own.

"Leon's welcome to you," he spat, his voice muffled by the handkerchief he held to his bloody nose. "Don't think you can go to your employer, either. They're locked in and I have the key. Sit down."

Phoebe was both astonished and relived that she'd hurt him enough to make him give up. She had no doubt that he would fire the gun if she disobeyed, so she moved over to the chair and sat down to wait.

What did Leon intend?

Alex's chest heaved as he sucked air into his lungs, sharp stabs of pain in his ribs, his right hand clutching his stinging arm. Before him, the innkeeper pulled the pitchfork out of Sarchet, one foot on his shoulder, ignoring his screams. The few remaining spectators drifted into the inn to settle their bets.

"Here." A tankard of ale was thrust in front of Alex, and he looked up to see Brevare.

"I'll survive," Alex said, answering the unspoken question on the other man's face. He glanced around, but Miss Deane was nowhere to be seen, nor Perrault. "What happened to the woman?"

"Perrault must have taken her inside."

Alex glared at him. "I told you to—"

"I went in to check that the Calvac women were still safely locked in." Brevare shrugged. "I was only gone a minute."

"Damn." Why had he expected any more of the man?

Alex took a pull of the ale, then put the tankard down. He couldn't see how bad the cut to his arm was in this light. He picked up his coats and draped them awkwardly over his left shoulder, then clasped his right hand over the cut again to try to stop the bleeding.

"Get some hot water and a bottle of brandy sent up to my room, will you?"

Brevare nodded, and Alex followed him inside. The parlour they had occupied earlier was empty, so Alex trudged up the stairs.

The woman first.

The door to his own room was ajar, so he pushed it open with one boot. Perrault rose from the bed, one hand holding a pistol and the other pressing a bloody handkerchief to his face. The pistol was not pointing at him but at Miss Deane, sitting by the unlit fire.

"Here you are, *citoyen*," Perrault said, his voice muffled through the cloth. "She's ready for you. Good luck taming the bitch."

Miss Deane appeared to be unharmed, despite her set mouth and wide eyes.

"Get out," Alex said to Perrault, and stood to one side while the man hobbled out of the room with a smirk. As he left, a maid arrived with a can of hot water, brandy, and a glass. Alex gestured at the table, and she set the brandy and the glass next to the lamp, the water on the floor beneath. She cast a curious glance at Miss Deane before Alex hustled her out.

He locked the door and leaned on it, his eyes closed. His legs felt as if they wouldn't hold him up much longer. There was a faint buzzing in his head, and he had a desperate compulsion to lie down. When opened his eyes, he saw that lying down wasn't going to be an option, at least for now.

Miss Deane had produced a pistol from somewhere. She held it with both hands, the business end pointing directly at him.

One of his pistols. The irony was almost amusing.

He hoped it was the one that had gone off in the parlour earlier, but he couldn't count on it. Now he thought about it, the coat over his shoulder felt lighter than it should.

He looked at the pistol, then lifted his gaze to study the woman's face. For all the tremble of her lips and the fine tremor in her hands, the pistol was steady enough to kill him if she fired it.

Will she really try to use it?

Unless she knew how to use a pistol, he could probably take it from her. On the other hand, she'd done some damage to Perrault without a pistol, and he was hurting enough as it was.

Can I get her to trust me?

"If you want to shoot me with that, you'll have to cock it first," he said, not moving from his position by the door. "The lever on the top —pull it back further."

Miss Deane glanced down at the pistol and pulled on the lever. It settled further with a loud click.

"It doesn't fire instantly when you pull the trigger," he went on conversationally. "Keep it pointing in the right direction until the powder explodes."

She stared at him without moving, and he wondered if this were the most stupid way he could have thought of to ease her fears.

"You'll need to keep both hands on it."

The pistol wavered as she looked at it, then back at him. She carefully laid it down on the floor by the chair and bent forwards, hands covering her face. Her shoulders moved as she took a couple of deep breaths, then she straightened, dashing one hand across her eyes. Tracks of tears shone in the lamplight, and she rubbed her face again before gripping her hands together in her lap.

"Could you have shot Perrault?" he asked, curious.

"I think so," she whispered.

Alex frowned, a sudden image from earlier flashing into his mind. "It was you who gave me the pitchfork?"

She nodded.

"Why?"

"Perrault seemed determined that someone should... should..." She unclenched one hand long enough to wave it in place of the words she clearly did not want to say. "At least you seem to be reasonably clean and don't reek of garlic," she added finally, her voice creditably steady.

It took a moment for what she had said to sink in, then Alex began to laugh. His knees gave way and he slid down the door until he sat with his back against it, trying to both hold his injured arm and his ribs against the pain there, made worse by his laughter.

He laughed until tears came to his eyes, then a sharper stabbing from his ribs sobered him. After a few more gasps for breath, he leaned his head on the door. Standing was too much effort.

Miss Deane hadn't moved from the chair. Although her posture had relaxed a little, she was still tense.

"I may have been clean before the fight," he said, looking at the mud coating his breeches and shirt. "I won't hurt you," he added quietly. Her eyes widened in alarm, and he realised how his words could be misinterpreted. "I mean, I will not harm you in any way. I am not Sarchet."

"But you said to Perrault—"

"I used an argument he would accept." She wasn't to know he would never force himself on a woman.

"You should go to your room now," he added. He should have said that as soon as he'd got rid of Perrault, of course, instead of prolonging her fear. But she might not have believed him; most men faced with a loaded pistol would say anything to avoid being shot.

"Perrault locked them in and took the key," she said. "He told me."

Alex drew his knees up, then used his good arm against the door to push himself painfully to his feet. He unlocked and opened the door; noise from the taproom below drifted into the room. Perrault was sitting on a chest on the landing, a mug of ale in one hand.

"Going well, *citoyen?*"

He had stopped dabbing his nose, but it was red and swollen. The bloody cloth lay beside him on the chest. Alex suppressed a smile.

"What the hell are you doing there, Perrault?"

"Just making sure the servant girl doesn't stab you like she did Sarchet."

"Well, make yourself useful. Your friend made a mess of me. I'm going to need more hot water, wood for the fire, and another glass for the brandy. And bring up anything that got left behind in the parlour."

Perrault didn't move.

"Unless *you* know how to contact the harridan's husband to get the ransom?" Alex added.

Perrault grimaced, but put down his ale and went down the stairs.

Phoebe wiped her eyes and blew her nose, putting her handkerchief away as Leon turned back into the room. He was hurt—that was clear from the way he was moving. In the last few minutes he had changed from an unpredictable threat into the kind-hearted man who had returned her sketchbook the day before.

The sick feeling in her stomach receded further. Taking a deep breath, she straightened in the chair. Tomorrow's troubles could wait.

"Perrault seems determined you will stay here," Leon said. "What did you do to him?"

"A lucky hit," she said, surprised to feel a little amusement. She'd never thought Joe's lessons would be so useful. "But then he pulled out his pistol."

"I can't explain now," Leon said, "but I'd prefer Perrault to continue to think I'm going to… to take advantage."

"I'm not sure my aunt would let me in, even if Perrault hadn't locked the door. I've been away from her long enough for her to assume…" She swallowed hard, shaking her head. There were more important things to worry about now than the loss of her reputation.

He was shivering. The room was cold, and he was standing there in a wet and bloody shirt.

"You're bleeding!" She could—*should*—do something about that. She took kindling and wood from a basket on the hearth and laid a fire. There was no tinderbox, so she twisted a page from her sketchbook into a spill and lit it from the lamp. The routine task calmed her, and she soon had flames flickering in the grate.

Someone knocked. Leon opened the door and a maid brought in a tray and a bundle of cloth. The key scraped as he locked the door behind her.

"Perrault is still out there," he said, handing the key to Phoebe. "I'd rather he couldn't just walk in here, but I'm not locking *you* in. You keep this."

He really *didn't* mean her harm. A feeling of lightness—and gratitude—spread through her as she took the key and placed it on the mantelpiece.

Leon peeled back his torn shirt sleeve. The long, jagged cut was seeping blood—it looked deep and painful. Phoebe winced in sympathy. There was blood on his breeches too, but he couldn't have lost too much or he wouldn't still be standing.

"Your arm needs seeing to," she said.

"I can manage."

"I'm sure you can, but I have *two* hands available to tend to it." She made another spill and used it to light the pair of candles standing on the mantelpiece.

"Sit down," she said, moving a chair closer to the fire.

His lips twitched. "Whatever you say, *citoyenne*." He sat, resting the elbow of his injured arm on his knee with his hand in the air, leaning over to try to inspect the damage.

Phoebe dragged a small table over, steadying the lamp on it. The brighter light allowed her to get a closer look.

"This isn't a job for you," he said. "If you would pass me that bowl and some water—"

"Nonsense," Phoebe said, firmly suppressing her own doubts. She'd seen her father deal with worse injuries, and she was all Leon had for the moment. "I'll need to clean it up so I can see how deep it is. What was it, a knife?"

"Broken bottle." He raised one eyebrow.

"My father was a doctor," she explained. "I helped him sometimes."

"Unusual." There was no condemnation in his expression.

"I know. He had quite a few unusual ideas." She swallowed a lump in her throat; she missed him, still.

Standing abruptly, she went to investigate the bundle the maid had left. It was the dress she'd been mending earlier. When she shook it out, her scissors clattered to the floor. Picking a spot, she made a snip in the fabric and pulled, smiling in satisfaction as it tore.

"What...?"

"My aunt's gown. The cleaner parts of it should do to start with. Now, can you turn your hand in a little more?"

She knelt on the floor at his feet, gently dabbing his arm with a dampened piece of the blue silk dress. It was good to have something to focus on, something useful to do. His skin felt cold to her touch at first as she gently soaked off the blood that had begun to congeal in the gash. As she worked, she was conscious of the rigid muscles beneath the skin she was cleaning, and the growing warmth of his flesh.

She kept her gaze firmly on her work until the cut was clean, occasionally pushing her hair out of her eyes with one wrist. When it was done, she sat back on her heels. Her father's instructions came back to her. *Check it's clean inside.* The broken bottle could have pushed dirt and bits of linen fibre into the wound.

"You've made it bleed again," Leon said, as if making conversation.

"I need to make sure there is no dirt in it," she said. "The Lord alone knows what you were rolling in out there." She paused. "Although as I can't smell anything particularly obnoxious, it may well only be mud rather than... than animal droppings."

She moved the lamp to illuminate the wound better and inspected it, spotting a few strands of fabric.

Clean all your instruments. Her father's colleagues had laughed at him for his insistence on cleanliness, but even if it did no good, it would surely do no harm. Rinsing her scissors in the bowl of water, she checked that all Sarchet's blood was cleaned off them, then poured some brandy into a glass and dipped them in that.

Using the scissor points as tweezers, she gently pulled out a couple of scraps of fabric. Breath hissing between Leon's teeth indicated that she'd hurt him, but she had no choice. Worse was to come.

"Finished?" he asked when she put the scissors down.

"No. I should wash it out with salty water."

He shook his head. "There's none here, and I'd rather neither of us left this room this evening. Is there another option?"

"Brandy." She picked up the bottle. "This will help to stop your arm getting infected. It's not ideal, but there isn't anything else to use. It will hurt, though."

"Go ahead." He shrugged. "It can't hurt more than the cut."

"Yes, it can. This will *really* hurt, especially now you're not fighting. Perhaps you'd better drink some brandy, too."

He obediently swallowed the drink she held out to him.

"Ready?"

He nodded.

She took hold of his wrist and gently poured brandy into the gash on his arm. His muscles tensed and he hissed in a breath, then swore. She used enough to wash out any bits of dirt, then waited while he rested his head on his good hand, dragging in deep breaths.

Better hurt now than infected limbs later. Her father's dictum made sense, but this was the first time she had inflicted such pain. She bit her lip, wishing she could help but knowing that all she could do was wait.

After a few minutes his breathing returned to normal and he sat up straight, rubbing a hand across his forehead.

"You were right," he admitted, his voice slightly shaky. "Finished?"

"No."

CHAPTER 8

"*B*andages?" Alex suggested.

"I can bandage it up, yes, and it will be fine if you wear a sling and don't move it for a few days." She peered at his arm once more, then at his face, doubt clear in her expression.

"You don't believe I'll rest my arm?" Alex asked.

"Will you?" She tilted her head to one side, her mouth curving up at the corners.

"What is the alternative?"

"I can stitch it up, but it will hurt."

"Stitches," he decided. Being able to use his arm was far more important than enduring a little more pain. He hadn't thrown up when she applied the brandy, although he'd come close. He would control himself again.

Miss Deane refilled his glass, and he sipped from it while she took needle and thread out of her pocket. She ran her hands through her hair, and Alex admired the way it reflected the lamplight in shades of orange and red as she twisted it into a tail behind her head and secured it. A shame, really, to tie it all back.

Filling the other glass with brandy, she dropped the needle and a length of thread in the liquid, and rubbed brandy on her hands. Her actions until now had been confident, but she hesitated when she had the needle threaded.

"Have you done this before?" Alex asked.

She nodded. "My father let me stitch up a cut leg, once." She appeared amused, but did not share the joke. "Are you sure you are happy for me to do this?"

"Happy isn't the right word, but it needs to be done."

Alex forced himself to keep his arm still, sucking air in through clenched teeth as she stuck a needle through his skin. After that he concentrated on not swearing, trying to avoid flinching as the thread pulled at his flesh.

Needing a distraction, he stopped watching the needle, staring instead at one red curl that fell over her shoulder. It rested on a fichu partly filling the low neckline of her dress. He tried to make out the curve of her breasts beneath the thin fabric, half-ashamed to be doing so while she was helping him.

"Done," she said, as she finished tying off the last stitch, looking rather pale.

"Thank you." He twisted his arm experimentally. It hurt, but compared to what she'd just put him through, it was nothing.

"Stop that," she scolded. "I'll bandage it up in a minute."

"How did your last patient get on after you had stitched him up?"

"The squire got several more years of hunting out of him," she said, her voice light as she picked up the torn strips of cloth.

"A horse?"

Her smile widened.

"You lied to me!"

"No."

As he recalled what she had said, he started to laugh. He finally sobered when his ribs hurt again, and met her gaze.

She wasn't laughing, but her smile lit her eyes, and the lamplight turned her hair to fire. He caught his breath, his muscles tensing as he resisted the impulse to reach out and run his fingers over the curls. The woman before him was far from the drab creature he'd first seen two days ago.

She returned his gaze, one brow raised.

"Sore ribs" he lied, looking away, his breathing gradually returning to normal. The sound of tearing silk broke into his thoughts.

"Bandage?" he asked

She examined the blue dress critically. "It's not very clean. At this point in a novel, the heroine usually sacrifices her petticoats," she added with another smile.

"I think I have a clean shirt left in my bag." Alex tried hard to dismiss a mental image of her lifting her skirts to make a bandage. He stood—too quickly. When the room had stopped moving, he went over to where he'd left his bag on the far side of the bed.

The clothing inside was jumbled. Someone had searched through his things: Perrault, most likely. There was nothing worth stealing in there, and he was too tired to worry about it. He extracted the shirt and handed it over, wanting to simply lie down and sleep, but Miss Deane beckoned him back to sit in the chair.

She cut a strip off the bottom of the shirt tail, doubled it over and laid it along his wound, fastening it in place with strips of blue silk.

"Very fetching," he said, approvingly.

Miss Deane emptied the bowl of bloody water out of the window, and poured in more clean water from the jug.

"I can manage the rest." Alex took the bowl and another piece of blue silk from her. They had to spend the night in the same room; best not to have her bathing his face while he gawped at her bosom again.

Dabbing gingerly at his jaw and eyes with the now-cold water, he discovered a lump on one temple, but his eyes didn't seem to be swelling. Hands and face clean, he decided to leave the rest.

"You have the bed," he said. "I'll sleep on the floor."

"You should put your nightshirt on," Miss Deane gestured towards the screen in the corner of the room. "Your clothes are wet. You'll take a chill."

That made sense. He pulled his nightshirt out and went behind the screen. Removing his shirt brought every sore muscle to his attention, but none were bad enough to impede his movement. When he emerged, Miss Deane had placed a blanket and pillow on the chair and turned down the remaining bed coverings. His coat and greatcoat hung on the hooks on the back of the door, and the pistol lay on a small table beside the bed.

"You lie on the bed until I'm ready," she said.

Too tired to even think of arguing, Alex did as he was told. There was something else he should have dealt with, he was sure, but he couldn't bring it to mind.

Something had woken him, but he didn't know what. He lay still, listening. It was dark, only the glow from the dying fire giving faint illumination to the room.

Moving his eyes, he took in as much of the room as he could without lifting his head. A shaft of light penetrated the darkness; he heard a faint scraping. Someone was opening the door.

Alex rolled his head, aware of the aches in his muscles. As he looked, the door opened wider. A figure blocked the light for an instant before quietly edging through the gap and into the shadow behind the door.

Miss Deane?

No, it was a man. Faint sounds of breathing, and of cloth moving, came from beside the fire as well as behind the door. Miss Deane was also awake.

Alex disentangled his arms from the bedclothes and reached out to the table beside the bed, praying he didn't knock anything off it before he found his pistol. Feeling cautiously, his fingers touched something cold—a glass. Then wood, metal. Curling his fingers around the butt of the pistol, he lifted it and brought it close to his body.

He pulled the hammer back, unable to muffle the sound as it clicked into the cocked position. The shadowy figure by the door moved swiftly, pulling the door to behind him as he left the room.

There was silence for a minute, broken only by a shifting log in the fire.

"He's gone," Miss Deane whispered. "Should I light a lamp?"

"Please." Alex pushed himself to a sitting position.

Her shape blocked the light from the fire as she bent down, holding a candle to the embers. She used that to light the lamp, then moved to the door and checked it was latched.

He kept his voice low. "Did you unlock it?"

"No." She crossed to the mantelpiece for the key he had given her earlier, and locked the door.

"Leave the key in the lock this time," Alex said. "Turn it a little so it can't be pushed out if he tries again. Someone obtained a spare key."

She nodded, and returned to her chair.

"Could you see who it was?"

"No," she replied, looking at the door. "Too tall for Perrault, though. Not Sarchet either. What do you think he wanted?"

"*Merde!*" He flung the bedcovers off and moved over to the door. Thrusting a hand into a pocket on his greatcoat, he felt around frantically, and swore again. How could he have been so stupid?

"What is wrong? Did he take something?"

"A packet."

"Oh." She fumbled in her skirts. "This fell out of your coat pocket when I stole your pistol."

Alex took it and examined the seal; it was still unbroken, and his shoulders sagged with relief. He tried not to contemplate what would be said if he'd lost this.

"You were supposed to use the bed," he said, putting the packet on the table. He must have fallen asleep very quickly.

"That's kind of you, but I think your need is greater than mine." She blew out the candle and turned the lamp down, then wrapped herself in the blanket and closed her eyes.

He knew he should argue, should give her the bed, but his eyes were already closing of their own accord.

Phoebe winced as pain shot through her neck. Turning her head slowly from side to side, she dug her fingers into her stiff muscles, then cautiously sat up to stretch her back. Eyes gritty from disturbed sleep, she took in the patch of grey where pre-dawn light filtered through the thin curtains. Sounds of activity from below stairs blended with the slow cadence of Leon's breathing.

A confusion of images and feelings from the previous evening tumbled through her mind, as they had done at frequent intervals during the night. She would not go back to sleep now, not in this uncomfortable chair.

Moving quietly, she untangled herself from the blanket and folded it, then stood and tightened her stays, straightening her clothing as best she could. Her hair she could do little about, but a pale glimmer on the floor near the door turned out to be the cap she had lost yesterday in the parlour. She bundled her hair into it and checked that her pockets were still securely tied beneath her gown.

The key turned with a quiet snick, and she paused to check she had not disturbed Leon. Sleep would help him heal. There was enough light in the room to make out his unmoving shape beneath the blankets, one of his pistols on the table next to the bed, along with the little packet she'd returned to him.

It was important to him, that much had been clear last night when he thought it had been stolen. To forget about it when he returned to the room, and then to simply leave it on the table, showed how hurt and tired he must have been.

Because of me.

She couldn't leave the room unlocked with his packet lying there, but she didn't want to lock him in the room with it, either. Picking it up, she turned it over, seeing only that it was sealed with a wafer. The temptation to open it was strong, but she tucked it between her chemise and her stays. She scribbled a note on a page from her sketchbook, and let herself out of the room.

The parlour door stood open. She hesitated as she heard Perrault's voice ordering coffee, and turned instead in the direction of the taproom. A woman wiping the tables went off to fetch coffee willingly enough when Phoebe asked. The room stank of spilled ale, pipe smoke, and unwashed bodies, so she took her drink out through the front door.

Deep breaths of the chill air cleared her head, even as the cold pierced her gown. She slipped slowly, warming her hands on the mug. Too chilled to stand still, she walked around the building into the stable yard at the back, and found a spot by the wall where she could catch the first rays of the rising sun.

The dark menace of the previous night had gone, and the yard was a bustle of activity. Men moved barrels and crates while ostlers forked piles of straw from the stables. The noise of clattering pots and pans from the kitchen told of breakfast being prepared. Phoebe stood for a short while, eyes closed against the sunlight, breathing the appetising smells of hot coffee and baking bread. She was beginning to feel more awake.

A crash and a volley of foul language roused her. One of the men had dropped the end of a crate, and sat on the damp cobbles holding his injured foot. She smiled as she recalled Leon's language the night before, when she'd poured brandy into his wounded arm. He, too, had come out with some interesting...

She thought back more carefully—some interesting *English* curses.

She had no idea how well, if at all, Leon spoke English, but surely a Frenchman would use his own language under such circumstances. If he were English, that could explain why he had stopped to help them.

Brevare—was he English too? She had no way of knowing. What *was* the connection between the two men?

CHAPTER 9

*A*lex woke slowly, at first conscious only of the ache in his limbs and short stabs of pain when he turned over. The fight, yes. Other fragmented memories came back as the stitches pulled against his skin: red curls and that smile, the burn of alcohol against his torn flesh, the shadowed hollow beneath her fichu hinting at the hidden curves, the stab of the needle.

She'd manoeuvred him into taking the bed again. Most ungentlemanly of him to accede, but he was grateful for it. He turned his head far enough to see the chair she'd occupied the night before. Only a pillow and a folded blanket on it gave any indication there had been a second occupant of the room.

The packet?

He sat up abruptly, cursing. Why had he left it on the table by the bed instead of putting it under his pillow?

It was not there now, but there was a piece of paper, weighed down by the room key. *I have it safe,* the note said.

Had she taken it as a bargaining tool? No—he could easily take it from her by force if she tried to negotiate with him, and she was too intelligent to try with Perrault.

Lying back in the bed, reluctant to leave its comfort, he mentally catalogued the damage. His ribs were fine as long as he didn't move too suddenly, but his injured arm ached. Peeling away one end of the bandage, he could see that the cut had sealed itself. The line of it was red and slightly swollen, but it didn't seem to be infected. Time would tell.

He continued his inventory. His knuckles were raw in places, and his hands felt stiff when he flexed his fingers, but that would wear off soon.

Reluctantly, he pushed the bedclothes back and stretched before standing up, feeling more alert than he had in days. The visitor in the night had woken him, but he must have slept soundly afterwards, as Miss Deane hadn't disturbed him when she left.

He shook his head. That was worrying in itself—he must be more careful.

The breeches and shirt he had been wearing the previous evening hung over a chair near the fireplace. The garments were dry, if filthy. He tried to brush the mud off, but soon gave up, bundled them both together, and stowed them in the bottom of his bag. He donned his spare breeches and the shirt Miss Deane had cut his dressing from, and carefully inserted his arms into his coat.

He winced at his reflection in the mirror above the fireplace. An ordinary face at the best of times, it would now be good for frightening ladies and young children. In addition to various cuts and grazes, the skin under one eye was turning black, even though the eye itself was not swollen. One thing was certain: he wasn't going to attempt to shave this morning.

He reloaded the pistol that had been fired and put both weapons in his greatcoat pockets. Holding the coat over his shoulder, he stepped into the short corridor leading to the stairs. The sound of voices made him pause—female voices speaking in English.

The comtesse.

Treading quietly, he moved closer to their door.

"—hasn't been back here all night."

"It wasn't her fault, Mama."

"Nonsense, she didn't try to get into the room."

The daughter's reply was a low murmur, even with his ear pressed to the door.

"She could have asked for a spare key," the comtesse said. "If she hadn't pretended to be a servant, none of this would have happened. Well, she won't be having a season with you this year."

His body tensed as he listened—that sounded horribly like triumph. Did the woman really think Miss Deane would not have gone back to their room if she had been able to?

Another low murmur from the daughter.

"Don't argue with me Hélène, she's obviously no better than she should be."

"But Mama, if you dislike her so much, why does she live with us?" Hélène's voice was louder now. "Georges likes her, and—"

"It was not my choice. Your father insisted."

Alex winced at the venom in the comtesse's tone. He banged on the door with his fist, finding some satisfaction in the answering shriek.

"Get dressed," he shouted, in French. "If you're not in the parlour in fifteen minutes, you'll go without breakfast." He lowered his voice. "And keep your voices down if you want to get to the coast."

Shrill complaints followed him down the stairs. Sticking his head around the parlour door, he saw only Perrault and Brevare, breakfasting at separate tables. He told Perrault to let the women out of their room.

A serving woman carrying a tray caught his eye and jerked her head towards the rear door. Puzzled, Alex walked out to the scene of the fight, to see Miss Deane standing in a patch of sunshine against the inn wall.

Naturally, the entire population of the inn assumes I...

His anger subsided as he realised that people were just going about their business. No-one was looking askance at her, or making snide comments.

"—no, no, Hélène. The grey gown."

That damned woman again—her voice carried through a window above them. He took in the droop of Miss Deane's shoulders, the downward curve of her lips; she must have overheard her aunt's earlier words.

"Are you all right?"

Phoebe jumped. She had been listening to her aunt to the exclusion of other sounds in the yard. Turning, she saw Leon's gaze on her, and noted the cuts and bruises on his face with concern.

"My aunt. Her voice carries." Her throat felt tight, and she swallowed. She knew her aunt didn't like her, but it hurt to find out that the comtesse hadn't wanted to take her in.

"Yes, I heard. I'm sorry." He looked away, his lips compressed.

"It's not your fault," Phoebe said. "Do you want your packet?"

"You have it safe?"

She put her hand to the neck of her gown, hesitating as one corner of his mouth quirked upwards.

"If you don't mind keeping it for me today, I think it's safer there than sewn into my pocket. Have you eaten?"

She lifted the empty mug in her hand. "Only coffee. But Perrault is in the parlour."

His eyes focused on her dress. "You must be cold. Your aunt will be breakfasting downstairs. Once they're out of their room, I can have your breakfast sent up there, if you wish? Your trunk should still be in there."

"Thank you."

"My pleasure." He smiled and went back into the inn. She followed, taking refuge in the taproom until she heard her aunt's voice coming from the parlour, then went to their bedchamber.

Phoebe locked the door of her aunt's room after a maid brought breakfast and hot water. Although the fresh bread smelled wonderful, feeling clean would be even better, so she undressed. The chill in the room caused goose bumps on her skin, but after she'd washed and donned a clean chemise she felt refreshed. She laced up her stays and considered the orange gown. The skirts were stained with mud and blood, and she doubted that sponging it down would get the marks out.

Her spare gown was a pastel peach colour, no more flattering than the orange one, but it was clean. Phoebe combed her hair, pinning it all up beneath a fresh cap, then stood straight and smoothed her skirts. Whatever her aunt thought, she had done nothing wrong and she would not act as if she had.

She ate and drank with appreciation, then stuffed all her belongings into the trunk. She struggled down the stairs with it and out through the front door of the inn.

The coach was ready, the horses standing harnessed with an ostler at their heads. She caught a glimpse of Perrault's profile inside, already claiming one of the forward-facing corners. Leon and Brevare stood nearby, Leon with his arms folded, looking impatient.

His expression lightened when he saw her. He came over and took the trunk from her hands, directing Brevare to get the remaining trunks brought down.

By the time the comtesse and Hélène appeared, Phoebe could hear Perrault muttering about 'damned aristos'. The comtesse swept past them, only looking around to send a disgusted glare in Phoebe's direction.

"Come, Hélène. You should not be associating with such a person."

"But Mama, Phoebe—"

"Now, Hélène!"

Hélène cast what could have been an apologetic look in Phoebe's direction, but followed her mother into the coach without further protest. Phoebe turned away, pressing her lips together, and came face to face with Brevare.

Brevare's eyes narrowed as he looked after the comtesse, then he returned his gaze to Phoebe. "I'll be driving. Would you like to ride on the box, Miss... er...?"

"Deane." Phoebe gave the tiniest of curtsies, then stood with her chin up and shoulders back. The best counter to her aunt's hostility was to not let it affect her.

"It will be cold," Brevare added. "Lend her your greatcoat, West... Leon. You won't need it inside the coach."

"Thank you, *citoyen*." Why did Brevare want her to ride with him? She glanced at Leon.

"Why not?" Leon said, after a momentary hesitation. Phoebe noticed a wince as he removed his greatcoat. He transferred something from one pocket to the day coat he had on beneath, then held the greatcoat so Phoebe could put her arms in. She took off her cloak and put the coat on. It was heavy, almost wrapping round her twice, and smelled strongly of horses. But it was warm.

Leon helped her scramble up onto the box and she tucked her cloak around her skirts. With that, and the oiled cloth the drivers used to cover their legs, she should be warm enough for a while. Regardless, not having to face her aunt's hostility would make up for the cold.

There was a heavy lump in the coat. Putting her hand in the pocket, she found that Leon had left one of his pistols there. She withdrew her hand carefully; she didn't trust the thing not to go off by accident. He had moved something from this greatcoat to the jacket he still wore, so he must have deliberately left this pistol for her. Did he think she might need it?

Leon and Brevare conferred, their heads bent together over a book as Leon pointed out something on the pages. Leon straightened, giving her an encouraging smile as Brevare climbed up and sorted out the reins. Below them, the coach door finally slammed, and Brevare flicked the whip to get the horses moving.

The earlier clouds had cleared and the wintry sun had a little warmth in it. Phoebe enjoyed looking at the scenery for a while as they passed through several villages, before turning her thoughts to Brevare. He was travelling with Leon, but if they were colleagues, why had he sat eating dinner in the inn where they'd been arrested instead of returning with a horse straight away? Where had he been during the fight? Leon could have been seriously injured or even killed.

He seemed to know where he was going, slowing only briefly to check the fingerposts, but after an hour or so, he felt in his pocket and handed a book to Phoebe. It looked like the one the two men had been consulting earlier.

"Here, take this, will you?" he said. "The page is marked."

It was a road guide, well thumbed.

"Which village should we be looking for next?"

Phoebe opened the book, fumbling in gloved fingers. There were pencil marks against some village names. She guessed that these were places they would pass through, but she hadn't been paying attention to the fingerposts and didn't know how far they had come.

"You *can* read, can't you?"

Surprised, Phoebe glanced at him. His attention was on the road and a particularly deep set of ruts.

"Yes," she said.

Brevare muttered a curse and pulled the horses to a stop. He took the book out of her hands, flicked through the pages, and jabbed a finger at the name of a village. "We have just been through there," he said, then moved his finger to the next name with a cross by it. "We are going there next. When we get there, tell me the name of the next village with a cross. Can you manage that?"

"Yes." Did he think she was an idiot?

"Is there a problem?" The voice was Leon's, calling from a coach window.

"Only checking directions," Brevare called back, urging the horses into motion again. They drove on through another village, and Phoebe pointed out the way at the next signpost.

"Just tell me the next village," Brevare snapped.

"Sainte-Marie."

Keeping one finger in the current page, Phoebe surreptitiously looked through the book, checking that the marked sequence of villages was taking them north-west, towards the coast somewhere near Caen or Le Havre. Then she tried to trace the way they'd come, but she hadn't been able to read fingerposts from inside the coach yesterday. Making a rough estimation of how far they'd travelled each day, she smiled. She couldn't be sure, but she suspected they'd been heading for Caen from the moment Leon took charge.

"Miss Deane!"

She looked up with a start, and turned to the correct page in the book. "Condret."

Brevare made the turn before he glanced at her. "Have you worked for the comtesse long?"

His tone had lost the earlier impatience, but he was frowning. Not merely making idle conversation, then? She faced forwards, keeping most of her face hidden from him by the rim of her bonnet.

"I have been with her for four years." Phoebe carefully phrased her reply to tell the truth, if not the whole truth.

"You *are* English, are you not?"

"Yes."

"You speak French well."

Phoebe decided to act the rather unintelligent servant he appeared to think her. "Thank you, sir." He sighed, and she suppressed a smile. She was annoying him nicely.

"Tell me how an English girl like you comes to speak French so well," he said.

"The comtesse visits her château and brings me with her."

"Do you like it in France? Or do you prefer England?"

"They both have very pretty countryside." What did he really want to know?

His lips thinned, but he didn't speak as he slowed through the next village, carefully guiding the coach past market stalls lining the road.

"Miss... er..."

"Deane."

"Yes," he said. "Miss Deane, are you loyal to your country?"

"Of course, sir."

"I.... I need your help with something."

"Yes, sir?"

"My... my colleague is carrying a message. I need to see it."

The packet. "A message, sir?"

"You don't need to know the details. You must trust my word on this. It is vital I see that message."

"But I don't know who you are."

"My name is Hugo de Brevare. I am... I was the Vicomte de Brevare."

That would fit with his accent.

"I need that message to... it is necessary to stop these revolutionaries. There'll be a few livres in it for you."

A few coins for betraying the man who had saved her? But it would not be wise to refuse outright. "I don't know what *I* can do, sir."

"You can begin by searching the pockets of that coat you have on."

So that was why he'd asked if she wished to ride on the box. Phoebe obediently felt in the pockets, showing him a handful of coins and a handkerchief. She didn't mention the pistol.

"Nothing else?" he asked, disappointed.

"No, sir."

"Feel the linings," he instructed. "The message may be sewn inside it somewhere."

Phoebe went through the motions of searching for the packet already tucked inside her stays. "There is nothing there," she said at last.

He cursed under his breath. "You must try to find it later," he said. "It is really *very* important. You should be able to search his bag and his other clothing tonight!"

Phoebe's amusement vanished. She turned her face away, afraid she could not control her expression. Not only did he think she was a servant, but he assumed Leon had bedded her and was going to do so again.

She took a deep breath. For a man of his class, such an assumption was not unexpected. She *had* spent the night in Leon's room, and had readily accepted his coat this morning. Muttering something that could be taken as agreement, she pretended to concentrate on the road guide until they stopped for refreshment.

CHAPTER 10

The inn where they stopped to eat wasn't busy, and there were plenty of tables to choose from in the dining room. Alex sat with Brevare, keeping a wary eye on everyone else as he ate. The comtesse was not deigning to speak to Miss Deane, and although Hélène cast a sympathetic glance at her cousin, the sentiment did not seem to be strong enough for her to go against her mama's orders. Nor did the comtesse wish Miss Deane to sit with them, pointedly choosing a table with space for only two.

Alex noted Miss Deane's hesitation, her lips turning down a little, then her shoulders squared as she took her plate over to a window seat. His dislike of the comtesse grew.

Perrault ate his way through a huge plate of food, occasionally brushing breadcrumbs from his coat, his eyes continually moving from one person to the next. Perrault had been alone in the carriage with the comtesse and her daughter for several minutes before they set off. Had either of the women said something they should not have done?

Casting a sideways glance at Brevare, Alex wondered what he'd said to Miss Deane while they were on the box of the coach. He could have made a grave error of judgement in asking her to look after his message and then leaving her alone with Brevare.

Brevare rose and went over to Miss Deane, his sudden movement pulling Alex from his worries. Brevare gestured towards their own table. Miss Deane's posture stiffened, and she stood abruptly, sending her chair scraping across the floor. Turning on her heel, she stalked out of the room, her food hardly touched.

Damn. None of this was her fault, yet she was being treated like a pariah by her family, and now Brevare had upset her as well.

Alex moved over to where Brevare still stood by the window. "What did you say to her?"

Brevare glanced at him. "Nothing," he muttered, and went back to eat the rest of his meal.

There was no sign of Miss Deane in the entrance hall. Remembering her preference for being outside this morning, he headed out of the building only to see her disappearing behind a team of horses being harnessed to a carriage. By the time he'd moved beyond the animals she had reached the road, striding at a brisk pace towards a crossroads.

She wasn't trying to escape or abscond with his message; she had more sense than that. Perhaps she was trying to walk off her feelings.

Sticking two fingers in his mouth, he whistled. She turned to face him, but made no move to return. Their way lay to the left at the crossroads, so he pointed. They would catch her up soon enough with the coach.

She took a few steps in the direction he'd indicated, then looked towards him. He waved a hand and went back into the inn.

Phoebe had stormed out of the inn without Leon's coat, but walking soon warmed her against the chill air. Had she misunderstood Brevare's suggestion? He'd said that sitting with Leon now would make it easier for her to get close to him tonight.

No, she had understood him perfectly well. It was little different from what he'd implied on the coach, and it was foolish of her to get so upset about it. True, he had made assumptions about both her and Leon's morals, but that reflected more on his own standards than hers. It was the idea that she should actively pursue the presumed liaison, following her aunt's snub, that had tipped her into anger.

Her pace slowed. What her aunt thought was more important—that could have a drastic effect on her future. A blackbird crossed her path, chattering in alarm. Phoebe, diverted from her worries, stopped to watch it swoop over the hedge and vanish into the adjacent field. Her uncle was a fair man; surely he would not hold the events of yesterday against her?

She marched on at a more moderate pace until she heard the clop of hooves behind her, appreciating the opportunity to get the blood moving in her limbs. Her mood lifted at the sight of Leon, rather than Brevare, in the driving seat. He was the nearest thing to a friend she had at the moment.

He pulled the horses to a halt and leaned over, holding out a hand to help her up onto the seat. She took it gladly. A cold ride on the box was far preferable to joining her aunt inside the coach.

"You'd better put that on again," he said, nodding towards his coat lying on the bench between them. She struggled into it as he flicked the horses into motion, and arranged its length under her bottom. He handed over his road guide when she had sorted herself out.

"Can you look after this? I might need it later." He gave her a small bundle wrapped in a napkin. "You'd better have this, too."

Unwrapping it, Phoebe found a bread roll and some cheese. "Thank you," she said, biting into the roll. The exercise had helped to calm her emotions; the food, and the kindness behind it, cured what remained of her irritability.

"Better now?"

"Much better, thank you." She settled against the backrest and looked around, beginning to enjoy the scenery. But the memory of Brevare's request—no, instruction—that morning returned too quickly, along with her conclusion that the two men were not working together.

She opened her mouth, about to ask him, but thought better of it.

"Out with it," Leon said, with a sideways glance.

"I beg your pardon?"

"You were going to say something, or ask something."

She didn't reply.

"Nice weather for the time of year, isn't it?" he offered blandly. "Lucky, really. It could be raining, or even snowing, then you'd have to choose between sitting in silence with your aunt glaring at you inside the coach, or sitting in silence with me getting cold and wet."

She shot a quick glance at his face—the bruises she had seen earlier were darkening, the black eye developing into a real shiner. Added to his unshaven jaw, the whole effect was completely disreputable. He must have intimidated the comtesse this morning in the coach, for Phoebe hadn't heard a single word from her. But he did not look as tired and strained as he had when she had first seen him, and she wasn't afraid of him any longer.

"I never thanked you for saving me from Sarchet," she said. "And for not..." Her voice faded out.

"You are very welcome. Although I had more than one reason for fighting him, and might not have won without your help." A sheepish grin spread across his face.

"You enjoyed it?"

"I'm afraid so. Right up to the point when he picked up that bottle. But at least we're rid of him now."

"And now there's one less person to share the ransom with."

The silence grew, and Phoebe wondered if she'd overstepped the bounds of his tolerance.

"What were you originally going to say?" He kept his eyes on the road, and his voice held little expression.

Beating about the bush wasn't going to get her anywhere with this man. She needed some answers: where they were really going, what further lies she might be forced to tell.

"Brevare—is he really a vicomte?"

"He told you that?" His voice was as expressionless as before.

"Yes. Is he your friend?"

"An acquaintance, rather than a friend. And yes, he is, or was, a vicomte. Why do you ask?"

"He asked me if I was loyal to England, and told me to look for a message you were carrying. He said it was necessary to stop the revolutionaries."

"You didn't show it to him?" His voice sounded remarkably calm after the consternation he'd shown in the night when he thought he'd lost it.

"No. I have it safe. Do you want it?" She put her hand inside her coat, but he shook his head.

"It's safer with you than me at the moment, if you don't mind keeping it."

"Very well." He trusted her—the notion spread a warm feeling through her chest.

"Why didn't you give it to him?" Leon's gaze searched her face.

"Why should I?"

"I haven't given you any reason not to," he said, turning back to the road. "Unless it was some kind of gratitude for last night?"

"Mostly that, I suppose. But also, you are our best chance for getting home. He's done nothing to help." She reconsidered her words. "That is, nothing deliberately to help."

"What do you mean?"

She hesitated, wondering if she was imagining things, reading too much into little details. "At the inn where Perrault tried to get us arrested, Brevare was eating in the taproom when we arrived, taking his time. If he'd gone back for you with the spare horse right away, you could both have eaten at the inn and been on your way long before we arrived."

"I thought he'd taken a long time." He was almost talking to himself.

"Why would he delay you?"

"I'm not sure. Have you noticed anything else?"

"I think it may have been him at the door in the night. Whoever was there was searching your coat, and today he asked me to look through its pockets."

79

"Which you did?"

"Oh yes. Strangely, I didn't find anything he was interested in." She smiled.

"You lied to him?"

"No."

"Hmm." He had his eyes on the road ahead, but she could see the curve of his lips before he spoke. "In the same way you didn't lie about the squire's horse."

She laughed this time. "Someone searched your bag, did they not?" she went on. "It wasn't Perrault—at least, not while he was in that room with me. It could have been Brevare. I didn't notice him in the yard when you were fighting Sarchet."

"You are very observant. But none of that proves whether either of us is acting in the interests of your country."

She switched to English. "My country and yours."

The reins jerked, making the horses toss their heads. "*Je ne vous comprends pas.*" He sounded as if he really hadn't understood what she'd said.

"Then why did my words surprise you?" Phoebe asked, reverting to French. Now she was more confident that she was correct. "You *are* English, aren't you? Brevare started to call you a different name this morning. An Englishman carrying something to England is more likely to be supporting England than France."

"Who else have you said that to?" His words were sharp, tension evident in the muscles of his jaw.

"No-one."

His face relaxed a little. "How did I give myself away?" he asked, resignation in his voice.

Phoebe closed her eyes, sighing with relief. She'd worried that what she *wanted* to be true might have clouded her reasoning. "There were some distinctly English oaths when I poured the brandy on your arm. I doubt anyone else would have any idea."

Leon shook his head. He drove in silence, coming out of his abstraction at turnings only to read the signposts. Phoebe watched him covertly, wanting to ask what he was doing here, but it was none of her business. He hadn't said so, but she knew now that he was taking them home—that should be enough.

"Why are you in France?" he asked eventually. "Does your uncle have estates here?"

"A château and lands at Calvac," Phoebe said. "My uncle moved us all to London over a year ago, when the situation became too dangerous. Then in January he went away somewhere on business. I think he sent Anson over here to collect some remaining documents." She stiffened, ashamed that she had given no thought to Anson over the last couple of days. "I don't know what happened to him."

"I sent him to the coast. I got him to pay off the servants you had with you before he left; they were happy enough to avoid trouble and go home. He's likely to be safer on the diligence than he would have been remaining in your aunt's company."

That was true. Although his French was poor, he would have the sense to remain inconspicuous while travelling on the public coaches.

"Go on. Anson was sent over…"

"While my uncle was away, the comtesse decided to accompany him. She said she had to collect some of her jewels that had been left at Calvac."

"Hmm."

Phoebe didn't believe it either. Anson could easily have been told where to find such things. She recalled the packet of letters she'd glimpsed. Old love letters, perhaps? Something that her aunt didn't want Anson—or even her uncle—to know about?

She put that idea out of her mind. She could think about that later when—if—they returned to England.

"Do you live with your aunt and uncle?"

"Yes."

Leon glanced at her, one eyebrow raised.

Phoebe hesitated, wondering why he was asking, but it could do no harm to answer his questions. "The comtesse is my mother's sister. Their father, my grandfather, was Viscount Wycombe. He did not approve of my mother marrying my father, so he cut her off."

"The doctor?"

She nodded. "When my parents died, four years ago, my uncle took me in."

"I'm sorry."

Phoebe managed a smile. "I miss them, and I miss my old life too. London is so… confined." She walked in the park, when a maid could be spared to go with her, or took outings with her ten-year-old cousin Georges and his governess.

Leon lapsed into silence again after that. Phoebe gazed at the passing hedges, coppices, and fields, but there was little of interest in the countryside hereabouts. Tiring of the scenery, she opened the road guide and tried to work out where they were and how far they had to go.

She found the page with the villages marked, but none of the names looked like any she had seen on signposts. Flicking back through the book, she found some names she recognised, then consulted a few more pages.

They were no longer heading for Caen.

Phoebe was debating whether to ask about their new destination when Leon switched the reins to his right hand, wincing as he flexed his left arm.

"We should stop before dark," she suggested. "It will hurt even more if you are going to drive all day tomorrow."

His head turned sharply in her direction. "Damn it, woman, are you a mind reader?" He didn't sound or look angry, in spite of his words. Curious, perhaps. "Why do you suggest I won't be getting Brevare to drive tomorrow?"

"Brevare was—is—travelling with you, but you don't trust him," she said. "You didn't trust him before I told you he wanted your message, did you? If you did, you wouldn't have left a pistol in this coat for me this morning."

He nodded.

"He knew that the notion my aunt was a spy was nonsense, and that you are heading for the coast," Phoebe continued. "He rode on the box with Sarchet yesterday, to direct him. Sarchet wouldn't have known we weren't heading for Paris, but Perrault might, so you kept him inside the carriage."

"Correct so far. How did *you* know yesterday that we weren't going to Paris?"

"I didn't guess until the afternoon. The sun was in the wrong direction. I checked in the road guide this morning."

"Go on."

"Last night you told Perrault we would go to Caen. And this morning's route was in roughly that direction. But now we are aiming for somewhere that Brevare doesn't know about either."

Leon shook his head.

"I'm wrong?" Where had her reasoning had gone astray?

"No, you're not wrong." His tone was resigned, or thoughtful, perhaps. "You are a most unusual woman," he said, after driving on for a while.

"Oh?" She hoped it was a compliment.

"You haven't asked me what is in the message, nor where we are going. Most people I know would have been pestering me with questions."

"What's the point? You wouldn't tell me."

He turned to look at her, but she couldn't decipher his expression.

"I might."

CHAPTER 11

*P*hoebe surveyed the small bedroom she'd been allocated. It was cold, with no fire laid in the grate, and contained only a narrow bed, a tiny wash-stand, and a chair. But it suited her far better than sharing her aunt and cousin's larger room. There was no key in the lock, but she could jam the back of the chair under the latch tonight. Laying her bonnet on the bed, she started to unpin her hair.

She tensed as the door opened, but it was only Hélène.

"Mama says you have to come to our room."

Phoebe sighed, and pushed the pins back into place.

"Phoebe… are you… have you…?"

Surprised, Phoebe noted Hélène's frown, and the hesitant way she had spoken.

"I mean… Mama said some things about…" Words appeared to fail Hélène, and she waved a hand.

"I am well, thank you." Despite her aunt's opinion about what had happened.

"Mama says you must—"

"I'll come." Refusing would be storing up trouble. If they did all get home safely, her future would still depend on her aunt.

In the larger room, colour glowed from the gowns strewn across the bed and spilling from the trunks. Her aunt had persuaded someone to bring all their luggage inside. The comtesse thrust a gold-coloured dress towards Phoebe. "Wear this tonight. It's long on Hélène, so it should be only a little short for you."

"That's one of Hélène's best gowns," Phoebe objected.

"It will be more becoming than what you are wearing," the comtesse said. "You'll never be a beauty like Hélène, but you'll look less pasty in that colour. It might help tone down your hair, too."

Phoebe made no move to take the gown, suspicious of her aunt's motives.

"Put it on," the comtesse said impatiently. "Then Hélène can help you with your hair."

"Why?"

"*That man* seems taken with you. If you... play the coquette... with him, he may not ask as much ransom. Hélène's come-out will be expensive."

And we will also try to avoid paying a ransom for poor relations, Phoebe thought bitterly.

"Don't just stand there, girl, put it on!"

Phoebe reluctantly unfastened the peach gown. The gold fabric was lovely, the sleeves ending with a fall of lace below the elbow. She resisted the temptation to stroke the material; under other circumstances she would have enjoyed wearing it. Donning the gown, she carefully checked that Leon's message was still tucked inside her stays while the other two were occupied with their own toilettes.

Phoebe sat before the mirror, scowling at Hélène's reflection as her cousin dressed her hair into a loose collection of curls and picked up a gold ribbon. Was Hélène so poisoned by her mother's pride and selfishness that she thought there was nothing wrong in helping Phoebe to prepare herself to seduce someone? For that was what it amounted to, if the comtesse had her way. Surely Hélène had *some* idea of what normally went on when a man and a woman were together?

"The sacrificial lamb is sufficiently adorned as it is." She lowered her voice to a forceful whisper. "How would you like to be sent to please Brevare so that *he* could help us get home?"

Hélène's eyes widened, the hand holding the ribbon stilled in mid-air.

"I... I didn't think..." Her lower lip began to tremble. "I'm sorry. Mama said—"

"I don't want to hear what she said," Phoebe hissed.

"He would not... I mean, he's a vicomte, he told us in the carriage today. He wouldn't ask a ransom for us. That man must have some hold on him."

"He's not nobility now," Phoebe pointed out, wondering what else Brevare had told her cousin.

"He said he has a château north of Paris. His mother and his sister live there."

Rank and honour seemed to go together in Hélène's mind, but Phoebe didn't agree. She turned to go back to her own room, picking up the peach gown she had taken off. Did Hélène's information have any bearing on Brevare's actions in recent days? He must be worried about his mother and sister, alone in a country gone mad.

When she closed her door, she looked at the gown over her arm, tempted to change into it again. But a good dress did not make a flirtation—the comtesse could not control her behaviour.

She compromised by adding a fichu to fill in the low neckline and redoing her hair in a plainer style. Satisfied with her appearance, she spent the time before dinner going over all that had been said that afternoon.

In the empty taproom, Alex was half-way through his meal when the comtesse swept in, speaking to someone behind her.

"Come in, Phoebe, for heaven's sake. Why are you loitering in the hallway?" Not waiting for an answer, the comtesse seated herself at the table laid for three. Once again, both mother and daughter were dressed as if for a formal dinner.

Miss Deane followed them into the room, her eyes downcast as she removed her shawl and draped it over a chair. Surprise, mingled with a stirring of attraction, filled him as he watched her discreetly. She, too, wore a decent gown instead of the usual shabby garments. Her hair was without its normal enveloping cap, and although she had it arranged in a rather severe style, it still made a fiery halo around her head.

The dress was clearly not hers. The colour lent her skin a creamy glow, but the skirt was a little too short, and the bodice too big. Another cast-off from her cousin? The sash pulled the gown in at her waist and showed off her figure well.

Not that he should be thinking about that, he told himself, forcing his attention back to his plate. He took several mouthfuls before noticing that Brevare was not eating, but looking at the comtesse and her daughter with an odd expression on his face.

"Aren't you hungry?" Alex asked.

Brevare started and cast a quick glance at Alex before picking up his fork. Alex glanced uneasily at the other tables in the room. He hadn't seen Perrault since they had got out of the coach earlier. The man's absence was worrying.

When they finished their meal, Alex leaned back in his chair, nursing a glass of wine. Keeping his gaze ostensibly on the fire, he watched the women from the corner of his eye. The innkeeper had produced pastries in addition to the roast chicken, and the comtesse and her daughter were eating them. Miss Deane was pushing pieces of chicken around her plate, her face expressionless.

He recalled their conversation on the coach. She was observant, that was certain. And she had drawn correct conclusions from the things she had noticed.

He'd told her that he might answer her questions. At the time, he hadn't been sure if he'd meant it, but the more he thought about it, the more the idea appealed to him. The situation had become complicated.

Brevare finished his meal and drained his glass. "More wine?"

"Not yet."

"I will." Brevare pushed his chair back. "I'm going to take a look in the cellar—see if they've got anything better than this." He flicked a disdainful finger at the empty wine bottle.

Alex watched him leave, wondering what he was really going to do.

"Come Hélène," the comtesse said, loudly enough for Alex to hear. "We will spend the evening in our room."

Keeping his face towards his wine glass, Alex turned his eyes their way and saw Miss Deane stand with them, and her aunt's glare.

"You'll stay here, miss," she hissed. "And take that off." The woman took hold of the fichu Miss Deane was wearing and pulled. It came away easily, leaving the low neckline of the gown gaping slightly. "And don't think you can sneak off to your room—I've locked it."

She swept towards the door. Hélène took a few steps after her, then hesitated, turning back towards Phoebe. But any notion she may have had of remaining was thwarted as the comtesse grasped her arm and pulled her out of the room. The door closed behind them with a bang.

Slumping back into her chair, Phoebe rested her head in her hands. How had her aunt locked her room?

"Wine?" Leon put a glass down on the table beside her. "You have a different gown."

Her cheeks grew hot as she sat up, pulling the shawl from the back of her chair and wrapping it around her shoulders. Leon was regarding her with... sympathy? Kindliness, at least, and he was looking at her face, not her bosom.

"It's nice, isn't it?" she said through tight lips. "My aunt hopes it might compensate for my hair and complexion, and make me attractive enough to please you. I'm an offering to try to reduce your asking price." She turned her face away.

He swore softly. In English.

"Watch your language," she muttered. She glanced upwards to see his quick frown, then a wry smile as he worked out what she meant.

"I would never take such advantage." He pushed the wine glass towards her. "Drink that—it'll make you feel better."

The wine helped calm her, but too much would be unwise on an empty stomach. Setting the glass down, she pulled the shawl more closely round her shoulders.

"May I join you?" He gestured at the chair opposite her.

"Do I have a choice?"

"Yes."

He hadn't moved; shame washed through her. "I'm sorry. None of this is your fault. Please, sit. You'd have been far better off if you had just ridden on and left us."

"I'm not so sure about that," he said, pulling out the closest chair and sitting down. He smiled. "You don't intend to do as your aunt says, do you?"

"No," she said, giving him a sharp look. "No," she repeated, her tone softening. She didn't think he'd meant it as a genuine question. "Apart from the obvious reason why not, it wouldn't make any difference anyway."

"How so?"

"Does it matter?"

"Humour me."

She shrugged. "For one thing, you have not been any of the people you've said you were. You're not from Grenoble, you don't work for the Committee of General Security there, you're not even French. It seems unlikely that you are a kidnapper."

"And for another thing?"

"It wouldn't work." She hugged the shawl tighter across her chest.

"Oh?"

She raised her eyes to look at him, knowing he wasn't that obtuse. "If you *were* going to ask for a ransom, you would still do it whether or not you... we..." The words caught in her throat as he returned her gaze, his eyes on hers, his mouth showing a faint curve.

It might not be the worst possible fate.

Her fingers fumbled for the glass, the red liquid sloshing up the sides as she dropped her gaze to hide her confusion. Where had that thought come from? She hadn't said it out loud—had she?

89

She took a sip of the wine, risking a quick glance his way. He was still looking enquiringly at her.

"And a third thing?" he asked.

"What do you mean?"

"I wondered if you had another reason."

She shook her head.

"Don't lie to me," he said.

She was surprised at the urgency in his voice. "I won't lie to you," she said simply. *But nor do I promise to tell you everything.*

He picked up the bottle of wine and went to top up Phoebe's glass.

She put her hand over the glass. "No, thank you."

He set the bottle down again. "I can see if they have anything better."

"Are you trying to get me intoxicated?" she challenged, tipping her head to one side.

He laughed. "No, not at all. I… well, I wanted to talk to you, and thought you might like a drink while we were talking." He looked at the remains of the dinner that had not yet been cleared, now congealed into an unappetising mess. "You didn't eat much."

"No."

"I can order something else if you wish? You should eat after sitting outside in the cold all day."

What did he want to talk to her about? Curiosity, and a sudden pang of hunger, made the decision easy.

"Yes, please."

He went to find the innkeeper, leaving Phoebe toying with her glass. She smiled at the irony: her aunt had wanted her to spend the evening with Leon, and she was doing so.

She turned her head as the door opened. It was Brevare, carrying a bottle of wine. He came over to the table.

"That's a much nicer gown they've given you," he said, appreciation colouring his tone. "It looks well on you."

He put out a hand to touch one of her curls. Phoebe resisted the impulse to slap his hand away.

"You know, you dress up well," he said, sounding surprised. "You get me that message and I'll see you don't lose by it. I'm sure we can come to some arrangement once we're in England. You can't be happy working for that woman."

Phoebe clenched her fingers around the glass, clamping her lips together. So, he was going to help her with her career as a courtesan? How *kind* of him.

Loosening her grip, she pretended to sip the wine, needing to do something to hide the trembling in her hands. Perhaps he would think she was nervous, rather than fighting off the temptation to fling the contents into his face.

She forced her thoughts back to what this insufferable man wanted, and why. "What happens, sir, if I can't find the message?" she asked, relieved to hear the steadiness of her voice.

"You look for it tonight and bring it to me. You can return it later."

He hadn't answered the question, but there was no point in persisting. "What if he catches me looking? What should I say?"

"Just don't get caught. He mustn't know it is missing."

Brevare nodded at her, as one would dismiss a servant, and went over to the door, calling for the innkeeper. He almost collided with Leon returning, followed by one of the serving women. "Ah, there you are," Brevare said to the woman. "Bring me a glass for the wine, and some cheese. And a bottle of brandy—something decent." He took his wine to the table nearest the fire and sat down.

Leon glanced over at Brevare, then put a key on the table next to Phoebe.

"Your room key," he said, his voice too low for Brevare to hear. "They had a spare. I've had them light a fire in there. You can go any time you wish."

She glanced up. He was looking at her hand, still gripping the glass too tightly. She made an effort to relax it.

"They have also lit a fire in the parlour," he added. "Would you prefer to eat in there?"

Brevare looked settled by the fire in here.

"Yes, that would be preferable, thank you."

CHAPTER 12

*P*hoebe shivered at the chill in the parlour and rubbed her arms. Leon pulled a table closer to the fire and held a chair for her. She smiled—the gentlemanly action seemed incongruous in the circumstances.

"They only had soup and cold food left," he said, as the serving woman pushed the door open and brought a laden tray over to their table. Phoebe's stomach rumbled at the savoury smell of the onion soup, and she picked up her spoon eagerly.

"It's good, then?" Leon asked, as she spooned the last few mouthfuls from the bowl.

She glanced up; he was leaning back in his chair, a smile curving his lips. She had completely ignored him while she ate. "I'm sorry."

"Don't be. Wine? They have some surprisingly good vintages here."

She nodded. He poured wine, and pushed a plate towards her with slices of cold meat and bread. A bowl of fruit and a platter of pastries stood ready for later. Leon helped himself to an apple.

"How is your arm?" she asked, catching a flash of blue silk beneath the cuff of his shirt.

"Fine," he said. "Have some more ham."

"Hmm. My father had several patients—all men—who would say

that whatever their injury." Had she been rude, effectively telling him he was lying? Perhaps not—his wry smile showed amusement.

"Very well. It aches like the blazes at the moment, but no doubt you'll say it's my own fault for driving all afternoon."

Phoebe looked down at her plate, feeling her cheeks heat. Those words had been on the tip of her tongue. Hearing a chuckle, she glanced at his face.

"Miss Deane, please just say what you think. I mean that."

No. Not when her thoughts were on the attractive creases beside his eyes when he smiled, the warm glow she felt at having someone concerned for her well-being.

What had she been saying? His arm... "No sign of increased redness? It doesn't feel hot?"

"No, not in the bit I've inspected. How long do your stitches need to stay in?"

"A week, or a few days longer, but you'll be in England by then."

He hesitated before he spoke. "I'm glad your father allowed you to help him."

Phoebe nodded, a lump coming to her throat.

"You still miss them," Leon said gently.

Blinking, she looked away. She was not accustomed to sympathy.

"Don't talk about it if you'd rather not."

She found she wanted to tell him, wanted someone else to appreciate what her parents had been like. "Papa cared for his patients, and Mama helped him with his practice. He caught scarlatina, and Mama fell ill while nursing him. Joe, my brother, was at sea." They had both died before her letter telling of their illness could have reached Joe.

"Your father was a physician?"

"He could have trained as one, but he chose to be a surgeon and an apothecary instead. He thought that would serve the people better."

"Something your aunt would not have agreed with."

"No, indeed." Although they had not been poor, they'd had to be careful with money, but she knew her mother would not have exchanged her situation for any amount of wealth or status. She felt an impulse to tell him more of her life and her parents, but did not. This could not be why he'd wanted to talk to her.

"Why am I here?" she asked, firmly turning the subject.

"Apart from eating, you mean?"

Phoebe raised an eyebrow. She knew prevarication when she heard it.

Leon got up to put more wood on the fire, then stood leaning on the mantelpiece.

"What is it you want?" she asked, her earlier curiosity returning.

Alex gazed into the fire, its crackling the only sound in the room. He still hadn't decided how much he should confide in her.

One of his problems was Brevare. He could start there without telling any of—any *more* of—his secrets. "What did Brevare say to upset you in the parlour?"

Her face reddened, and she turned her eyes to the table.

"Miss Deane?"

She met his eyes briefly. "He asked—no, *instructed*—me to steal the message tonight and take it to him. I was to put it back later so you didn't know it had been taken."

His muscles tensed. "He assumed I'd be taking advantage of you—"

She shook her head. "That says more about his morals than yours. But I don't need to worry," she added, the corners of her mouth turning down. "He said we could come to some arrangement, so I won't lose out when the comtesse dismisses me."

Damn Brevare! He would not let her be subject to that. "Your uncle...?"

"I don't think he'll cast me out," she said. Her tone was certain, but her expression said there were other things she was concerned about.

"Don't be too concerned. I'll make sure you come to no harm—and *not* in the way Brevare implied." Bella would help, if he asked her, but that was a problem for later. Then the last part of her sentence sunk in. "He still thinks you're her *servant*?"

"He really isn't very observant, is he?" Her pursed mouth now looked as if she were suppressing a laugh.

"Unlike you—you would make an excellent spy." It was true. She was intelligent and perceptive; resilient, too, to be sitting here talking with him calmly, after all she'd been through.

Brevare didn't want to take the message—he wanted to copy it. That was new information; what would Miss Deane make of it? Reaching his decision, he resumed his seat. He poured himself more wine and offered her the pastries.

"I need an ally," he said. "Getting the message to England was originally simple enough, but Brevare turned up, and now I've got Perrault to deal with. I told Perrault he'll get a share of the ransom, but I don't think he believes me, and he seems to have absconded. Then there's your aunt, who will antagonise everyone she comes across unless she is kept under control."

Miss Deane had become increasingly wide-eyed as he spoke, the pastry ignored on the plate in front of her. "You think you can trust me?" she asked. "You don't really know much about me."

He knew enough. "*You* trust *me*," he said. "You wouldn't be in here alone with me otherwise."

She nodded, her expression thoughtful.

"I suppose we are both taking a bit of a gamble," he added.

"Very well." She held her glass up. "Allies."

"Confusion to our enemies," he said, touching his glass to hers.

"Brevare being the main enemy?"

"Perrault, too, but I'll come to that later. I can't work out why Brevare hasn't just stuck a knife in my back and taken the packet."

Her mouth fell open for a moment. He'd shocked her, but it wasn't fair to gloss over the possible dangers. "You can change your mind," he said, hoping she wouldn't. "Go to bed—you'll be safe if you lock yourself in. We should reach the coast tomorrow, and you'll be on the boat the day after."

"I won't change my mind." Her chin lifted as she spoke. "I'll help if I can, but I don't know what I can do."

"Listen, think. You're perceptive, you work things out—I'd like to hear what you make of it all."

Her cheeks reddened again, and she took a sip of wine.

"I've been finding contacts," he began. "People who might be useful for supplying information or hiding someone. The message is a list of their details."

"Only you, not Brevare?"

"Only me."

"Is there too much on the list for you to remember?"

"Yes. I could probably recall a fair amount of it, but not enough. Not all the addresses and code words. If the French authorities get hold of the list, it will be disastrous for the people on it."

Her brows creased as she thought. "It mustn't fall into the wrong hands," she said slowly. "Is that more important than delivering it?"

He nodded—he *had* been right to take her into his confidence. She'd worked out his main worry straight away.

"You could destroy the paper."

"I will if I have to." Even though that would waste months of effort.

"So Brevare is working for the French?"

That was what he'd been trying to reason out. "He must be in some way, obviously, but not directly. I've been acquainted with him for a few years, seeing him at race meetings, clubs, and so on. A couple of days before we came across your party, Brevare found me. He said he'd been sent to warn me that the authorities knew where I was and what I was doing, and it was time to leave before they caught up with me."

"But you didn't believe him."

"It wasn't a bad story, but I was about return in any case and my... my superior knew that, so why would he send Brevare to find me? There were also certain safeguards—"

"Code words?"

"Something like that, yes. He didn't have them. But until you told me he had asked for my list, I didn't know for certain why he'd come. And now it appears he wants a copy of the list, not to steal it."

She sipped her wine, her gaze on the fire. He had his own ideas, but he'd been thinking about it too long and wanted to see what she made of it all.

"How did he know where you were? He can't have been wandering France looking for you."

Another good question. "He knew. What does that tell you?"

"Someone in your... organisation... is working for France," she said slowly, as if working through the implications as she spoke. "They have some information—where to find you—but they don't know everything. The code words, for example."

He nodded. "Go on."

"If this person is part of your organisation, why didn't he wait until you got back to get the names? Would it be harder to steal them once you have passed the information on?"

"Not necessarily." Not if Marstone wasn't aware they had a traitor in their midst. "It might be harder to copy it without being found out."

"That's it," she said, eyes glowing. She sat forward, leaning her arms on the table. "If they know you have a list of... well, spies... if they get the names without you knowing, by copying the list... when others contact those people, or visit them, the... the net widens. Whoever it is gains more from copying the list than they would from stealing it," she finished, leaning back in her chair, the shawl slipping off her shoulders.

He forced himself to concentrate on her words. "Yes—that explanation makes perfect sense."

"It doesn't explain why they sent someone as inept as Brevare," she pointed out. "I suppose he knows what you look like, but if they knew where you were, they must have known what name you were using..." She hesitated. "At least... what *is* your name?"

"Alex Westbrook, at your service." He bowed his head. "Alexander rather than Alexandre though. I use a variety of names, so they probably needed someone who could recognise me." He looked at her glass. "More wine?"

She shook her head. "I'd prefer coffee, please."

He glanced at the clock above the fire, surprised to see they had been in here over an hour. "I'll see what they can do."

. . .

Leon—Westbrook—walked to the door, shutting it behind him as he went out. Phoebe rubbed her temples. Had she really just held a conversation with a spy?

The packet she was carrying—she had guessed it might be troop locations, or numbers of cannon or warships, information that could affect the coming war. The real message carried responsibilities on a more personal level; many people could be arrested and executed if the authorities obtained the paper.

Moving over to the door she listened, then opened it a crack. She could hear the murmur of Westbrook's voice from the taproom, but that was all. She put her hand down the front of her dress and retrieved the sealed packet.

A serving woman followed Westbrook into the room, setting a coffee pot and cups on the table. She cleared the dishes, leaving only a plate of pastries. Westbrook closed the door behind her, then took his seat and poured the coffee.

Phoebe held the message out. "I'm not sure I should be keeping this."

He made no move to take it from her. "It's safer with you than with me, as long as Brevare thinks I've still got it. If you don't mind looking after it, that is."

She looked at it doubtfully, turning it over in her hands. Knowing its contents made his trust in her even more surprising. The knowledge also piqued her curiosity. "Is it a list of names?"

"Open it."

She glanced up at him, not sure she'd heard correctly.

"Go ahead."

She broke the seal, unfolding the sheets of paper to find row after row of numbers. "Code?" Of course it was in code. "Will they know how to decode this if they *do* get it? I mean, would you decode it yourself when you get to London, or does someone in the organisation know what to do?"

"Excellent question. One or two people know. As the traitor found out where I was travelling, it is possible they also discovered the key."

"How—? No. I don't need to know," Phoebe said firmly, shaking her head. In fact, it was safer if she did not.

Westbrook's lips curved. "But you want to, naturally." There was a definite twinkle in his eyes.

"Naturally!" She couldn't help her answering smile.

"It's a book code—the numbers represent pages and letters on the page. However, now I know there's a traitor in the organisation, I should re-code it, in case it does fall into their hands."

"Would it...?" Phoebe broke off, wondering if it was her place to suggest things. He *had* asked her to help. "Would it be better if it was coded with a book you haven't been carrying around with you? Brevare might—"

"Good idea, yes. Providing someone in London can obtain the same edition."

"It's a new book. Shall I get it? You could re-code it now."

"Do you have paper as well? I'd rather not ask the innkeeper."

"My sketchbook."

Westbrook went to the door and opened it cautiously, sticking his head out into the passage. He beckoned, and Phoebe slipped out and up the stairs.

Her room was warm, as he had promised. The fire was dying, so she added some wood from the pile before turning to her trunk. The clothing appeared undisturbed, and she lifted out the novel and her sketchbook. She stilled, gazing at them, then sat down on the bed.

So far, the events of this journey had been forced upon her; now she was on the point of *choosing* to participate in something dangerous. Even if it were no more than lending a book and carrying the message for another day, she could be putting herself in more danger. If she chose to stay here he would not come in search of her, she was sure.

She should do it to repay him for rescuing them, but gratitude wasn't the only reason she returned to the parlour, or even the main one.

Westbrook's fingers brushed hers lightly as he took the novel. *"The Pirate's Cavern?"* He smiled, then laughed. "That should do nicely."

He locked the parlour door and placed his road guide on the table. Phoebe stared at it—he'd coded his message using the book Brevare had handed to her this morning?

"Really?"

He raised his brows, the quirk of his lips showing he wasn't offended by her remark. "There is an added layer of coding—some numbers to add or subtract from the page and letter numbers. Nor would anyone wonder why I have this particular book with me." He pulled his chair closer to the table. "If I turn the code back into names and addresses, you can redo it using your novel, if you will?"

Phoebe settled herself at the table while he decoded the first few lines onto sheets torn from her sketchbook. His fingers traced across the pages of the road guide as he counted letters, working with concentration. He had strong, square hands, the scrapes and cuts from the fight healing but still obvious.

She drank the coffee he'd poured, but it wasn't the drink that made her feel alert, with a fluttery feeling of anticipation. A corner of her mouth lifted; it was likely to be a tedious, painstaking task, but she felt excited nonetheless.

Westbrook moved his chair round to sit beside her while he explained the method, coding one line himself as he talked. It was not difficult, and she worked on the next line while he watched, aware of his closeness but determined not to be distracted by it. She completed one more line before he moved his chair away again to continue decoding the original.

He worked much faster than Phoebe, giving her the last set of details while she was still only half-way through. Once he had finished, he sat and stared into the fire, nursing another glass of wine.

When she had finally completed her task, she handed over the papers. Westbrook tore up the original paper and the plain text version he'd just made, throwing them onto the flames and stirring with the poker until there were only tiny flakes of ash left.

"What should we do with this?" Phoebe asked, holding out her new version.

"I have an idea," he said. "But it might be dangerous, so please do not feel obliged to accept."

"Tell me more," she demanded, without hesitation.

"You carry two messages. This one," he tapped her newly coded lists, "and another, nonsensical one. The real one you hide very well, the second one, not so well."

Merely putting it inside her dress was not enough, but she had needle and thread. "I could sew it into my stays?"

His lips twitched, but he only nodded.

"What do I do with them?"

"The most important thing you do with the second one is to give it up immediately if Brevare—anyone—threatens you. A safety ruse."

Phoebe frowned. "But... no, it will take them some time to work out that it *is* nonsense."

"Exactly. I'm hoping you'll be out of France tomorrow night, so it's only for a day."

"You said 'the most important thing'—is there something else?"

"You deliver them in London for me. I'll work—"

"You're not returning with us?"

He shook his head. "Probably not. I'll work out the details tonight, but if you still have the decoy note by then, there might be a way of finding out the identity of the traitor who sent Brevare."

Something of her sudden, empty feeling must have shown on her face.

"Don't worry," he said. "The people I'm sending you with will make sure you get home safely."

She nodded, managing a small smile. That wasn't why she'd felt so dismayed.

He eyed the plate of pastries. "Have you eaten enough?"

She was no longer hungry, although she hadn't eaten much more than the soup. Picking up a couple of the pastries, she wrapped them in a napkin. "I'd better go to my room," she said, with regret. "I have some sewing to do."

He stood. "Sleep well."

CHAPTER 13

*P*hoebe awoke to a loud banging, her eyes gritty.

"*Citoyenne*, it's time for you to get up."

She didn't recognise the voice; it was probably one of the serving women. Light filtering through the curtains revealed that it was already full daylight, even though she felt as if she had only just gone to sleep.

"*Citoyenne?*" The door rattled.

"I'm coming," Phoebe called, and the rattling stopped. Shivering in the cold air, she dressed and splashed water on her face. It had been long after midnight when she finished sewing, and her clothing was still strewn about the room. Hastily bundling up the gold dress, she stuffed it into her trunk with her sewing things. Hesitating over *The Pirate's Cavern*, she finally put it into her pocket with her sketchbook.

Her trunk was heavy, and she was glad to give it up to an ostler at the inn door. Hélène and her aunt waited by the coach, impatience clear in her aunt's stiff posture and down-turned mouth. As Phoebe approached, the comtesse turned and climbed in.

Hélène took a step towards Phoebe, with what appeared to be concern on her face, before a sharp word from inside the coach made her turn away. Brevare followed her in and slammed the door.

Westbrook came to stand beside her, garbed in greatcoat, muffler, and hat. "I persuaded the innkeeper to part with this," he said, holding out a coat. "The comtesse doesn't appear to be in the mood for your company, and you won't be warm enough in that cloak."

Phoebe smiled her thanks, slipping her arms into the coat as he held it for her. This one fitted her better than his greatcoat had, and she turned up its high collar. Westbrook helped her onto the box, handed up a cloth-wrapped parcel, then climbed up himself. She wrapped her cloak around her legs as he sorted out the reins.

"Breakfast," he said, indicating the parcel. He gave her a stoneware bottle as well. The bottle felt warm, and when she removed the stopper the rich smell of coffee wafted upwards. The napkins held fresh rolls and slices of ham, and she ate hungrily.

"Enough?" he asked as she wiped her fingers and tucked the empty wrappings under the seat.

"Yes, thank you."

"I thought you'd need as much sleep as you could get," he said. "Otherwise I'd have had them send up breakfast."

She rubbed her eyes, still feeling half-asleep. It wasn't until she finished the coffee that she realised something was wrong.

"Is Perrault in the coach?" She hadn't seen him, but he could have been in a dark corner.

"No-one's seen him this morning," Alex said.

"That's not good. Where do you think he's gone?"

"I don't know," he said, his expression grim. "I suspect he may have gone to find someone in authority to arrest us—he still thinks he'll get some kind of reward. He's had plenty of time since I last saw him before dinner yesterday."

"Does he know where we're going?"

"He *didn't*, but it's possible Brevare might. If he does, I wouldn't put it past him to have let something slip. There's an inn we use beyond Granville, a place to leave messages or to arrange for a boat." He glanced down at her. "Don't worry too much. The Dumont brothers who run the inn are regular contacts; they won't betray us. I sent Anson to them, so if he's arrived they'll know to be extra careful. We'll have to see what the situation is when we get there."

Phoebe nodded, rubbing her eyes again, too tired to worry about it now.

"You could ride inside," he suggested.

He must have seen the change in her expression, for she heard a chuckle. Her eyes were closing of their own accord. She couldn't sleep sitting up like this, but if she leaned to one side...

Jerking herself upright, she took a deep breath of the cold air, now damp with a fine drizzle. Leaning against Westbrook would be improper. People would think... no, it would make no difference. Her eyes closed. Her aunt already thought the worst of her... Westbrook did not... it was much more comfortable leaning sideways against his shoulder...

Alex shifted position cautiously, glancing down at Phoebe—Miss Deane—resting against him, her face concealed by the dripping brim of her bonnet. Her huddled form seemed far more vulnerable than the animated and perceptive woman he had confided in. He should never have involved her.

Returning his gaze to the road ahead, he forced himself to review the last few days dispassionately. His actions had indirectly led to Sarchet's assault, but it was difficult to see what else he could have done under the circumstances.

Last night? He had given her several opportunities to change her mind about getting involved; she could have stayed in her room instead of returning with the novel, and she could have declined the decoy note idea. But she'd understood the need for it, and contributed ideas of her own.

A sudden squall brought heavier rain, and he felt her stir. She sat up, casting a quick glance in his direction and sliding away along the seat. She turned her head from side to side, one hand rubbing her neck. The wind whipped strands of hair across her face, and she hunched her shoulders.

"Easterly wind," he said. "It will be easy for the *Lily*—the boat—to get under way after she's picked you up."

He caught the movement of her bonnet out of the corner of his eye as she looked at him, crossing her arms over her chest.

"You're cold—move a bit closer."

"I'm all right," she said, not moving.

"You may be, but I'm not," he said. "It will be warmer."

She was still for a moment, then she shuffled closer until her shoulder touched his. The extra warmth was minimal, but it felt good to have her so close again. The sky to their left was brighter, a few clear patches visible in the distance promising better weather soon.

"Is Brevare short of money?" she asked.

He smiled. "A random thought?"

"Sorry. I was thinking about Brevare..."

His smile vanished.

"Why he's here, I mean. He's... well, he doesn't seem particularly competent. You said he might have been sent because he could recognise you, but why did *he* agree to come?"

He'd wondered that himself, but the obvious conclusion didn't fit what he knew of the man. What would she make of it?

"Money is the most likely reason," he said. "Although I don't think he's any worse off than other émigrés, and gambles no more than anyone else."

"There are some French nobles who sympathise with the revolutionaries."

Alex shook his head. "I don't know him well, but I've never heard him say anything remotely like that."

"Blackmail?"

"Why do you say that?"

"Do you ever answer 'yes' or 'no'?" Phoebe asked, exasperation clear in her voice. "This is worse than being in the schoolroom! Am I making any sense?"

He couldn't resist a tease. "Yes, and yes."

She chuckled. "Yes, I'm making sense?"

"Yes, you are. Brevare is likely to be a danger to us, but if he's being blackmailed, I'd rather not have to kill him."

The pressure of her shoulder on his lessened as she pulled away from him.

"That surprised you?" His lips twisted. Of course it had—it would shock anyone not involved in his business.

"Yes." She stared at him, meeting his eyes for a moment before gazing back at the road. "Perhaps it should not have."

"I presume your normal conversations do not involve such matters?"

She ignored his attempt at levity. "If it's a choice between one man and all the people on your list..." She shook her head.

He drove on in silence for a few minutes, pleased when she resumed her former position. Blackmail was a possibility he hadn't considered.

"Why do you suggest he is being blackmailed?" he asked.

"Little things, really. It's probably a silly idea."

"Tell me anyway. Small things taken together can be important."

She did not speak immediately. Marshalling her thoughts?

"He's not a very good spy, as we said last night."

"Go on."

"He could have killed you and made up a story about coming across your body by accident. If he just reported your death to the... the Foreign Office, your organisation would never have known anyone else had your list. Instead, he delays you on the road, doesn't help you win the fight, and generally impedes things without doing anything directly."

"So they picked an incompetent traitor?"

Phoebe shook her head. "Perhaps they chose someone they could control. Someone who could not get more money by betraying *them* to the government."

That was an excellent point.

"Hélène says he has a mother and sister living in a château somewhere north of Paris," Phoebe continued.

Alex frowned. "I think I remember him saying something about a sister."

"He spends a lot of time watching Hélène," Phoebe said. "You may not have noticed—he's fairly discreet about it."

"Well she's an exceedingly beautiful girl." His lips curved. "Hen-witted, though, it has to be said."

"Yes, but I've seen other men who admire her, and he doesn't look at her in the same way. He backed you up when you rescued us from Perrault, and he would have been in as much danger as you. When I caught him looking at her later, I wondered if she reminded him of some other woman—his sister perhaps? Or a sweetheart? Is it possible that she—or they—are being held by the revolutionaries?"

"We won't know unless we ask him. He and I have never discussed our families, so it would seem odd for me to start now. You might be able to find out, if he lets anything slip."

"I'll try."

He looked at her. "Phoebe, I'm *not* suggesting you ask him directly."

Phoebe met his eyes, seeming startled at the vehemence in his tone.

"If he is being blackmailed, he could become desperate," Alex went on. "Finding out isn't important enough to put yourself into danger." He kept his gaze on hers until she nodded, then returned his attention to the road.

What she said had given him an idea. He turned it over in his mind as he drove.

"This decoy idea..."

She turned her head towards him.

"I was originally going to stay behind in France only a day or so, to give Brevare or his handler a chance to get the decoy from you. But if I can find out where the rest of his family is and take them to England—"

"You might be able to persuade Brevare himself to tell you who the traitor is?" She'd understood instantly—of course.

"If he knows. The traitor might be using an intermediary."

Phoebe nodded. "And even if he doesn't know anything useful, his family will be out of harm's way and the traitor will no longer have a hold over Brevare. If we're right about the blackmail, of course."

Westbrook's plan made sense, and it would give him—or his superiors—another possible way of identifying the traitor. She didn't like it, though. Going to look for Brevare's family would be far more dangerous than merely waiting at the coast for a few days.

He's a spy. That's the kind of thing spies do.

It made no difference, she told herself firmly. They would have parted ways as soon as they reached English soil in any case.

Bare hedges lined the road, with muddy fields punctuated by copses of leafless trees beyond. As the coach rattled on, the rain stopped and occasional patches of sunshine cheered the landscape and the villages along their route. Phoebe found it difficult to correlate the stories of violence and terror she'd read in the newspapers with this peaceful setting.

"Can you drive?" Westbrook asked, bringing her back to the here and now.

"Yes," she said, picturing driving her father on his rounds. She bit her lip as she realised she might be overstating her skills. "I mean, I used to drive my father's gig," she added. "But only one horse, not four, and that was years ago."

"I might need you to drive later, only for a mile or so."

Phoebe gazed at the four horses in front of them.

"These aren't the most taxing animals," he added.

"Couldn't Brevare drive?"

"No, I don't want him to know what's happening."

It was important then. She straightened her spine. "I'll try. What do I do?"

His expression lightened. "I'll show you. Hold out your left hand."

She did as he said, and he looped the reins through her gloved fingers.

"That's it, hold them like that—there's nothing complicated while we're going in a straight line. Now try slowing them down." He reached across her awkwardly with his left hand, then muttered under his breath and moved back to put his arm round her shoulders instead. Now he could twist a little and use his right hand to guide her hands on the reins.

Phoebe drew in a breath.

"Do you mind?" he asked, straightening up again.

She shook her head, not minding at all. In fact, it felt rather nice. Ignoring the warmth coming from him, she concentrated on the horses. He showed her how to loop the leaders' reins when they came to a bend. After making a few turns without needing his guidance, she began to enjoy herself.

Westbrook divided his gaze between her hands and the way ahead, occasionally consulting the road guide. Her left hand and arm ached after she'd driven a few miles, and she gave the reins back. Flexing her hand, she tried to massage the pains out of it.

"You did well," Westbrook said. "You'll be fine if you need to drive them later." He gave her the road guide.

"Oh," she said, before he could speak. "I've still got the book I used to code the message. Shouldn't we get rid of it?"

"You've hidden the message?"

"Yes, but it would be stupid to be caught with the message *and* the key to it."

"Throw it over the hedge," he said.

"What?"

"Why not?"

Phoebe thought about it. Why not, indeed? If the message were found, the authorities were hardly likely to search the countryside for a book. She took it from her pocket. How far could she throw it from a seated position?

"Here, I'll do it," Westbrook said, taking the book out of her hand. It sailed off over the hedge into a stand of trees. "Everyone knows girls can't throw," he said in a bland tone, spoiling the effect by giving her a wary, sideways glance.

"Just as they cannot read maps and follow signposts?" Phoebe asked, her tone honeyed. For once he didn't have a reply, and she laughed. "I cannot throw as far as you, that's certain." She held up the road guide. "What did you want me to do with this?"

"We need to skirt Avranches." He waved a hand towards the road ahead. "I've been in this area before, but I don't usually need to avoid the towns. I don't know the way through the lanes. When we've passed Avranches we head for the coast beyond Granville, but avoid that town too."

Phoebe flicked through the pages, finding the towns he'd mentioned. Entering them, or even a village of any size, risked someone wanting to examine their papers, or her aunt doing something that would get them arrested. She worked out a route, turning down the corners of the pages she'd need.

CHAPTER 14

*A*n hour later, Phoebe took the reins for more practice. This time Westbrook knotted them so she didn't need to grip them with her fingers to maintain the correct length. He explained how the horses worked together in harness and how much continual but light pressure was needed to keep the animals ready to respond. She listened intently, glad for a chance to learn. It was something she missed greatly about her father—he didn't care much for what was proper or right for a woman to do. He'd simply taught her what she'd wanted to know, talking to her as he might have done to another adult. Forcing back her sadness at the memories, she kept her concentration on the road and the horses.

The mental effort, as well as handling the reins, tired her and she was glad to let Westbrook take over once again. She checked the road guide, then asked a question that had been in the back of her mind since she first suspected he was a spy.

"What do you do in France?"

He looked surprised. "I told you last—"

"Sorry. I meant…I was wondering what it is other people think you are doing in France." She grimaced as the question came out;

perhaps she shouldn't have asked. "But it's none of my business, really."

"That part's no secret," he said. "I set up trading deals. I find goods that should sell well in England, and put the sellers in contact with my uncle's trading company in Devon."

Phoebe suppressed a smile. If her aunt did not already detest 'that man', knowing she was associating with someone in trade would have made her turn her nose up.

"You really do that?" It sounded an interesting way of making a living. "Are you a successful trader?"

"Reasonably. It helps to have a true reason for being here."

"How did you learn that trade?"

"After I finished my schooling I went to work for Pendrick's—my uncle's firm. An import and trading business seemed more attractive than studying to become an attorney."

"That's what your parents wanted?"

He hesitated. "It was interesting for a while, but then Marstone offered me something more interesting. Marstone—the Earl of Marstone, I should say—runs agents in France, and probably elsewhere."

Phoebe nodded, wanting him to continue but not feeling she should press him.

"Marstone suggested to Pendrick that I'd be better employed looking for new sources of goods on the continent. They already had their own people doing that, of course, but I suspect he made... well, an investment of some kind, so they agreed."

"Gathering information for him while buying goods for Pendrick?" He didn't seem to mind talking.

"Exactly."

"And you liked that better? It sounds lonely."

"I didn't notice that at first. There was the novelty of seeing new places, but it's not as enjoyable when you have to always be on your guard—whether for business or other matters." He paused for a moment. "I suppose there was an element of danger too, and it was better than being a glorified warehouse clerk."

Lonely or not, it sounded both interesting and useful. "What do you trade in?"

"It depends on where I need to be. Wine, quite often. Brandy, fabrics…"

"Smuggled?"

"Most of it is legitimate trade," he said, one brow rising as he turned to her. "Why did you think I was a smuggler?"

"I'm sorry," she said, hoping she hadn't offended him.

"Don't be." His lips curled up. "I *am* sometimes a smuggler. I was wondering why you thought so."

She had jumped to that conclusion, but there had been enough clues. "I imagine the packet boats won't be running now we're at war, but you know that we can get a boat to pick us up at a beach somewhere. It sounds like a regular arrangement."

"Yes. Smuggling is a good excuse for boats crossing the channel at odd times. No-one questions it—other than the Revenue men, of course. Smuggling keeps the skipper familiar with private little beaches."

Phoebe sighed.

"Phoebe?"

"Your life sounds so much more interesting than mine." When had he started to call her Phoebe? She suppressed a smile—perhaps being used as a pillow gave him that right.

"You don't enjoy living in London?" he asked.

"I prefer the country. I used to go for long walks or rides when my parents were alive; at Calvac, too. In London there is only the park. I spend a lot of my time with my uncle's travel books."

"No balls and entertainments?"

"Not yet. My uncle said I was to come out with Hélène this spring. She's looking forward to it, but it all seems rather pointless to me."

"Many people enjoy dancing," he said, a note of enquiry in his voice.

"Oh, I do enjoy dancing, but from what my aunt and Hélène have been discussing, it is likely to be every evening, with social calls all day." She grimaced. "There's only so much I can say about fashion and gossip."

"Hmm, I take your point." His smile was wry. "Perhaps an unexciting life will seem more appealing after this week's events."

Perhaps.

They skirted Granville early in the afternoon and drove on northwards. The warmth of the sun on her face was welcome, helping to counter the wind biting through her coat. They had not talked much more, but the quiet felt companionable, a friendly silence.

"The inn we're aiming for is about a mile further on," Westbrook said, as he turned the carriage down yet another narrow lane. "If Brevare told Perrault about the place, there might already be soldiers there."

"We could stop here and you could check on foot," Phoebe suggested.

He shook his head. "If there is trouble and the Dumonts have escaped, there's a rendezvous further on. I'd rather you were safely beyond the inn before I start looking. We must drive along the road as if we're passing through."

He handed her the reins. "There's a copse a little way beyond the turning to the inn—I'll jump off as you go behind that. In another mile you'll come to some woodland. Stop there and wait. I shouldn't be long."

He felt in the pocket of his coat. "You'd better have this." He showed her a pistol and then put it into one of her coat pockets.

"Am I likely to need that?"

"Let us hope not, but you can use it to discourage Brevare in case he tries to take charge while I'm away," he said.

Using a pistol was a little more than she'd bargained for.

"Stay on the box if you can, and use it to keep him away from you if that becomes necessary. It isn't cocked. You remember the catch on the top you have to pull back?"

Phoebe nodded. That scene was graven on her memory.

As the inn came into sight she slowed the horses, examining the building. "Are some of the windows open?" she asked.

"It looks that way, and not enough chimneys smoking," Westbrook confirmed. "Something's definitely wrong."

Phoebe swallowed a lump in her throat, slowing once again as they neared the copse. Westbrook moved to the edge of the bench and swung himself partway down.

"Are you sure you'll manage?" he asked.

Phoebe wanted to tell him to be careful, and to ask what they should do if he did not come back, but she couldn't delay him. She nodded, and he dropped to the road, staying crouched until the coach had passed so the occupants did not see him through the windows.

She felt her pulse accelerate—she was on her own now, in charge of four horses and the people inside the carriage. The lane curved, and she pulled on the reins as she'd been taught, calming as she realised the horses were behaving no differently from before. Westbrook would be returning soon, she told herself firmly. He was going to reconnoitre, not to fight anyone.

Trees appeared ahead once she rounded another bend in the lane. The hedges give way to bushy undergrowth as they approached the patch of woodland. Phoebe slowed the horses to a walk, bringing them to a halt where the road widened a little. Someone coming along the road would see them, but the coach would not be visible from a distance.

"What's happening? Why have we stopped here?" The comtesse's shrill tones were clearly audible, even through the closed doors of the coach. Phoebe pulled the pistol out of her pocket and put it down carefully on the seat beside her, keeping a firm grasp on the reins with her left hand. The door opened, and Phoebe twisted round on the seat to see Brevare climb out.

"Why have we stopped?" He looked around, then up at her on the box. "Where's... what are you doing up there on your own?"

Some of Phoebe's tension dissipated. She must not underestimate him, but at the moment he didn't appear to be a threat. The temptation to become the rather dim servant was overwhelming.

"I'm holding the horses."

"Why?"

"So they don't run away." She bit her lip at his scowl.

"Where's Leon?"

"He got off."

"Yes, I can see that!"

"What is happening?" the comtesse demanded again from inside the coach.

Brevare ignored her. "*Where* did he get off?"

"Back there a bit," Phoebe said, twisting round and pointing the way they had come. Brevare said something she couldn't quite make out, but from the look on his face she suspected it was rude. She kept her face bland with an effort; it would not do for her to laugh at him.

"Where are we? Here, give me that road guide."

Phoebe handed it over, and he flicked through the pages, his impatience growing as he failed to find their location.

"Where are we?" he repeated.

A crackle of undergrowth drew her attention away from Brevare's sputtering demands. She caught a flash of movement between the trees, then a stranger stepped onto the road. Her pulse racing, she slipped her hand down to the pistol beside her, gripping it but not lifting it. Westbrook had mentioned his friends—Dumont, that was the name.

From the corner of her eye, she saw Brevare's mouth snap closed as the man approached the horses, reaching out to take the reins close to the leading animals' bits. Brevare cursed as he stepped back into the coach.

The man was smartly dressed—a respectable tradesman, Phoebe guessed, although the effect was spoiled by splashes of mud on his coat and breeches. He drew a pistol from his coat pocket, holding it loosely with the barrel pointing at the ground. Not a soldier. And not, she thought, one of Perrault's associates.

"Your bonnet, *citoyenne*—remove it if you please?"

"Unhand those horses!" Brevare emerged from the coach, pointing his own pistol. "Release them at once!"

The man ignored the shouting, keeping his gaze on her while pointing his gun towards Brevare. "Your bonnet," he repeated.

She pulled the ribbons undone and slid her bonnet off. Guessing what the man might want, she pulled her cap off too—her hair was her most identifiable feature.

The man nodded.

"Are you deaf, man?" Brevare stepped forwards, still waving his pistol.

"Your name, *citoyen?*" Phoebe called, ignoring Brevare's incoherent protest.

"Pierre Dumont." He touched his hat.

"Brevare," Phoebe called, cocking Westbrook's pistol. Brevare froze, his jaw dropping.

"You need to get off the road," Dumont said, putting his weapon away. "There is a track ahead. I will lead them."

"Lead them on, then." She let the reins go slack. "Put the pistol away," she said to Brevare. "This man is helping us."

"Have you gone mad, woman?"

"Just doing what I was told, sir."

Brevare muttered something under his breath and climbed back into the now-moving coach, stumbling as the wheels lurched into a rut. The door slammed hard behind him. There was a terse reply to yet another demand from the comtesse, and then quiet from inside.

Phoebe carefully released the lever on the pistol as the coach moved into the trees. If Dumont knew to look out for her, Anson must have arrived here safely. Her relief was short-lived, however— Dumont's presence here also meant there must be soldiers at the inn.

As the coach came to rest behind a thicket she tucked her hair into her cap and put her bonnet back on. The ground looked a long way off, but she scrambled down without mishap.

"Where is Westbrook?" Dumont asked in a low voice as she approached him.

"He thought there was something wrong at the inn when we passed," she explained. "He went to investigate. He told me to wait in this wood for him."

"How long ago?"

"Ten minutes? Not long, he could not have walked here yet."

He met her gaze and nodded once more. "*Bien.* We wait."

"How did you know to be here?" It surely could not be a coincidence, the way he had appeared so quickly.

"Monsieur Anson arrived yesterday. This is a meeting place." Dumont looked towards the road and then back to Phoebe. "You will stay here?"

"Yes." She couldn't turn the horses round on her own anyway.

"If Westbrook arrives, tell him to wait here."

Phoebe wanted to ask where he was going, but he had already faded into the bushes. She wrapped her coat more tightly round her, choosing to lean on the outside of the coach rather than join her aunt inside.

Finally she heard the crack of a dry stick, a metallic jingle, then a low murmur of voices. Pierre Dumont emerged from the trees, leading a horse with a small girl on its back. He was followed by another man with a horse, this one with a plump woman carrying a baby in a sling, her skirts hitched up to ride astride. Both men and horses were also laden with bags and boxes.

"My brother, Henri," Pierre said, jerking a thumb towards the other man. Henri was taller, but the two brothers bore a strong facial resemblance.

Pierre helped the girl and woman dismount, then climbed up onto the coach, stowing the bags Henri threw up to him on the roof. The woman opened the coach door and climbed in, her daughter behind her.

"Plenty of room here, isn't it?" the woman said. "Move along a bit, my lady. Come on, Sophie, *cariad*, sit you down here."

"Pierre's wife is Welsh," said a familiar voice in her ear.

Phoebe jumped. "You don't say!" she retorted, her pulse settling at the sound of his chuckle. "What did you—?"

"I'll tell you later," Westbrook said. "We need to get a bit further from the inn. You'll have to travel inside, I'm afraid, but we're not going far." As he spoke, Pierre finished tying the bags down and climbed forward onto the box. Henri brought the two riding horses over.

Inside, the girl sat between Hélène and the comtesse. Brevare glowered from the opposite seat, his arms folded. As Phoebe climbed in, Dumont's wife shuffled along and patted the narrow space beside her.

"Here you are, see. Plenty of room." The woman settled back comfortably and adjusted the baby on her lap. The coach jolted into motion, and Phoebe almost fell into the gap, muttering her thanks.

"Who are these people...? What...?" Words were failing the comtesse. Phoebe smiled, not caring if her aunt saw it.

"Can't you *do* something?" the comtesse said to Brevare. His scowl deepened, and he shook his head.

There wasn't much to see through the window, only hedges and trees. After about half an hour of jolting along a rutted track, the coach came to a halt. Westbrook opened the door and helped Phoebe and Madame Dumont to alight.

"You will be more comfortable if you stay here for the moment, *citoyenne*," Westbrook said to the comtesse. "Brevare, come and help."

The men busied themselves unharnessing the horses and unloading the baggage. Phoebe could be no help to them, so she walked to the edge of the woodland and breathed deeply of the salt air. Sand dunes rose before her, and the sound of surf was faint in the distance, almost masked by the wind in the trees.

CHAPTER 15

*A*lex turned back to the coach as the Dumonts walked past Phoebe and headed off into the dunes, laden with bags and boxes.

"You can have one trunk each," he said, sticking his head inside. "Sort out what you want to take."

"Don't be ridiculous, that's—"

"If you don't sort it out, we'll leave it *all* behind." He turned away, ignoring the gasp of anger from the comtesse. Thank God he wouldn't have to deal with the woman after today.

Now for Brevare.

"Down to the hut on the beach," he said, pointing the way the Dumonts had gone. Brevare made no move, so he pulled a pistol from his coat pocket.

"Beach. Now!"

Brevare's mouth opened and closed, then he turned and began to walk.

Alex put the pistol back and hoisted Phoebe's trunk onto one shoulder. "You come too, please," he said as he passed her.

As they neared the hut, a drift of smoke rose from its chimney. Gwen Dumont had wasted no time in lighting a fire. Alex added

Phoebe's trunk to the Dumonts' pile of baggage and gestured for Brevare and Phoebe to walk on. The Dumont brothers followed them.

"What's going on, Westbrook?" Brevare asked as they stopped a dozen yards from the hut.

Alex ignored him, turning to Pierre. "There were soldiers at the inn."

"They arrived this morning," Pierre confirmed. "I saw them coming and got Gwen and the girls out. Henri went to the nearby farms."

"Nothing wrong at the farms," Henri said, his face expressionless as his gaze brushed over Brevare. "They only came to our inn. They were to wait for a grand coach with two men and three women."

"How do you know that?" Brevare asked. Alex glanced his way; despite the cold, there was a sheen of sweat on his forehead.

"I listened," Henri said.

"Why didn't they keep proper watch on the road?" Alex asked. He'd had little difficulty getting close to the inn without being spotted.

"Drunk, probably. I left the cellar door unlocked."

Alex nodded and turned to Brevare. He was now certain that Brevare had betrayed them; whether deliberately or accidentally he had yet to determine. "How did they know to come to *this* inn? And who to look for?"

"Perrault must have told them." Brevare's gaze dropped as he spoke.

"And how did Perrault know where we were going?" Alex kept his voice level, despite his rising anger.

"I didn't tell him!" Brevare's head snapped up, his eyes wide. "For God's sake, I want to get out of this damned country just as much as you! Why would I tell him?"

"So you *did* know this was where we were headed?" He watched as Brevare's jaw fell open; the man was clearly searching for a response.

"Well, yes. When they sent me…"

Alex waited, but Brevare did not explain further.

"Who did you tell?" Alex prompted, making an effort not to shout.

Alex could almost see the moment Brevare realised what he had done.

"I, er… I asked the innkeeper last night how far it was to Granville," he said, his gaze darting around the group before dropping to his boots. "Perrault may have overheard."

"Pierre, could they have found out in Granville that we might be coming here?"

Pierre shrugged. "Many people know about the smuggling. It is possible."

Alex swore. "What else did you say, Brevare?"

"N…nothing!" Brevare stammered.

Damned liar!

Alex pulled his pistol out of his pocket again. "Do you know how we will get home from here?"

Brevare's face turned ashen. Good; the fool had enough sense to be afraid. "There… there will be a boat—"

The click as Alex cocked the pistol was loud. He put it close to Brevare's temple, his hand almost trembling with the desire to pull the trigger.

"The name of this boat?"

"I don't know." Sweat beaded on Brevare's forehead. "I… I only know there is a boat." He swallowed hard. "I said nothing about a boat to Perrault."

"Or to anyone else?"

"No, really, I did not!"

Alex was so furious with the man's stupidity that he didn't know whether to trust his own judgement. He glanced first at Phoebe, her face white and eyes wide, then at Pierre.

"I… I think he's telling the truth," Phoebe said.

Pierre nodded. Alex reluctantly released the catch on the pistol and put it back in his pocket. Brevare was more use alive than dead; he might lead them to the traitor in the Foreign Office.

"Very well. Brevare, go to the coach and make sure those women are sorting out one bag each."

Brevare's gaze flicked from Alex to Phoebe, then he turned abruptly and set off along the path, almost running.

Phoebe watched Brevare leave, her pulse gradually slowing. She had really thought Westbrook was going to shoot him in front of her. Westbrook's jaw was still set, but the whiteness around his mouth was fading. She saw his chest rise as he took a deep breath before turning to face the three of them.

"We need to decide what to do next," he said, his voice calmer. "I was expecting to leave about now in any case, so Trasker should have had the *Lily* ready for a few days. The usual arrangement is to meet in Granville. He knows this pick-up point, but not when we were to be here."

Pierre shook his head. "There'll be soldiers in Granville, too, looking for you. And we're known in the town." His gesture took in his brother as well. "Someone there must have told them about our inn, so they will be looking for us too."

"I'll go then," Westbrook said. "When is high tide?"

"An hour or so before midnight, or thereabouts," Henri said. "A few hours either side is good enough at Granville."

Westbrook nodded.

"You'll be rather conspicuous," Phoebe pointed out, before he could say anything else.

"What do you mean?"

"Have you looked in a mirror lately? Your eye..." Not to mention the other bruises. "Perrault only needs to have told them to look out for a man with a black eye."

Westbrook swore. "Brevare's useless, even if he didn't intend to betray us," he said, after a moment's thought. "Gwen would be as recognisable as you," he said to Pierre.

To Phoebe, the solution was clear. Her stomach knotted at the idea, but there seemed to be no other option.

"And it's too dangerous to send a woman," Westbrook finished.

He was looking at Pierre, not her. Unaccountably annoyed, her hesitation dissipated. She had no wish to put herself in danger, but surely it was more dangerous for Westbrook—dangerous for all of them, not only him.

"I could go," she said.

Three faces turned towards her, Westbrook frowning. "No," he said, shaking his head.

Pierre looked her up and down, and raised one brow. "Why not?"

"If Perrault has given the authorities detailed descriptions, she'll be just as recognisable as me," Westbrook objected.

"I can hide my hair—you cannot hide your face. Not without looking like a highwayman."

Westbrook opened his mouth and then closed it again. He nodded, but the set of his lips showed he wasn't happy with the idea.

A thought struck her: there was something that might rule out her involvement as well. "Will Perrault be there?"

Westbrook frowned, but eventually shook his head. "He may be in the vicinity somewhere, but I can't see an officer using him for anything other than identifying us if we are caught." His lips curled, but the smile was humourless. "With any luck, when we are *not* caught, he'll be in trouble for wasting the time of the authorities."

A part of her was sorry not to have an excuse, but she couldn't change her mind now. "What will I have to do in Granville?"

"I'll take you into the town," Westbrook said. "What we do there depends on whether they have soldiers on the look-out, and where Trasker and the crew are. You might need to go into a tavern to find them." He looked into her eyes, his expression grim. "They won't be the kinds of places we've been staying at. Much rougher."

Phoebe took a deep breath. "Do we have a choice?"

"No." He held her gaze. "But Phoebe, you're playing with fire."

"Not *playing.*"

"No, not playing. And it's your choice to make." He paused, and rubbed a hand across his forehead. "Thank you. You have an hour or so—we don't want to get there until after dark. Try to get some rest. We'll go and see to the horses." A jerk of his head included the Dumonts.

Phoebe watched him walk off into the trees before going into the hut. The interior was dim, but she made out the girl Sophie sitting holding the baby.

"Coffee," Madame Dumont said, taking a battered pot from the fire. She poured some of the brew into a cup, and handed it to Phoebe. "I'm Gwen," she added.

"Thank you, Gwen," Phoebe said. "I'm Phoebe."

"We didn't have time to pack much," Gwen went on, seeming glad to have someone to talk to. "Had to leave in a hurry, see? Still, it will be good to be back home where I can understand properly what folks are saying."

Gwen had taken her coat and bonnet off, and brown curls escaped from beneath her cap. Her plumpness was due to her being well on the way to her third child.

Perrault would have described a redhead, not a pregnant brunette.

"Gwen, did you bring any spare gowns?"

Alex ignored Brevare and the two women as they passed in the woods, and went on to help the Dumont brothers with the horses. He found a couple of buckets in the boot of the coach and helped Henri fill them at a nearby stream for the carriage horses to drink.

"We ride those two to Paris?" Henri asked, jerking his head towards the two saddled horses Pierre was leading towards the stream.

"Not all the way. Until it is safe to use the diligence." Travelling on horseback would allow them to dodge into fields or woods to avoid any soldiers they encountered, but after that they would attract less attention on the public coaches than as travellers needing to rest their mounts at regular intervals.

"The *Lily*? If there are soldiers?"

He'd been thinking about that. Another decoy? "You and I will build a signal fire a mile north of here. I'll get Trasker to drop a boat off here but sail the *Lily* closer to the fire before signalling."

Henri nodded. "The soldiers will head for the fire, yes."

It was by no means foolproof, but it could divert any attention for long enough to get Phoebe... get the whole party away safely.

The sun was setting as they returned to the hut. Gwen handed them fresh coffee, and the Dumont brothers sat down to drink it. The comtesse and Hélène huddled in one corner, their faces sullen, but Phoebe wasn't there. He found her on the sheltered side of the hut, out of the wind, a brown dress visible beneath her coat. The garment hung baggily on her—an even worse fit than the dresses she'd been wearing before. She had a bundle slung around her shoulders and, apart from a few escaped curls, her hair was completely hidden under her cap.

"You need—" He looked again. The curls were brown—she'd done something to her eyebrows, too.

Her eyes crinkled with amusement. "Gwen's," she explained. "If I have brown hair on display, no-one will even wonder if I have red hair."

"Good thinking." The possibility would never have occurred to him. "Ready to go?"

She sobered, her chin lifting. "Yes."

They picked their way carefully along the path, the gathering dusk masking tree roots and rocks. Alex checked the harnesses and hitched the saddled horses to the back of the coach before helping Phoebe onto the box and settling himself next to her.

The sky was almost dark, but a gibbous moon hung on the horizon and gave enough light for Alex to follow the road south towards Granville without using the lanterns.

"Why the coach?" Phoebe asked as they regained the road and turned south.

"Too easy to find if we leave it here," Alex said. "We're going to abandon it in a field outside Granville. If someone does spot it, it should mean that anyone looking for us will waste time searching the town."

"And we ride back on the horses?"

"Yes. Henri and I will need them later as well." He caught the sudden turn of her head in the edge of his vision. "A diversion for when the *Lily* picks you up, if needed, then we'll use them for the start of our trip to Paris. That's the best place to begin a search for Brevare's family."

She didn't reply immediately. He wondered what she was thinking, but the light was too dim to work out her expression.

"Tell me what I need to do," she said at last.

"The idea is that you hold onto the real message until you can give it to the Earl of Marstone. When Brevare asks you for it—and he will—hand over the decoy if he threatens you."

Phoebe nodded. "I will. But if he doesn't...?"

"Tell him you are to give it to the Earl of Marstone at the Foreign Office. With any luck, he'll introduce you to his controller pretending to be Marstone, and you give him the decoy."

"I take a good look at him?"

"Yes. See Marstone first—the real one, that is—and he'll help to keep you safe." He explained the details and she repeated the main points back to him, word perfect. If only the others he'd worked with in the past had been as quick to understand.

Alex drove the coach into a field on the edge of Granville, stopping behind a high hedge. Phoebe helped him to unhitch the horses, both of them fumbling with the unfamiliar buckles in the dim light. Alex turned the coach horses loose and left the saddled horses tied to a tree.

Leading the way into the town, he kept to the shadows, skirting the old town wall until they came to the harbour. The smell of salt-laden air and dead fish was strong here, and the slap of ropes against masts and spars joined the splash of waves on the harbour walls. A few seagulls still called in the dark.

Alex stopped in the shadow of a building, cursing under his breath as he scanned the scene. Twenty or more boats were moored against the quay, some quite large, and a few more bobbed at anchor a little further out. Moonlight reflecting from the water turned them into inky silhouettes. A few had a light shining from a cabin; most were dark.

"Which one's the *Lily*?" Phoebe asked quietly.

127

"She'll be one of the larger ones, and against the quay, I hope, but I can't tell from here. We need to get closer. Best to check she's here before we try to find Trasker."

They crept along a bit further, then Phoebe put out a hand. Following her pointing finger, he saw four soldiers spaced out along the quay. As he watched, one of them challenged a man walking towards the boats. He was allowed to go on his way, but Alex didn't want to risk such an encounter.

"Damn."

"You can't spot the *Lily* from here?"

"No."

He felt, rather than heard, Phoebe fumbling in her coat, then she pulled out a little pot and unscrewed the lid.

"What's that?" Alex whispered.

"Face paint. I stole it from my aunt's box and mixed a little mud in. Turn around."

"What for?"

"It won't hide your black eye in good light, but it should stop it being so obvious out here." Her lips twitched. "You're lucky it's not perfumed."

"Oh, if you insist," he said, seeing the sense of it. He took the pot and smeared a liberal dose of the stuff under his eye before putting the little pot into his pocket.

She gazed at his face, inspecting his work before using a finger to rub the cream in, her fingers gentle. The intimacy of the act made his breath catch. Finally, she nodded in satisfaction.

Returning his attention to the soldiers on the quay, he turned over possibilities in his mind. He was not dressed as a fisherman would be; what believable excuse could he give for walking here?

Beside him, Phoebe was rearranging her clothing, whispering an apology as her elbow jabbed him in the arm. Turning, he saw she had removed the bundle from her back and was pushing something up under her skirts.

"What—?" Alex asked.

"Shh. You'll see."

Standing up straight, she shook out her skirts, leaving a distinct bulge at the front. Ah—the ill-fitting gown belonged to Gwen, who was expecting her next child. Phoebe's coat was unfastened; she cupped one hand beneath the bump, looking for all the world as if she were only a couple of months from her time.

"They're not looking for a pregnant woman," Phoebe whispered. "If you take my arm, we're merely a married couple taking the air. Less suspicious than skulking along in the shadows."

It was a good idea—certainly better than anything he could have come up with. Escorting her onto the quay was no more dangerous than bringing her to Granville to find Trasker in a tavern, and he'd had to accept that.

He nodded and held out his arm. She rested her hand on it and they stepped onto the quay, Phoebe on the side nearer the water so he could look at the boats while pretending his attention was on her.

Phoebe set a slow pace, waddling as if she were struggling with the weight of a pregnancy. Alex scanned the boats as they passed them, but none looked familiar. As they approached the first soldier, Phoebe leaned more heavily on him. Suppressing a surge of unease as the soldier took a step in their direction, he bent his head closer to hers.

"Feeling a little better, *cherie*?" Alex asked, aware of her hand tense on his arm. The soldier took another step closer. Alex looked him in the face and gave what he hoped would pass for a courteous nod before returning his attention to Phoebe.

She stopped and arched her back, pressing one hand into it and turning so her bump would be clearly visible. "The exercise is helping. Let us walk up to the end."

Her voice was loud enough for the soldier to hear. His eyes moved from her face down to the bump in her gown, then he lost interest and resumed his pacing. Alex's shoulders relaxed as he heard Phoebe release a breath, and he patted her hand as she returned it to his arm.

The shape of one of the boats beyond the second soldier looked familiar, but he'd need to be closer to be sure it was the *Lily*. Keeping a wary eye on the soldier, he was prepared to repeat their previous performance, but the man nodded at them without interest and waved them on.

It *was* Trasker's boat; light spilling from the cabin of the vessel moored ahead of it was enough to make out the name along her bow. He walked on until they were in earshot of the third man before addressing Phoebe.

"You are cold, *cherie*. We should go back."

They retraced their steps, turning into a side street and slipping into a deep shadow.

CHAPTER 16

Once they were out of sight of the men on the quay Phoebe leaned against the wall, eyes closed, and took a few deep breaths. Her knees felt wobbly. She had managed to carry off their little act, but she suspected a harder task lay ahead.

"You did well," Westbrook said quietly. "The *Lily* is there—no lights, though. They'll have left someone on board, but most of them will be in a tavern."

"Do you know which one?"

"There are a couple of favourites," he said. "If we're lucky we might be able to hear which one Trasker's in. He's rather... loud."

"How is it that an English boat and crew are safe here?" Phoebe kept her voice low as they walked along the street, one hand on his arm, the other still supporting the bump in her dress.

"They may not be for long. But smuggling makes money for the local people—they won't be in too much hurry to let that go."

Turning into another alley, Phoebe heard tavern sounds getting louder as they moved—voices, someone singing off key, and an argument beginning.

A shaft of light spilled onto the street as the tavern door opened, and a crowd of men surged out of the door. Westbrook stopped and pushed her gently but firmly until she stood with her back to the wall. He leaned towards her with his hands on the stones, one each side of her head.

"What—?"

"Shhh." His face was turned away, watching the men. In the darkness, she could make out only the glimmer of light on his eyes and the hard line of his mouth. Then he leaned closer and put his head down next to hers.

"Don't move," he said softly, his breath tickling her ear and sending a warm shiver through her. The men's voices were getting closer, some calling unfamiliar words. Westbrook leaned closer still, his body pressing her into the wall, squashing the bundle of Gwen's petticoats and shawls uncomfortably between them. Realising what he was pretending to do, heat burned in her face as she briefly wondered what it would be like if he really wanted to kiss her. After a brief hesitation, she reached up to put one hand around his neck.

The men were walking, staggering, in their direction. Now that Phoebe *could* understand what they were saying, her flush deepened. Westbrook raised his head and told them to find their own light-skirt in language equally as crude, and the men lost interest and staggered on.

He waited until the sounds of their revelry faded, leaving only the noise from inside the tavern. She checked that her bump was still in place as he pushed himself away.

"I'm sorry," he said.

There was enough light from the tavern windows for her to make out his expression. He looked particularly grim.

"I shouldn't have brought you here."

"You didn't have a choice," she said, as briskly as she could manage in a whisper. "It's certainly expanding my vocabulary!"

His expression softened, one corner of his mouth lifting.

"Is Trasker in there, do you think?" She needed to concentrate on their plan, not on how her heart was racing, or the way his breath had felt warm on her cheek.

"I can't tell. We'll listen outside the other one. This way."

Phoebe lost her bearings as they walked, but Westbrook seemed to be familiar with the town, leading them confidently down a series of narrow alleys.

They came to a halt by the window of another tavern, listening to the raucous laughter and raised voices. This time it was only a moment or two before Westbrook whispered that he could hear Trasker's voice. He put his eye to a gap in the ill-fitting shutters, but shook his head when Phoebe asked him if he could see anything.

"I think there are a couple of soldiers inside," he explained. "I caught a few words. They may be keeping a watch on the *Lily*'s crew."

"Can we wait until they return to the boat?"

"They could be in there all night, but the *Lily* needs to leave within a few hours to use the high tide."

"So we have to get Trasker out of there?"

"Yes. If the soldiers *are* watching the *Lily*'s crew, that might make them suspicious, but I don't see what else we can do." The grim look was back on his face.

Phoebe's stomach knotted. This was what she had come here for, what she had volunteered for, and she hadn't expected it to be easy. She didn't know what Trasker looked like, so she couldn't just sneak in and talk to him quietly.

She hitched up the shawls, and an idea flashed across her mind. Someone being hunted would not go into a tavern and announce their presence, so doing so might allay the suspicions of the soldiers. Bold and fast would help to reduce the chance that she would be accosted by the other drinkers.

"Trasker, is he quick to grasp things?"

"Yes—he's been successfully dodging revenue men for ten years. Dumont sent Anson to find him, so he should be expecting someone to contact him."

"I've got an idea," she whispered. "Give me a name—a name he knows, but someone who could not possibly be here, in France. A French name, if possible."

Westbrook thought, then his brow cleared. "There's Michel Paquet, one of his crew, drowned a few years ago."

"Other people here won't know he's dead?"

"I don't think so. Well, only his crew. Paquet came from Dieppe."

"What's Trasker's first name? What does he look like?"

"Dan. Or Danny to his… er… lady friends. He looks nothing out of the ordinary, unfortunately. About my height, black hair. Fond of rather bright waistcoats. From the noise he's making, he's not far from this window." He peered at her in the near-dark. "What are you planning?"

Phoebe closed her eyes and recalled a time, six years ago now, with her father on his rounds. It had been a tavern brawl, tables and chairs overturned, and three men leaning on the bar, all looking much the worse for wear. One of the miscreants was being scolded by his wife when they arrived, and she heard again the accusation in the woman's voice.

Bracing her shoulders, she opened her eyes and checked that the shawl and petticoats were still giving her a respectable bump in the right place. Westbrook was looking at her, waiting for her answer.

"I'm going to demand Danny makes an honest woman of me," she whispered in his ear, then took a deep breath and headed for the tavern door.

Westbrook cursed, but made no move to stop her. Turning before she pushed the door open, she caught a brisk nod, noting with a shiver that he now held a pistol in one hand.

In the taproom, Phoebe tried not to wince at the din and the rank smells of ale, smoke, and fish. On the opposite side of the room two soldiers sat at a table by the fire, the tavern's other patrons leaving a clear space around them. She was only a few steps inside the door, looking for Trasker, when she realised the noise had quietened and several sets of eyes were running over her. She couldn't see a bright waistcoat anywhere.

"Danny Trasker!" she shouted into the room, her voice shrill with nerves.

The room became silent. Now every eye was on her, faces filled with curiosity, disapproval, or salacious interest. The reality of this taproom full of men was more terrifying than she had expected. Perhaps the shrillness was all to the good.

"Danny Trasker, you lying bastard," she called, forcing her voice to remain steady. "I saw Michel Paquet in Avranches—he said you've been here for days."

Some men began talking to each other, a few laughed, and one or two pointed towards the window with suggestive winks.

There. A man in a red and blue striped waistcoat, looking her way with a quizzical expression. Phoebe took another breath and started again, facing him directly this time.

Don't think about what will happen if he's not *Danny Trasker.*

"Days!" she carried on with determination, her voice rising in pitch. "Why haven't you come to see me? *Quel salaud!*"

Some of the men snickered and one of the soldiers got to his feet. The man in the gaudy waistcoat started to make his way towards her. She kept her eyes fixed firmly on him, pretending not to see the soldier approaching. "You promised you'd take care of me, but I have to come here to find you!"

"I'll look after you tonight, *cherie*," said a voice beside her, and a hand squeezed her bottom. Keeping one arm firmly under the bump, she turned and dealt the man a ringing slap to his face. His friends cheered as he pushed his chair back and stood up with an oath, but by then the man in the waistcoat had reached her.

"Danny." She grasped the collar of his jacket.

Trasker glared at the man she'd slapped, and Phoebe breathed a sigh of relief as he turned away.

"Who's this?" the soldier said.

Trasker put one arm around her waist. "Why, this is Colette," he said, planting a smacking kiss on her cheek. "What's it to you?" Even the smell of ale on his breath was welcome, she decided, her racing pulse slowing a little.

"We're watching for some women."

"Well she's not one of them." He pulled her closer. "The love of my life, she is." Trasker's smile was more of a leer, but the soldier's gaze went from the brown curl escaping her cap down to the bump, then he shrugged and moved a few steps away.

"Danny, my love, we need to talk." She pulled on his collar, pitching her voice to a wheedling whisper, loud enough for the men nearby to hear. "*Please*! We can't do it here!"

To her relief, Trasker nodded, walking with her to the door and ignoring shouted remarks about living under the cat's foot. Once outside, they walked along the alley, his arm still on her waist.

Phoebe attempted to pull away, but Trasker's arm was unyielding. "They might still be watching," he said, his voice only a murmur. "Where's Westbrook?"

"Nearby." He had to be. He would not have gone far.

Trasker guided them around the corner and Phoebe glanced back towards the tavern door. There *was* a soldier watching them.

"You can let go of her now, Trasker," Westbrook hissed from the shadows, taking Phoebe's arm and pulling her from Trasker's grasp. "Let's get further away."

Alex led them around another corner, one hand against Phoebe's back to guide her. He could feel her trembling, hear her breath coming in gasps.

"This'll do," he said in her ear, ducking into the doorway of a closed shop. "It's done now; you're safe. You were very brave."

"What's the plan?" Trasker asked.

"Get the *Lily* to sea," Alex said. Was Phoebe cold? He pulled her gently towards him, opening his coat and wrapping it around her.

"Westbrook!"

Alex returned his attention to Trasker. "Pick them up at the beach near the hut. Henri and I will make a fire a mile up the coast, as a decoy. If you drop a boat near the hut, you can sail on a bit before you signal, in case anyone's watching, then head back for the boat."

"How many people?"

"Miss Deane, here." She'd stopped trembling, but he was in no hurry to release her. She would be warmer under his coat, he told himself.

"And...?"

Concentrate!

"Er, Pierre, Gwen and the children, Miss Deane's aunt and cousin, and Hugo de Brevare, the *ci-devant* Vicomte de Brevare." He almost spat the last name.

"There's a story there?"

"Miss Deane is carrying something for me. Make sure the treacherous bastard doesn't bother her, either on the voyage or on the way to London. Choose your destination by the wind, but check with Miss Deane." There was enough light for Alex to see Trasker's eyebrows rise, but he made no protest.

"The *Lily's* ready for sea," Trasker said. "Tide'll be high enough by the time I get the crew on board. Pick-up at eleven o'clock?"

"Fine."

Trasker gazed down the street, brow furrowed. "We'll need a good diversion to keep the soldiers occupied." His teeth showed white in a grin. "A little goodbye present for Clothilde and Suzette, perhaps," he said. "Enough to buy them some brand new gowns."

"Ha, yes, that should do the trick!" A fight involving clothing being torn would certainly attract attention.

"Right, then." Trasker clapped Alex on the shoulder, and vanished down the alley.

"Phoebe?" Alex asked, ducking his head to try to see her face. "Phoebe, are you feeling better now?"

Phoebe nodded, then realised that he probably couldn't see her at all. "Yes." Standing beneath his coat had been comforting; she *was* beginning to calm down.

"I'm so sorry I got you into this."

"I volunteered, remember?" She took a deep breath—it was time she pulled herself together.

"Yes, but you didn't know—"

137

"It's done now." Thank goodness. "How will we know when Trasker's distraction is ready?"

"We'll know." There was a smile in his voice.

"What's he going to do?" Was she talking too much? He didn't seem to mind. "New gowns—oh!" A giggle rose in her throat as she worked out the implications. "To guarantee the full attention of their audience?"

"Exactly! How's the baby?"

The change of topic made her chuckle again. "About to keep my neck warm!" She took a step back and away from him, shivering as she left the warmth of his coat, and wound the shawls around her neck. She leaned on the wall beside him as they waited for Trasker's friends to start their diversion.

It was only a few more minutes before two women began screaming at each other, the shrill sounds echoing in the narrow streets.

"Let's go," Westbrook said, and led her through the town, avoiding streets with taverns or too many people. Phoebe hurried to keep up, glad to be leaving. A few men moved towards the source of the noise, but took no notice of the pair of them.

Back in the field, Westbrook checked the saddle girths on the horses and made a step with his hand to help her to mount. Clumsily, being used to a side-saddle, she swung one leg over the horse and found the stirrups, cold air biting her legs as Gwen's skirts bunched uncomfortably beneath her thighs.

"All set?" Westbrook asked.

"Yes." She dug her heels in, thankful the horse seemed to be a placid animal, and followed Westbrook's mount into the lane. Beside her, his face showed pale in the moonlight as he turned in her direction.

"Can you manage a trot? Best we're not overtaken if anyone comes after us."

"Yes." She sounded more confident than she felt. Riding astride was much more secure than using a side saddle, but it was over a year since she'd been on horseback. Urging the horse faster, she was relieved to find it easy to control, and soon settled into the new rhythm.

The landscape was featureless, reduced to silhouettes of trees against thin clouds, lit from behind by the moon. At last they turned into a track through woodland, and Westbrook slowed the horses to a walk, then dismounted in the same clearing as before. She slid off her mount and stood beside him, both using the horses to shield them from the wind.

It was time to say goodbye.

CHAPTER 17

"Can you remember the plan?" Alex asked. "There won't be time for any private talk when we get to the hut."

"Yes." Her voice held certainty.

"Be careful, Phoebe," he said forcefully. His feelings told him he should never have involved her further in this business, but the rational part of him acknowledged that she was a valuable ally. Albeit an inexperienced one. "They won't all be as inept as Brevare—and Brevare himself could be dangerous, for all his lack of observation. Don't expose yourself to danger; abandon the plan if you have to. Remember, the main thing is for the list not to fall into the wrong hands. Destroy it if—"

"I know," Phoebe said. "I will."

"And if you need help with anything else, go to Lady Carterton, in Brook Street."

"You told me. I *do* remember." She sounded impatient and he smiled in the darkness. *That* was why he'd thought it was a workable idea.

"Sorry, it's... oh, hell!" He took her by the shoulders. "When you went into that tavern—I... well, I knew I shouldn't have got you into all this. It's too dangerous. Just burn the damned message!"

140

"I will if it becomes necessary," she promised. "But if I don't even try, we've wasted months of your time."

"Better that than—"

"You saved all of us. At *best* we'd be in prison now, or being held somewhere for ransom. By someone who *would* intend to collect."

He saw the pale oval of her face as she looked up at him, but there was not enough light beneath the trees to make out her expression.

"And this plan is worth trying, isn't it?" she asked.

He sighed. "Yes." But he'd made the plan before he'd had to wait outside that damned tavern. Fear like that for someone else, made worse because he was powerless to act, was new to him. "I still don't like it. Be careful."

"You be careful too!" She sounded almost indignant now. "You will be taking far more of a risk than I am."

"It's my job. I volunteered."

"So did I."

"It's not the sa—" A movement behind Phoebe caught his eye; Henri, with a lantern. He swore under his breath, a suppressed little snort from Phoebe indicating that his curses hadn't been as quiet as he'd thought.

"It is arranged?" Henri asked, in French.

Alex cursed again, silently this time. He hadn't realised he'd been talking to Phoebe in English. That was dangerous—if he couldn't remember something that simple, perhaps it was time for a rest.

"Yes, Trasker will do as we planned. We leave in half an hour."

Henri nodded. "Good. Gwen has some coffee and food. Come." He led the way back to the hut. Inside, the comtesse and Hélène sat in one corner, keeping a disdainful distance between themselves and the Dumont family.

"Phoebe, where have you—?" The comtesse's sharp enquiry was silenced by a glare from Pierre.

"Brevare?" Alex asked.

Pierre jerked his head towards the door. "We told him to watch for the *Lily*."

"But she's not due for another couple of hours."

Pierre shrugged, and Alex shook his head. "You'd better relieve him soon. After Henri and I have left," he added.

Gwen handed him a piece of day-old bread and a cup of coffee, and he ate and drank gratefully, leaning against the wall. Phoebe sat next to Gwen and removed her cap. She unpinned Gwen's lock of hair and took down her own hair, smoothing it with her fingers before twisting it up into a knot. What would it be like to run his own fingers through it? Looking away hastily, he stepped closer to Pierre to run over the plans once more.

While Henri fixed new candles in a couple of lanterns, Gwen handed over wrapped packets of bread and cheese, and Alex pocketed them with a word of thanks.

"We'll get some wood together," Pierre said, following his brother out of the hut.

Alex went after them, but stopped outside the door. Phoebe followed him, although he hadn't given any indication that she should. He thrust his doubts away as he faced her.

"Be careful," she said. Had that been a faint tremor in her voice? "You should soak that bandage off in a day or so. See if you can find some honey to spread on it, then put a clean bandage on. And find someone to take the stitches out for you."

She sounded more business-like now, but he could see a crease in her brow, a twist of her lips that was not quite a smile.

"Yes, doctor," he said quietly.

Good, that looked more like a proper smile. She hadn't put that enveloping cap back on, and her hair curled about her head, a few strands slipping down onto her shoulders.

Her smile turned into something more intimate—inviting even— and he did what he knew he should not. He raised one hand to tuck a loose curl behind her ear, then rested it on the wall beside her. The memory of adopting a similar position in Granville sent his heart beating faster; he dipped his head down towards hers, brushing her mouth lightly at first, giving her plenty of time to pull away.

She didn't. Instead, she leaned into him, winding her arms around his neck. He brushed her lips again. Wanting—needing—to be closer, he moved one hand to her waist and pulled her gently towards him.

Once more she met him, pressing herself forwards with uptilted face, her lips slightly parted, her breath warm on his cheek. This time he put his mouth on hers, running his tongue along her soft lower lip. Heat flooded through him at the feel of her body against his, the way her lips parted further. She responded tentatively at first, then more confidently, testing his control as she put a hand up to the back of his head, fingers tangling in his hair, pulling him closer.

He deepened the kiss, wanting more, to touch more of her, without their layers of clothing in the way. That thought finally made him lift his head and relax his hold on her. They stood close while his breath slowed.

"I'm sorry." He didn't know why he was apologising. Nothing could some of it, but he wasn't sorry in the least, no matter how much he should have been.

Phoebe put a finger on his lips. "Don't be." Her eyes searched his again. "Don't be sorry—be careful. Come home safely!"

He took her hand and kissed her palm briefly, then picked up a bundle and set off after the Dumont brothers, with one more look behind him as he entered the trees.

Phoebe leaned on the wall of the hut, watching him go, her heart still beating uncomfortably fast. She put a hand to her lips. Whoever would have thought a kiss could melt her insides, reach right down to her knees and turn them to jelly?

"You only met him five days ago," she told herself. So why did this farewell leave her feeling so empty?

Closing her eyes, she concentrated on the sharp tang of the salt air, the sounds of surf in the distance, until her pulse returned to normal. They were not safe yet, and she had the message to deal with as well.

She stood there until Pierre returned, saying something about fetching Brevare before he walked on down to the shore. Not wanting Brevare to find her standing outside on his return, she entered the hut and sat down next to Gwen. She knew she should rest until it was time for the boat, but the warm memory of that kiss kept her from sleep.

Pierre roused everyone an hour later. Phoebe had reduced her things to only a small bag, abandoning the orange dress without a qualm. At a word from Gwen, she took their little girl's hand and waited outside. Pierre, laden with his family's possessions, led the way through the dunes onto the beach, a darkened lantern in his free hand. Phoebe waited until everyone else had left the hut then brought up the rear, feet sliding in the loose sand.

A light shone off to the north, large enough to be a bonfire—that must be Alex's diversion. She could not think of him as Westbrook now, not after that kiss.

Further west, a faint flicker of light showed against the black void of the sea. Although the wind was blowing from the land, waves broke on the beach.

"Is that our boat?" Brevare shouted to Pierre, his voice almost lost in the noise of the surf.

Pierre nodded.

"It's miles away! What's it doing over there?" Brevare looked around. "Where's Westbrook?"

Ignoring him, Pierre walked on across the sand and into the shelter of a rocky spit. Phoebe sat next to Gwen on a protruding rock slab, happy to be out of the wind. She settled herself to wait, hoping the boat would arrive soon and soldiers would not. Hélène sat in miserable silence while the comtesse complained bitterly and long about the wind, the noise, the sand in her shoes, the lack of respect from the others. Keeping her eyes on the surf, which was glowing faintly in the moonlight, Phoebe shut out her aunt's voice.

By the water's edge, Pierre fiddled with his lantern, opening a shutter to allow a narrow beam of light to show, then directing it out to sea. Gazing across the water, Phoebe finally made out the pale splash of oars beyond the waves breaking on the sand. The shadowed form of a boat drew closer. Four men rowed, one oar each.

Wading into the surf, Pierre grabbed the prow and dragged the boat onto the beach. He turned and waved. Gwen, ready and waiting with the baby fastened to her front by a pair of knotted shawls, moved forward with her daughter, Phoebe close behind. One of the oarsmen scrambled out and ran up the beach, giving Gwen a swift hug before picking up the girl in one arm and a bag in the other. Pierre swung Gwen and the baby into the boat and Sophie and the bag followed.

Phoebe stood by the prow, bag in hand, gasping as she was lifted with similar lack of ceremony into the boat. A hand reached out to steady her, and she sat down as Pierre passed over the rest of the family's luggage and then Hélène. Phoebe made space for her cousin beside her, and ducked her head at the shriek emitted when the comtesse was dumped on board.

Brevare hung back. "Where's Westbrook?"

"Get in the boat," Pierre said. "Westbrook is not coming."

"What? But he—we must wait!"

Pierre shrugged. "Wait if you want to." He pushed the boat until it was afloat before scrambling aboard and sitting down next to his wife.

Phoebe turned her head, wondering what Brevare would do. His gaze swung back and forth between the beach and the boat. At the last minute, he waded into the water up to his waist, grasping the gunwale and making the boat rock alarmingly. Pierre swore and grabbed his coat, pulling until Brevare landed in ungainly heap in the bottom of the boat.

Her aunt shrieked again as the boat pulled out into the swell and began to pitch, plunging up and down as the waves passed under them. Neither Pierre nor the oarsmen looked at all concerned, so Phoebe gave Hélène an encouraging smile and took a firm grip on the gunwale. As they cleared the breaking swells, the motion of the boat eased and her grip relaxed as she relished the wind and spray in her face.

Squinting against the moisture-laden wind, she spotted an intermittent gleam of light out at sea, and could hear shouted commands and the slap of canvas as it grew closer. Finally a shadow loomed large against the moonlit streaks of cloud.

Their boat came alongside the larger vessel, two of the oarsmen grasping a rope ladder let down over the side. The others shipped their oars, gesturing to the passengers. Pierre helped Gwen onto the ladder and climbed it right behind her, clearly ready to support her if she slipped. At a shout from Pierre, one of the oarsmen did the same with Sophie. From the way they moved, Phoebe guessed that this was not the first time they had boarded a boat in such a way.

She tucked up her skirts as Gwen had done and gingerly stepped up to the gunwale of the rocking boat. The remaining oarsman steadied her as she pulled herself up the ladder, the ropes rough and wet in her hands. Then her arms were grasped from above and she scrambled up onto the deck, staggering as they let her go. Jostled by the men bustling around the ladder, she moved over to the rail, almost falling onto it as the *Lily* rolled.

Looking over the side, she watched with amusement as the men remaining in the rowing boat gave up trying to persuade her aunt and cousin to climb the ladder. They caught ropes flung down to them, making them fast at the prow and stern. The boat was hauled upwards, complete with baggage and whimpering women. Once on the deck and unloaded it was quickly lashed down.

Another shout to 'get those damned women out of the way' prompted Gwen to usher the comtesse and Hélène through a door that must lead below decks. Phoebe was about to follow them when she felt a hand on her arm. It was the sailor who had hugged Gwen.

"You'll be all right here, miss, if you want to stay out for a bit. Not enough room to swing a cat in the cabin."

His accent brought a smile of recognition to her lips. "You're not from these parts, then?"

"Gwen's brother, Owen Jones."

"I'm pleased to meet you, Mr Jones," Phoebe said.

A series of shouted orders had men pulling on ropes, and the *Lily* heeled over and turned west, dark sails filling with wind. Phoebe looked towards the land, trying to make out the signal fire.

"You'll have to share a cabin with Gwen and young Sophie," Owen went on, leaning on the rail beside her. "Unless you want to go in with your... your aunt, is it?"

"It is," said Phoebe. "But we do not get to choose our relations."

There was a snort of laughter.

"Won't Gwen be with Pierre?" she asked.

"Not enough space for this many passengers," he said. "Pierre and that fancy man who nearly got left behind, they'll have hammocks with the rest of the crew."

Phoebe nodded, giving him only part of her attention. She'd finally spotted the speck of light that was the decoy bonfire. Was Alex still there? Had someone worked out where to send the soldiers from Granville?

"They will be fine," Owen said in reassuring tones. "Been dodging revenue men for years, see?" He pointed to a couple of lanterns being hauled up into the rigging. "That's the signal that you are safe on board. Watch for the answering signal."

Phoebe glanced up as the lights rose from the deck, then turned her gaze to the land again. At least Alex would be able to do his job without worrying about her and her relatives.

"Don't stay out too long, miss. It'll be cold."

His footsteps retreated across the deck, but she kept her eyes on the shore. There—a light some distance from the dying fire. Of course, any soldiers would be heading for the fire.

The lanterns in the rigging were lowered. Letting out a breath, Phoebe watched until she was sure there would be no further signal from the land, then went to find Gwen's cabin.

Alex and Henri huddled in the shelter of a hedge, Alex keeping an eye on the bonfire half a mile to their south while Henri's attention was fixed on the sea. The fire would burn for another half-hour or so without attention, by which time the *Lily* should have spotted it. So far, there was no sign of anyone approaching: no precautionary shots, no shapes passing in front of its light.

Henri's elbow dug into Alex's ribs, and Alex followed the man's pointing finger. At last, a light—one more step in the plan. This rendezvous pick-up felt different, more nerve-racking than usual. It was the first time he'd been concerned about more than the success of the mission, but that kind of sentiment could be dangerous.

Taking out his watch, he squinted at it in the moonlight, wondering how long they'd have to wait for the *Lily*'s signal.

Henri settled back, his face impassive. What was the man thinking? Brevare's actions had put the Dumonts out of a home, and although Marstone would see them set up somewhere else, that would likely mean settling in Britain. He doubted Gwen would mind, not with another baby on the way, but what about Henri?

Perhaps it was just as well. The soldiers had come to the inn quickly enough, so the Dumonts may have been under suspicion already. At least now Pierre and Gwen were on their way to safety.

Reminding Henri to keep an eye out for the *Lily*'s signal, Alex stood and walked around a curve in the hedge to where they'd left the horses. He tightened the saddle girths so they were ready to leave; they hadn't seen any soldiers so far, but that didn't mean it was safe to stay this close to the pick-up point. They would ride inland for a while before finding somewhere to spend what was left of the night.

"Westbrook!" Henri's voice was barely loud enough to be heard above the wind. Out at sea, Alex could make out two lights, one above the other, and some of the tension in his body relaxed. Phoebe should be safe enough on the *Lily*—he'd have Trasker's guts if anything happened to her.

He caught a flash of light as Henri returned the signal then, dousing the lantern, Henri joined him and mounted his horse. Alex kicked his own mount into motion, and followed Henri across the field.

CHAPTER 18

*P*hoebe breathed the smell of coffee, becoming aware of creaking wood and the sound of rushing water, a hard mattress beneath her.

"Coffee, Miss Deane?"

Opening her eyes, Phoebe blinked at the beams only a couple of feet above her head, beaded with condensation. She turned on her side; Gwen's face was level with her own, dim in the lamplight.

"Careful now," Gwen said. "Ceiling's low."

"What time is it?" With no window, there was no clue from outside.

"Middle of the morning. Lovely day outside, it is. Owen thought you'd be wanting something to eat by now."

Phoebe rubbed her face, her thoughts finally coming together and her stomach giving her the answer. "Yes, please." She propped herself up on one elbow and took the steaming mug from Gwen.

"I'll tell him you'll be out soon." Gwen smiled. "There's water there, if you're wanting a wash. Food'll be in Cap'n Trasker's day cabin, down the passageway."

Phoebe drank the coffee, beginning to feel more awake. She

stretched as well as she could in the cramped space before scrambling down to the cabin floor.

Last night, she'd stayed awake long enough to remove her gown and stays, but she felt sticky and grubby. There was a piece of towelling next to the bucket of warm water, and she had a quick all-over wash which made her feel much better. Oh, for a bath, though!

Phoebe pulled her bag from beneath the bottom bunk. She chose the cleaner of her two spare chemises and donned the peach gown again before going in search of food.

The day cabin had windows across the stern of the vessel, giving a view of blue sky with puffy clouds and the white streak of the *Lily*'s wake across the rolling swell. A table took up over half the floor, with a bench seat around three sides of it. The only sign of life was a place set with a bowl of stew, a hunk of bread, and a spoon. Phoebe's stomach rumbled at the savoury smell; stew for breakfast was unusual, but she wasn't going to complain. She slid awkwardly into the seat and tucked into her meal with relish.

She was wiping the bowl with a piece of bread, glad no-one could see her poor table manners, when Owen entered and asked if she wanted more.

"Yes, please. Are you the cook? It's very good."

"We don't have a cook, miss, not properly. I do a bit when we have passengers. But mainly taking buckets to her ladyship, I am." This last was said with a grimace as he filled her bowl again.

"Are they both seasick?"

"Only the old bi... er, biddy. But it's not proper for Lady Hélène to dine with us common sailor folk without a proper chaperone, see?" Owen's words sounded matter-of-fact, but Phoebe caught a twinkle in his eye.

"I don't count as a chaperone?"

"I haven't told her you've woken up, miss. Thought you'd like a bit of peace to eat first." He winked.

Owen had only just left when her uncle's steward came in, looking tired and rumpled, but with a smile of greeting on his face.

"Anson!" She stood, staggering slightly at the motion of the ship, and held out her hand. "Oh, I'm so pleased to see you!"

"And I you, Miss Deane." He shook her hand briefly, then sat at the opposite end of the table. "I wasn't sure I should have taken orders from that Mr Westbrook, but it seems to have turned out for the best."

"What did you do?"

"He told me to take the diligence to Avranches and then find the Dumont brothers near Granville. They got word to Captain Trasker, and I've been staying on board while we waited for you. It was remarkably easy. No-one took any notice of me."

"I'm glad you didn't get caught up in the trouble my aunt caused."

Anson allowed himself a rueful smile when their eyes met, then turned his head as the door opened. Hélène entered, glancing around the cabin with a frown. Owen followed her in, carrying a tray. He placed a plate of stew in front of Anson, then one near Phoebe, clearly intended for Hélène.

"Good morning, Hélène," Phoebe said politely. "I hope you slept well?"

"In that tiny cabin, with Mama being—?" She shook her head. "The accommodation might be the kind of thing you're used to, but not me."

"None of us is used to taking passage on a smuggling vessel," Phoebe pointed out.

"Smugglers?" Hélène's eyes became round.

A retort sprang to Phoebe's lips, but she didn't speak. She couldn't be bothered with Hélène's naivety, especially as there were likely to be far more interesting things to see up on deck. She quickly ate her second helping and excused herself, leaving Anson and Hélène finishing their meal. Collecting the disreputable coat from her cabin, she wrapped a shawl around her neck and scrambled up the steep stairway to the deck.

The cold, salt-laden breeze took her breath away at first. Phoebe tried to remember some of the books she had read about sailing, and Joe's impatient lessons in the proper language to use about ships. The wind was coming from the front of the vessel, on the starboard bow.

They were heading northwards, she thought, leaning on the rail and taking in the sun sparkling on the white tops of the waves, and the way they seemed to roll endlessly on to the horizon.

She soon retreated to stand by the mast, making the most of the meagre shelter it offered from the wind. The trip between Dover and Calais never had this feeling of being far from land, the sense of adventures to come. Her lips twisted in a wry smile; she'd had adventure enough in the last few days, although she couldn't regret anything that had happened. This was different, though—the sense of unknown possibilities, new places, different people. No matter that things would change when they were safely back in London, or that she would appreciate it more with Alex beside her; she would enjoy the moment.

"Ah, there you are."

Brevare's voice made Phoebe jump, her heart accelerating as she spun around. The wind in the rigging had masked the sound of his footsteps, and now he stood glowering beside her—too close. She took a step away, but he put a hand on her arm. He didn't grip tightly, but she sensed that he would if she tried to move further.

"You were supposed to bring me that message." There was anger in his voice.

Phoebe resisted the temptation to pull away, glancing sideways but seeing no-one nearby. She'd hoped to avoid this confrontation, but had forgotten about Brevare in her excitement at coming on deck. Being here alone had been a mistake.

"Well, girl?"

"I've got it," she said.

"I suppose that's better than nothing." His frown smoothed. "Does he know you stole it, or hasn't he missed it yet?"

"I didn't steal it."

"What? Stop messing about and give it to me." He held a hand out.

Did he still think of her as a rather dim servant? It was worth a try. "No, sir," she said, allowing her voice to quaver a little. No servant would wish to antagonise a member of the upper classes.

He stared at her, nonplussed, then his lips tightened, his mouth forming a sneer. "It will be safer with me—what do you think you can do with it?"

"Take it to the Earl of Marstone, sir. That's what Mr Westbrook told me to do."

"Nonsense! He wouldn't trust you with something of such importance. I'll see it gets to where it needs to go."

Phoebe shook her head.

"Come, girl, do as you are told!" This time he was almost snarling, his face close to hers, menacing.

She swallowed, trying to keep her voice steady. "I *am* doing as I was told, sir." If she had to, she could give him the decoy note.

"Everything all right, miss?"

Phoebe let out a long breath as Dan Trasker appeared behind Brevare, two of his crew beside him.

"I wanted a word, Miss Deane, if you have a moment." Trasker nodded to Brevare and extended an arm in invitation.

Brevare's grip tightened momentarily. Trasker raised an eyebrow and glanced towards the two crewmen, and Brevare finally let go.

"Excuse us, sir," Trasker said. "This way, miss."

Phoebe took his arm, and he led her aft, steadying her against the movement of the ship. They stopped in the shelter of the small wheelhouse.

"Best if you don't come on deck alone," Trasker said. "Ask Owen to show you the ropes, or have Pierre Dumont with you."

"I will, thank you."

"That wasn't what I wanted, though. The wind is still easterly. I wished to discuss our destination with you."

Phoebe's eyes widened. She had heard Alex tell him to consult her, but she hadn't believed he would.

"The original plan was to put you ashore near Brighton to make the overland part of your journey short and give that fool," he jerked his head in Brevare's direction, "as little chance as possible to... bother you."

Phoebe tried to bring a map of the south coast to mind. "The wind...?"

Trasker smiled. "Indeed, Miss Deane. It could take a day or two to beat up the Channel—longer if the wind strengthens. If you don't mind a longer coach journey, we could make for Ashmouth. That's the *Lily*'s home port, in Devonshire. With the wind fair on this heading, we could be there this evening. It will take two days to London from there, perhaps three, but we can find a coach and driver for you all, and someone to be a lady's maid as well. They can make sure Brevare doesn't bother you."

"Ashmouth, I think, under the circumstances," she said.

Trasker nodded in satisfaction. Phoebe suspected he had already made up his mind, but was pleased to have his choice approved.

"Would you have taken us to Sussex if I'd chosen that?"

"Westbrook put you in charge, Miss Deane. I trust his judgement."

She could detect no trace of resentment in his words or his expression, which was as surprising as Alex's instruction. She found herself standing straighter, while hoping their confidence was not misplaced. "Have you worked with him long?"

"A few years, off and on," Trasker said, which didn't tell Phoebe much at all. She sensed she wouldn't get more out of him. In Granville, the two men had seemed to know each other well, but there was no reason why Trasker should speak freely to her. She changed the subject, asking him to tell her about the *Lily*.

"She's quite big for a cutter—I've twenty-eight hands," he said, chest swelling with pride as he turned and gestured towards the bow. "Fast, too, when her bottom's clean."

"Is she yours?"

"I've been in command five years," he said, with only the slightest hesitation.

Phoebe, wondering if she was becoming too suspicious of everyone, interpreted this as meaning that the *Lily* did not belong to him, but he wasn't going to tell her who the owner was. Rather than persist, she asked him to explain what some of the seeming hundreds of ropes did.

Trasker's disbelieving expression turned into a smile of pleasure when she assured him she really was interested. Walking along the deck beside him, she could hardly keep up as nautical terms flew at her: braces and shrouds, halyards and sheets, masts, yards, and bowsprits. She must have looked bemused, for he apologised with a rueful grin.

"No, don't be sorry!" Phoebe said hastily. "It is such a lot to take in —but I *am* interested. My brother is..." She wondered if smugglers regarded the Royal Navy as their enemies, but ploughed on. "Joe is in the navy. Now I can better understand his stories. Do you... will it be all right if I do some sketching?" She waved her hand to indicate the sails and sea.

"Of course. I'll keep an eye on Brevare while you get your things, then I'll send Owen or Pierre up with a chair for you."

An hour later she looked up guiltily as she heard Trasker barking out orders for trimming the sails. Members of his crew surrounded her chair, and she belatedly wondered if some of them were supposed to be doing other things. They had certainly kept Brevare away from her; he still stood by the rail, his gaze alternating between her and the horizon.

"Am I distracting them from their duties?" she asked as Trasker approached. "I'm sorry." She showed him her sketchbook, and was relieved to see Trasker's lips twitch as he regarded the portrait of one of his men, with added eyepatch, cutlass, and bicorne hat complete with skull and crossbones.

"I allus fancied mesel' as a pirate," the subject of the portrait, said. "Jemmy there wanted to be a gennelman with a fancy hat."

Jem showed his picture, and Trasker laughed. "No need to hurry, Miss Deane," he said. "Finish the one you're doing."

She quickly added the final lines and tore out the page, handing it to the crewman. She waited until the men had gone about their duties before she turned back to Trasker. "You will have to let me, or Mr Anson, know how much we owe you. I think... I hope we have enough money left."

"No charge, Miss Deane. Besides, I reckon you've earned your own passage anyway, entertaining my crew like that!" He shook his head. "Now, what I came to say was, we can make port within a few hours if we keep all sail on, and you could be on your way this evening. Or we could arrive late enough for you to need to stay the night in Ashmouth. Mr Anson could go on ahead; he thought it might be wise if he travelled post to London to carry the news of your arrival."

Her uncle must have returned to London from his business trip some days ago. Having Anson tell him the unadorned version of events first seemed an excellent idea to Phoebe.

"That sounds the best plan," Phoebe agreed, still enjoying the novelty of having her opinion solicited. She could see a faint smudge ahead where the sea joined the sky. "Is that land?"

"Yes. We'll heave to here and wait for a few hours." Trasker gave orders to the mate and shouts sent men scrambling up the rigging.

Phoebe tensed as Brevare finally left his position by the rail and made his way towards them. "What's going on?" he asked Trasker. "Why are you taking in sail here?"

"Can't get into the harbour until later this evening," Trasker told him, his expression bland. "Tides."

"Ah, very well."

Brevare stood glaring at Trasker, who showed no sign of leaving her side. Phoebe suppressed a smile, then gave the captain a small nod. Trasker moved off, but stopped only a few yards away—out of earshot, but close enough to see what Brevare was doing.

"I'm sorry if I frightened you earlier," Brevare said, almost sounding sincere. "But that message is extremely important."

"I *will* give it to the earl, sir, as I promised." Now was probably the time to give him a hint. If he had a plan to obtain the message in London, he was less likely to try to get it from her on the journey. "I'm supposed to take it to the Foreign Office, sir, but I'm not sure where that is. Do you think they will let me in?"

Brevare's face brightened. "I can help you there," he said. "I know the earl, and I'm sure I can arrange for him to meet you. I'm told they are not very friendly there, unless you are a member of the *ton*. The Calvacs reside in Berkeley Square, do they not?"

"Yes, sir."

"I'll send a note when I've arranged the meeting. You will be able to slip out?"

Phoebe nodded, almost pleased with him for falling in so well with Alex's plan. He was about to say something else when Trasker, with excellent timing, returned.

"Excuse me, Miss Deane, but her ladyship is asking for you," he said.

Phoebe sighed, until she caught his quick wink.

"Thought you wouldn't want to spend too long with him," Trasker muttered quietly as Phoebe moved away.

"Thank you, Captain," Phoebe said, and gladly escaped.

CHAPTER 19

*P*hoebe sighed with pleasure as she sank into the hot water. After the sea voyage and two very long days on the road to London, it was bliss to be allowed to soak in peace, scented soap to hand and a steaming cup of chocolate on a table by the bath. By the time they had reached the house last night, she had been too exhausted to do anything other than retire to bed.

The *Lily* had moored in Ashmouth harbour after dark, and Owen and Trasker escorted them all to the village's single inn. As soon as the comtesse and Hélène had been shown to their rooms, Anson arranged for the inn's gig to take him to Exeter that night, hoping to get a seat on the mail coach. Phoebe, sorry to see him go but appreciating the need, had been relieved when Brevare said he would join him. That had removed any worry about the journey to London, and now they were back on English soil her aunt's injudicious remarks could cause no further trouble.

Phoebe had risen early the next morning and walked around the village, knowing it was the only exercise she was likely to get over the following couple of days. Seen in daylight, Ashmouth was a pretty little place, houses lining a cleft in the sandstone cliffs running inland from the harbour. Standing on the short sea wall with gulls calling above her, she wondered if Alex had ever stood here looking at this view.

The east wind was biting, and she had not stayed out long. She had returned to find that the comtesse and Hélène had breakfasted and Trasker had organised a coach and driver. Owen Jones was to act as guard, and the innkeeper's daughter, Ellie, would be their maid. It had felt rather odd, at first, to be travelling inside a coach again, but Ellie's presence inside, and her aunt's tiredness from the crossing, resulted in a relatively peaceful journey. All had gone to plan so far.

Her part in the plan, at least. Where was Alex now? She sat up and soaped herself, feeling a pang of guilt for luxuriating in her bath when he was probably crammed into a jolting diligence somewhere. He hadn't explained how he would go about finding Brevare's family, but she couldn't imagine he would be able to relax properly until he was back in England.

Phoebe donned a robe while she towelled her hair, thinking how things would change here at home. She was looking forward to seeing her young cousin Georges again, and his governess. Before this last trip to France, she and Alice Bryant had shared confidences—now there was much she couldn't tell.

They would be happy to see her again, she told herself, giving her curls a final rub. She hoped that her uncle would, too, unless her aunt had already poisoned him against her.

No, he *was* a fair man, and would at least ask for her version of events.

Ellie's knock was a welcome interruption to these thoughts, and the maid's cheery smile helped to lighten Phoebe's mood. "M'sewer le Comte said to join 'im fer breakfast, miss." She eyed the yellow gown Phoebe had laid on the bed. "Shall I 'elp you on with that, miss?"

"Yes, please. But why are you waiting on me? I thought you were only taken on for the journey. Aren't you supposed to be going back to Devonshire?"

Ellie bobbed a curtsey. "The 'ousekeeper said as how I should make myself useful while I be 'ere." Ellie finished lacing Phoebe's gown. "I was wonderin', miss…"

"Yes?"

"Well, I was wonderin' if I could be your maid for a bit. It'd be nice to see Lunnun. And Mrs Kidd said as how Lady Hélène's maid would be busy lookin' after 'er ladyship as well, 'til she gets a new maid, so there baint no-one for you. I baint trained, like, but I can get gowns clean and pressed, and I learns fast and I allus used to do my sister's hair, and—"

"Stop!" Phoebe begged, laughing. "If Mrs Kidd agrees, I'd love to have you as my maid!"

"Thank you, miss!" Ellie beamed, dropping a quick curtsey, then turned to unpack Phoebe's bag.

"What time is it?"

"It be gone ten o'clock, miss."

No wonder she felt so ravenous.

The Comte de Calvac looked up as Phoebe entered the breakfast room. He was seated at one end of the table, wearing his usual matching waistcoat, coat and breeches—of plain cloth but well cut—and his grey wig. He smiled and put aside his newspaper.

"Ah, Phoebe! Welcome back."

"Thank you, sir," Phoebe said, appreciating his unfailing courtesy. How different he was from his wife in that respect.

"I hear from Anson that you had a bit of difficulty?"

What had Anson said to the comte? Helping herself to eggs and toast, she thought she would have to see the steward in private—the sooner the better.

"Yes, sir, but all ended well." A footman brought her some fresh coffee.

"I have not yet spoken to your aunt in detail, but she did not sound happy when you arrived last night." The comte's voice held an unspoken question.

"Her maid left us to return home only two days after we left Calvac," Phoebe explained. "She didn't like having to manage without servants." Which was the truth, although it omitted all the important details.

The comte nodded and returned to his newspaper while Phoebe

ate. He must have been watching her, as he put his paper down as soon as she finished her meal.

"You may leave us, Green," he said to the footman.

Green bowed, closing the door as he left.

"Now, Phoebe, I would like more detail, please."

Phoebe took a sip of coffee, wondering how much she should—or could—tell her uncle.

"We were travelling in short stages, sir, from Calvac. On the third day we were accused of being spies when we stopped at an inn. Luckily the local magistrate was not available, and a passing gentleman persuaded them to let us travel on. He escorted us to the coast and found us a passage home." That was all true.

"The name of this gentleman?"

"Mr Westbrook. He was travelling with the Vicomte de Brevare."

"My wife said…"

Phoebe was fascinated to see her uncle's face turning red. She guessed that her aunt had told her own version of events, and the comte was trying to think of a way to put his question delicately.

He cleared his throat. "She seemed to think that you were… that your reputation…" He faltered to a halt again.

Phoebe took pity on him. "If someone wanted to put the worst possible interpretation on what happened, then some happenings could lead to that view." Which, of course, was exactly what her aunt had done.

The comte digested this. "But you were not… did not…"

"No, sir. Nothing like that."

Apart from that kiss. Phoebe felt heat rise to her face, and hurriedly took another mouthful of coffee, hoping the cup would hide her momentary confusion.

"Good… good." He nodded, seeming relieved to have got that out of the way.

Phoebe suspected that this would not be the end of the matter. The comtesse was not one to let complaints drop.

"May I ask you a question, Uncle? Without explaining *why* I want to know?"

"That might depend on the question."

"Do you know of the Earl of Marstone?"

"I have met him, yes, but do not claim a good acquaintance. He is not particularly active in the Lords, as far as I know, but I believe he has some links with the government." His brows drew together. "What do you want to know?"

"Just whether he is a… a man of integrity."

"I believe so, yes."

"Thank you."

The comte's lips twitched. "Perhaps one day you will tell me why you need to ask?"

"Perhaps," she replied composedly. "If you will excuse me, sir?"

He smiled, and Phoebe went in search of the housekeeper, relieved that she hadn't had to explain in any more detail.

Mrs Kidd was happy to take on Ellie as Phoebe's maid for a few weeks. As Phoebe made her way back up to her room, Georges appeared on the landing.

"You're back!"

"Georges!"

Her cousin flung his arms around her waist, then recalled some of the dignity required of the ten-year-old heir. "That is, I am glad you are back safe, cousin." His hauteur slipped again. "Bryant is so stuffy. Will you come and play cricket with me in the gardens?"

Phoebe laughed. "*Miss* Bryant is supposed to be giving you lessons —she's not stuffy! But I will come with you and ask her if you may play later." In the meantime, she should work out how she could arrange to see the Earl of Marstone.

An hour later, Phoebe descended the front steps and crossed the road to the gardens in the middle of Berkeley Square. Unlocking the gate, she wandered around the path inside the railings, the sun warm on her face. She was grateful that the houses on the square had access to this bit of greenery, but it wasn't the same as being in the country. The sound of horses and carriages on the cobbles was only slightly muffled by the vegetation, and the tops of the surrounding houses were visible above the trees.

Georges' chatter broke the relative peace, and Phoebe headed back towards the gate. Green and Ellie followed Alice Bryant and her charge into the gardens, and Georges soon had Green bowling for him and Ellie running to fetch the ball. Alice stood watching, and Phoebe went to stand next to her.

Alice Bryant's arrival last year as Georges' new governess had made Phoebe's life more pleasant. Unlike the previous woman, Alice was only a few years older than Phoebe. Although her light brown hair was always pulled tightly into a chignon, her ready smile, and the twinkle often in her eyes, removed any hint of severity. Phoebe had joined her on some of her outings with Georges, enjoying trips to the parks as well as excursions to museums. Alice was also someone she could talk to easily, the governess' background as the daughter of a landed farmer being close to Phoebe's own.

"I've heard you had some trouble in France?" Alice said, keeping her voice low.

Phoebe sighed. Ellie's presence in place of the comtesse's former maid must have made it plain that the journey had not been straightforward. She gave Alice the same pared down story she had told her uncle at breakfast. She wished she could say more, but most of it was not her story to tell.

"Phoebe, come and play!" Georges called.

Alice gave her an apologetic glance at this interruption, but Phoebe shook her head and smiled. "I'll supervise if you'd like some time to yourself," she offered.

"Thank you." Alice returned Phoebe's smile and went back into the house.

Green bowled well, ensuring that Georges had to make some effort to hit the balls. Phoebe and Ellie dutifully attempted to field Georges' hits, Phoebe tossing the ball into the air in glee when she caught Georges out.

Phoebe, running for the ball again, slowed to a halt as she noticed a man in labourer's clothing approaching them. He was not one of the regular gardeners. Green, too, must have felt uneasy, for he pushed Georges behind him. She let out a breath of relief when the man merely asked if one of the women was called Deane. She nodded, and the man thrust a note into her hand, then turned and walked off.

The note was sealed with a blob of wax, but with no impression in it. "I think we'd better go back in," Phoebe said. "Now, Georges, please," she added, as Georges opened his mouth to complain. "If your mother hears that rough men have been in the square she may not let you play out here again."

That was enough to make Georges comply, and they made their way indoors. Unfortunately the comtesse was descending the stairs as they crossed the hall. She compressed her lips in disapproval but, for once, did not say anything.

Phoebe went to her room to read the note. It was from Brevare, as she'd suspected. The scrawled text told her to meet him in Hyde Park at four o'clock, bringing the message. It gave detailed directions, and finished with the statement that he would call in person at Berkeley Square to collect it if she did not meet him as instructed.

Phoebe's heart sank. Brevare must not come to the house—there would be too many explanations required, and her task would be secret no longer. The plan had been for her to contact the Earl of Marstone first—the real earl, not the make-believe one she and Alex suspected that Brevare would take her to see. Brevare had organised the meeting much sooner than she'd expected.

If only Alex were here, she could talk over the situation with him. That was a nonsensical idea, though. If he were not still risking his life in France, none of this would be happening.

She was on her own, and she must do the best she could.

The clock on the mantelpiece showed it was just after one o'clock. It would take less than half an hour to walk to the park, so she had time for something to eat first. She had just started using her last empty sketchbook, so if anyone asked her where she was going, she could truthfully say she needed to go out to buy drawing materials.

CHAPTER 20

*P*hoebe climbed the area steps with Ellie behind her, hoping her aunt wasn't looking onto the street as they hurried away. She was wearing her oldest pelisse and bonnet. And, after thinking about what Brevare might do when she refused to hand over a message, she had put only a few items in her pocket.

"Where be we goin', miss?" Ellie asked. "I'd love to see the sights while I be 'ere."

"Nothing very exciting today, I'm afraid, Ellie." She hoped that was true. "But we'll see what we can do another day." Phoebe stopped at the corner of the square, out of sight of the house. "I'm going to buy some sketching paper, and I have another errand to do as well. If anyone asks, we went to lots of different shops until I found the paper I wanted. Do you understand?"

Ellie nodded. "This baint about a young man, miss?" she asked warily.

"No."

"Best say no more, then, miss."

"You don't seem surprised?"

"Mr Trasker said he thought you needed a maid who could keep 'er mouth shut."

"Is that all he said?"

"Yes, miss. I'd rather not know more. But should you be 'avin' Owen Jones along as well?"

"Owen? He didn't go back to Ashmouth?"

"No, miss. I'm to send a message to the Crown if 'e's wanted. It's only a few streets away."

Phoebe suddenly felt a lot less nervous about the coming encounter. Owen wasn't Alex, but his presence would be reassuring nonetheless. She scribbled a short note on a page torn from her sketchbook and Ellie took it to an urchin lurking nearby.

Once Owen joined them, Phoebe felt safer. He and Ellie were obviously trusted by Trasker—they might be able to get a good look at whoever Brevare had summoned her to meet, in case this was the only chance. If her idea worked, though, she should be able to meet the man again with some of Lord Marstone's men nearby to observe.

She told Owen and Ellie her plan as she walked between them towards Hyde Park, explaining that the man she was seeing thought she was a servant. They were all brisk walkers, soon making up the time they'd spent waiting for Owen. It was refreshing not to have to dawdle along at the slow stroll adopted by the comtesse and Hélène when they visited the park.

Stopping outside the park gates, Phoebe peered around the gate posts, but Brevare was not in sight. She would just have to follow his directions and hope he had not picked too secluded a spot.

On Phoebe's nod, Owen and Ellie set off arm in arm, walking slowly and giving a good impression of lovers enjoying their half-day off together. Watching them, Phoebe clenched her hands together, hoping she didn't look as nervous as she felt. A rueful smile accompanied the realisation that it didn't matter—a servant entrusted with delivering an important paper might well look ill at ease.

Phoebe set off as Owen and Ellie turned into the path leading towards the Serpentine, passing them just before they reached the copse described in Brevare's letter. Brevare was there, holding the reins of a pair of matched greys harnessed to a plain landau with the top down. An older man sat in the vehicle, his coat encrusted with lace and his wig heavily powdered. Brevare's anxious expression turned to one of relief as he saw her approaching. The other man did not get down from the landau, forcing Phoebe to peer up at him.

"This is the woman with the message, my lord," Brevare said.

"You are Miss Deane?" the man asked.

"Yes, my lord." Phoebe bobbed a curtsey. "You are the Earl of Marstone?"

"I am. Thank you for bringing the message, although it would have been more convenient if you had given it to Brevare here, as he asked."

"I was given specific instructions, my lord," Phoebe said, dropping her eyes.

"Well, girl, let's have it then," he said impatiently.

Phoebe looked up at him. "No, my lord. Mr Westbrook told me to give it to you at the Foreign Office. If you tell me when you'll be there, and where I must go, I will give it to you then."

Brevare cursed under his breath. The man in the landau shook his head slightly, his brows drawing together. Phoebe noted his expression with interest—he appeared confused, rather than angry or annoyed.

"Don't be ridiculous," Brevare said. "He cannot possibly have meant you had to actually *be* in the Foreign Office. He was only telling you where you would have to find... his lordship. You do not need to go there now that I am helping you."

"I'm only doing what I was told," Phoebe said, trying for the stubborn determination of a not terribly bright servant. "He said I was to take it to the Foreign Office. He never said anything about handing it over in a park!"

Brevare swore again, more loudly this time. He let go of the horses and moved towards her. "Give me your pocket."

Phoebe fumbled beneath her skirts to undo the strings, and handed it over. He emptied its contents onto the grass, her small sketchbook falling next to a comb and a few coins. Brevare flicked the pages of the sketchbook, finding nothing. Muttering a curse, he put a hand inside the pocket and drew out a handkerchief.

Phoebe wished she'd blown her nose on it before they set out.

"Where is it?" he demanded.

"I have it safe, sir," Phoebe said, opening her eyes wide in what she hoped was a gaze conveying bovine incomprehension.

She kept her face as expressionless as she could, watching a frown gathering on Brevare's brow. At the edge of her vision, Owen and Ellie strolled past. Phoebe struggled to keep her eyes on Brevare's face as his gaze appeared to look through her. Although he was standing uncomfortably close, he made no move to touch her. Was he trying to work out what to do?

"Very well," Brevare finally said through tight lips, holding her pocket out. "I will send you a note to tell you when his lordship can see you. Make sure you bring the message with you next time."

Phoebe curtseyed as Brevare swung himself up into the landau and flicked the reins. She picked up her pocket, watching the landau until it was out of sight behind some trees.

"All right, miss?" Ellie's voice came from behind her, and she turned.

"Yes. Yes, thank you Ellie." Phoebe went to sit on a nearby bench. She made a rapid sketch of the man in the landau while she could still remember his face, Owen and Ellie peering over her shoulder.

"Did you manage to see him?" she asked, as she added the finishing touches.

"Not very well, miss, 'e was too far away. But that's a right good likeness, far as I can tell."

"Thank you."

She could try to see Lord Marstone directly, but Alex had thought it would be easier to keep her visit secret if she asked Lady Carterton to help. She could call on the way home.

"I need to buy something to explain where I've been this morning," she said. "Owen, can you go and buy me another sketchbook? Take this one, so you get something similar." She tore out the picture of the man in the landau and handed him the rest, together with a few coins. "I have another call to make on the way back, but I should be safe with Ellie now."

"Right, miss."

⁓

Alex lay on the lumpy bed, hands behind his head, trying to ignore the screaming argument from the room below. The grimy windows blocked most of the light provided by the feeble February sun. A foul stench from the yard behind the tenements permeated the whole building.

His lips twisted as he looked at the damp stains on the ceiling. This was a far cry from what most people imagined of Paris—the former city of fashion, favoured destination for the aristocracy. Damn Brevare, he thought, not for the first time. If it wasn't for him, he'd have travelled back on the *Lily*, standing on deck with Phoebe, strands of her hair whipping in the wind. She should be safely on English soil by now, all being well.

He half wished he hadn't thrown that novel into a field in Normandy; it would have given him something to do with his time while he waited for Henri to return. Whoever thought the life of a spy was exciting had not endured the long stretches of tedium and discomfort that were always involved. He hadn't really minded the boredom when he began making these expeditions to France, but now the periods of inaction seemed to be getting longer. And lonelier.

Alex sat up and swung his feet to the floor at the sound of foot-steps approaching. A muttered *"C'est moi"* accompanied a tap on the door, and he relaxed as Henri slipped in.

"Any luck?" One of Alex's old contacts, an apothecary, had found the address of the Brevare townhouse in the Marais district. Henri had gone to find out if it was still occupied.

"Some. My contact didn't know anything about it, but he has sent someone to investigate."

That was fair enough—Henri's acquaintances in Paris were past investors in the smuggling operation, not spies. He and Henri could watch the house themselves, of course, but it was quicker if someone local could ask around in the area—someone who would not arouse suspicion.

"He will report this evening, in Le Chat Gris. I gave him your description. I'm going for some food now—want anything?"

Alex shook his head, and Henri left. Another vision of red hair and smiling eyes flashed into his mind, and he tried to dismiss it. Phoebe probably knew little more about Paris than he did, although he could at least have talked things over with her. He suppressed the thought that talking things over could be the least of the benefits of Phoebe's presence. She was a lady, or as near to it as made no difference, and ladies did not deal in espionage or reside in filthy garrets like this one. Nor did they consort with men like him.

He was safer alone, and he should keep it that way.

The alley leading to the inn stank of rubbish, rotting food, and worse things that Alex did not care to imagine. Thankfully the darkness hid most of the details from sight. The steady drizzle did not improve his mood, nor the cold wind funnelling between the tall buildings. The interior of Le Chat Gris was warm, but smelled little better. Slipping inside, he pushed a coin across the scarred and sticky wood of the bar, then took his ale to an empty seat in one corner. He sprawled back in his chair and tipped his hat forward over his eyes, cradling the tankard in his hand as he prepared to wait. The last thing he wanted at the moment was to be drawn into conversation.

"Leon?" The man addressing him was unshaven, his clothing worn, blending in well with the rest of the clientele. He held a tankard of ale in one hand.

"*Oui.*" Alex gestured, as if the man had just asked if he could take the seat beside him.

The man sat down. "House is empty apart from one old man and his wife. Caretakers."

"How long?" Alex asked.

"Months, perhaps longer. The family—the *ci-devants*—have not been seen there for four or five months, at least."

"Does anyone know where they are?"

"There's a château half a day away—they could be there. It's a few leagues north of Beauvais."

That was all the man had, but it was enough. Phoebe had found out only that the château was somewhere north of Paris—now he knew where to look.

Alex slid the agreed payment onto the table and the man pocketed it, drained his tankard, and left without a backward glance. To Alex, it seemed rather obvious they'd had an assignation, but no-one else was taking any interest in his corner of the room. He contemplated leaving too, but this place made a change from their dismal rented room. He waved at the bartender, and the man brought another ale.

"I've got a nice, quiet room," a husky voice said.

Lifting his eyes from his drink, Alex took in a red skirt, remarkably clean considering the clientele in here. Above that was a generous bosom, then a face with scarlet lips and a knowing gaze.

"You look like a man who needs a bit of pleasant company," the woman said, raising one shaped eyebrow and curving her lips into a smile.

Alex pushed his hat back and inspected her more closely. She had the kind of figure and blonde prettiness that he'd always found attractive, and she was young enough to not yet be showing the ravages of her way of life.

His gaze slid sideways, taking in the tavern's other occupants. "This can't be your usual location."

"My last customer brought me here." She took a step closer.

At any other time, that would have been the signal for Alex to allow her to sit on his knee and wind her arms around his neck.

He didn't move, still holding the tankard in front of his chest. She inched forward, then made a moue of disappointment and moved on.

Alex watched as she propositioned an older man sitting a few tables away, wondering at his own actions. A month ago, he would probably have done what she wanted—enjoyed a night with her in exchange for a few coins, and parted in the morning with no regrets, no ties, no involvement.

He sat there until he'd finished his ale, then left. Outside he filled his lungs with the chill air then stepped out briskly—safer to be in their lodgings than wandering the streets, and safer alone.

No involvement, no ties, had been his life for years. It still was—but it was much harder when there was someone he would like very much to be involved with.

Very much indeed.

CHAPTER 21

The next morning Phoebe awoke early, and had the dining room to herself as she ate breakfast. She had to go to Brook Street this morning—Lady Carterton had not been at home to visitors yesterday, but the maid she'd talked to suggested she try after breakfast this morning. However it was not yet time for that, so she whiled away an hour or two in the library.

The shelves lining the walls overflowed with books, both the volumes that had been bought with the house and the ones brought over from the château at Calvac. The slightly worn carpet and leather armchairs were comfortable rather than fashionable. This was Phoebe's favourite room in the house—she had spent many a happy hour here poring over atlases and accounts of voyages and explorations. It was also a room that the comtesse rarely visited.

The book she'd been reading before her aunt took them to France was a weighty tome, bound in leather, and too big for Phoebe to comfortably read on her lap. Setting it on the central table, she drew up a chair, found her page, and was soon lost in detailed descriptions of South Sea islands and native rituals. So absorbed was she that she didn't hear her uncle enter until he spoke behind her.

"Phoebe, what are you doing here?"

Phoebe looked up. Why was he surprised to find her here? She often used this room.

"I'm sorry, sir. I'll leave if you—"

"No, no." He waved a hand at her book. "I only came in to get some papers. But why aren't you out visiting with your aunt? She and Hélène have gone to meet Lady Brotherton."

"I'm quite happy reading here, sir. As long as you don't mind, that is?"

"Of course not," the comte said. "You know you can use the library whenever you please. But you should really be out meeting other people. Better to make some acquaintances before you start going to balls, *n'est-ce pas?*"

Lady Brotherton? That malicious gossip?

Phoebe was glad her aunt had not found her—the last thing she wanted was to have to sit politely while Lady Brotherton and her daughters made snide remarks about her appearance and prospects.

"You do not seem to be looking forward to the season," he said.

Phoebe realised she hadn't hidden her feelings well enough—or her uncle was more perceptive, and perhaps more sympathetic, than she had thought.

"Your aunt said something yesterday about not wanting to take you visiting because of your hoydenish behaviour," he added with a smile.

"I had been playing cricket with Georges in the square, with a couple of the servants," Phoebe explained, relieved he didn't seem to agree with his wife

"Well, it might not be the most proper behaviour for a young lady, but Georges enjoys it. He does seem happier now you are home."

"I'm sure he's pleased to see his mama again," she said, hoping she didn't sound as insincere as she felt. Her aunt's attention to her son was haphazard. "In truth, sir, I am not looking forward to going into society," she went on, unconsciously smoothing the gown she was wearing. It was one of her better ones, in a pale primrose colour, but the fit was still loose on her, and the ruffle lengthening the skirts did not quite match the style of the rest of the gown. It would be good to meet some new people but, dressed as she was, she was likely to end up becoming a wallflower—a boring as well as embarrassing experience.

She saw the comte's gaze drop to her hand. "You would feel more confident in better gowns, would you not?" he asked.

"I spend all my pin money on drawing materials, sir."

His brows drew together.

"I'm sorry, sir, if I sound ungrateful," she said hastily, relieved when he shook his head with a smile. "I am truly thankful you gave me a home when my parents died."

Glancing at the clock, she saw it was time to set out to see Lady Carterton again. "If you will excuse me, I have an errand to run."

The comte nodded absently, and Phoebe went upstairs for her pelisse.

The house on Brook Street was of a similar size to her uncle's house. As when they'd enquired yesterday, Phoebe and Ellie descended the area steps to knock at the servants' entrance. The same scullery maid opened the door, glancing with surprise at Phoebe's gown before taking the folded note Phoebe held out.

"This is a message for Lady Carterton," Phoebe said. "I'm to wait for a reply. May we sit inside, please?" She stepped forward as she spoke, as if there was no doubt she would be let in.

The maid shrugged and stood aside to let them pass, and showed them to a couple of chairs in a corner of the passage where they could wait.

The two women sat, breathing in the smell of baking bread, watching the bustle as footmen carried trays containing the remains of breakfast and handed them over to the scullery maids.

"Her ladyship will see you now, miss," a footman said, coming to stand before them. "Follow me, if you please."

Signalling for Ellie to stay where she was, Phoebe followed the footman up the narrow service stairs to the ground floor, then through a baize-covered door into the family's part of the house. He showed her into a light and airy parlour overlooking the street.

Lady Carterton was sitting at an escritoire near the window, and turned to face Phoebe as she was shown in, setting her pen in its holder. She was an attractive woman, with blue eyes and dark curling hair dressed on top of her head. Her round gown was plain in style, but well cut. From her unlined skin, Phoebe guessed she was in her late twenties. Alex hadn't explained his relationship to her and Phoebe had assumed she would be much older.

"Miss Deane," she said, holding up Phoebe's note. "You say Westbrook sent you." Her expression was wary, but at least not hostile.

"Yes, my lady. Thank you for seeing me." Phoebe curtseyed.

"Is he well?"

"He was when I last saw him." He was still, she hoped.

"When, and where, was that?"

Phoebe hesitated, not sure how much she should say. "A few days ago, when we returned from France. He… he helped me and my relatives to escape."

Lady Carterton's expression softened. "Won't you sit down?" She stood, and moved to a pair of chairs near the fire. "Where is he now?"

"I do not know." That was true—she didn't know *exactly* where he was.

"You say you were in France—who were you with?"

"My aunt, the Comtesse de Calvac, and her daughter. I live with the Comte and his family."

Lady Carterton finally smiled. "How can I help you, Miss Deane?"

"I need to see the Earl of Marstone. But it would be best if no-one knows I have done so."

Lady Carterton's eyebrows rose.

"Mr Westbrook said you could help me," Phoebe went on. "Do you know the earl?"

The eyebrows rose higher. "You could say so. He's my brother."

That explained why Alex thought Lady Carterton could help her, but not why she *should*. Phoebe felt a sudden desire to ask just how well Alex knew Lady Carterton, and why her ladyship should help her only because Alex had asked.

"Miss Deane?"

Telling herself sternly that it was none of her business, she forced her attention back to Lady Carterton.

"Is this urgent?" Lady Carterton asked.

"I think so, my lady. I cannot say whether the earl would agree."

Lady Carterton tapped her lip thoughtfully, then rose to ring the bell. She moved back to her escritoire and drew out a sheet of writing paper.

"My lady?" the butler said as he entered the room.

"I need someone to go to Grosvenor Square, Hobson. Please send Barrington in for instructions. And have some fresh tea sent up, too."

The butler bowed himself out, and a few minutes later a footman entered. He took the note that Lady Carterton held out.

"This is for the earl," she instructed. "If he is at home, you are to wait for a reply. If he is not at home, leave the note but make sure Langton knows it is urgent. And ask when the earl is expected back. Is that clear?"

"Yes, my lady."

Phoebe eyed the papers on Lady Carterton's desk. "I'm sorry to have interrupted you, my lady."

Lady Carterton smiled. "Oh, don't worry about that. I'm only making notes about yesterday's Paupers' Fund meeting. I can easily finish it later. Now, Phoebe... you don't mind me calling you Phoebe?"

Phoebe shook her head.

"Tell me how you met Alex."

By the time the footman returned from Grosvenor Square, Lady Carterton had extracted most of Phoebe's life history and, to her surprise, had instructed Phoebe to call her Bella when they were in private. Phoebe had also been given exhaustive details of her three children and the Cartertons' estate in Sussex. She felt as if she had been put through a mangle.

Lady Carterton opened the note. "Good, he can see us now." She

177

turned back to Phoebe. "I think your maid should stay here, but lend you her cloak. You shall be my maid. Do you think that will answer?"

"Yes, thank you." It should work, Phoebe thought, as long as she covered her hair.

"Are your staff...?" Phoebe started to ask as they set off, then thought better of it. Questioning the quality of Lady Carterton's servants was not polite.

"Very discreet," Lady Carterton said, eyes twinkling. "Unless they are asked not to be."

They were soon in Grosvenor Square, and Phoebe gazed upwards at the Greek columns flanking the door as Lady Carterton plied the knocker.

Wryly amused to be acting the part of a servant again, Phoebe kept a pace behind as she followed Lady Carterton into the black and white tiled hallway. After a brief word with the butler, they were shown into the library.

"I will inform his lordship of your presence, my lady." The butler left.

Phoebe gazed with mixed awe and envy at the large room: its floor to ceiling shelving held far more books than her uncle's library. Then her attention fixed on a family portrait hanging above the mantelpiece. Examining it, she saw a man of thirty or so, dressed in the fashion of some years past. He stood with his hand on the shoulder of a slightly younger woman, her dark brown hair dressed high, but unpowdered. She held a babe in her arms, and two small girls played at their feet. The scenery behind them showed wooded slopes and a glimpse of sea.

"My brother and his family," Lady Carterton said. "I think it was painted about ten years ago—they've had another son since then and another daughter. I'm the youngest of my generation—he's more than ten years older than I am. Lady Marstone doesn't care much for London, or Marstone Park. That was painted at—"

Lady Carterton broke off as they heard the door open behind them, and Phoebe turned to see the real version of the man in the portrait. The Earl of Marstone was a little above medium height, his face stern, with a straight nose and square jaw, and the same blue eyes as Lady Carterton. Something about him felt vaguely familiar—but then she had just been inspecting his portrait.

"What is it, Bella?" the earl asked, impatience clear in his tone. "Your note didn't say. I really am busy, you know!"

"This is Miss Phoebe Deane," said his sister calmly. "She has something to tell you."

As the earl turned his gaze on Phoebe, she reminded herself that Alex had told her to come here, and she was not wasting this man's time. She raised her chin as he assessed her appearance from head to toe, his face now unnervingly expressionless. His gaze seemed to pierce through her, but she refused to drop her eyes.

"I don't think my presence is required," Lady Carterton said. "I'll call back in… half an hour or so?" Phoebe nodded as Lady Carterton glanced her way. "Now, if you'll lend me a maid she can wear Phoebe's cloak."

"Very mysterious, Bella," said the earl repressively.

"Oh, don't deny me my bit of fun, Will," Lady Carterton laughed.

Phoebe asked Lady Carterton to buy a copy of *The Pirate's Cavern* while she was away, keeping her voice too low for the earl to hear, then handed over Ellie's cloak. Lady Carterton laughed again as she departed, and Phoebe was left to face the earl.

CHAPTER 22

"*D*o sit, Miss Deane." Lord Marstone waved her to a chair in front of his desk, seating himself in the leather-covered chair behind it. She saw his gaze slide sideways—was he looking at the clock already?

Phoebe took a deep breath, annoyance beginning to overcome her nervousness. If she could face a tavern full of drunken Frenchmen, she should not be quailing before an English lord, no matter how forbidding he appeared.

"Well, Miss Deane?" He sounded impatient still.

"I have a message for you from Mr Westbrook," Phoebe said, getting straight to the point. It appeared social niceties were not required.

"Is he well?"

"Yes, my lord." At least, he had been the last time she saw him.

"Good. How do you come to be his messenger?"

"He helped me and some members of my family escape from France."

The earl's brows rose. "Details, if you please."

Phoebe told her story. As well as the outline she had given to Lady Carterton, she briefly described the discussions with Alex about

Brevare's actions and possible motives. Her irritation abated as he listened intently, interrupting only to clarify a point now and then.

"So," he said when she had finished. "Westbrook has gone on some wild goose chase in search of the Vicomte de Brevare's mother and sister, who may or may not be residing in Paris or at a château at some unknown location north of there, leaving you to bring back both the real information and a decoy note."

It didn't sound very sensible, put like that.

"Yes, my lord. The decoy part of the plan required he not return with us. And he thought that if Brevare was being blackmailed, having his family safe might allow him to tell—"

"Yes, I understood that. What would have happened if Brevare had tried to take the message, or messages, from you by force?" His expression had not changed, but Phoebe thought she detected disapproval in his tone.

"He would only have obtained the decoy."

"How so?"

"The real one is... er... sewn into my stays." Phoebe hoped she was not blushing.

The earl surprised her by giving a short laugh. "Should I leave you alone for a few minutes, then?" he asked.

"A maid and a pair of scissors would also be useful, if you please."

Still chuckling, the earl left the room. Shortly afterwards a maid appeared and led Phoebe upstairs to an unoccupied bedroom. Phoebe took in her surroundings with interest while the maid helped her unlace her gown and stays. The room was not large, having space enough for only a single bed, a chair, and a chest, but it was richly furnished with heavy brocade curtains at the windows and around the bed. The size and location of the house already spoke of wealth; the furnishings reinforced the impression.

Once down to her chemise, Phoebe quickly unpicked seams to retrieve the letter, then dressed again—she could mend her stays when she got home. When she returned to the library, she was surprised to see a younger man with the earl.

"Phineas Kellet," the earl said. "My private secretary."

Kellet bowed in greeting. Phoebe held out the message to the earl, who took it and glanced briefly at the numbers before handing it on to Kellet.

"My thanks, Miss Deane."

Kellet sat down at one end of the desk. As she seated herself, Phoebe saw him take a book from a drawer; it looked like the French road guide Alex had been using. She suppressed a smile as he started turning pages and counting words. How long would it take him to work out that he could not decode it using that book?

"Now, Miss Deane, you still have the decoy message as well?"

"Yes, my lord." She handed it over. "Although that part of the plan has not quite worked as we... as Mr Westbrook planned."

"That was probably to be expected," he said, his tone dry. "But do go on."

"I hoped to be able to speak to you before Brevare contacted me, so you could set people to watch him. However, he summoned me to Hyde Park yesterday, and told me to hand the message over to a man he introduced as the Earl of Marstone."

Phoebe was pleased to see she had surprised him.

"You refused?"

"Yes—I told him I had been instructed to hand it to you at the Foreign Office."

"He accepted that?" The earl's eyebrows were once again rising.

"He had no choice; I didn't have it with me."

"Hmm. You took a risk. Now, can you describe the man with Brevare?"

Phoebe pulled the sketch from her pocket, passing it to the earl. He studied the drawing carefully before handing it to his secretary.

"Do you recognise the face, Kellet? I'm afraid I do not."

The secretary shook his head.

"He may have been an actor," Phoebe said. "He didn't know what to say when I refused to give him the message. Brevare was in charge of the meeting, not this man."

The earl steepled his hands, resting his chin on them. "What does the decoy message say?"

"I think it is just a set of undecipherable numbers, but written to look as if it is in the correct code."

The earl placed it on the desk next to the real message Kellet was scratching his head over. He put his finger on the decoy.

"This is in Westbrook's hand," he stated. "The real one is not. Who coded the real information?" Phoebe detected a note of censure in his voice.

"I did."

The earl's mouth became a tight line. "Why did he entrust you with this... sensitive information?"

"You would have to ask him." She wished he were here to be asked.

"How many *other* people know about this?"

Anger rose—Alex had made the best judgement he could in the circumstances, and this man was criticising him. Had *he* ever been in a situation where he risked arrest and probable execution?

Sitting forward in her chair, she began to tick people off on her fingers, her voice sharp. "The captain of the *Lily* knows I am bringing a message that Brevare wants, but he does not know what the message is. The same applies to one of his crew, who was sent to London with me. As Mr Trasker appears to play a large part in the smuggling oper-ations, I assume anyone he sends is trustworthy."

She paused there, keeping her gaze on his face, awaiting some acknowledgement of what she'd said. His eyes narrowed, but then he nodded, so she continued.

"Mr Trasker also sent a maid, who knows Brevare wants some-thing that I am... I was carrying, but she doesn't know where I am now."

"And you involved my sister in this?"

Was he implying that Lady Carterton was indiscreet, or worried about her safety? His expression gave nothing away.

"She only knows that I wanted to talk to you. I also asked my uncle, the Comte de Calvac, where you live and what your reputation is, to ensure I gave the paper to the correct person, but he doesn't know *why* I wanted to know. My aunt and cousin know nothing about a message. The only person who knows I am here, in this house, is Lady Carterton."

Phoebe drew a deep breath, closing her eyes. That was the first time she'd given an earl a set-down.

Her eyes flew open again as she heard a quiet chuckle.

"My apologies, Miss Deane. I will have to rely on Westbrook's judgement in this matter, but so far his trust appears to be justified."

Phoebe's ire began to dissipate, a warm feeling spreading through her as she recalled that Alex *had* trusted her, from the beginning.

"Kellet, could you first confirm that the decoy is, in fact, nonsense?"

The secretary put aside the real message, turning his attention to the decoy. The earl regarded Phoebe for a few moments, until she felt self-conscious enough to speak.

"My lord?"

"My apologies again, Miss Deane. I was considering possibilities." He leaned towards her, resting his forearms on the desk. "As I see it, you have a choice now. You have completed the main task you were entrusted with very competently, for which you have my thanks. At this point you could end the matter. If Brevare contacts you again you need only say your uncle has passed the message to me so you no longer have it."

"And my other option?" Phoebe asked. She should be glad to be done with the business, instead of feeling disappointed at missing its conclusion.

"Your other choice is to continue with the decoy plan, or a variation of it." The earl sat back in his chair, his head tilted slightly to one side. "I have recently discovered that there *is* someone passing information from... from within my department, as you suspected. Possibly the same person responsible for sending Brevare."

Phoebe nodded. "Should you...? I mean, this must be secret..."

"Are you going to tell anyone else?"

She stiffened. "No, of course not!"

"Then there is no reason why I should not tell you, is there? Do you think you could bring yourself to continue?"

"I... yes, I will help if I can." Surely it could not be any riskier than that tavern in Granville.

"No hesitation, Miss Deane? You are playing with fire—this could be dangerous."

"I... well, it is a novel experience to be useful." She wasn't accustomed to being *asked* to do something, either, rather than being told.

"Very well," the earl said. "Now, you have told Brevare you will only hand over the document when you visit me at the Foreign Office. It occurs to me that he is in fact more likely to arrange for the message to be stolen from you—probably when you are on the way to a meeting he has arranged."

"Yes, my lord. That is why I wanted to see you today."

"What did you think I could do?"

"You could have me followed, then the watchers could follow the people who take the message. I would be sure not to try too hard to prevent them taking anything," she added, her stomach fluttering at the idea.

The earl was once again watching her over his steepled hands. "How successful do you think this plan would be?"

"It could easily go wrong." She tried to imagine the scene—a crowded street full of bustle and movement. "It cannot be easy to follow people who rob others—they must be used to avoiding attention or eluding pursuit."

"I agree. Nevertheless it is worth a try—there is nothing lost, after all, if the watchers lose track of them."

Unless I an injured.

It was too late for second thoughts.

"We could perhaps add another string to our bow," the earl added. "Kellet?"

Kellet looked up from his deciphering attempts. "The decoy message *is* indecipherable, my lord, but so—"

"In a minute," the earl waved him quiet. "Kellet, do you think we could compose a message that may make our traitor do something to betray himself?"

The secretary scratched his head, his unfocussed gaze on the far wall. "It's possible," he said eventually. "It will take some consideration."

"Miss Deane. You are aware of the potential danger in this—are you sure you are willing to take part?"

Phoebe swallowed hard. She could change her mind now if she wanted to, and no-one would think any the worse of her. *She* would, though. Alex and people like him were risking their lives daily to help protect England; she should play her part too. It wasn't likely to be *very* dangerous, after all.

"Yes, but…"

"But…?" the earl prompted.

"May I know who will be watching? So I know who I need *not* worry about?"

"Certainly. Kellet, please ask Brownlee and Chatham to step in, then see if Lady Carterton has returned. Let her know we are nearly finished."

Phoebe toyed with the fabric of her gown. She hadn't explained Brevare's mistaken impression of her status.

"A problem, Miss Deane?"

"My lord, Brevare still thinks I am my aunt's servant. Might it give away what we… what you are trying to do when he finds out I am not? My cousin is having her come-out this spring, so we may meet socially."

The earl considered for a minute. "That might even work to our advantage," he said. "But let me think about it. Now, I will send you a replacement message early tomorrow. What is the best way of getting it to you?"

"Have someone take it to the servants' entrance, directed to Ellie Denton. I will warn her to expect it."

"And your… escorts?"

"I will tell Owen to stay close, but not too close."

The earl smiled. "Good, good." He indicated the two liveried footmen now standing just inside the library door. "Now, these men will be your watchers, wearing other clothing, naturally. Brownlee,

Chatham, take a good look at Miss Deane. I will give you further instructions later."

Phoebe stood and returned their scrutiny. Would she recognise them again? Chatham did have a slightly bent nose—broken at some time in the past, she guessed. Other than that their appearance was not remarkable, although their direct gazes conveyed an air of purpose, of determination, that reminded her of Alex. She was glad they were on her side.

The earl dismissed the two footmen as Lady Carterton came into the room. She handed Phoebe a package. "Is that the correct one?"

Unwrapping the paper, Phoebe thought the book was the same edition as the one now mouldering in a field in France.

"My lord?" Kellet tried to attract the earl's attention. "The real message—?"

"Mr Kellet might enjoy reading this," Phoebe interrupted, handing the book to the earl and exchanging a smile with Lady Carterton.

The earl read the title on the spine. *"The Pirate's Cavern—A Romance,"* he said, a smile growing as he skimmed the first page. "The information was obviously even more secure than I thought. Thank you, I think Kellet will find this book... informative. Here, Kellet, try using this for deciphering." He passed the book over. "Miss Deane, I apologise again for doubting you earlier."

Phoebe flushed with pleasure as the two women took their leave.

CHAPTER 23

*B*ack home again, Phoebe took off her pelisse in the hallway and handed it to the butler. She needed to sit quietly for a while and think over what had just been said at Marstone House. Her heart sank as the comtesse emerged from her uncle's study. Had she been waiting for Phoebe to return?

"I don't know where you've been all morning," the comtesse said. "Wherever it was, you should have asked first. Your uncle wishes to see you."

A cold knot settled in Phoebe's stomach. The comtesse must have given her husband more details of her version of events in France.

The comte followed his wife out of his study, shaking his head. "Lavinia, I'll see Hélène first. Phoebe, can you find Hélène and send her to me, please?"

"No, no, Edouard, I'll find her," the comtesse said quickly, turning to face him. "Phoebe's here, why don't you find out what—?"

"No, Lavinia." The comte took her arm and led her towards the stairs. "I think you should go upstairs for a rest. Phoebe can find Hélène."

Phoebe glanced from one to the other as her uncle looked around the hallway, the cold feeling beginning to dissipate. Whatever her aunt had said, it seemed her uncle was not going to take his wife's word without corroboration.

"Green, send Madame's maid up."

Her aunt's mouth turned down at the corners. "But Edouard—"

"Now, Lavinia!"

Phoebe had never heard him speak so sternly, nor seen her aunt look so shocked. The comte released his wife's arm and made a gesture upwards. She started up the staircase, turning after only a few steps, but the comte was already walking back towards Phoebe.

"Phoebe, I'd like to see you later. Please do not go out again. Now, can you send Hélène to me, please?"

"Yes, sir," Phoebe said, relieved at his polite tone.

"Try the back parlour, Miss Deane," the butler advised.

Phoebe found Hélène, as Cookson had said, in the back parlour on the first floor, and told her to go to her father. Hélène didn't meet her eyes as she put down her novel and left.

Phoebe shrugged, too tired to puzzle out her cousin's behaviour. She needed something to drink, so she rang the bell. The tea, when it came, revived her a little. Her uncle's conclusions may well depend on what Hélène said, she thought gloomily. If Hélène confirmed whatever tale her mother had told the comte...

Well, she would know soon enough. She resolutely turned her mind to what would happen when Brevare arranged the next rendezvous.

When Phoebe was summoned back down to the study half an hour later, she found that Hélène had gone. Her uncle sat behind his desk, looking tired and rather grim, with the fingers of one hand pressed against his temple.

"Sit down, Phoebe."

Phoebe settled into a chair facing him, her body tense. Her future could depend on what was said here.

"Yesterday, you told me something of your journey," the comte went on. "Now I want more details. No doubt it will be yet another different version of events," he added, almost under his breath.

"I will not lie to you, sir," Phoebe said. Either her aunt or cousin must have already lied to him, if their stories were different.

"I'm not accusing anyone of lying. Not yet," he said wearily. "Begin with why this man…" He looked at some scribbled notes on his desk. "Why this man Perrault thought you should all be arrested."

Phoebe described the scene in the inn, giving only enough detail of her aunt's actions and words to make clear how she had attracted Perrault's attention. It would not do to paint too black a picture of her aunt.

"That tallies more or less with what Hélène said," he commented, when she had finished.

Had the comtesse told a different story? That must be why she'd wanted to speak to Hélène before the comte saw her. Phoebe felt some of the tension leave her body as she realised that her uncle must have considered this possibility.

"Now, your aunt refers to Westbrook as a common, rough fellow."

"I don't think so, sir. I don't know much about him, but he speaks like a gentleman, and always behaved towards me in a gentleman-like manner." The few things she did know about him could not be passed on to her uncle.

The comte said nothing, seemingly waiting for her to go on.

"He… er… the part he was forced to play to prevent our arrest required that he treat our party with…" She wondered how to convey what Alex had done without making it seem worse than it was. "With less respect than Madame thinks is her due."

"A very diplomatic way of putting it," the comte said. "Now, the next night, there was an argument between Westbrook and Perrault. Tell me about that, in detail."

In detail? Would he believe what his wife had done?

"The truth, Phoebe," the comte said. "I know that at least one of the three of you is prevaricating. I want to hear what happened, no matter how uncomfortable it makes you feel." He kept his gaze on her, his mouth turning down at the corners. "Nor how uncomfortable you think it may make *me* feel."

Phoebe sighed, then briefly related what had happened up to the point when Hélène had said that a ransom would be paid for Phoebe as well. "Madame did not agree immediately, then Mr Westbrook had them taken out of the room." That did not reflect well on Alex, she realised. "It was important for Mr Westbrook to maintain the fiction that I was a servant, otherwise Perrault would have been more suspicious of *him*, too."

She raised her chin—all her aunt had needed to say was 'yes', and she had not. None of it was Alex's fault.

"What happened next?"

"Mr Westbrook fought Sarchet and won. He had pretended he... he wanted me himself as that was what Sarchet would understand. Afterwards..." She stopped and took a deep breath. "Afterwards, Madame and Hélène had been locked in their room. Perrault was watching and Mr Westbrook needed to continue to act the role he had assumed, so I stayed in the same room. I slept in the chair." She met her uncle's gaze squarely. "Madame assumed the worst."

"I see. And the following night?"

Phoebe hesitated again.

"Just tell me, Phoebe."

Describing her aunt's attempt to prostitute her brought back the hurt of betrayal, as painful now as it had been at the time. Her uncle's face grew steadily grimmer as she talked, one hand massaging his temple again. He looked more disappointed than angry.

"And then?"

"Mr Westbrook obtained a spare key to my room. I slept there, alone." Admitting to spending most of the evening with Alex in a private parlour was not wise. Uncomfortably aware that omitting a relevant point was almost as bad as a lie, she told herself that nothing had happened, after all—at least, not the kind of thing her aunt was implying.

The comte consulted his notes again. "You spent a lot of time with him during the day?"

"You think we were... improper... on the box of a coach? In *February?*"

"I did think that was rather unlikely," the comte allowed. "But your aunt also mentioned something about going off together while you were waiting for the boat to arrive?"

The tavern in Granville was not a place for respectable young ladies, but the details of that did not seem relevant to her aunt's accusations. "He needed my help to arrange for the boat. He also gave me a paper to deliver to the Earl of Marstone."

The comte raised his eyebrows. "What is the connection between this Westbrook and the Earl of Marstone?"

"I think Mr Westbrook works for him, sir." Should she admit to already having seen the earl?

"In what capacity? A steward? A business representative in France?"

Although that last guess was close to Alex's cover story, it would be best to say as little as possible. "I do not know the details, sir." She bit her lip. "If I did, I am not sure that I should tell anyone."

The comte gazed at her for almost a minute. Phoebe tried not to shift uncomfortably under his scrutiny; her uncle was as astute as the Earl of Marstone, and must be aware that she had omitted some details from her story.

"Very well. Go now; I need to think. Send Cookson in, if you would."

He nodded dismissal. Phoebe let out a breath of relief as she left the room.

They were summoned to the study again an hour later. Phoebe was surprised to see all her gowns draped over a couple of chairs brought in from the dining room. The comtesse and Hélène followed her in, their gazes sliding away from the meagre collection of garments.

"Sit down," the comte instructed.

"I hope you agree with me, my dear," the comtesse began, her tone sounding almost pleading to Phoebe's ears. "Under the circumstances it would be totally inappropriate to introduce Phoebe into society at the same time as Hélène. Her presence could severely reduce Hélène's chances of making a brilliant match. Now that you know the truth about what happened in France—"

"Pray let me speak, madame," her husband said, his tone cold. "I will come to that shortly, but there is another matter to address first."

The comtesse looked at the pile of gowns, one hand twisting the fabric of her skirts. Phoebe shivered at the comte's stern expression as he fixed his gaze on his wife.

"I increased the allowance I gave you quite considerably when Phoebe came to live with us," he stated. "This was to allow for gowns and all the other things that Phoebe would need. These bills—" The comte indicated a pile of papers on his desk. "—these bills indicate that you did, indeed, spend all of this increased allowance on gowns, shoes, bonnets and so on. But when I asked Phoebe's maid about her gowns, those appear to be all she owns."

Phoebe listened to this speech with widening eyes. The taunts about her clothing she had endured during social calls—they were ultimately her aunt's fault. Why had her aunt done such a thing? Greed?

Not just greed, she thought, remembering the comtesse's frequent statements that Phoebe should not come out with Hélène, as Phoebe's clothing would disgrace the family. More like deliberate spite.

Her uncle was still talking.

"...tell the maid where Phoebe's other gowns are kept? The maid says she has brought down all the ones kept in Phoebe's room."

Phoebe opened her mouth to speak, but the comte waved her to silence.

"Some are kept in Hélène's room," the comtesse said.

"Why? Because you gave Phoebe one of the smallest rooms in the house?"

The comtesse glanced away without responding.

"Please ask your maid to bring one of Phoebe's other gowns down." When the comtesse did not reply, he reached for the bell cord. "Well, madame?"

"The gold one is in my room, Mama," Hélène said, her voice strained.

"Just the one?" enquired the comte. "How many gowns do you have, Hélène?"

Hélène flushed. "I don't know exactly, Papa."

"Ten? Twenty? Thirty? Come now, you must have *some* idea!" Hélène hung her head. "A lot more than Phoebe, I assume?"

"Yes, Papa," Hélène whispered.

"And why should she not?" the comtesse snapped. "Hélène is *our* daughter, after all!"

"Phoebe is still family," the comte reminded her, his voice quiet. "Now, do I need to get someone to bring down the gowns you say are Phoebe's? Or will one of you tell me the truth?"

Another tense silence fell on the room. Phoebe's amusement at her aunt's discomfort was countered by thoughts of the effect it was likely to have on her temper later.

"Very well," the comte said, and rang the bell. When a footman entered he instructed him to send Phoebe's maid to them. Ellie appeared so quickly that Phoebe suspected she had been listening outside the door.

"You are…"

"Ellie Denton, milord," Ellie bobbed a curtsey.

"Good. Now, you will go with Miss Deane and help her to change into the… the gold gown of hers that is kept in Lady Hélène's room."

"Beg pardon, sir, but I don't know of any of Miss Deane's gowns what are kept elsewhere. I brung down all the ones she had when Mr Cookson told me to."

"She's new," said the comtesse. "She doesn't know. I told you that."

"Yes, you did. I am beginning to find this tedious, as well as disappointing," the comte said. "Can you assure me, madame, that if I send Phoebe to change into this gold gown Hélène mentioned, or any of the others you say she has, they will fit her as well as the gowns you and Hélène are wearing fit you?"

Phoebe awaited her aunt's reply with interest—did the comtesse really think her husband could not see through her lies?

The comtesse muttered something about a trainee seamstress. The comte waved dismissal to Ellie and the interested footman hovering in the doorway, and waited until the door had closed behind them.

"So if I send for..." He consulted the bills in front of him. "If I send for Mademoiselle Laurent, she will explain how she came to give only Phoebe's gowns to an incompetent trainee to make?"

The comtesse had the sense to keep silent this time.

"You have insulted my intelligence, madame, as well as the honour of this family. And your lack of honesty in this matter calls into question your candour about what happened in France." He stood up. "You will none of you leave the house again today. I will be dining at my club. I will speak to you all in the morning."

The comtesse, face flaming red, got up and stalked out of the room. Phoebe gave her time to get beyond the hall and then followed, going to ground in the back parlour to take stock.

She sat looking out over the small garden behind the house, a smile gradually spreading over her face. Her aunt had well and truly been hoist with her own petard. If she hadn't been so stupid and spiteful in France, it could have been some time before the comte discovered what she'd been doing with Phoebe's allowance.

But that was not responsible for the feeling of lightness within her now—that was due to her uncle. Although he was not her blood relation, he had far more care for her than her aunt. Affection, she wasn't sure about—he was a reserved man, unfailingly polite, and normally hid his feelings well. For him to have rebuked his wife in front of herself and Hélène, he must have been angry indeed.

Whatever the comte decided to do, Phoebe's situation was not likely to get any worse. Even if he believed his wife and banished Phoebe to the country somewhere, she would probably have more freedom than she did now.

CHAPTER 24

*P*hoebe awoke the next morning to the smell of chocolate. Ellie put the cup down beside the bed, and handed Phoebe a small packet.

"This come to me, miss, to be given to you. I ent told no-one about it."

"Thank you, Ellie."

Phoebe was relieved to see that her name was written in small, neat handwriting, quite unlike Brevare's scrawl.

"Be you wanting breakfast up here, miss?"

"Yes, please, Ellie. Coffee and toast will do." That would get Ellie out of the room.

The packet contained a sealed note—the new decoy message—and a folded paper from the Earl of Marstone. It stated that the house was being watched as planned, and instructed her to send someone to tell the watcher when she had heard from her contact. Her 'contact' must be Brevare.

Quickly dressing herself, she fastened a pocket beneath her gown and put the sealed note in it. The folded paper went in the fire. Her apprehension about the plan was overshadowed by worry about the coming interview with her uncle. Had he believed her story, or would her aunt prevent her being introduced into society? Either result could have its advantages, as long as the comte did not cast her off completely.

"Miss, I'm supposed to help you dress," Ellie protested as she returned with breakfast.

"I can manage perfectly well, Ellie. I've been doing it for years."

Ellie's mouth turned down. "But you won't need me, then, miss. Do you want me to go back to Devonshire?"

Phoebe laughed. "Of course not—if you don't tell Mrs Kidd I can dress myself, I won't either. It's more important to me that you don't gossip."

"Ooh, I like a good bit o' gossip, miss," said Ellie, with a grin. "But not about you, never that!" She shook her head emphatically as she spoke.

Cookson directed Phoebe to the dining room when she went downstairs. Her uncle was breakfasting there alone; her heart sank at the stern expression on his face.

He set down his cup and waved Phoebe into the place set next to his own. "Good morning, Phoebe."

"Good morning, sir." She took the indicated seat, her hands clenched in her lap.

"There is no need to be quite so apprehensive, Phoebe. I believe your version of events—but I hope you can understand why I am not pleased about what happened."

"Yes, sir. And thank you."

"I saw the Earl of Marstone yesterday," he went on. "I am aware, from my conversation with him, that there are some aspects of your story that you did not share—" He put up a hand as Phoebe opened her mouth to speak. "—that you did not share with me. However, he did vouch for Westbrook."

Phoebe bit her lip. Why had she not considered that her uncle might check with the earl?

"Phoebe." The comte leaned toward her, his gaze fixed on her eyes. "I want you to give me your assurance—your *word*—on something."

She nodded.

197

"Do the parts of your story you omitted have any bearing on my wife's concern for your... your virtue?"

"No, sir, they do not. I give you my word." Her nails bit into her palms as she awaited his reply. His gaze held her own for an uncomfortably long time before he looked away, one hand rubbing his temple.

"Very well. I believe you, but that is not likely to endear you to my wife. I will be making it clear that any gossip about your reputation will also reflect badly on Hélène. You and Hélène will *both* go into society this spring. If you are not invited to an event, she does not go either."

Phoebe glanced down at her gown.

"Don't worry about that," her uncle continued. "I am giving you the total of the allowance that should have been spent on you since you came to live with us. Four hundred pounds is a lot of money to spend at once, but it appears that the state of your wardrobe necessitates it."

"Sir, you can't spend all that on me!"

"Phoebe, I am sorry affairs have reached their current state. I have been too absent from family matters of late, but that is about to change." He patted her hand where it rested on the table. "I am not a demonstrative man, and although you and Joseph are not of my blood I do regard you both as family. And you have been good to Georges, from what Miss Bryant tells me." He gave a small smile. "I hope you will still find some time for Georges once you are involved in balls and assemblies."

"Yes, sir, I enjoy spending time with him."

"That's good. Anson will discuss arrangements for your allowance with you. Have bills sent directly to him. I am assuming I can trust you to not overspend?"

"Yes, sir. Sir, I don't know how I can thank you—"

"Family, Phoebe. Family." But he seemed pleased with her thanks as he waved dismissal.

Phoebe came down to earth again abruptly when she went back to her room. Ellie was waiting for her, holding another sealed note.

"This come for you miss. Dunno who come with it—it was left in the kitchen."

Phoebe took it and broke the seal.

Be at the west end of the canal in St James' Park at 8 a.m. tomorrow. I will take you to the FO.

Brevare was at least pretending to take her to the Foreign Office; she'd have to cross St James' Park to get there from Berkeley Square. She refolded the note.

"Can you take this to Owen? Without anyone else knowing?"

"Yes, miss."

"Tell him he's to tell the watchers."

Ellie nodded.

"I have to meet the vicomte tomorrow morning at eight o'clock in the park, but I will go with only Owen to escort me."

Ellie's eyes grew round.

"No-one else is to know, Ellie," Phoebe warned.

"No, miss." Ellie bobbed a curtsey and took the note.

Phoebe's plans for a quiet afternoon reading came to nothing, as the comtesse had arranged for them all to visit Mademoiselle Laurent's salon. Now there was money to be spent on Phoebe's clothing, the comtesse seemed to want to get on with it as quickly as possible.

This was Phoebe's first visit to a fashionable mantua-maker. She gazed around the room, taking in the imitation gilded Greek columns against the walls with floor to ceiling mirrors between them, the ornately upholstered sofas, and the marble-topped tables holding pattern books and cloth samples. No wonder mantua-makers' charges were so high, if their customers expected such surroundings. To Phoebe's eye, it was overdone and tasteless.

Mademoiselle Laurent was a tall, angular Frenchwoman with sharp features, dressed in a deep purple gown of simple cut. "Madame de Calvac, it is always a pleasure to see you and your beautiful daughter," she said, gesturing for the comtesse and Hélène to seat themselves. She looked at Phoebe, her gaze travelling quickly from her hair to her gown, then acknowledged her with a brief nod before turning her attention back to the comtesse.

"What can I do for you today, Madame? I have some lovely new fabrics that would look wonderful on Lady Hélène."

Phoebe's lips tightened as Mademoiselle Laurent snapped her fingers to a waiting assistant. This visit was supposed to be for her own gowns. Did she really want to spend all her money with this woman?

The assistant returned with a bolt of white lustring, its sheen picked out by tiny silver threads running through it.

"This will suit for a ball gown, *n'est-ce pas?*" Mademoiselle Laurent said.

"Oh, Mama, that is lovely," Hélène gasped. "When will my first ball be?"

"I had planned on introducing you at Lady Brotherton's musicale in a few days' time, Hélène, but your first proper ball will be next week, at Lady Sandrich's."

Lady Brotherton's two daughters would also be making their come-outs this year. Phoebe had put up with their scorn and rudeness during too many social calls to wish to attend the musicale, but she would have little choice in the matter.

"That reminds me, Hélène," the comtesse went on. "We must get a dancing master to make sure you remember your steps properly. You must look elegant when you dance."

"This style, Mama?" Hélène's attention was focused on a fashion plate. Phoebe sighed, recalling the tedious conversations during recent days on the road.

"Ah, no, Lady Hélène," Mademoiselle Laurent said. "Something simpler for your first season. We need only to frame your beauty, not enhance it. How could we enhance perfection?"

Hélène stood up and allowed Mademoiselle Laurent to drape the fabric across her, turning her head to admire her reflection from all angles in the mirrors. Phoebe listened as Mademoiselle Laurent continued to praise Hélène's complexion, her figure, and her hair, wondering how Hélène put up with the woman's obsequious manner. Glancing from the comtesse to Hélène, she realised they believed every word, the comtesse looking as pleased as if praise for her daughter were praise for herself.

Phoebe waited with mounting impatience until the discussion of Hélène's gown finally ended and her aunt remembered that Phoebe, too, needed new gowns.

"Oh, my niece will need a gown for the ball, too. Whatever you can manage in the same time. Stand up, Phoebe."

Phoebe stood, forcing her body to stay relaxed as Mademoiselle Laurent walked around her, raking her eyes up and down and taking in every detail of the ill-fitting primrose gown.

"It is a shame about the hair and the figure," she said to the comtesse, talking as if Phoebe were not present. "Perhaps we can powder this red to something less... glaring." She walked around Phoebe once more. "Marie will take her to be measured, and we will choose the style. A challenge, eh?"

The assistant came to stand by Phoebe, but Phoebe ignored her. "Mademoiselle Laurent, what—?"

"So this design, in the white," the comtesse said, handing Mademoiselle Laurent a fashion plate. "We will come back for fittings in two days. Phoebe, why are you still standing there? Go and get measured!"

"One moment," Phoebe said, determined to be heard. "What material and design am I having?"

Mademoiselle Laurent waved the fashion plate in front of her. "This one will improve you greatly. And this white—the colour is good for younger ladies, n'est-ce pas?" She pointed to a fabric sample.

The design was unexceptional, although Phoebe wondered if the lack of lace and trimming was due to considerations of cost rather than what might suit her. The fabric, too, was adequate, but it did not have the sheen of the material chosen for Hélène, and she always thought her skin blended too much into her dress when she wore white.

"Come, Phoebe, we haven't got all day." The comtesse's voice was sharp now.

"How much will this gown cost?" Phoebe asked the mantua-maker. "This will not be charged to my aunt's account."

Mademoiselle Laurent raised her brows. "You have your own—?"

"Phoebe, don't fuss," the comtesse interrupted. "It is vulgar to discuss money in that way."

Phoebe took in the anxious expression on her aunt's face. Was there something more there than impatience to be gone?

"I do not like the colour or the style," she said firmly. "I also need day dresses and walking dresses. If you do not have time to consult *me* about my gowns, and choose styles and colours to suit me, I will take my custom elsewhere. I will not be buying any gowns from you at all."

She swept towards the door, not caring whether her aunt and Hélène followed her.

"Oh, but you misunderstand!" Mademoiselle Laurent said hastily, hurrying after her. "Of course we can show you other designs. Please, Miss… er… Miss…"

"Surely the loss of one ball gown cannot be so important?" Phoebe shook off the hand that the woman had put on her arm. "Particularly as you haven't even bothered to ask my name!"

"I'm sure Mademoiselle Laurent can show you some nicer fabric, Phoebe," the comtesse said, not meeting her eyes. "It will all be paid for, Mademoiselle, I assure you."

Understanding dawned on Phoebe.

"Just how many gowns *were* you going to charge to my account?" she asked. Hélène looked confused, but the comtesse's expression told Phoebe that she had guessed correctly.

"For goodness' sake, Phoebe, stop arguing! Mademoiselle Laurent knows what she is doing. You can choose your other things later. You need to order it now so that it is ready in time."

Phoebe recalled her uncle's comment that morning. If she did not go to the ball, Hélène would not either. Looking her aunt in the eye, she shrugged. "If I do not have a ball gown, I won't go to the ball. I haven't enjoyed the few social events you have taken me to so far, so I won't mind missing it."

The comtesse glared at her, but Phoebe stood her ground.

"Oh, very well," the comtesse said at last. "Mademoiselle Laurent, make up the one for Hélène. I'll bring my niece back when I've talked some sense into her."

Once in the carriage, Phoebe had to listen to a diatribe about her selfishness, poor manners, and unfortunate appearance all the way back to Berkeley Square. Hélène glanced at Phoebe with something approaching sympathy in her face. Phoebe smiled inwardly. It appeared that sometimes her aunt could be too much even for her own daughter. Phoebe let it all wash over her, feeling instead a quiet satisfaction as she kept her gaze on the passing scenes beyond the carriage. Thanks to her uncle's sense of fairness, she had won this minor battle.

The comtesse continued her monologue as they entered the house, but the comte happened to be crossing the hall as they entered and, catching his eye, the comtesse gradually subsided.

Phoebe suppressed a smile, and went in search of Anson. She would ask to see her aunt's accounts from Mademoiselle Laurent, and use those to help her to work out the garments she needed. Then she'd send a note to Lady Carterton. She needed an ally.

CHAPTER 25

*P*hoebe crept up the area steps at half past seven the next morning, wearing the same old dress she'd had on when she met Brevare in Hyde Park two days before, topped with Ellie's cloak. This time, she carried a small basket with the decoy message hidden beneath an old, folded petticoat. The weather was cloudy, the damp feel to the air promising rain to come.

Owen awaited her at the far corner of the square.

"Watchers?" Phoebe asked in a low voice, and he indicated someone sweeping outside a house half-way along the street, and another man loitering on a corner further up. Phoebe pressed a hand to her stomach; she was feeling slightly nauseous. Agreeing to this plan had seemed easy two days ago when she was talking to the earl, but the reality felt rather different. If only this were over, and she were on her way to the meeting Lady Carterton had arranged in reply to her note.

"You don't have to do this, miss," Owen said.

Phoebe took a deep breath. "I'll do it." She'd wanted adventure, hadn't she? "You will stay close, Owen, in case they try to do more than take my basket?" she added, pleased to find that her voice sounded normal.

"Of course, miss."

She checked again that the earl's message was in her basket—although it couldn't possibly have gone anywhere since the last time she checked it five minutes ago. She didn't want to make things too difficult if she *was* going to be robbed, and hoped they'd take the basket and look through it first before attempting to steal a pocket.

"All right, Owen?"

"Lead on, miss. I'll not be far behind."

The streets were busy with delivery men and their carts, and noisy with street sellers calling out their wares. Phoebe resisted the need to look behind her—a servant on her way to the Foreign Office would not be expecting anything to happen to her on these streets.

The shortest route to her destination was down the edge of Green Park. It was peaceful amongst the trees and grass, with grazing cows and deer nearby, but the relative lack of people also meant that Owen could not stay so close without appearing suspicious. She found she was eyeing each tree she passed, in case someone sprang from behind it, and told herself not to be foolish. No-one could know the route she planned. Her stomach knotted as she crossed the Mall into St James's Park.

The canal was just ahead, most of the people present walking purposefully as if on their way to work. Turning her gaze from side to side, she tried to spot Brevare, but a sudden push in the small of her back made her stumble. Her arm was wrenched backwards and she tripped, legs tangling in her skirts.

She found herself on her knees, her left palm stinging from contact with the ground. Her basket was gone.

Taking deep breaths, she tried to steady the trembling in her arms, then pushed herself to her feet. Her legs wobbled as she looked around. Whoever had done it was now far enough away to be indistinguishable from anyone else in the park.

"You all right, love?" A young woman with a basket of daffodils put a hand out to steady her.

Phoebe swallowed, nodding mutely. She had expected the basket to be taken, but not the sudden assault.

"It ain't right, robbin' someone who ain't got much anyway," the woman went on. "I 'ope you didn't 'ave a lot in that?"

Phoebe shook her head. "No, not much." She looked down at her gown, muddy now where her knees had hit the ground. Brushing at the mess only made it worse. She finally noticed Owen standing behind the flower girl.

"Oh, Mr Jones!" she said, not needing to feign the relief in her voice. "I'm glad to see you."

"Here, let me take you home," Owen said, taking his cue. He held out his arm and Phoebe took it gratefully.

"Thank you for helping me," she said to the flower girl. The girl smiled and turned away, trying to sell some daffodils to a plump woman carrying a basket of bread.

"Did you see who did it?" she asked when they had left the park.

"Yes, but I don't know if I could describe him. He was just ordinary. Saw that Frenchie standing watching, though. Are you all right, miss?"

"Yes, I'll be fine." Already the exercise was working off the wobbles in her legs. "Did the watchers see as well?"

"I think so."

"Good. That's over then."

She wondered what Alex would have said about it, remembering his resistance when she'd volunteered to go into Granville. She smiled at the thought, enjoying the feeling of relief that it was over. At the same time, she felt slightly flat—was this her last connection with Alex and his business?

Phoebe re-entered the house through the kitchens and took the servants' stairs up to her bedroom. She couldn't explain to her aunt why she was dressed as she was, nor the mud on her gown and hands. Once she was safely in her room, she rang for Ellie.

"Oh, miss, what 'appened to you? You shouldn't of—"

"I'm perfectly all right Ellie, really," Phoebe said. Apart from bruised knees and a sore wrist. Luckily she hadn't grazed her hand, so there would be no outward signs of her fall once she had donned a clean gown. "Help me change, please. After breakfast I'm going to visit a mantua-maker with Lady Carterton."

Ellie's eyes and mouth grew round. "New gowns, miss?"

"Yes," Phoebe smiled. "And Lady Carterton told me to bring you along as well."

"Me, miss?" Ellie's voice was a squeak. "What for?"

"I'm not sure yet," Phoebe admitted; Lady Carterton's note had not explained.

Phoebe and Ellie arrived at Miss Fletcher's premises in Henrietta Street in good time. On explaining that she was to meet Lady Carterton there, Phoebe and Ellie were shown in and asked to sit. The reception room was similar to Mademoiselle Laurent's in some ways —both had large mirrors on the walls, and tables with pattern books and fabric swatches. Unlike Mademoiselle Laurent's, however, the walls were papered with a pale pattern in cream and yellow, the tables were polished wood, and the sofas looked comfortable. The whole effect was of good taste, without being ostentatious—a promising sign, Phoebe thought. Lady Carterton's dress had exuded a similar air of quality, but Phoebe wondered uneasily how expensive that kind of apparent simplicity would be.

Her speculations were cut short as Lady Carterton entered.

"It's good of you to help me, my lady," Phoebe said, standing up. "Especially at such short notice."

"Nonsense, Phoebe, it will be great fun! I'm glad I'd already made an appointment today. It's an age since I had an excuse to buy dozens of gowns—it will be years before I can buy ball gowns for my daughters."

"Hardly dozens, my lady." Phoebe protested.

"We'll see." Lady Carterton sat down and helped herself to some biscuits from the tray. She glanced at Ellie. "This is your personal maid?"

"Yes, this is Ellie. She's not been a maid long."

"Hmm. If you have the time, we'll go back to Brook Street and my maid can show her some better ways of doing your hair."

"I be right keen to learn, my lady," Ellie said.

A slim woman in her thirties entered the room. "Lady Carterton," she said, dropping a curtsey.

"Good morning, Miss Fletcher," Lady Carterton said. "A slight change of plan, today, if you will. This is Miss Deane, a friend of mine. She needs a complete wardrobe. *Everything!*"

"What about your gowns, my lady?"

"They can wait. Now, Phoebe, do you know what engagements your aunt has planned?"

"I think only social calls this week, and a musicale one evening. Then Lady Sandrich's ball next week."

"So, a day dress and an evening gown urgently, and a ball gown for next week," Miss Fletcher said, noting the requirements down in a little book.

"That sounds a sensible start to me," Lady Carterton said. "What do you think, Phoebe?"

Phoebe pulled a piece of paper out of her pocket, glancing down the list of items and prices she had estimated. Would it be thought vulgar to discuss money now?

Ready for embarrassment, she handed the list to Miss Fletcher. "I made a list of what I think I will need. I cannot spend more than the total here."

She was relieved to see Lady Carterton smiling with approval at her approach. Miss Fletcher took the list, studying it carefully.

"This is for the whole season? Do you already have some gowns?"

Phoebe shook her head. "This is my best one," she explained, indicating her primrose gown.

Miss Fletcher tutted and turned back to the list. "You will have to wear the same gown many times. Most ladies don't. Is that acceptable?"

"Yes—this is far more than I was expecting to have," she said. "I don't want to give a false impression of wealth."

Miss Fletcher seemed to accept that, tucking the list into the back of her notebook and waving a hand to the empty space in the middle of the room. "Please stand there, Miss Deane. We will begin by considering colours and styles."

Phoebe obediently took up the indicated position. Miss Fletcher walked around her, scrutinising her from top to bottom. "Your hair will be a challenge," she said.

Phoebe's heart sank; the words were so close to those of Mademoiselle Laurent. Was she really so hard to dress?

"I don't think she means what you think she means," Lady Carterton said.

Phoebe looked at her, realising that her dismay must have shown on her face.

"You wish for honesty?" Miss Fletcher asked.

Phoebe wasn't sure she did, but whatever Miss Fletcher said couldn't be worse than the things she'd already been told—by her aunt, her cousin, the Brotherton girls, not to mention Mademoiselle Laurent. She clenched her jaw and nodded.

"Your figure is good—" Miss Fletcher smiled in response to Phoebe's expression. "Oh yes, a large chest is not everything! It is easier to design for those with slimmer figures. Your complexion is good, and your hair is a remarkable colour."

Phoebe put her chin up, determined not to let the woman see her confidence draining away again.

"That was not a criticism, Miss Deane." Miss Fletcher's smile broadened. "Please sit down and we will talk." She beckoned to her assistant and murmured a few words to her, taking a seat as the woman disappeared through the door at the back.

"Now, the reason I mention your hair is because of the fashion for younger ladies to wear only pale colours. Some will suit you, but many will not."

Phoebe thought of the peach dress, and had to agree.

"Your hair will be magnificent—"

Magnificent? Really?

"—when you are dressed in the proper colours—deep greens, for example. We can find some paler colours, but I do not think white will suit."

Phoebe began to feel that she might actually enjoy this visit.

"How old are you, Phoebe?" Lady Carterton asked.

"Twenty." Too old, her aunt had said. Repeatedly.

"I think that if you do not mind people knowing that you are older than most young ladies in their first season, you will get away with wearing darker colours," Lady Carterton said. "You should aim to be an Original, rather than an Incomparable—but you will need confidence to carry it off. Can you do it?"

I can. Her pulse accelerated as she recalled the determination she'd needed to enter that horrible tavern in search of Dan Trasker. Nothing the *ton* could do or say would be as bad as that.

"Yes. I can do it."

The assistant reappeared, followed by two other girls, all carrying bolts of cloth of different colours.

"Amy, who is the next appointment?" Miss Fletcher asked.

"Lady Jesson."

"Ah, she won't mind cancelling if I explain," Lady Carterton said. "In fact, if you let me have paper and pen, I'll get my footman to take a note round now."

Amy asked Phoebe to follow her. In the dressing room, she started by removing Phoebe's stays and giving her a new set. "These are a better shape for you," she explained. "They are not the best—we need to get a set made to your measurements—but they are better than the ones you had on." She stood back and regarded Phoebe's re-laced figure. "If you want to look more... full in the chest, we can get another set made for evening wear that will push you up a bit."

Not used to having her personal attributes discussed so dispassionately, Phoebe felt a blush rising up her neck. She shook her head.

"Good, only one set of measurements to do, then." Amy glanced at Phoebe's face. "You don't need... enhancing, you know," she added reassuringly. "It is just that some women think men only look at their bosoms."

"Some men do," Phoebe pointed out as Amy started to measure her.

"But they aren't the ones you want to attract." Amy worked efficiently down Phoebe's body, then handed her a robe. "If you would put this on, miss? You will get your dress back later."

Back in the main room, the table was covered in fashion plates, and a few gowns hung from a rail in one corner.

"Miss Fletcher thinks these designs will suit," Lady Carterton said. "See what you think."

Phoebe liked the styles the women had chosen. The ruffles and frills on them were subtle, enhancing the lines of the gowns. They were quite unlike the styles favoured by the comtesse and Hélène.

Half an hour later her head was spinning, but she had a list in her hand of gowns to be made up, two more appointments for fittings, and a shopping list for chemises, shoes, gloves, and bonnets. Miss Fletcher had carefully chosen colours that suited her, but also specified colours for shoes and bonnets that could be worn with several different gowns.

"Can I really get all this without overspending?" Phoebe asked, looking at the list doubtfully.

"Yes," Miss Fletcher said with confidence. "You do not need expensive fabrics to look good, just the right colours. And several of these I already have partly made up for someone who cannot pay, so they will be cheaper. And... when anyone compliments you on your gowns or appearance, you will mention me," she instructed.

Phoebe's surprise must have been evident in her face, as Lady Carterton smiled encouragingly.

"Anyone can dress a woman of normal colouring," Miss Fletcher went on. "Other women with unusual colouring will want to know about a mantua-maker who can choose the best colours for them."

"You might not believe her now," Lady Carterton said. "Wait until you come for your first fitting—you'll see."

Amy came into the room with the primrose gown. Phoebe caught the smell of lavender as the assistant guided it down over her head and settled it in place. She ran her hands down the bodice as Amy laced it up—it now fit snugly over her new stays.

"Look in the mirror, Phoebe," Lady Carterton said, a laugh in her voice.

She couldn't help but gasp. They must have worked fast. The ruffle that had lengthened the skirt was gone, replaced with a strip of pale green fabric, a darker green ribbon hiding the join. A matching ribbon marked the waist and a narrower version of the same thing outlined the neckline and the ends of the sleeves. The changes were small, but the dress now looked as if it had been made for *her*. It was not as elegant as Lady Carterton's gown, but it was vastly better than it had been. The only thing that could now be criticised... she put a hand to her hair, still curling uncontrollably after the damp air outside.

"We'll sort that out back at my house," Lady Carterton said.

"I've already taken too much of your time," Phoebe said, doubtfully. "I'm very grateful—"

Lady Carterton waved a hand. "Nonsense—I enjoyed it. I need some tea, then I have calls to make. You, however, will be left with Hopkins, my dresser, for further instruction."

When they arrived back in the Brook Street house, Hopkins took Ellie off somewhere and Phoebe had a welcome cup of tea while Lady Carterton talked about her own future engagements.

Lady Carterton—" Phoebe interrupted.

"Call me Bella, please."

Phoebe smiled. "Bella. I don't know if my aunt has invitations for all those balls and other things."

"Oh, don't worry about that. I'll make sure you get invitations."

Would she fit in if she *did* go? She smoothed the skirts of the refashioned gown; perhaps she would, with a decent wardrobe. "I can't thank you enough for your help."

Bella shrugged. "You are the friend of... of a friend. I also know something of your aunt and, to be blunt, it is a pleasure to help someone stand up to her." She smiled, her eyes dancing. "No doubt she will be surprised when she sees you in your new gowns."

Surprised, but not pleased, Phoebe suspected.

"Where did we meet? I mean, my aunt will ask, and I don't want to tell her about going to see Lord Marstone."

Bella thought. "I bumped into you in a bookshop?"

"And I dropped all my books on the floor?"

"So I took you to the Pot and Pine Apple for tea and cakes."

They exchanged conspiratorial smiles, and Phoebe felt she had found a true friend.

CHAPTER 26

"Did you get anything useful?" Alex asked, as Henri closed the door and sat on his bed. Their trip to the Château Brevare had determined only that the vicomtesse and her daughter had not been seen there for months. Gossip in the local tavern had indicated that Brevare's mother was not popular amongst ex-servants at the château—'fit for the guillotine' had been mentioned—but the daughter appeared to have been well liked. No-one knew for sure, but the general impression was that they had gone to Paris. Now Alex had to undertake the far riskier task of getting help to locate the women in the city. Henri had approached some of his contacts again on their return to the capital.

"The apothecary won't speak to me again," Henri said. "He's frightened. What do we do now?"

"I have one or two people we could try. Let me think about it. Go and get something to eat."

Henri grunted agreement and left again, while Alex turned his attention to finding someone who could help them locate the two women. If, as he suspected, there was a traitor within the Foreign Office or in Marstone's clandestine organisation, then the contacts in

Paris could already be compromised. They would have to check carefully before approaching any of them.

Phoebe should have seen Marstone by now and told her story. Would Marstone believe her? And agree with their conclusions? He suppressed a smile as he imagined the interview—Marstone had a way of doubting reports that goaded his subordinates into outright rudeness at times, until they got used to his way. Her eyes would be flashing fire.

Concentrate!

He spread a street map out on the threadbare counterpane. The names were ones he had memorised a year ago. Even without the possible traitor, the troubles in Paris could well have rendered them useless, or even dangerous to contact. He would have to go very carefully indeed.

Should he have gone back to England with the rest of the party? It would have been far simpler, but finding Brevare's family could help them identify the traitor. He rubbed his arm, where the almost-healed cut itched. It was a week since he'd seen Phoebe—it might be time to have the stitches removed.

Alex glanced doubtfully around the shabby hall as he waited for someone to answer his knock. There was no rubbish on the stairs, but they clearly hadn't been swept for some time and his hand came away grubby when he touched the banister.

"*Oui?*"

The woman standing in the open doorway had a pinched appearance, but wore a clean apron and cap.

Alex removed his hat. "May I see the doctor?"

She inspected him from head to foot, then stood to one side to allow him to enter. The door opened into a tiny inner hallway, and the woman pointed to another door, gesturing him to go in.

The consulting room was more reassuring. It was furnished with a narrow bed, covered with a clean sheet, an upright wooden chair, and a desk with a leather-covered chair behind it. A locked glass-fronted cupboard on the wall held an array of instruments whose purpose Alex didn't want to even guess.

A tall man entered, waving Alex to the wooden chair as he took his own seat behind the desk. He was old, with thinning grey hair and a lined face.

"What can I do for you, *citoyen?*"

Alex took off his coat and rolled up his shirt sleeve, showing the doctor the cut on his arm. "Is it time to take the stitches out?" he asked.

"You can pay?"

Feeling in the pocket of his coat, Alex took out some coins and deposited them on the desk.

The doctor grunted and beckoned him closer. Taking off his spectacles, he peered at the cut, touching it gently with a finger.

"It is looking healthy," the doctor said. He unlocked the cupboard behind him, taking out a bowl, scissors, and a pair of tweezers. Moving his chair closer, he busied himself snipping and pulling, while Alex clenched his teeth against the sharp tug of the strands of silk moving through his healing flesh. He couldn't help wishing it were Phoebe doing it.

"Spread some salve on it," the doctor said, returning his instruments to the cupboard. "There's an apothecary's shop on the next street—ask there."

Alex stood, and put his coat back on. The doctor escorted him to the door and closed it firmly behind him without a further word. Mildly amused, Alex shook his head—he had been told no names were required, and that the doctor was quick, but he hadn't expected the description to be so accurate.

He soon found the apothecary's shop, but hesitated before going in, his mind on Phoebe again. This time the memory was not of her smile or her hair, but of the way she'd washed her hands with brandy, and dipped the needle and thread in it.

The doctor had used instruments from his cupboard, and returned them without cleaning them. Admittedly, pulling stitches out wasn't the same as putting them in—the doctor hadn't poked needles through his flesh—but it made him wonder about the efficacy of whatever salve the apothecary might sell him.

Making up his mind, he walked on, looking for somewhere he could buy brandy and honey.

～

"It looks really nice, miss," Ellie said, as the Carterton carriage picked its way through the busy streets. Phoebe's hand rose involuntarily to pat her hair. She smiled, remembering her initial dismay as Hopkins snipped away, but Bella's dresser knew what she was doing. Her hair still curled tightly, but was now tamed with a bandeau, and Ellie had been taught how to put it up into a chignon.

"Lovely, you'll be, when your new gowns come." Ellie clutched a box on her lap, containing pots of face powder and coloured paste. They had both been shown how to apply the cosmetics, too—only enough to make Phoebe's skin subtly warmer, and her lips a little more red, all without the appearance of wearing any cosmetics at all.

Newly confident, Phoebe entered the house in Berkeley Square by the front door. The footman cleared his throat.

"Madame la comtesse asked to be informed when you arrived back, miss," he said. "And said you were to go straight to her."

Going to her aunt in her improved gown would cause a confrontation, she was sure. The comtesse would not be pleased that Phoebe had found her own mantua-maker.

"Thank you, Green. You may tell her I will come back down directly."

Once in her room, Ellie helped her to change into one of her older gowns. She should keep the primrose one clean, she told herself, in case she needed to wear it before her new ones were ready.

She paused before entering the parlour, her muscles tense at the prospect of another argument. Straightening her back, she walked in. "You wanted to see me, madame?"

"Yes, I did," her aunt said sharply, her lips pinched. Her gaze fixed on Phoebe's hair, her expression souring even further. "I also instructed Cookson and Green to send you to me *the moment* you came in."

"Green did pass on the message, madame, but it would not be polite to come to you in all the dust of the street. I only took five minutes to tidy myself."

"Quite right, Phoebe," said a voice behind them. Both women swung round to see the comte in the doorway. "I've asked for tea; I thought we might have it together," he added.

Phoebe saw her aunt's mouth open, then close again; she was clearly surprised at this unusual suggestion. It was only a momentary respite, however.

"Where have you been? You have been out all day, without asking my permission. Your reputation—"

"I had Ellie with me, madame," Phoebe replied. "There was no impropriety."

"You were supposed to come to Mademoiselle Laurent's with me to order your gowns."

"I didn't know you were expecting me to accompany you." Phoebe injected a hint of surprise into her voice.

"How else are you to be ready for the musicale in two days' time?"

"Oh, I can wear one of the gowns I have," Phoebe asserted, her imp of mischief taking over. "After all, until a couple of days ago you thought they would be sufficient for my season."

Phoebe wondered if she would have dared to taunt the comtesse if her uncle had not been present—although she'd said nothing but the truth. A quick glance at the comte showed a slight curve to his lips that could be amusement.

"I'm sure people will realise I am only Hélène's cousin—"

"If you are going to musicales and balls you must be dressed properly—it will reflect badly on all of us if you are not." The comtesse's voice sharpened. "You must come to Mademoiselle Laurent first thing tomorrow—I may be able to persuade her to make up something in time for the musicale."

"I will not be ordering any gowns from Mademoiselle Laurent." Phoebe said.

The comte coughed. "I'm sure we can get something ready in time," he said. "But I think it would be best if—"

He broke off at a tap on the door, followed by a maid entering with a tray of tea. The conversation stopped while Phoebe poured the tea and handed around the cups.

"It will be best if there is a plan for each week," the comte resumed when the servants had left. "Phoebe, you will need to know which engagements your aunt has accepted so that you are prepared. However, you do not need to be with Hélène's or your aunt at all times, as long as you are accompanied by your maid. If you have engagements of your own, you will inform your aunt of them, as a matter of courtesy."

That sounded sensible. Phoebe nodded agreement as the comte looked at her.

"Lavinia?"

The comtesse's brows lowered and her mouth pursed. "Oh, very well," she said at last. "Phoebe, I will expect you to come with me to Mademoiselle Laurent in the morning, and we will be making social calls in the afternoon."

"Mademoiselle Laurent does not produce gowns that suit me, madame, and overcharges." Waiting for an argument, Phoebe smiled inwardly as her aunt wisely did not answer. "And I am already engaged tomorrow afternoon, so I cannot accompany you."

"Engaged? How can you have an engagement—?"

"I am accompanying Miss Bryant and Georges on an educational visit," Phoebe said.

"Nonsense! Miss Bryant is quite capable of looking after Georges herself. Else why do we pay her?"

"I think Georges enjoys Phoebe's company, my dear," the comte injected.

"He's only a child; he will do perfectly well with Miss Bryant."

"Have you agreed to accompany Georges?" the comte asked Phoebe.

"Yes, sir."

"Well, one should not break promises unless there is a good

reason," the comte said. He waited, but it became clear the comtesse was not going to argue this point.

He turned back to Phoebe. "Where are you going?"

"We will be studying natural history, sir," said Phoebe, doubting that her aunt would approve of the planned visit.

"Very well," the comte said. "Now, I think I would like to attend this musicale with you all later this week. I'm sure, my dear, you can get the invitation extended to me?"

The comtesse gazed at him.

"Lavinia?"

"You...? Well, yes, I suppose—"

"That's settled, then." He put down his cup and plate and stood up. Phoebe rose as well.

"May I go, madame?" she asked. The comtesse waved a hand and Phoebe followed the comte out into the hall.

"Phoebe." The comte halted before his study door and she turned back to him.

"Where *are* you going tomorrow afternoon?" He looked her in the eye. "The truth, if you please."

"There is a performance at Astley's Amphitheatre, sir. My maid, Ellie, also wishes to see it."

"Natural history?"

"Yes," Phoebe nodded. "Horses, and the varied nature of the human condition."

The comte smiled. "Most educational! But take Green with you as well. I should imagine the company can sometimes be rather rough."

"Thank you, sir," Phoebe said.

"Your hair... it suits you well." He smiled. "You have obtained some gowns?"

"I will not disgrace you, sir," she promised.

Back in her room, Phoebe sat at her dressing table, admiring her new haircut in the mirror—her previous barely controlled mass of curls was now a proper style, framing her face. Her new gowns would give her more confidence when accompanying her aunt. What a difference a few days made.

The most important change, though, was that she now had allies here in London. A feeling of lightness spread through her as she recalled how Bella had willingly given up her time to help, and how her uncle had over-ruled his wife. She hadn't expected that much support from him.

Another thought crept in. Alex knew Bella well enough to be on first-name terms. She felt ashamed of her earlier suspicions that there might be more than friendship between them—Bella was not that kind of person, nor did she believe it of Alex. And perhaps Bella's friendship would make it more likely that she'd see Alex when he got back to England.

There was a knock on the door, and Ellie entered, holding a sealed note. "This was left in the kitchen, miss. No-one seen who left it."

Phoebe took the note, her mood sobering. It looked like Brevare's scrawl.

"Thank you, Ellie. I won't need you again until this evening."

When Ellie had gone, she broke the seal, letting out a breath of relief as she read it.

The thief was caught and the note has been safely delivered to the Earl of Marstone.

If she hadn't already known the thief was working for Brevare, she might have wondered how he knew the note had been stolen. He wasn't a very good spy, as she and Alex had agreed.

She put the note on the fire. Brevare must have written to discourage her from making further efforts to contact Lord Marstone.

That was over then. Her part in it, at least, not Alex's. Her brow creased as she considered the implications of whatever false information the earl had written. Brevare, or whoever was controlling him, thought the stolen message had come from Alex. But Alex would be able to repeat any information he had gathered when he returned. Would they try to... to kill Alex to stop him seeing Marstone?

Alex wouldn't know about the earl's deception; he thought the message she would be passing on was undecipherable.

Could he be warned? Would Lord Marstone think to do so?

CHAPTER 27

wo mornings later, Phoebe looked up from her buttered eggs as Alice Bryant followed Georges into the dining room.

The comte put down his newspaper. "Good morning Georges, Miss Bryant."

"Good morning, sir," Georges said. Phoebe suppressed a smile at his unusually serious tone. "Thank you for allowing me to have breakfast with you."

He took a seat at the table. Alice brought him a glass of milk and a plate of toast, then dipped a curtsey and turned towards the door.

"Do join us, Miss Bryant," the comte said.

"Thank you, monsieur, but I have already eaten."

"Some coffee, then?"

Phoebe caught the eye of the footman waiting by the sideboard. Green brought over a cup and poured coffee as Alice took a place at the table next to Phoebe.

"I thought I would hear about your... ah... natural history expedition yesterday," the comte added.

"Monsieur knows where we went," Phoebe said quietly, seeing a flush rise on Alice's cheeks.

"Well, Georges, did you enjoy it?"

Phoebe lifted her cup to hide her smile as Georges' face lit up, and he hurriedly swallowed his mouthful of toast. The comte had been out of the house yesterday when they returned, so had missed his normal afternoon visit to his son in the nursery.

She let the descriptions of the horses and their tricks wash over her—she'd been present herself, and Georges had talked about it all the way back in the carriage. Instead, she watched her uncle's face as he listened to his son. Until recently, the comte had spent most of his time at home ensconced in his study, leaving the management of the household to his wife. Her aunt's lies about the happenings in France seemed to have made him pay more attention to his family—including her, for which she was very grateful.

"And how did you enjoy it, Phoebe?" her uncle asked, when Georges had finally wound down.

"Very much, sir. I am glad you suggested taking Green; some of the company *was* a little rough."

Alice told Georges to eat his breakfast, and he obediently took another bite of toast.

"Have you other excursions planned?" the comte asked. Georges finished his mouthful, but Alice reminded him not to interrupt when other people were holding a conversation.

"There is the menagerie at the Tower, sir," Phoebe said.

"More nature studies." The comte's mouth turned up at one end. "Have you been to the British Museum?"

"Several times, sir. I enjoy sketching some of the exhibits." Phoebe glanced sideways; Georges' eyes were switching from her to his father as they talked, a piece of toast unheeded in one hand. "Georges enjoys looking at old weapons."

The comte's eyebrows rose, and Phoebe thought she detected a twitch of his lips. "I wonder what music we will be forced… we will hear tonight," he said, keeping his gaze on her. "Let us hope there are not too many sopranos. They screech rather than sing in far too many cases. What is your opinion, Phoebe?"

"Sir, I think Georges will burst!"

"Eh? Oh, did you have something else to say, Georges?" the comte asked. "It was good of you not to interrupt us."

Phoebe turned away to hide her amusement, and got up to help herself to more breakfast. Her uncle continued to surprise her—she hadn't thought him the type to tease his son like that.

"Sir, when can I have some riding lessons? I haven't been riding since we left my pony behind at Calvac. Please, sir."

"Riding only, Georges, not tricks!"

"Yes, sir."

"Very well, I will arrange it. Now finish your breakfast." The comte turned to Phoebe. "Do you wish to ride, too, Phoebe?" he asked. "I assume Hélène does not?"

"I don't think she likes it, sir. I used to enjoy riding around the estate at Calvac." She hesitated, not wanting to sound ungrateful for the offer. "I understand it is fashionable to be seen driving or riding in the park, but I admit to not seeing the attraction in such a limited space. I do thank you for the offer, though."

To her relief, her uncle smiled. "If you are sure?"

"I think I will have enough of riding by listening to Georges' accounts of his lessons."

"Indeed." His glance at his son held affection as well as amusement, and Phoebe marvelled again at how her dismal expectations for the season were turning out to be wrong.

Some of Phoebe's new dresses were delivered that afternoon. She spent a happy hour trying them on, discussing with Ellie which ribbons, gloves, and shoes should be paired with each. Between them, they chose Phoebe's outfit for the musicale: a moss-green gown with simple gold trim, to be worn with a gold ribbon threaded through her hair.

As she regarded herself in the mirror, Phoebe felt as if she were standing taller, and she was actually looking forward to meeting people now she was confident in her appearance.

Would Alex like it?

She turned from the mirror abruptly, picking up her cloak and draping it around her shoulders. She should not assume he'd want to see her again when he returned from France. For now, she should concentrate on making new acquaintances at the musicale.

"What are you hiding beneath that cloak, miss?" her aunt said sharply as Phoebe reached the bottom of the stairs.

Phoebe sighed, opening her cloak. Her aunt would have to see her gown at some point.

"Very nice," the comte said. To Phoebe's surprise, Hélène also gave an approving nod.

The comtesse sniffed. "It is not at all appropriate," she said. "Young girls should be wearing white, or the palest pastels—"

"Do you think she is unsuitably dressed for this musicale?" the comte asked quietly. "I made it plain, did I not, that if Phoebe does not go, Hélène does not attend either?"

"Mama!" Hélène protested.

"I... I didn't... I mean..." The comtesse struggled for words. "What do I say if people comment on her gown?"

"You could say that you think it becomes her well." He looked around. "You are ready, Hélène? Phoebe?"

Lady Brotherton gushed a welcome to the Calvacs and raised her eyebrows at Phoebe's dress. Phoebe was surprised that her ladyship didn't look particularly pleased to see Hélène either. When she saw Sophia and Sarah Brotherton, she understood. Sophia, the elder of the two, wore her blonde locks in a style similar to Hélène's, but Hélène's hair had a more lustrous gold tint, and her features were a little more regular.

Phoebe smiled as Lady Brotherton whisked her daughters off to their seats in the front row of chairs, ensuring no-one could make a direct comparison between Hélène and Sophia. Phoebe followed her uncle and aunt to the back of the room as Sir Alfred Brotherton introduced the first singer. For a while, all talking stopped as people listened to the woman's sweet voice, accompanied by a skilful pianist.

The next performer was a soprano singing operatic arias. Phoebe had to admit that her uncle's comment about screeching had some justice, and looked around to see how the other guests were enjoying the performance. She cringed at a particularly jarring note, catching Bella's eye across the room as she grimaced. Bella waved briefly at Phoebe and said a few words to the man sitting next to her before turning her attention back to the singer. Phoebe's eyes wandered on, gazing at the other guests, most of them frustratingly anonymous from her position at the back of the room. A lot of heads were turning and a murmur of talk began; she wasn't the only one unimpressed by the performance.

To Phoebe's relief, the soprano finally gave way to a man with a pleasant tenor voice, then there was a break for refreshments. She took a glass of champagne as a footman offered a tray to the Calvac party. She took a sip, almost sneezing when it bubbled interestingly up her nose.

"Hello Phoebe," Bella said, appearing beside her. "You look lovely tonight." She turned to her companion, who had dark blond hair and a friendly smile. "Nick, this is Phoebe Deane. Phoebe, my husband, Lord Carterton."

"My lord." Phoebe managed a small curtsey without spilling her champagne. From the corner of her eye she saw the comtesse's surprise.

"Lord Carterton, may I present my aunt, the Comtesse de Calvac?"

She wasn't sure she'd got the precedence correct—a French comtesse was probably of higher rank than a baron, but then the comtesse's title no longer officially existed. And if she had to choose which of them to offend, it wasn't going to be Lord Carterton. The comtesse introduced Hélène, but the comte and Lord Carterton had already met at their club.

As the men exchanged pleasantries, Phoebe stepped closer to Bella. "Is Lord Marstone here?"

"No, he hates these affairs. My own enjoyment depends on the quality of the entertainment—most of the performers this evening are good."

"I wanted to ask him something," Phoebe said. "It wouldn't take long, but I don't want to put it in writing."

Bella's forehead creased, then she nodded. "Can you be at Bateson's bookshop tomorrow—at eleven o'clock? I'll see what I can do."

"Thank you." Phoebe's gaze lifted as a tall, dark-haired man stopped beside Bella.

"Lady Carterton, won't you introduce me to your friends?" he asked. His gesture took in the whole family, but his eyes were fixed on Hélène.

Phoebe detected a quirk in Bella's lips as she obliged. "My lord, this is the Comte and Comtesse de Calvac, their daughter Lady Hélène, and their niece Miss Deane. Monsieur de Calvac, the Marquess of Harlford."

Lord Harlford's attention being still focused on Hélène, Phoebe had time to examine him. His nose was distinctly Roman, but that added to his looks rather than detracting from them, and his face had a slight colour that showed he spent some time out of doors. She thought his plain dark coat and breeches made a refreshing change to the dazzling array of colours worn by most of the other male guests. A ruby pin in his neckcloth and a watch fob were his only items of jewellery, and gave Phoebe an impression of elegance rather than ostentation.

Harlford bowed over the comtesse's hand first, as propriety demanded, then over Hélène's. Phoebe exchanged a rueful glance with Bella as he seemed to have forgotten her existence. Bella's gaze shifted to somewhere behind Phoebe and she gave a little wave of her hand. A cheerful-looking young man in scarlet regimentals made his way through the throng and kissed Bella's cheek.

"Miss Deane, may I introduce a cousin of my husband, Captain Richard Synton?"

"Pleased to meet you, Miss Deane," the captain said, as Bella turned to talk to someone else.

"And you, Captain." His gaze dropped, and there was a short silence before he spoke again.

"Er, I haven't seen you around before."

"This is my first venture into society," Phoebe explained. "Are you enjoying the entertainment, sir?"

"It passes the time and saves me—that is, yes, most enjoyable." He shifted his weight from one foot to the other.

"Even the second singer?" Phoebe asked, wondering if there was something wrong with her, or if the captain was just ill at ease in company.

His face lightened. "Well, perhaps—" He was interrupted by the discordant sound of a violin being tuned. "I should return to my seat, Miss Deane. Please excuse me."

She had time only for a nod as he bowed and moved off. Smoothing a hand down her skirt, she realised she had not thought about her appearance other than when Bella complimented her—that was a pleasant change from her previous social encounters.

Her aunt and cousin whispered throughout the next few performances, earning annoyed glances from the comte. Phoebe had to bite her lip at his expression of relief when the recitals ended, and he hurriedly declared that they had done enough socialising for one evening and it was time to return home.

The next morning Phoebe wrote a brief note to be sent to the comtesse with her breakfast tray, and then set off for the bookshop with Ellie.

She loved the smell of books, and the possibilities within their pages. She'd had her fill of novels from reading the ones Hélène had taken to Calvac, so she wandered along the non-fiction shelves. *Reflections on the Revolutions in France* seemed an apt title in light of her recent experience, and she leafed through the pages, only looking up as she heard footsteps approach.

"That is rather serious reading for a young lady, is it not?" The Earl of Marstone stood before her, his expression quizzical. She closed the book and was about to replace it on the shelf when the earl took it from her.

"It would be best to be seen discussing a book, don't you think?" he asked, glancing at people browsing the shelves nearby. "Bella said you needed to see me."

"I... I'm sorry, my lord, I didn't intend to cause you inconvenience."

"No matter, Miss Deane. How can I help you?"

She could detect no sign of impatience in his tone or face. "I was just wondering about... about Mr Westbrook," she said, keeping her voice low. "I mean, now they have a message that is supposed to come from him, they will want to stop you getting it. So when he comes back they might—"

"Don't worry, Miss Deane," the earl said. "Westbrook is not in the habit of publicly announcing his arrival. It is likely I will see him before anyone else is aware he has returned. I may have cause to try to communicate with him while he is away; if so, I will add a warning. Will that do?"

"Thank you. Yes, that is reassuring." She felt her cheeks grow hot. "I'm so sorry to have brought you out for—"

"Tell me, Miss Deane," the earl interrupted. "Aren't you the least bit curious as to the success of our endeavour?"

"Well, yes," Phoebe said. "But there is no reason at all why you should tell me, so there didn't seem to be any point in asking."

"Most unusual," the earl said, as if talking to himself. "As you predicted, Brownlee and Chatham did not manage to keep the thief in sight for long enough to identify the final recipient. However, we still have some hope that the content of the message may prove... productive. Have you heard from Brevare again?"

Phoebe told him about the note she had received, and he nodded, then turned his attention to the book he was still holding. "I would have thought your uncle would have a copy of this."

"He may have, but until now I have mostly searched his library for books on explorations or natural history."

"And now?"

"Having encountered first-hand some results of the revolution, I think I would like to know more about it. I will see what is in the library."

Phoebe wondered if she'd said something peculiar, as the earl seemed to stare through her. He blinked, and put the book back on the shelf.

"If that was all, Miss Deane, I'll leave you to your education," he said.

"Yes, thank you, my lord." Phoebe watched him walk away, hoping he didn't think she'd made a fuss over nothing.

When Phoebe returned home, Green informed her that the comte wished her to join him in the parlour. After going to her room to freshen up, she found her aunt sitting with her uncle.

"I hear Hélène is to go driving with the Marquess of Harlford tomorrow," the comte said to his wife, after Phoebe had explained where she'd been.

A satisfied smile spread across the comtesse's face. "Yes, he called earlier. He could only stay a few minutes, but he was extremely complimentary. That would be an excellent connection."

"And you had a caller too, I believe, Phoebe?" the comte said. "He left you a note, did he not?"

"Green didn't give me a note, sir." Nor had there been anything left in her room.

"Perhaps you were about to give Phoebe her message?" the comte suggested to his wife.

The comtesse flushed, taking a folded paper from her pocket. "I wanted to check Phoebe was making... suitable acquaintances," she said as she handed it over. "I don't know who the young man is."

The note was an invitation to drive with Captain Synton.

"Lady Carterton introduced me to Captain Synton at the musicale," Phoebe explained. "He is Lord Carterton's cousin."

"That seems unexceptionable, *n'est-ce pas*?" the comte said.

The comtesse's lips thinned, but she had to agree.

"And you have no other activities in mind for tomorrow at...?" He looked at Phoebe.

"Four o'clock, sir."

"Four o'clock. I hope not; it would be a shame for Hélène to have to miss her drive with Lord Harlford. He is due just before then, I think?"

"No, no other plans," the comtesse admitted, although it looked to Phoebe as if she had to force the words out.

"Excellent. I'm glad that's all clear."

CHAPTER 28

*A*lex leaned against the wall in a street near the Place de la Révolution. He lifted one foot and turned it to inspect the sole of his boot, using the movement to cast one final glance behind him. Yesterday's walk through this area had not generated any undue interest in him or his business here, and he was now confident that no-one had followed him this morning. That was just as well— discreet enquiries about his only other contact had revealed that the man had left Paris several months ago.

Seen through the window, Couillard's shop appeared empty of customers, so Alex crossed the street and went in. A man in a leather apron looked up from the shoe he was sewing.

Alex turned up his boot again. "Can you mend these boots while I wait?"

The man nodded, and gestured to a chair. Alex pulled off his boots and handed them over, allowing himself a small smile at the happy coincidence of his contact being a shoemaker at a time when his boots did indeed need mending.

He looked around at the shelves of shoes and boots adorned with paper labels, awaiting repair or collection. Once the man was stitching a new sole, Alex asked casually if he ever made shoes out of pig-skin.

The man's hand jerked slightly, but he did not look away from his work. "There's no call for it these days," he muttered. "Nor sheepskin."

Satisfied, Alex stood looking out of the window in his stockinged feet until his boots were repaired, then paid for the work.

"Don't come here again," the shoemaker said quietly as Alex took his change. "I cannot do any more... repairs."

Alex pulled his boots on, feeling a lump beneath his left instep. Glancing at the shoemaker, he could see tension in the man's neck, knuckles too white in the hand that gripped the money he'd taken. He could have ignored the code words, Alex thought, but he had acknowledged them, and the lump indicated that he'd passed on a message.

Courage deserved to be rewarded.

"Business might be better if you moved," Alex suggested. "I couldn't guarantee how well the journey itself would go, but I'm sure you could make a living in a new location."

"That is an interesting thought," Couillard said, after a moment's hesitation. "Do you have other shoes in need of repair? You could leave them here tomorrow."

"My friend may have some work to be done," Alex said. He did not think he should show his face here again. "He might be interested in buying some red shoes for a lady friend."

Couillard nodded and followed him to the entrance, locking the door behind him and turning the card in the window to show *Fermé*.

Back in their lodgings, Alex extracted the lump from his boot. It was, as he had suspected, a folded paper Couillard had hidden there while he was stitching. He took the road guide from his bag and sat at the small table to start decoding, pencilling in the translated letters above the original message.

Ten minutes later he leaned back in the rickety chair and stretched, running his hands through his hair in frustration. The message did not make sense. It must be coded using the road guide, as that was the only book he had with him—and the only book that Marstone *knew* he would have with him. Neither a straight decoding nor one using the extra numbers to add and subtract produced recognisable words.

The door rattled and he hurriedly folded the paper.

"Who's there?"

"Henri."

Alex relaxed, and went to unlock the door. Henri followed him back into the room, putting a wrapped loaf and wedge of cheese on the table before stretching out on the bed. "*Ça va?*"

"No luck with it yet," Alex replied. Henri grunted, and appeared to go to sleep. The man seemed to have a far bigger store of patience than Alex.

He looked at the original message again—it was a string of numbers, so it must be a book code. Using those numbers and his road guide produced a sequence of letters, but they had no meaning.

There must be a further layer of coding on top of the usual one. If there really was a traitor somewhere within the organisation, it made sense to encrypt the message further. However, whoever sent it must also have assumed he would be able to decode it.

Thinking back, he recalled the codes they had used, years ago, based on a single word or phrase. Marstone may have done that, using a phrase he thought Alex would guess.

He took a blank piece of paper and wrote out his name, omitting repeated letters, then followed it with the rest of the alphabet.

WESTBROKACDF...

Under that he wrote the alphabet normally—A under the W, B under the E. Using that key to transform the first few words of the half-decoded message produced another string of meaningless letters. He tried the same thing several times, using different starting words: his full name, Marstone, Kellet. He even tried Phoebe Deane.

He threw down his pencil in disgust and ran his hands through his hair again. These failures should not be surprising. The names he'd tried could be guessed by someone in the Foreign Office. What significant words would both he and the earl know about that others would not?

Was he using the wrong book to translate the initial numbers into letters? But Marstone could only rely on him having the road guide.

Books…?

Could Marstone have used the title of a book as the key phrase? Perhaps the one Phoebe had used to code the message he'd sent back with her—something to do with a cave. No, not cave. Cavern?

'Smuggler's Cavern' did not work, but when he tried 'Pirate's Cavern' the first words became Sixteen Rue des Fleurs.

He grunted in satisfaction and continued with the rest of the message, instantly feeling both relieved and much more optimistic. If Marstone knew about *The Pirate's Cavern*, then not only must Phoebe have got back to London safely, but she had seen Marstone and he had believed her story.

Two mornings later, Phoebe retreated to the library after breakfast. The promised drive with Captain Synton had been pleasant, once she'd got the captain talking about horses. Now she was looking forward to a quiet morning before visiting Miss Fletcher to have the final fitting for her ball gowns.

She turned to the parcel of books that had just been delivered. One was the book she had been looking at in the shop when Lord Marstone found her—*Reflections on the Revolution in France* by Edmund Burke. Two of the others were on similar lines, although they appeared from first glance to be taking the opposite point of view to Mr Burke. Finally there was *A Vindication of the Rights of Woman* by Mary Wollstonecraft. An unsigned note suggested that the books should be read in the order in which they were published.

The parcel could only have been sent by the earl. But why had he sent them? She'd said her uncle probably had a copy of the first book.

Lord Marstone must have had a reason for suggesting the reading order, so she picked up Burke's book. It was heavy going—the man never seemed to use one word when he could use five or six. She was a few pages into it when a piece of paper fell out and fluttered to the floor. Phoebe picked it up, wondering if it was a receipt for the books.

It looked like a tailor's account, but it was written in the same hand as the note that had accompanied the books. The sums of money looked odd, too—even the most extravagant sprig of fashion could not possibly pay five pounds for a neckcloth. Not only that, but whoever had written it appeared to think there could be more than twenty shillings to the pound.

She put the paper on the table, pushing Burke to one side. The book was new, so the paper must have been left in it on purpose, almost certainly by Lord Marstone. He, or his secretary, had written it out himself, so the words and numbers must mean something. A code? Was it some kind of challenge?

Smiling, she found paper, pens, and ink in the comte's desk. All the amounts were whole numbers of shillings, no pence. Could the number for the pounds be a page number and the shillings be the letters? The paper had been tucked into Burke's book, so she began to turn pages and count letters, pushing aside a warm memory of sitting with Alex in that French inn doing the same thing.

After a minute she sat back in disappointment—the results made no sense. She was using the same method she had used when putting Alex's list of names and addresses into code, but in reverse.

It *must* be a message of some kind—why else would the paper have been in the book? However, Lord Marstone wasn't likely to be sending her names that needed spelling out letter by letter. If the message could be expressed in ordinary words...?

This time she used the shillings to count the words on the pages instead of the letters. She beamed in satisfaction as the short message appeared before her.

Would you and your guardian care to join me at dinner?

That was all, although it was surprising enough.

How should she respond? The idea of being invited to dinner by the earl was both flattering and frightening. Her uncle had been invited as well, but she wasn't sure that she should, or even could, explain to him how she had come by the invitation. A formal invitation from Lord Marstone would be better.

She started turning pages and writing down numbers on a new sheet of paper. Then she rang the bell and asked for Green.

When Phoebe arrived at Miss Fletcher's salon that afternoon, she was surprised to see Bella there, perusing pattern books.

"Hello, Phoebe," Bella said. "I've come to see how your gowns look on you."

"If you'll come this way, Miss Deane?" Amy gestured towards the changing room.

"Bring her back in here to be pinned, please, Amy," Bella said.

"Yes, my lady."

Once in the back room, Amy helped Phoebe to change into the first of the ball gowns she'd ordered. This one was pale gold in colour, with an overdress in a deeper shade. Delicate, creamy lace trimmed the neckline and sleeves. Back in the salon, she stood in the spot Amy indicated, gazing in awe at her image in the mirrors.

"It's lovely, Phoebe," Bella said, getting up to walk around her.

"Don't move, miss," Amy warned through a mouthful of pins.

"How did you enjoy your outing with Captain Synton?" Bella asked.

"Oh, well enough." Phoebe smiled at the memory of the awkward start to their conversation. "Thank you for sending him."

Bella tutted. "He told you I'd sent him? The man has no manners."

Phoebe laughed, and this time Amy tutted.

"Not in so many words," Phoebe explained. "It was a little difficult at first, but we got on splendidly after I asked him about the horses."

"Yes, Nick said he's asked to borrow the phaeton and pair again tomorrow. He said you wanted to drive them?"

Phoebe remembered just in time not to turn around, and caught Bella's eye in one of the mirrors instead. "Yes. I had to—I drove a coach for a few miles in France, and I thought it would be interesting to learn properly." When there were no soldiers to evade. "Does Lord Carterton mind?"

Bella shook her head. "Not at all. He trusts Richard to take care of them."

"Step up on here, please, Miss Deane," Amy said, indicating a broad box. Phoebe did so, and Amy crouched to check the hem.

Phoebe recalled the start of her outing, and couldn't stop her lips curving.

"Do tell," Bella said. "What amuses you so?"

"The captain was due to call half an hour after Lord Harlford called for Hélène," Phoebe began, wondering if she was being fair to her cousin in relating the story. Perhaps she wasn't, but Hélène had brought it on herself, after all.

"Richard was late?"

"Oh no," Phoebe said, turning to Amy's command. "He was on time, as was Lord Harlford. Hélène kept him waiting for half an hour."

Bella's eyebrows rose. Phoebe had wondered if keeping a suitor waiting was normal, but it appeared not.

"He was not best pleased?"

"No. Well, it wasn't that." Phoebe turned again, and made a fresh start. "Hélène had planned a grand entrance, floating down the stairs in her finery."

"Her suitor more appreciative for having waited?" Bella suggested.

"I believe that was the idea. She made her entrance just as the captain arrived and was being introduced, so no-one noticed." From the chagrin on Hélène's face, she was sure her cousin had been late on purpose. She wondered if it had been Hélène's idea, or if the comtesse had suggested it.

"Ha!" Bella said. "An unwise strategy. Harlford's a stickler for punctuality, from what I've heard."

"There, miss," Amy said, finally standing.

Phoebe drew in a breath as she took in her appearance in the mirror. The bodice hugged her figure, the skirt flaring out from the waist. Bella stood and pulled a few curls from Phoebe's bandeau, draping them over her shoulder.

"Stunning," she said.

Phoebe swallowed. This gown surpassed the others she'd already received from Miss Fletcher—and made her into a totally different person from the dowdy poor relation in the orange dress. She twisted to see her back view, hardly hearing Amy's entreaty to be careful not to stab herself on the pins.

It seemed silly to feel so much more confident because of a gown, but she was now looking forward to the ball tomorrow evening.

CHAPTER 29

*P*hoebe gazed at Lady Sandrich's ballroom from her place in the line of guests, and tried to hide her awe at the grandeur. Swags of green, gold, and white cloth adorned the walls, and dozens of pots of daffodils and purple crocuses in full bloom gave the appearance of spring. The fresh feel of the colours did not extend to the air, which was warm and heavy with the smell of burning candles and cloying perfumes.

Once their small party moved past the receiving line, several acquaintances of the comtesse approached them, introducing sons or nephews or cousins; they all wished to secure a dance with the fair Lady Hélène, ravishing tonight in white, the edges of her bodice and sleeves outlined in silver thread, and tiny silver flowers and ribbons woven into her hair.

Phoebe, happy in her own new gown, no longer felt the poor relation and accepted gracefully when several of Hélène's would-be suitors were polite enough to also ask her for a dance as she was introduced. She concentrated on her steps at first, but soon gained enough confidence to exchange general remarks with her various partners about the ballroom, the weather, and occasionally the other dancers.

Bella arrived with her husband and Captain Synton while Phoebe was sitting down, glad to rest her feet.

"Well, Phoebe, are you enjoying yourself?" Bella asked, sitting beside her.

"Yes, very much, thank you."

"No partner?"

As she spoke, Sir Peter Tynwood appeared with the lemonade he had gone to procure. Phoebe made the introductions, then he excused himself and went off to find his next partner.

"A conquest?" Bella asked.

"Oh, definitely," said Phoebe, with a wry look. "He was keen to see me tomorrow afternoon in the park... when he learned that I will be accompanying my aunt and cousin for a drive."

"I say, that's a bit much!" Captain Synton said.

Phoebe laughed. "Oh, he was fairly subtle about it," she said. She suspected that several of her partners had been hoping she could help them get close to her cousin, but she was surprised to find that she didn't mind as long as they didn't make it too obvious.

"Have *you* met my cousin, Captain Synton?"

"No, but Bella pointed her out as we came over. Miss Deane, are you engaged for the supper dance?"

"No."

"May I?"

"By all means. Thank you, Captain." He smiled, and then left in the direction of the card room.

"He should be fit for polite society with another few years' training," Bella said, straight-faced, as she watched him go. "But at least he has the sense not to fall at your cousin's feet."

"I must thank you once again for introducing me to Miss Fletcher," Phoebe said. She saw a passing lady pause as she spoke, then turn and move towards them.

"Miss Fletcher?" the newcomer asked. "You must be the reason my appointment was cancelled last week."

"Maria, this is Miss Phoebe Dean," Bella said. "Phoebe, this is my good friend Lady Jesson."

Lady Jesson was in her mid-thirties, dressed in shades of light purple and silvery grey, her gown cleverly minimising a rather plump waistline. The few fine lines fanning out from the corners of her eyes looked to Phoebe more like laughter lines than signs of age.

"I am pleased to meet you, my lady," Phoebe said, making a curtsey. "I'm sorry to have taken your appointment, but I cannot regret the results." She glanced down at her gown as she spoke.

Lady Jesson regarded her for a few moments, then smiled. They *were* laughter lines. "You'll do, I like a girl who can be honest! Who's presenting you?"

"I live with my uncle, the Comte de Calvac. My aunt is presenting me along with her own daughter."

"Oh, yes, the new Incomparable is Lavinia's daughter." Lady Jesson looked Phoebe over, her gaze running from Phoebe's hair right down to her slippers. Phoebe kept her chin up, determined not to show her discomfort at being inspected in this way. Finally, Lady Jesson smiled at her.

"We'll see," she said cryptically, then nodded to Bella and walked off.

Phoebe looked at Bella, surprised to see her smiling.

"She's rather a gossip," Bella explained, "but she's not at all spiteful with it, unlike some."

Bella was claimed by another acquaintance a few minutes later, and Phoebe was happy to spend the rest of that set observing the company. She saw the Marquess of Harlford arrive and make his way over to Hélène, and later Hélène was on his arm going into the supper room, a triumphant smile on her face.

Phoebe enjoyed her own supper with Bella, Lord Carterton, and the captain, and had enough partners during the second half of the evening to call her first ball a success. She enjoyed the dancing, although she did wonder how much of it was due to the attraction of novelty. Conversations with her partners had consisted mainly of the platitudes she'd expected, quite unlike her talks with Alex. To be fair, it was difficult to hold a serious conversation during a dance.

It would have been lovely if she could have danced with Alex.

~

Alex ordered another cup of the swill the eating house called coffee, and stared morosely out of the window. He shouldn't complain too much, he thought, as a gust of rain spattered against the glass. At least he was sitting in the warm and dry waiting for Henri to return.

Marstone's coded message had provided several new contacts, one of whom had managed to find out that two women answering the description of the vicomtesse and her daughter were being kept in a house further down this street. Over the last few days they'd seen glimpses of two roughly dressed men who could be guards. There was also a girl in servants' garb who ventured out with a basket each afternoon.

He rubbed one hand across his face and looked at the newspaper he was supposedly reading, but his thoughts were on Brevare. The man was French, so some might say that he was not betraying his country in attempting to get Alex's list of names. But not many of the aristocracy sided with the republicans, and Alex guessed the numbers would be fewer still now the king had been executed. Brevare would be regarded as a traitor in some quarters.

Alex roused himself from his musings as Henri placed a steaming bowl of cassoulet and a plate of bread on the table and slumped into the adjacent chair. Hoping the food was better than the coffee, Alex caught the eye of a waiter and soon had his own meal before him.

"You talked to her?" he asked Henri.

"*Oui*. It *is* the Brevare women. Aimée looks after them—cooks for them and two guards."

"Does she know why they're there?"

Henri shook his head, his mouth full. "Told not to talk to anyone," he said. "But it can't be an official arrest—they'd be in prison if it was."

Alex nodded, dipping his bread into the juices in his dish—it wasn't the best cassoulet he'd eaten, but it would do.

Confirmation of the prisoners' identities backed up their theory that Brevare was being blackmailed. But finding the women wasn't enough—getting them to England might allow Marstone to find out who Brevare was working for.

"Is there any sign that they are about to be moved?"

"She didn't say anything about that, but the guards probably wouldn't tell Aimée anyway."

"Would she have told you if they had?" If Aimée was a good revolutionary, she wouldn't want to help a pair of aristos to escape.

Henri paused, considering the question. "I think so," he said. "She didn't seem happy with the situation."

"Will she help them escape?"

"I don't know. I only talked to her for a few minutes." Henri put his fork down. "And it would be dangerous for her, especially if we fail. I will talk to her again tomorrow."

"It will take a day or two to prepare," Alex said. They'd need travel papers, a coach, a diversion. The shoemaker was making arrangements to get himself and his wife to one of the rendezvous points on the coast that Marstone had detailed in his message. But it might be better if they all travelled together—anyone searching for the Brevare women might overlook a larger party.

"*Bien.* I will persuade her. She can come with us if she wishes, yes?"

"Of course."

Alex's estimate of two days was optimistic. It was three nights later that he and Henri climbed over a wall and into the dark back yard of the house where the Brevare women were being held. Only a dim light shone from what must be the kitchen windows, but it was enough for them to avoid alerting the inhabitants by kicking over buckets or other bits of rubbish strewn about.

As promised, the rear door was not locked. Pushing it slowly, Alex released his breath when the hinges made no sound. Good, they could get in quietly when it was time. He pulled the door to again without latching it, and moved back out and into the shadow beneath the window to bide his time.

He checked the priming of his pistols again while they waited;

Henri did the same. Alex partially drew his sword to make sure it moved easily in its scabbard. He wasn't used to wearing it and hoped he wasn't going to trip over the damned thing, but two pistols only gave two shots.

Ten minutes later shouts reached them from the street in front of the house, then pistol shots and the screams of panicking horses. Alex and Henri allowed a couple of minutes for anyone in the house to move to the front windows to see what was going on, then quietly let themselves into the kitchen. A candle stuck to the corner of a large table guttered in the draught from the open door. Henri picked it up and they made their way to the inner door. Everything so far was as Aimée had told Henri.

"No servants' stairs," Henri reminded him.

They'd have to pass whoever was on guard at the front of the house. Easing open the door between the servants' area and the main part of the house, Alex saw the hall lit with flickering orange light. A large man stood by the open front door, silhouetted against flambeaux in the street with his hands on his hips. His attention was on the developing riot in the street, but he was only a few feet from the bottom of the main staircase.

They crept forward, Alex with a cocked pistol in one hand. He could have sworn they made no noise, but the guard turned just as Henri reached the foot of the stairs.

"*Quoi?*" He stepped towards them.

Alex raised his pistol, but Henri dashed past, running at the guard and knocking him over. The guard reached up with a shout of rage, one hand grabbing Henri by the throat and the fingers of the other aiming at his eyes.

Henri twisted his face away and punched the man on the side of the head, but he didn't let go. Alex sidled round the flailing legs and took hold of the barrel of his pistol. The guard went limp as the butt of the pistol struck his temple.

Henri scrambled to his feet and they both stood in silence for a moment, listening. The only sounds came from the street. There was no indication that anyone was coming to investigate the disturbance.

"Drag him into the kitchen," Alex whispered, and went to shut and bolt the front door. He didn't want any surprises arriving from that direction.

Henri tied up the unconscious guard, leaving him in a dark corner of the kitchen, and they set off up the stairs. The first floor landing was lit by a lantern standing on the floor, its wick turned down low. A guard snored on a chair, a bottle of wine on the floor beside him. He didn't move even when Alex held the muzzle of a pistol against his temple. He bent down—there was alcohol on the man's breath, but the bottle on the floor was still half full.

"Drugged?" he whispered as Henri stopped beside him, then his attention was caught by the movement of a door half-way along the landing. A small hand came out and beckoned. Henri gave him a shove and they moved past the guard and through the door a girl was holding open for them. From her dress, Alex deduced that the girl was Aimée.

This room was better lit. Alex heard Henri's indrawn breath at the same time as he noticed a livid bruise across Aimée's cheek and another on the arm she had beckoned with. But there was no time for wondering who or why. Another young woman perched nervously on a sofa, this one clad in well-made and warm travelling clothes, her eyes enormous in a pale face. Beside her slumped a much older woman, breathing heavily but not reacting at all to their presence.

"I had to drug her," Aimée said quietly. "She does not believe she is truly in danger here—she thinks it is all a mistake that will be put right soon."

"And her?" Alex jerked his head towards the woman who must be Brevare's sister.

"She believes me. She will come quietly. But you will have to carry the vicomtesse."

Alex looked at Henri—Alex was the better shot.

"I'll take her," Henri said, and unceremoniously hoisted the sleeping woman over his shoulder. "We need to go now."

Henri carried the inert vicomtesse down the stairs and out through the kitchen door. The bound guard was beginning to regain consciousness, his eyes glittering as Alex held the lantern over him, but his bonds held firm. He'd be found as soon as his comrade came round, so Alex left him there.

Once they were outside, louder sounds of breaking glass and gunshots indicated that the arranged diversion was getting out of hand. Alex hoped it wouldn't bring the authorities down on them before they'd made a clean escape. He climbed the wall and took the unconscious woman from Henri, letting her gently down the other side. The two younger women were easily lifted over.

Henri dumped the vicomtesse into the waiting carriage while Alex paid off the lad minding it and scrambled up onto the box. Now they were to pick up the shoemaker and his wife, and wait somewhere inconspicuous until the barricades opened in the morning. Alex hoped Aimée had enough of the drug to keep the vicomtesse unconscious. A sudden vision of Phoebe's aunt came into his head—if this woman was anything like her, they'd be well advised to keep her unconscious as long as possible.

Tomorrow, he and Henri would be the coachmen for a merchant and his wife and sickly mother, plus their daughter and a maid. Three days' driving—avoiding towns and villages—and the *Lily* would be waiting for them off a secluded beach west of Dieppe.

Rubbing a hand over his face, he wondered if he would see Phoebe in London.

CHAPTER 30

$\mathcal{J}$t was well past midnight when Alex drew the hired carriage to a halt into the mews behind Grosvenor Square. Alex helped the two Brevare women down and lead them to the rear servants' entrance. He tapped gently on the door. A footman answered his knock, nodding in recognition as he ushered them into the kitchen.

"I need money, Brownlee," Alex said.

"His lordship is still out, sir, but I think Langton is waiting up for him. I'll fetch him."

"And wake one of the maids, please."

Brownlee glanced at the women before disappearing along the corridor leading towards the front of the house. Alex sat the women at the kitchen table, the vicomtesse looking around her with the corners of her mouth turned down. Her daughter looked so tired that Alex wondered if she was going to faint. He found a glass and poured her some water, then went back outside to help Henri turn the carriage round. When he returned, the butler was there holding a purse.

"How much do you need, sir?" Langton asked.

Alex tipped the coins out into his hand then returned them to the purse. "This should be sufficient, thank you. Can you find a room for the ladies? It is not to be known they are here. I'll need a bed as well. It would be best to get Doctor Cavenor to examine the ladies in the morning—discreetly—to make sure they are well."

"Yes, sir."

While Langton headed off to organise rooms, Alex went out to the coach and handed the purse to Henri. "Stop outside the city and find an inn, then send word where you are. I'll get money and a driver and groom sent to you—they'll know the way to Marstone's place in Devonshire. You can manage enough English until then?"

Henri just grunted. Alex put his head into the carriage. The shoe-maker's wife slept on her husband's shoulder; Aimée sat next to them, wide-eyed and with her hands clenched in her lap.

"All is well," Alex said quietly. "Only another hour's travelling tonight."

"Thank you, monsieur," Couillard said.

"Madame de Brevare, will she want me to attend her?" Aimée's voice trembled.

"You need have nothing more to do with her," Alex reassured the girl. "Unless you wish it."

Aimée shook her head.

"Lady Marstone will help you. She will find you a job, and help you to learn English. She is very friendly."

Alex gave them a final nod and closed the door. He suspected that Lady Marstone's intervention would not be necessary—Henri was showing all the signs of a man smitten. He watched until the carriage left the square again, uncomfortably aware that he was in a similar situation himself.

He staggered slightly as he re-entered the house. The crossing had been rough, making sleep impossible, then he had driven most of the way from Dover so that Henri would be rested for his onward jour-ney. The effects of the whole affair were catching up with him.

Someone had set a jug of ale and a plate of bread and cheese on the table, so he sat down to eat and drink. He asked Brownlee for pen and paper when the footman returned, scribbled a brief note, and gave instructions for its delivery to Berkeley Square in the morning. No doubt Marstone would prefer him not to tell anyone he was back, but he owed it to Phoebe to tell her he was safe.

At least, he *hoped* she'd want to know. Shaking his head against such thoughts, he finished the food and ale, then took a candle and retired to the room in the attic he used when his presence in London was to be kept secret.

"Wake up, sir."

Alex's hand reached for his pistol before he even opened his eyes. The man standing by his bed took a hasty step backwards. Blinking, Alex recognised the small attic bedroom and the earl's valet.

My apologies, sir," Harrison said. "His lordship wants to see you in the library in half an hour."

Alex laid the pistol on the floor beside the bed and rubbed his eyes. He was in a nightshirt, but he didn't remember undressing himself. The room was dim, the thick curtains closed. "What time is it?"

"Midday, sir. You have slept for nearly nine hours."

Alex groaned, and reluctantly pushed the bedclothes aside. He would have to explain himself to Marstone at some point—he may as well get it over with.

"I have had a bath filled for you in the next room, sir, and I have laid out some of the clothing you left last time you were here."

A hot bath might be worth the effort of getting up.

Half an hour later he was clean, shaven—and hungry. He waved away Harrison's offer of help, quickly dressing and knotting his own neckcloth.

"You asked to see me, sir?" Alex said as he entered the library.

Marstone looked up with his usual welcoming smile, then stood and came around his desk and clapped him on the shoulder. "I'm glad you're back safely, Alex."

Alex was about to speak when the rich smell of roast beef and gravy made him pause, his stomach rumbling. Kellet carried in a tray

251

and set it on one end of the desk. He pulled chairs to the desk, and poured coffee for everyone.

"Eat first," Marstone said, waving a hand at the food.

He didn't need to be told twice. He got through most of the thick slices of beef and a large pile of potatoes and vegetables before the earl ran out of patience and cleared his throat.

Alex reluctantly pushed his plate aside and leaned back in his chair, holding his cup of coffee. He started to relate his travels in France over the last few months, and the contacts he had made.

"Yes," the earl interrupted. "I've got the details of your contacts—you did well there. At the moment, I'm more interested in this business with the Vicomte de Brevare. That seems to be tied up in some way with the Calvac women—tell me how you came to escort them."

As Alex outlined what had happened when he came across the Calvac party, the earl went to stand before the fire. He leaned one arm on the mantelpiece and gazed down at the flames; only an occasional movement of his head indicated that he was listening.

"What possessed you to risk yourself by doing such a thing?" he asked, when Alex finished. "The information you brought back is worth far more than the lives of a few women."

Alex couldn't read his expression. "It was an impulse," he admitted. "Miss Deane had been friendly, and..." He shrugged. "I couldn't abandon them to their fate."

"Impulsive decisions can be dangerous," Marstone said, returning to sit at his desk.

"It worked out well in the end," Alex said. He'd expected more criticism, and its absence made him wonder what impulsive decisions Marstone had made in the past.

"Possibly better than you imagine." The earl's tone seemed amused rather than offended.

What did that mean? Alex glanced at Kellet, but the secretary raised his shoulders in a shrug.

"But you couldn't have known it would," the earl went on.

"True. But I would do the same again." Vague thoughts from the last weeks crystallised in his head. "I think that I'm no longer fit for that kind of work."

To Alex's surprise, Marstone didn't look displeased. "Well, we'll think about that when you're properly rested. Now, retrieving the Brevare women, how did that go?"

Relieved at the change of subject, Alex outlined what he and Henri had done. Kellet made notes as Alex spoke.

"The new men you sent details for were useful," Alex concluded. "I doubt we would have achieved anything without their assistance. The people in Paris whose details I already had are no longer usable. By the way, you have acquired a shoemaker and his wife—a loan to set him up in business would come in useful."

Marstone agreed, as Alex expected. "See to it, will you, Kellet?" He turned back to Alex. "Doctor Cavenor examined the vicomtesse and the daughter this morning. He prescribed a day of rest before they move on—but they will have had a day by tomorrow morning. The vicomtesse was complaining that you had sent her maid away."

Alex remembered the way the woman had spoken to her maid on the journey from Dover. Reluctantly, he had kept the vicomtesse drowsy with laudanum for most of the journey through France—one wrong word from her could have sent the whole party to the guillotine. But the last effects of the drug had worn off while they were on the *Lily*.

"The maid had a bruised face when we got them out of the house in Paris," he said, answering the implied question. "I assumed at first that she'd got it from one of the guards there, but I think it was actually the vicomtesse. The maid is currently acting as servant to Couillard and his wife, but I suspect Henri Dumont will end up looking after her."

"You seem to be making a habit of rescuing harridans." The earl was definitely amused.

"You've met the Comtesse de Calvac, then?" Alex asked with a wry smile.

"Only for a few moments at a ball. Bella told me about her. But back to business. I am glad you had them put into the special guest room—I'd prefer to keep their presence in England secret for a while."

"Have you got any idea who might be blackmailing Brevare?" Alex assumed Phoebe would have already explained their reasoning—possibly sitting in this very chair.

"No, but things have come to light since you left that convince me there *is* a traitor within the organisation somewhere. I have talked to both the Brevare women, but they don't know anything that might help us to identify him." The earl steepled his fingers. "Why did you take Miss Deane into your confidence? Surely it would have been better to maintain your pose as a Frenchman?"

"No doubt, but she worked most of it out herself. I gave myself away when she was stitching up my arm."

"Stitching up...?" The earl's eyebrows rose. "Explain."

Alex described the fight and its aftermath, the earl's brows, and Kellet's, rising even further as the tale progressed.

"So," Marstone said when Alex had finished. "She backed up your improvised fabrication without foreknowledge, stabbed this man Sarchet with a pair of scissors, stole your pistol, handed you a pitch-fork, which likely saved you from far worse injury, punched the other Frenchie and damaged him elsewhere, then played doctor?"

"That about sums that part of it up," said Alex with a grin. It sounded remarkable, but she was the most remarkable woman he'd ever met. His mind filled with the vision of her smiling at him, the firelight in her hair, and the memory of that kiss.

"There's more?"

Alex brought himself back to the present. "Yes. Braving a tavern-full of drunken fishermen, smugglers, and soldiers, driving the coach —I think that about covers it. Perhaps you should recruit her instead of me?"

The earl's expression remained suspiciously blank.

"I was joking!" Alex added sharply.

The earl waved a hand casually. "Of course you were."

"There has been no public talk about... well, about me and Miss Deane?" he asked. "The comtesse held some unfounded suspicions."

"Not that I have heard—you could check with Bella though, if you wish. I don't want you to show your face in public yet, but Nick's staff are discreet."

Alex nodded, aware that Marstone was studying his expression.

"Would it matter?" Marstone asked. "You could do worse for a wife if her reputation requires marriage."

Marriage—he'd tried to dismiss that idea when it had occurred to him. Marstone was right; if he were to marry, he couldn't do better. But she could.

"I don't want to *have* to marry anyone," he said sharply. "Nor should she be forced into a marriage because of rumour." Marrying someone he wanted but who did not want him could turn out to be the worst kind of hell. And he was *not* going to discuss it with Marstone, particularly with Kellet as an interested observer.

"No need to get angry about it, Alex. There appears to be no necessity at the moment. Now, the decoy note—Brevare hired an actor to pose as me, and tried to get Miss Deane to give it to him in the park."

"Tried?"

"She didn't give me many details, but I gather she played the stupid servant obeying her orders literally." The earl gave a small smile. "She then persuaded Bella to bring her here without anyone knowing. Kellet helped me to write a replacement that we hope will flush out our traitor."

"Did you get a look at who she gave it to?"

"It was stolen when she was on her way to an arranged meeting, but unfortunately the watchers did not manage to follow the thief far enough to see who it was finally given to."

Alex sat up straight. "Watchers? You were *expecting* the note to be stolen?"

"It seemed the most likely way they would obtain it. She had insisted on being taken to me at the Foreign Office before she would hand it over."

"You put her in danger from a common thief?" Alex asked, trying to keep the anger out of his voice.

"She volunteered," Marstone said mildly. "And she came to no harm. She had already worked out they were likely to try to steal the note from her before she could meet the fake me."

"But you let her?" Alex stood up abruptly, making an effort to keep his voice down. It was bad enough that he had done so in France, but there had been little choice then. Surely the earl could have found some other way?

"I suspect she is not an easy woman to dissuade once she has made her mind up."

Alex's tense shoulders gradually relaxed, and he gave a rueful laugh. "You could be right, sir. Has it worked? The new decoy note, I mean?"

"Nothing so far. You've heard nothing, Kellet?" Marstone's gaze turned to his secretary, who shook his head.

"The note was supposedly from you stating that you had evidence against certain members of the organisation," the earl said. "But you needed to confirm a few details before naming them and you needed to go to Paris to do so."

"So as far as they are concerned, I am still in Paris and they do not yet need to flee?"

"Correct. So your public reappearance may initiate something. Nevertheless I think it best if you escort the two women to Ashton Tracey tomorrow. My wife will ensure they are kept in seclusion while they are there. If someone has been using threats against the women to make Brevare act for them, I'd rather they continued to do so. I wish to choose the time at which I tell him that he no longer needs to fear for their safety."

"Why don't you just ask him who's responsible?"

"Whoever has been dealing with Brevare may not be the only one involved, and may not be the one in charge. I need to get more out of him than one name."

"You can be rather ruthless at times, sir," Alex said, although he could understand the reasoning.

The earl did not appear to take offence at this comment. "As you've said before. But the greater good, eh?"

Alex sighed. "Very well. I'll ride escort—I'm not spending two days cooped up in a carriage with that woman."

"Make sure no-one recognises you. And you had best not tell anyone else you are back, either."

"Too late for that," Alex said.

"What? Who?"

"Oh, don't worry, no word will get out." He stood and headed for the door before the earl could say anything else. "I'll call on Bella, then I'm for my bed again."

CHAPTER 31

*E*llie knocked and carried a tray of coffee into Phoebe's room. "Lovely day it is, miss," she said, once she had set down the tray and opened the curtains. "This come for you earlier," she added, handing Phoebe a twist of paper. "Leastways, we think it was meant for you."

"What do you mean?" Phoebe asked, sitting up in bed and taking it.

"Some scruffy urchin brung it round to the kitchen. Said it was for the lady with the red hair."

"That must be me." Phoebe flattened it out, her heart lifting when she saw the few scrawled words.

Back safe. A.

She folded the paper up again, glancing at the clock. "Oh, I'm late for breakfast."

"The green gown, miss?" Ellie asked, taking it from the closet. Phoebe nodded, and Ellie helped her with the fastenings.

"Thank you, Ellie."

Phoebe opened the note once more—she was relieved that Alex

had returned, but why had he sent such a short note? She'd hoped to see him, to find out…

She shook her head and picked up her book, determined to put Alex out of her mind for now.

To her surprise, her uncle was still at the breakfast table.

"Good morning, Phoebe," he said. "You looked well in your gown when you all set off for the ball last night."

"Thank you, sir." She felt a warm glow of pleasure at his words.

"I'm sorry I could not accompany you. You enjoyed yourself?"

"Yes, indeed." She had been without a partner for only a few dances, and her companion for supper hadn't been too obviously obsessed with Hélène's attractions. Glancing down at the dark green sleeve of the round gown she wore in the house, she was still impressed at the added confidence her new appearance gave her. Enough to realise that at least a few of her partners last evening had chosen her for herself, not merely for being Hélène's cousin.

"I must thank you again, sir, for—"

"Family, Phoebe, as I said." The comte waved away her thanks, but she thought he looked pleased. He glanced at the book next to her plate, one brow rising. "Burke?"

"Yes, sir."

"What do you think of it?" he asked.

"I think I don't know enough about what happened to start the revolution," Phoebe admitted. "This book gives only his interpretation of things, and I doubt that he's an unbiased commentator."

"You would find it difficult to find anyone unbiased," the comte said. "I deeply regret the way things are going, but some change was inevitable."

"You sympathise with the revolutionaries?" Phoebe asked, surprised.

The comte's gaze become unfocused, and Phoebe wondered if she had offended him.

"No, not really—certainly not their methods of enforcing change," he said. He rubbed one temple. "There were many injustices that needed to be addressed, but I'm afraid I was not so sympathetic that I tried to do anything about it. I opted for a quiet life, and so moved you all here, out of the way. I am likely to lose Calvac, but I have sufficient investments in London to maintain us. "

"What happened?" Phoebe hesitated—that was a sweeping question, inviting a detailed answer. "I'm sorry," she added, "It isn't something that can be answered quickly. You—"

The comte held up a hand. "Are you seriously interested?"

"Yes, sir."

He poured himself another coffee and settled back in his chair. "To understand the revolution, you need to first know what life was like in France beforehand." He went on to describe how power was more concentrated in the monarchy in France than in England, and the way the tax system supported the aristocracy at the expense of the peasants and middle classes.

Phoebe glanced around the dining room as he talked, taking in the roaring fire, the polished wood and decorated china, the landscape painting above the fireplace. She smoothed her skirt, uneasily aware that the amount she'd just spent on clothing could have fed and housed a number of labouring families for some time.

"If you are still interested, Phoebe, we could meet after breakfast once or twice each week. When you have read that—" He indicated Burke's book. "—you may have more questions."

"Thank you, sir, I would like that."

He took a folded paper from his pocket and handed it to her. "On another matter, this invitation was delivered this morning. Do you know anything about it?"

Phoebe opened it—it was an invitation for the Calvac family, including Phoebe, to a dinner with the Earl of Marstone.

"You don't seem surprised," the comte said.

"Not entirely," she admitted. "His lordship sent me Burke's book and a couple of others after he came across me in a bookshop. There was a message in one of the books." Best not to mention the code. "I wondered if he was joking, so I wrote to say that I was sure that you would accept a formal invitation."

"It is most unusual," the comte said, taking the letter back and looking over it again. "I have heard of Marstone's dinners. They are for conversation—no cards or other entertainments. Political discussion, I gather."

It wasn't the kind of dinner her aunt or Hélène would appreciate. Phoebe wasn't sure she would enjoy it either—she knew little of politics as yet, but she *could* listen.

The comte stood and moved over to the mantelpiece, perusing the invitations propped up on it. "There is an invitation here for a ball on the fourth of March. Should you mind missing that?"

"No, sir. My aunt, though—"

"I would like to accept Marstone's invitation, but your aunt will not. However, I do not think Marstone will be offended if only you and I go. I will arrange it."

"Thank you, sir."

The day continued fine, with hazy sunshine and hardly a breath of wind. Phoebe was glad for an excuse to be out of doors again, even if it was only to play cricket with Georges. She asked Cookson to allow Green to bowl, while Phoebe and Ellie acted as fielders.

When Georges finally tired of batting, Ellie took a turn, providing much amusement for Georges and Green with her wild swings. Phoebe, having been roped into Joe's games when younger, decided to show them that not all women were hopeless with a cricket bat.

Her first swing connected with a satisfying smack, sending the ball into a clump of bushes, and she paid Georges back for his earlier laughter by making him crawl into the undergrowth to retrieve it. Her second ball went further, narrowly missing a gentleman entering the gardens.

Recognising the elegant clothing and bearing of the Marquess of Harlford, she hurriedly handed the bat to Ellie, straightened her gown, and tucked a few stray curls back into place. The marquess had invited Hélène to go driving this afternoon. What was he doing here?

"Miss Deane," Lord Harlford said with a bow. "I came to enquire whether you would like to attend a balloon ascension."

"That would be interesting, thank you my lord." She hoped she'd kept the surprise from her voice. She hadn't thought he even knew her name. "When is it?"

"A balloon?" Georges exclaimed. "Oh, that would be excellent!"

Lord Harlford glanced at Georges, then back to Phoebe, his face expressionless; he did not have the look of a man who wished for the pleasure of her company. "It is in an hour, Miss Deane," he said. "We would need to leave now."

Phoebe hesitated.

His lips compressed as he awaited her answer. "Your uncle suggested I ask you," he added.

Ah. He was supposed to be taking Hélène, but she must be once again trying to show her power by keeping him waiting. She felt a quick flash of anger and hurt, for who would want to be merely a last minute replacement? Georges shuffled his feet beside her, and her mood lightened.

She smiled sweetly. "Thank you. We would be pleased to accept!" She turned to Ellie and winked. "Please inform Monsieur le Comte that Georges and I have accepted Lord Harlford's kind invitation."

Ellie looked surprised, then she bobbed a quick curtsey and went off with a grin.

Lord Harlford stood as if turned to stone. Phoebe retrieved her pelisse from a nearby bench, then helped Georges to fasten his coat.

"I'm in my phaeton—"

"I don't take up much space, my lord. It will be a squash, but I'm sure Georges won't mind. It is so kind of you to offer." She bit her lip, trying not to betray her amusement at his dismay. It served him right.

"Come, Georges," she said, sweeping out of the gardens as Lord Harlford's tiger appeared with the phaeton. The poor man must be getting used to walking the horses while his master was waiting for Hélène.

His face still set, the marquess helped her up, then Georges, before climbing in himself and taking the reins. Georges, oblivious to the fact that the marquess had not actually invited him, pelted him with questions about the balloon they were going to see.

Phoebe, from her position at the other end of the seat, watched the conversation between the two with interest. Lord Harlford, stiff and cold at first, unbent a little as he explained the basics of ballooning to Georges, all the while guiding the phaeton with a skill that made it look easy. He almost appeared enthusiastic when Georges' questions turned to the matched greys. They were a magnificent pair, Phoebe thought, and was surprised to hear he'd bred them himself.

The park was crowded, a host of carriages already gathered around the roped-off area where the balloon was being readied. Lord Harlford must have reserved a space, for he pulled the phaeton up in a position with a good view of the balloon, and the tiger climbed down from his perch to take the horses' heads.

"There is time for some refreshment before the ascent," Lord Harlford announced. Phoebe felt an unexpected pang of sympathy for the man, having his plans disarranged by Hélène's deliberate tardiness.

Unusually, Georges wasn't impressed by the prospect of food. "Can we go right up to the balloon, Lord Harlford? Please?"

The marquess looked doubtfully at Phoebe over Georges' head. "Wouldn't you rather watch in comfort from here? The ground is rather muddy."

"It would be interesting to take a closer look, my lord," Phoebe said. "We should have time to do that, *and* to watch the ascent from here."

"If you wish, Miss Deane," he said, his eyebrows rising. He helped them down, then offered his arm to Phoebe as they pushed through the crowd. Coins discreetly changed hands, then one of the men keeping the spectators at a safe distance lifted the rope and allowed them through.

"Do they use hot air?" Phoebe asked, dredging from her memory the few things she had heard about balloons. There was no indication of a fire here, only a large, barrel-like object below the inflated balloon, and some pipes.

It was clearly Lord Harlford's day for surprises, Phoebe thought, noticing his expression.

"This balloon is filled with hydrogen, Miss Deane. Like hot air, it is lighter than the air around us, and so provides buoyancy to lift the balloon upwards."

"Where's the hygen come from?" Georges asked. Lord Harlford glanced at him, but addressed his answer to them both.

"Inside that barrel, there is a way of adding oil of vitriol to iron; the chemical combination generates the gas."

"Is that not dangerous?" Phoebe asked. "Oil of vitriol?"

"Indeed it is. The gas produced is very inflammable too—safety procedures must be followed strictly."

Not to mention the dangers of rising into the air, Phoebe thought.

"What's the balloon made from?" Georges wanted to know. Phoebe listened in snatches as the marquess answered the stream of questions.

"...varnished silk, so the gas does not leak out..."

To Phoebe, Lord Harlford looked as enthusiastic as her young cousin as he provided Georges with a detailed description of the balloon's construction.

"...where the wind takes it..."

She wondered if her sense of adventure would be up to a balloon voyage, should she ever have the chance.

"...let gas out of the top..."

The marquess' explanation was cut short by one of the aeronauts. "My lord, we are almost ready to ascend, if you would be so good as to leave us now."

"Can't we stay here?" Georges asked.

"I'm afraid not," Lord Harlford said. "These men need space to finish their preparations. Come, it is time to eat." He turned to the balloonist. "Thank you, sir, for allowing us to inspect your vessel."

The man touched his cap and went back to his preparations. Phoebe put her hand on Georges' shoulder to forestall any further protests, and followed closely as Lord Harlford pushed his way back to the phaeton.

The tiger had opened the basket of provisions and set out plates of sandwiches and small pastries on a tiny folding table. There was also a chilled bottle of champagne, and one of lemonade.

"I suggest you and young Georges sit in the phaeton, Miss Deane," Lord Harlford said. "I can eat standing up. Now, what can I get you? A little of everything?"

"Thank you, my lord." Phoebe helped Georges into the phaeton, and scrambled up herself while Lord Harlford filled their plates and handed them up. So far, the expedition had been far more enjoyable than she'd expected. Lord Harlford had coped with Georges' enthusiasm surprisingly well.

They ate in silence while the men bustled about the balloon, the high perch of Lord Harlford's phaeton giving them a clear view over the heads of the other spectators. Phoebe watched with interest as the two aeronauts finally climbed into the basket. Some of the ground anchors were released and the balloon abruptly rose a few feet, stopping with a bounce when the remaining rope pulled taut.

"It looks like a racehorse ready to start," she said to herself.

Lord Harlford looked at her. Phoebe wondered if she'd said something foolish, but he smiled. "Indeed," was all he said, returning his attention to the balloon as the last rope was released. He was quite attractive when he wasn't wearing one of his severe expressions.

The next moment she had to grab the back of Georges' jacket as the balloon rose into the sky. Without her restraint, he would have fallen out of the phaeton in his excitement. The cheers from the crowd rang in her ears as she turned her head to follow the balloon drift slowly westwards. What would it feel like to float above the earth, looking down on everything below?

Cold, she told herself firmly, as Georges began his questions— where would the balloon go, how long would it stay up, how could it be landed safely and could they follow it?

"I'm afraid not, Georges. I have another appointment shortly," Lord Harlford said smoothly. "It is time for me to take you home."

Georges took this refusal in good part. The tiger soon had the picnic things packed up and they set off back through the streets.

"I really do have an appointment," Lord Harlford said, as he handed Phoebe down in Berkeley Square. Georges was already inside and running up the stairs to tell Miss Bryant about his trip.

"Thank you for the excursion, my lord. It was very interesting."

"Thank *you* for your company, Miss Deane. I enjoyed it."

She wasn't sure if he meant the balloon ascension or her company. It would be nice if it were the latter—she had appreciated conversing about something other than the generalities she'd shared with her dancing partners.

"Do you go to the Carringtons' ball later this week?" he asked.

"I believe so, my lord."

"I shall see you there, then. Good day." He touched his hat, then remounted the phaeton and flicked the whip to start the horses.

Phoebe watched him go before entering the house. Cookson was holding the door, waiting for her. "Monsieur asks that you join him in the parlour, miss," he said.

Her aunt was no doubt angered by Phoebe's acceptance of Harlford's invitation. Squaring her shoulders, she entered the parlour.

The confrontation wasn't as bad as Phoebe had feared. The comte began by thanking Phoebe for accepting Lord Harlford's invitation. "If he had left any later, he would have missed the ascension altogether. I'm glad he took up my suggestion."

The comtesse's lips were turning down, and Hélène had a definite pout, but they said nothing. Phoebe suspected they had already had their say while she was out.

"It was kind of him to invite Georges along as well," Phoebe said. From the twinkle in his eye, she suspected her uncle already knew how Georges had become part of the expedition. "If you will excuse me, sir?"

The comte waved a hand, and Phoebe went up to her room. She would let Georges' enthusiasm wear itself out, then go and talk with Alice herself. Alice would be interested to learn about the balloon, and she suspected that her young cousin's explanations would be less than coherent.

Phoebe took the note from Alex from her pocket again and smoothed it out, wondering what he was doing now. Had he been in a hurry when he wrote it, or wary in case someone else read it? Why else had he not even mentioned if he had found Brevare's family?

She folded it in half, and put it in the pocket beneath her gown.

CHAPTER 32

$\mathcal{T}$he following afternoon, Phoebe was curled up in a chair in the back parlour, listening to the patter of rain on the window. She was reading Burke's book, and was almost finished. Her progress was slow, as she tried to understand the implications of what was written and made notes of questions for her uncle. The whole situation was far too complex for her to take in at once, but she hoped to make sense of it eventually.

The sound of knocking echoed up the stairs—a welcome distraction. Curious, she went to the door and, hearing a voice she recognised, she dropped her book and dashed out onto the landing and down the stairs. Cookson was taking the visitor's hat and heavy cloak.

"Joe!"

Phoebe ran towards him. He picked her up and swung her around, before hugging her close.

"Pleased to see me then, sister dear?" His grin was almost as wide as hers. "You are looking splendid!"

"Oh, Joe! We didn't expect you yet!" She searched his face in sudden anxiety. He was tanned, but there were shadows beneath his eyes. "You look tired—very tired—but you are well? What happened when your ship was wrecked?"

"No fevers here, Fee, but we've had a long journey up from Falmouth. I'll tell you about the ship some other time. I'm afraid I've come in all my dirt; we've only just arrived."

There was a tut from behind them. Phoebe turned to see her aunt watching from the bottom of the stairs.

"Joseph," the comtesse said, without any warmth in her voice. "I suppose you'll be expecting to stay here?"

"Pleased to see you as well, Aunt Lavinia," said Joe, sweeping a low bow.

Phoebe bit her lip—she was sure Joe was overdoing it on purpose.

The library door opened. "Of course you must stay here, Joseph," the comte said, approaching Joe and shaking his hand. "Welcome back. Are you here for long? You must be hungry, let me order—"

"No, sir, but thank you. I'm staying with a friend. I... er, he..."

"Join us for dinner, then," the comte suggested. "Bring your friend too."

"But Eduoard," the comtesse protested. "We are playing cards with the Brothertons this evening."

"I don't suppose Lady Brotherton will mind if Phoebe doesn't go," the comte said. "I was not intending to go in any case. You can make Phoebe's excuses."

Phoebe smiled. Dinner with Joe was a much more attractive proposition than the card party.

"Oh, very well," the comtesse said, and went back up the stairs.

"Thank you, sir," Joe said. "I'll be pleased to come. I left a trunk of clothes here last time I was in England. Could you get it sent over?"

"Give Cookson the address of your lodgings. I'll have someone look it out and send it over."

"Thank you, sir. Until this evening." He gave Phoebe another swift hug. "Sorry, Fee, but I've got a lot of things to sort out. I'll see you later."

Later would do, now she knew he was back and safe.

. . .

That evening Phoebe was descending the stairs as Joe and his friend arrived, and observed them unseen while they handed hats and coats to Green. Joe looked smart in his dark coat and breeches. His friend, too, was attired correctly for a dinner engagement, apart from having his right arm in a sling, a bandaged hand showing. Phoebe drew in a sharp breath as he turned and she saw a jagged, livid scar running from his right eye almost down to his chin. Poor man—but thank heavens Joe had not been hurt.

"Fee!" Joe called when he caught sight of her. "Fee, may I introduce Lieutenant Andrew Marlow? Marlow, my sister Phoebe."

Lieutenant Marlow bowed politely, his expression shuttered.

Phoebe smiled, keeping her gaze on his eyes and not on his scarred cheek. "I am pleased to meet you, Lieutenant," she said. "Won't you come into the parlour?"

The comte arrived as they took seats near the fire, and soon they were all settled with glasses of wine.

"We weren't expecting you back for months, Joe," Phoebe said. "Longer. Is it because of your ship being wrecked? Will you tell us about it?"

Phoebe's stomach knotted as Joe related a sad tale of incompetence on the part of his captain. Knowing that fighting at sea was dangerous was very different from hearing the details of her brother's narrow escape. Although the ship had been wrecked, no men had been lost and a court martial had exonerated Marlow and Joe, the second and third lieutenants, from any blame.

Dinner was served, and over food and wine the talk moved on to less gloomy tales of incidents at sea and on land. Lieutenant Marlow gradually relaxed and became more talkative, relating amusing anecdotes with a dry wit. It wasn't long before Phoebe didn't even notice the scar, or the clumsiness with which he cut up his meal with his bandaged hand.

As they talked, Phoebe wondered how harsh their life at sea was. It was not something Joe was ever likely to be honest about, having passed off all such enquiries in the past with some flippant comment. Whatever their discomforts, though, it was clear that both men were proud to be serving their country. She knew that Joe, at least, had wanted that career.

With their uncle present, and Lieutenant Marlow too, there was no opportunity for Joe and Phoebe to exchange more personal news, so as the party broke up Phoebe arranged for Joe to accompany her on a walk in the park the following morning.

"But not too early," he pleaded. "We're still both short of sleep after our travelling. There'll be plenty of time for you to tell me everything you've been doing."

Phoebe retired to her room and let Ellie help her undress. What would she say to Joe the following morning? The trip to France had been an adventure, as had the events surrounding the decoy note, but she wasn't sure how much of that she could tell her brother. That chapter of her life might well be over now anyway, and what else did her future have in store?

When Ellie had gone, she walked over to the closet and opened the door, gazing at the array of gowns hanging there—all new. That was her lot, she thought, looking at them with less of the pleasure their colours and fabrics had given her before. These were designed to make her sufficiently attractive to snare a husband. That was her purpose in life.

Joe had little more than the small trunk of clothing her uncle had sent over to his rooms earlier that day. But he had the satisfaction of doing a useful job for his country. And unlike Alex, Joe and Lieutenant Marlow were acknowledged to be doing so.

Until now, she'd never really questioned her mother's willingness to forgo her aristocratic upbringing to become a surgeon's wife, accepting that it was the way things were. Perhaps she was beginning to understand. Although not rich by many people's standards, her family had been comfortably off. More importantly, to Phoebe's dawning realisation, her mother had spent her life helping others. Being useful.

Closing the closet door firmly, she got into bed and pulled the covers up to her chin. She was happy that Joe was home, and safe for the moment. There was nothing she could do to change society's expectations for women of her class, so she had better make sure she chose a husband who could give her the opportunity to do something useful.

Alex would…

Joe was already in the library when Phoebe went downstairs ready for their walk. Georges and her uncle were there, too, Georges pestering Joe with questions about ships, how they worked, and whether Joe could take him to see one.

"I'm afraid I'm not in charge of anything," Joe said. He looked at the comte for help.

"I might be able to arrange something," said the comte. "But Georges, you must give Joseph time to talk to his sister! And—"

"—pay attention to Miss Bryant," Georges finished for him as Joe and Phoebe took their leave.

They set out down Berkeley Street to Green Park, Phoebe's hand on Joe's arm, and were soon strolling on the grass. She related the bare details of their trip to France, and after he'd exclaimed at their aunt's stupidity, she told him about the comtesse's subterfuge with her allowance.

"She really spent it all on herself?" Joe asked, turning to face her.

"And Hélène."

Joe shook his head. "It's all sorted out now, is it? I have to say you're looking really well, Fee. Not what I expected from your letters, at all."

"It wasn't what I expected either," she said. So much had changed since their escape from France.

"Are you enjoying yourself?"

"Mostly." She caught a turn of his head, his raised brows. "I enjoy dancing, but it has the attraction of novelty. I can't imagine doing the same thing year after year."

"God, no," Joe said, with feeling.

"I'm learning to drive," she added, with more enthusiasm.

"You used to drive the gig at home, didn't you?"

"Sometimes, yes," she said.

"I'm driving a pair, now," she went on. "But I'd like to learn to drive four as well. Could you take me driving?"

"I haven't got any horses, Fee," he protested.

"You could hire them? Or Uncle Edouard might lend some?"

He hesitated again. "Well…"

"Can *you* drive a pair?" Phoebe asked.

He laughed and shook his head. "There's not much call for driving at sea," he pointed out. "And where would I have learnt before I signed on? I was only thirteen, remember?"

"I never thought of that," Phoebe admitted. "Never mind, I'll have to ask someone else."

"Why do you want to? Most women don't drive, do they?"

That was a poor reason *not* to do something. "I enjoy being able to control the horses," she said slowly, thinking it through as she spoke. All that power, hers to command, if she knew how to do it properly. "I'd like to be able to do it well—to be competent at something." There was satisfaction in being able to do anything well.

"You can draw—"

"Something *useful*," she interrupted. Was that so wrong?

Guessing Joe's reaction, she asked her next question anyway. "How about shooting, then? You must be able to fire a pistol in the navy."

"Yes, of course, but—"

"Can you teach me?"

"Why on earth would you want to? Ladies have no need to do things like that."

"Ladies don't need to learn how to swim, either. And if they did, there are better ways of learning than being thrown in the pond by their brother!"

Joe had the grace to look ashamed. "I was a lot younger then." He looked down at her. "You are serious?"

"Yes."

"Why?"

The confidence gained from knowing how to shoot might have helped her in France, even though she hadn't needed to fire a pistol in

273

the end. Although there was little reason to suppose she would need to use one in the future, she still wanted to know that she could.

"I like learning how to do things," she said, not wanting to describe those events to Joe. "Don't you?"

"Yes, but I've no desire to learn how to embroider. That's women's work—pistols are not."

Phoebe sighed, trying to put out of her mind the idea that Alex would not have said such a thing.

"I wanted to ask you something," Joe went on. "Marlow's mama is pressing him to find a wife. She insists he attends balls and other events while he's on leave. Personally, I'd tell her to go to the devil, but he's…"

"A dutiful son?" Phoebe suggested.

"Would you dance with him if he asked you?"

"Yes, why ever shouldn't I?"

"His face is—"

"Don't be silly. He can't help that! Besides, I stopped noticing last night."

"She's got him an invitation to the Carringtons' ball tomorrow."

"We're going to that. So I'll see you there?"

He started to shake his head, but she caught his eye and he gave a rueful grin. "It looks as though I may be attending after all."

Alex glanced at a milestone as the hired post chaise ahead of him rounded a bend. It would be another few hours to Andover, where they would stop for the night. Madame de Brevare would have to put up with a maid from whichever inn received the dubious privilege of their custom, although he hoped she would be too tired to protest much by the time they arrived.

His mind turned to Phoebe, as it had for most of the journey. When he'd visited Bella the day before, he'd been pleased to find that she had taken Phoebe under her wing. She'd talked of Phoebe's new wardrobe, and her enjoyment of her season so far. He was pleased for Phoebe—her success was more than she'd been expecting.

Marstone had made a comment about marriage. He'd thought about that, of course, but his longing for her was not just wanting her in his bed, but having her with him, working with him as a partner. He could see now how impractical that was; he was tiring of the life himself—he could not inflict it on someone else, even if she were willing.

What else could he do, though? Marstone would still have *some* use for him—preferably something more interesting than returning to work at Pendrick's. It would undoubtedly involve travelling, too, even if only as a courier. That wasn't a good life for a wife either, whoever she might be: sitting at home waiting for a long-absent husband who might possibly not return.

He was making too much of that final kiss, he told himself. In all his imagining, he'd assumed that she would want to be with him. It had been a dangerous evening, and she must have been terrified inside that tavern. The kiss was a fairly natural result of being so close for several days. She'd not said anything other than wishing him safe, and *he* had made no promises to her. He had no reason to think she would want to see him again.

On that depressing thought he spurred the horse on, overtaking the chaise to have a word with the postilions.

CHAPTER 33

*P*hoebe stood behind her aunt and cousin in the queue for the receiving line in Carrington House, looking around for any familiar faces. Peering back down the line of guests, she could see no sign of Joe. However, they had arrived on time, for once, and she doubted he'd be an early arrival.

"Do you think Lord Harlford will be here tonight, Mama?" Hélène said. Her manner towards Phoebe had been distinctly cool since the balloon ascension.

"I do hope so, my dear," the comtesse said. "You have saved dances for him, haven't you? It would be a feather in your cap if you can attach him."

Lord Harlford had said to Phoebe that he'd be here. She was beginning to wish she'd told Hélène, to stop this endless speculation.

"Oh, yes, the supper dance and one afterwards." Hélène turned to peer at the waiting crowd. "He must have been away, Mama, or he would have called on me before now." Of course, Hélène would not attribute his absence to a dislike of being kept waiting.

"If he is not here tonight, I'm sure he will call on you as soon as he returns. You must make sure not to accept too many invitations from your other suitors."

"Yes, Mama."

Thankfully they had now reached their hosts and, once greetings had been exchanged with Lord and Lady Carrington, Phoebe was free to move away.

"Our dance, I believe, Miss Deane?" Lord Tresham stood before her—one of Hélène's court, but willing enough to dance with Phoebe when his goddess was not available. Exchanging the usual pleasantries with him was undemanding, and at the end of the set, he thanked her with sincerity and escorted her to a seat by the wall. She found herself beside Lady Jesson.

"My lady," Phoebe said, warily recalling Bella's description of her as a gossip.

"Miss Deane." Lady Jesson inspected her gown, then smiled. "Miss Fletcher has done you proud again, I see. That pale gold suits you well."

Relaxing, Phoebe returned the smile, smoothing her skirt.

"Your cousin has found her target," Lady Jesson said, nodding towards the steps down from the entrance to the ballroom, where the Marquess of Harlford stood talking to Hélène. His countenance had lost the besotted look she'd noticed during his first encounters with her cousin.

"Silly girl," Lady Jesson said. "That game of keeping her suitors waiting—bound to go wrong. I wonder if it was her idea or Lavinia's."

Phoebe felt her jaw slackening—how did Lady Jesson know about that? She heard a chuckle.

"That *is* why you and your younger cousin accompanied him to see the balloon, is it not?" Lady Jesson wore an innocently enquiring expression, but Phoebe was not deceived.

"I think you already know that, my lady," she said, trying not to smile too broadly.

Lady Jesson chuckled, her eyes on the latest new arrivals. "Hmm. I think Lady Brotherton could use Miss Fletcher's advice, don't you? Although she dresses her daughters well."

The Brothertons moved on into the ballroom, Lady Brotherton frowning as she passed the marquess. Lady Jesson kept Phoebe entertained with snippets of gossip, but although some of the comments were poking gentle fun at their targets, they felt good-natured.

"Your brother has arrived," Lady Jesson said as the next set was nearing its end. She waved a hand. "Do go and dance with him before he escapes to the card room."

Phoebe was half-way across the floor before it occurred to her to wonder how Lady Jesson knew who Joe was, and that he would avoid dancing if he could.

She enjoyed her sets with Joe, then with Lieutenant Marlow. She danced until supper, when Marlow and Joe escorted her to the dining room and went to fetch plates of food.

While they were gone, Lord Harlford appeared with Hélène on his arm, and asked if he might join their table. As Phoebe agreed, Hélène's tightened lips indicated that it had not been her idea. She made the introductions when the men returned.

Unfortunately, Hélène appeared to be one of the people who could see Lieutenant Marlow only as a scar and not as a person. Phoebe was annoyed on Marlow's behalf when Hélène did not look at him directly, even on the few occasions when she replied to something he said. After a couple of short responses, Marlow gave up.

"I have an interest in gunnery," Lord Harlford said into the resulting awkward silence. "However, I have talked mainly to artillery officers. What do you see as the main differences between operations?"

"Rolling decks," Joe said, with a laugh. "The ground doesn't normally move as you are trying to aim!"

Hélène looked from Lord Harlford to Joe as the men talked, a crease gradually forming between her brows.

"...spent as much time on the gun deck as I have, Deane, you wouldn't say..."

Phoebe listened with interest, gleaning more of Joe's experiences at sea from the discussion than she ever would have done if she'd asked him herself.

"...chain shot to destroy rigging and spars..."

"These pastries are delicious," Hélène said, cutting across Joe's description of a stern chase. "Would you bring me some more?" She fluttered her lashes at Lord Harlford.

"Allow me, Lady Hélène," Marlow said, and went off to fetch them.

"I'm sorry, Lady Hélène," Lord Harlford said. "I thought you would be interested in your cousin's stories."

Hélène quickly changed her pout into a smile. "I...of course I am, my lord. Do carry on, please, Cousin Joseph."

"I think the music is about to start again," Phoebe put in. She knew why Hélène was annoyed and was irritated by her shallowness, but it wouldn't do for her to say something rude in front of her cousin's most important suitor.

"If you wish for more information, my lord, a message to Berkeley Square will reach me," Joe said.

Lord Harlford thanked him and turned to Phoebe. "Are you free for the next dance, Miss Deane?"

She should not have been surprised, for he had asked if she would be attending.

Hélène spoke before Phoebe could reply. "*I* was saving that dance for you, my lord!"

He looked down at her, his face expressionless. "I do not recall asking you."

"I know, but you always have two dances with me," Hélène said coyly. "Any more would be improper."

"True," he said, his voice cool. "However, I prefer to arrange my own partners."

"But I will have no-one to dance with!" Hélène's pout just avoided the appearance of a sulk.

"A novel experience," Joe muttered under his breath. Phoebe jabbed her elbow at him.

"I would be honoured to dance with you, Lady Hélène," Lieutenant Marlow said.

"Thank you," Hélène said, but turned to Joe with a smile. "But I should dance with my cousin," she said. "It's such an age since I've seen you, Joseph!"

"Don't play your games with me, Hélène," said Joe. "Come, Marlow, you said you only wanted to stay until supper."

Phoebe glanced at Marlow, wondering if Hélène had hurt his feelings, and was relieved to see what looked like a rueful smile and not the set expression he had worn at the beginning of the evening. They made their bows, leaving Phoebe with Hélène and Lord Harlford.

Harlford returned his attention to Phoebe, his expression holding a hint of a smile. "Miss Deane?"

"I am not engaged for the next, my lord."

"Then may I have the pleasure?"

"Yes, thank you."

The marquess was a good dancer, but Phoebe felt awkward. His conversation was stilted, and limited to the usual comments about the weather, and she found none of the shared enjoyment of the activity shown by most of her other partners. Was he dancing with her only to punish Hélène?

After contributing a few remarks herself about the ballroom, she fell silent. His face displayed polite boredom; unsure whether the cause was her talk or her silence, she concentrated her gaze on the ruby pin in his neckcloth. He had talked readily enough when they had been watching the balloon, but that was mostly about technicalities. Even the vapid comments made by some of her other partners were better than this uncomfortable silence. She thought, with a pang, of the easy way she and Alex had conversed, and wished he were here.

"Did you enjoy the balloon ascension, my lord?" she asked eventually, determined not to dance in silence any longer. "I have never seen one before, and found it most interesting."

He looked at her rather searchingly, and then finally smiled.

"I should apologise for foisting my young cousin on you," Phoebe added.

"On the contrary," he replied. "It is encouraging to witness such enthusiasm."

"It can be rather wearing," said Phoebe ruefully, winning another, slightly wider smile. This time it reached his eyes, making him look much friendlier. The rest of the set passed in companionable discussion of various sights worth seeing in London, then he led her to a chair.

"Would you care to drive in the park with me, Miss Deane?"

"That would depend, my lord," said Phoebe. He looked surprised, and rather taken aback. She guessed he was not used to receiving anything but a grateful acceptance.

"On what, may I ask?" He did at least sound polite.

"On whether you truly wish to take me for a drive, or if you are still annoyed with my cousin, as you were when you invited me to view the balloon ascension."

His eyes slid away from hers.

"I don't hold that against you," Phoebe went on. "I think bringing Georges along was sufficient revenge."

"Touché, Miss Deane," he said, a smile giving an attractive curve to his lips. "I would enjoy your company on a drive, if you are willing."

"In that case, yes, thank you."

"Tomorrow? Around four o'clock?"

She agreed, and he bowed and took his leave. She was surprised to see that he left the ballroom soon afterwards, not going back to rejoin Hélène's crowd of admirers.

When they arrived home, the comte emerged from the library and asked them all to join him in the parlour.

"How did you enjoy the ball, Phoebe?" he asked.

"Very well, sir. I danced most of the dances, with some pleasant gentlemen. It was—"

"She made Harlford dance with her after supper," Hélène interrupted.

"Really?" asked the comte. "How did she make him do that?"

Phoebe watched with scarcely concealed amusement as Hélène's mouth opened but no words came out. She closed it again, her lower lip sticking out.

"Phoebe puts herself forward far too much for one of her rank, Edouard," the comtesse said. "I have always said so."

"So you asked Lord Harlford for a dance?" the comte asked Phoebe, ignoring his wife.

"No, sir. He asked to join us for supper—he wanted to talk to Joe and Lieutenant Marlow about gunnery. Then he requested the next dance." She kept her eyes on her uncle, sensing her aunt's glare. It would be better to break the worse news to the comtesse and Hélène while her uncle was there. "He also asked me to go driving with him tomorrow afternoon."

"Interesting," the comte said, looking towards his wife. "Perhaps some men value punctuality. Now, I'm sure Phoebe can be excused any calls you may have had in mind for tomorrow afternoon."

The comtesse nodded reluctantly, and Phoebe suppressed a sigh of relief. As she mounted the stairs to her bedroom, she wondered whether driving with Lord Harlford would be worth the resulting resentment from her aunt and cousin.

CHAPTER 34

$\mathcal{A}$lex slowed his horse to a walk as he rode up the drive at Ashton Tracey. The setting sun cast long shadows across the gravel and glinted off the windows on the house. He dismounted by the steps and knocked on the door as the post-chaise approached behind him.

"Mr Westbrook." The butler greeted him with a sedate bow. "We were not expecting you, sir."

"Mackenzie." Alex smiled. "Lord Marstone has a sudden need to provide hospitality for the Vicomtesse de Brevare and her daughter. They will be staying for an indeterminate time."

"Very good, sir. If you will excuse me."

Mackenzie didn't wait for Alex's acknowledgement, but turned and summoned a footman, who dashed up the staircase. Going to find Lady Marstone, no doubt.

Alex went back outside as the carriage pulled up, opening the door and lowering the step before handing the vicomtesse down. Overdone politeness to the woman now might ease the burden on the staff who would have to look after her.

The vicomtesse stood on the gravel, her gaze running over the building before her. Ashton Tracey was one of Marstone's smaller estates, but he and his wife seemed to prefer it above their other properties.

Mackenzie returned, and ushered the vicomtesse into the house with a low bow. Alex helped the daughter down, then offered his arm. Inside, the vicomtesse surveyed the marble tiles and polished oak staircase, the thick velvet curtains framing the windows, and the crystal chandelier above, all with a faint air of superiority.

Lady Marstone descended the stairs. Alex watched in admiration as she appeared to sum up the vicomtesse instantly, giving a low curtsey even though her own rank was higher than that of her guest.

"My lady, welcome to my home. You must be exhausted after your journey. Let me escort you to your room myself, so I may ensure all is in order. You can rest and change."

That was a mistake, Alex thought, shaking his head at Lady Marstone over the vicomtesse's shoulder. One of the woman's complaints had been that Alex had not brought any of her clothing out of Paris with them.

Lady Marstone's glance flicked to him then to the hall behind him, where any luggage would have been placed. "I'm sure we can find something to fit until we can summon a seamstress to look after your needs," she said, with barely a moment's hesitation. "Won't you come with me?"

The vicomtesse followed Lady Marstone upstairs without a backward glance at her daughter. Alex felt the girl's hand tighten on his arm, and looked down. Suzanne de Brevare's face was pale and drawn, but she held herself straight with her shoulders back.

"Mrs Hunt will show mademoiselle to her room, sir," Mackenzie said. "And provide refreshment."

About to hand Suzanne over to the housekeeper, Alex paused as he felt a small tug on his arm.

"Please, monsieur, may I walk outside for a little time? I would like to speak with you."

"If you wish, mademoiselle." He glanced at the butler. "Please ask for refreshments in twenty minutes. I'll be staying overnight, too."

"Very good, sir."

Alex led the girl back out of the front door and into the formal garden beside the house, which was still catching the last of the afternoon sun. Why did she wish to talk to him now? He had hardly spoken to her during the journey. At first he'd been driving, and then on the *Lily* she'd never been apart from her mother, who did not deign to talk to the help.

"I have to thank you, monsieur, for rescuing us," Suzanne said, in a quiet voice. "I do not think my mother will do so."

"You are welcome, mademoiselle."

"However, I understand we are still prisoners, in some degree?"

"Not exactly prisoners." But with no money of their own, where could they go? "What did his lordship say to you?"

He should have asked Marstone himself, but the earl had not been in when he returned from seeing Bella, and they had set off early the next morning.

"He asked me about my brother, and when we last saw him." She stopped walking, and took her hand from his arm.

Alex turned to face her. "When *did* you last see him?"

She stared into his face, then raised her shoulders in a shrug. "Many months ago, after he had to sell our other estates." Turning, she started walking again, speaking as if she was reciting words already said once. "He is not good with money, but he means well. We could have managed, except for the trouble in France. Two months ago, some men came with guns, and made us go to Paris with them. We have been there ever since, and we have not heard from Hugo."

"That is what you told Lord Marstone?"

She nodded. "Is Hugo all right?"

"Did Marstone tell you anything else?" Alex asked.

"He said Hugo was safe, that's all." She bit her lip, and he saw the glint of tears in her eyes.

"He was safe three weeks ago," Alex said. "That is all I know, mademoiselle."

"Why is Lord Marstone interested in my brother?"

Alex could hear a tremble in her voice now. He walked on,

wondering how much to tell her, if anything. It would not reassure her to know that Brevare was suspected of treasonous activities.

Glancing down, he could see some resemblance to Phoebe's cousin—a similarly shaped face, and both girls had golden hair. When Suzanne was rested and happier, she *would* remind someone of Hélène. Or, rather, Hélène would remind an anxious brother of Suzanne. Phoebe's supposition had been correct—naturally, he thought with a wry smile. The two mothers were similar in some ways, too, although the comtesse did seem to have some affection for her daughter—he'd seen little of that from the Vicomtesse de Brevare.

This Suzanne, though, was more resilient than she looked, certainly more so than Hélène. She had uttered no word of complaint about the hurried journey or rough crossing.

The truth, he decided.

"Marstone, and I, suspect that Brevare is being blackmailed with the threat of harm to you and your mother."

The girl nodded, as though this was not a new idea.

"I wondered if it was something like that," she said. "What has he done? Is he now a criminal here?"

He heard the wobble in her voice again.

"Not yet." Although if Brevare did anything to endanger Phoebe he'd not only be a criminal but would certainly come to harm at Alex's hands.

"That is why you rescued us."

"Yes. That is also why Marstone wishes you to stay here. He hopes to find out who is doing this to your brother."

Suzanne nodded again. "I do not like our situation, but it would be worse without your actions." She bit her lip again. "Monsieur, it would not be wise to repeat this to my mother."

"Very well." The sun had dipped below the horizon and the early spring chill was sharp. "Shall we go back in now?"

Inside, the housekeeper took Suzanne upstairs and Alex retired to Marstone's library to sample his brandy. He'd rest tonight, then set off back to London in the morning. He contemplated using the mail coach from Exeter, but decided to ride. He didn't want to be cooped up with strangers for so long.

Then he'd have to decide whether he should call on Phoebe.

Phoebe awaited the marquess in the library the next afternoon, standing at the window to look out over the square for his arrival. She'd finished Burke's book and was part way through Paine's *Rights of Man*, currently lying open but disregarded on the table.

Watching Lord Harlford draw up in his phaeton, at four o'clock precisely, she wondered what he would think of Paine's proposal to eliminate hereditary titles. She wasn't sure she should broach that topic though, not to a marquess.

Lord Harlford was shown into the library, still wearing his many-caped driving coat.

"Would you like some refreshment first, my lord?" she asked as he made his bow.

"If you are ready, Miss Deane, leaving now would be preferable."

"Certainly."

Phoebe was again impressed at the skilful way Lord Harlford manoeuvred his phaeton around carts, coaches, and other less expertly driven leisure vehicles. The greys seemed fresher than on the day of the balloon ascension, or perhaps the marquess was driving faster now because he didn't have a small boy pestering him with questions. She watched his hands, noting the way they hardly seemed to move on the reins.

"Are you quite well, Miss Deane?" the marquess asked, after some minutes of silence.

"Yes, thank you my lord." She'd been preoccupied, but had also thought that he would initiate any conversation they were to have.

"You seem rather quiet."

He did look concerned. She bit her lip as it occurred to her that he was used to Hélène's chatter.

"I did not wish to distract you on the busy roads," she explained. "And I was admiring your horses. They seem to respond to the tiniest movements of your hands."

"They are a good pair," he replied. "Soft-mouthed. Fast, too, although there is not much opportunity to demonstrate that in Town."

"Does being soft-mouthed make them easier to drive?" Phoebe asked, remembering aching arms after driving with Captain Synton in the park.

"That depends on the horses. If a soft or hard mouth were the only difference, then yes, you would not have to pull on the reins as hard. But it also depends on their temperaments. Why do you ask?"

"I have been practising driving a pair, and find my arms and hands get tired quite quickly. I was wondering if that pair have harder mouths."

Lord Harlford regarded her, wariness in his expression. Phoebe wondered if she had said something wrong.

"Was that a hint, Miss Deane?"

"A hint, my lord?"

"That you wish to drive my greys."

"No. Well, I mean, yes…"

She would love to, but from the way he had spoken of them she didn't think he would be happy with someone so inexperienced handling the reins. "I would love to try driving them, but if I were you I wouldn't want me to drive them." That had been somewhat incoherent. "If you see what I mean?"

"I think so." He sounded friendlier this time. "Have you been driving your uncle's carriage?"

"He doesn't have a carriage at the moment," Phoebe said. "I believe he is going to purchase one, but it will be a coach rather than a phaeton. Not really the kind of thing to take for a drive in the park."

"What have you been driving?"

"Captain Synton is a cousin of Lord Carterton. He took me in his lordship's phaeton and pair."

"Carterton's blacks?"

"Yes."

"They must be a bit of a handful for you." He said nothing further while he negotiated the carriages almost blocking the entrance to the park. "I wish people would go *into* the park instead of greeting each other at the gate!" he muttered irritably as he finally got through the crowd.

They drove on into the park, their progress slow as riders and people in other carriages stopped to greet the marquess. Some attempted to start conversations about the weather or the latest *on-dits*, but the marquess didn't have much to say in return, and each encounter lasted only a short time. Glancing at his face as he urged his pair on again, Phoebe wondered if he was as bored with the common-place remarks as she was.

Driving on, they came eventually to the location of the balloon ascension, now just a muddy area where the gas-generating machine had stood. Recalling the way the balloon had disappeared into the distance, Phoebe asked the marquess how far such a balloon could travel.

"It depends on the wind, Miss Deane, and on how quickly the gas leaks through the fabric of the balloon."

That wasn't a very informative answer. "Could they cross the Channel?" she persisted. "I was wondering if the French could use balloons to spy on our ports, for example."

"The wind would have to be..." His voice trailed off as the phaeton slowed to a halt.

She must have said something foolish, although she didn't know what. Perhaps he considered such a discussion unsuitable for a woman—he hadn't minded discussing such things at the ascension, but Georges had been with her then.

"My lord?" she said, putting her chin up. It would be polite to apol-ogise, even if she didn't really mean it. "I'm sorry if I—"

"No, no, Miss Deane." He met her eyes, a wry smile twisting his mouth. "I should apologise for becoming distracted."

"It was probably a silly idea." She looked at her gloved hands, folded in her lap.

"No, indeed. I believe balloons could be useful to the army as well, to locate enemy positions, for example. But there are difficulties."

"The wind direction?" she asked, interested to learn more.

"Yes. There is also manufacture of the oil of vitriol, some of the materials—"

Breaking off, he shook his head as he flicked his whip above the horses' heads, setting the phaeton into motion again. "I'm sorry, I must be boring you."

"Not at all. The oil of vitriol is for making the hydrogen, is it not? Is it difficult to manufacture?"

"I was thinking that some of the materials needed for making it are also needed in the manufacture of gunpowder," he said, guiding the phaeton back out through the park gates.

Phoebe digested this information. "I had not considered the complexities of such things," she admitted at last. "I suppose an efficient supply of materials is as important in warfare as ships and men."

"Efficient is often the last word to describe it," he muttered, turning off Piccadilly onto Berkeley Street.

Intrigued, Phoebe wondered if he was involved in government in some way. She hadn't come across his name in the newspapers, but there must be many men working behind the scenes.

"I've enjoyed our drive, Miss Deane," he said as he pulled up outside the house. "Would you care to drive again? I am free the day after tomorrow. If you wish, I could find a nice quiet pair, suitable for a lady. We could go in the morning, when the park is empty."

Phoebe wasn't too sure about the 'nice, quiet pair', but perhaps quieter horses would allow her to concentrate on her technique. He *had* taken her wish to drive more seriously than Joe had.

"Thank you, my lord, I would enjoy that."

"The day after tomorrow, then?" he said, helping her down and bowing over her hand.

Phoebe stood in the doorway, looking after him with mixed feelings. She'd enjoyed watching his expert driving, and their conversation had been interesting once they were no longer attempting the usual social pleasantries, but she did not feel totally at ease with him.

She still wondered if he was trying to teach Hélène a lesson, in spite of what he'd said at the ball. A man of his station wouldn't be seriously courting someone like her, with no title and no dowry. It didn't really matter—she'd enjoyed the drive, and would enjoy his company again.

CHAPTER 35

*P*hoebe sipped her wine as she looked around the parlour at Marstone House. This room was decorated in a very different fashion from the dark wood and rich colours of the library, which was the only other room she'd seen here. Pale green walls and delicately patterned curtains gave it a light feel, and the paintings depicted countryside scenes and seascapes.

Her gaze passed over the other guests, as she tried to recall everyone's name. She was by far the youngest person present, with Bella a close second. Why had Lord Marstone invited her? If he wanted to talk to the comte, an invitation to her aunt and uncle would have sufficed.

Listening to snippets of the conversations going on around her, she felt ill-qualified to join any of them. The talk was all of Fox's continuing disagreements with other Whigs, or the expectation of some regions of France rising up against the revolutionary government.

There were uneven numbers of ladies and gentlemen, and Phoebe supposed there must be more guests yet to arrive. However, the butler entered the room to announce that dinner was served, and the earl approached with the only two people she had not been introduced to.

"Fenton, may I present Miss Phoebe Deane. Miss Deane, Admiral Lord Fenton." The admiral was older than Lord Marstone, with iron-grey hair and a weather-beaten face. Lord Hilvern, the remaining guest, was portly, with a florid complexion and developing jowls.

"These dinners are rather informal, Miss Deane, as you may have gathered," Marstone continued. "We do not stand on ceremony. Fenton, if you would escort Miss Deane?"

The admiral offered his arm, and the whole party made their way into the dining room across the hall. Phoebe was seated between the admiral and Lord Hilvern. Bella sat beyond Hilvern, at the foot of the table. The comte was almost opposite, and gave Phoebe an encouraging smile as he sat down.

The meal was good, but not outstanding; many of the guests appeared to be giving more attention to their conversations than their dinners. Phoebe sat without talking for a while, concentrating on controlling her nerves and watching the other diners. Then Bella brought her conversation with Lord Hilvern to a close. As Lord Hilvern turned ponderously towards Phoebe, Bella caught her eye with a quick grimace before giving her attention to the comte on her other side.

"Well, and what brings you here, Miss... er..." Hilvern looked down his nose at her—quite a feat, Phoebe thought, as he wasn't much taller than she was.

"Deane, my lord."

"I haven't seen you before." He spoke as if that were her fault.

"I have only just come into society."

"Hmm. Niece to Calvac, eh? Who's your father?"

"I doubt you will have heard of him." Really, this felt like an interrogation rather than a conversation.

"You seem young for one of Marstone's guests." Hilvern took another mouthful of roast pigeon.

"Time will cure that, my lord," she assured him. She wondered if she had been too impolite, but a soft snort from the end of the table reassured her. Bella was listening—the thought gave her a small glow of confidence.

"Miss Deane," the admiral addressed her, and she turned to her left. "We have not met before tonight, but the name seems familiar."

"My brother is a lieutenant in the navy, my lord," Phoebe said. The admiral seemed both friendlier and more polite than Lord Hilvern. "You may have seen his name on some list?"

"It seems I have come across it recently."

With a slight sinking of her heart, Phoebe wondered if the loss of Joe's ship had come to his notice. "He was serving on the *Galene*, sir, and returned to England a few days ago."

"Ah, yes. Unfortunate affair that." A fleeting look of disapproval crossed his face.

"My brother was absolved of any blame," Phoebe added.

"Quite so, quite so." He gestured to a footman who came to refill their glasses; more servants entered to clear the dishes and bring in the next course.

"You do not seem convinced, my lord," she said.

"I do not recall the details, Miss Deane. I will, of course, be guided by the findings of the men who conducted the court martial."

"Come, Miss Deane," Lord Hilvern spoke from her other side. "You should leave these matters to those in charge. They need not concern you. *Sutor, ne ultra crepidam*, and all that, you know?"

"I beg your pardon, my lord? I'm afraid I have never learnt Latin."

"Naturally not," Lord Hilvern said, looking down his nose again. "Females are unsuited to it, addles their brains."

Phoebe took a deep breath and let it out slowly, wondering if she should just swallow the insult. Beyond Hilvern, Bella gave her a smile and a nod.

"That must have made life very difficult for the Romans," Phoebe said.

"What...?" Hilvern frowned.

"The Romans spoke Latin, did they not?" She widened her eyes a little. "How did the men speak to their wives?"

"What? Of course their wives spoke Latin!"

"But you said that females were unsuited to it, my lord?" Phoebe raised her eyebrows and fluttered her eyelashes as Hélène often did, hoping she wasn't overdoing it.

"Well, it must be different if they are taught from childhood. Obviously."

"Oh, I see." She narrowed her eyes, as if thinking. "So the Romans brought their own female servants with them when they first came here?"

Hilvern stared at her for several long moments, then turned to his plate without speaking.

Phoebe's lips twitched and she picked up her glass. Before she could drink, Bella leaned forward.

"Why would they need to bring their servants with them, Phoebe?" she asked, a definite laugh in her eyes.

"If females can only learn Latin when they are children, they would not be able to get any British female servants to learn their language," Phoebe said. "They would have to train up new servants from childhood."

"That's a good point, Hilvern," the admiral chipped in from her other side. Phoebe glanced around, uneasily aware that the rest of the guests were now listening to this exchange.

"That's a part of history they never taught me." The admiral shook his head in wonderment. "Amazing the details they omit."

Hilvern's jaw dropped, before he closed it with a snap, his jowls wobbling. "Nonsense!" he said. "You're letting the chit make fun of you, Fenton."

"Oh, I think I know who is looking the butt of this joke, Hilvern," the admiral said. "I know many women who speak other languages."

"Yes, well, they speak French—that's a different matter completely. The female brain is not suited to the classical languages."

"Lord Hilvern, are you suggesting that *no* females can learn Latin?" Bella said.

"Not suited to it, as I said." Lord Hilvern's face was becoming flushed, and he pulled out a handkerchief and mopped his brow.

"That's odd. I'm sure Lady Mary—"

"Oh, leave him alone to lick his wounds, Bella," Lord Marstone said from the far end of the table, a wicked gleam in his eye. He turned back to his neighbour. "Now, Tresham, I doubt this repulsion of the French attempt to take Sardinia is as significant as you—"

"How did you find attitudes in the countryside during your trip to France, Miss Deane?"

Phoebe turned to the admiral with relief as Hilvern glared at his plate. "It was difficult to tell, my lord. We avoided contact with others as far as possible."

"Of course—very wise."

"Fenton, could I ask you a favour?" Her uncle spoke across the table—by now Phoebe wasn't surprised that no-one took any notice of what was usually a social solecism.

"My son is ten years old, and at an age when he wishes to know about everything," the comte went on. "His latest desire is to see a warship. No doubt he would wish for a ship of the line, but a frigate would do. Is there any possibility of something of that nature?"

"I'm sure there must be something suitable at Greenwich," the admiral said. "Failing that, at Deptford or near Woolwich. I'll see what I can arrange."

"My thanks, Fenton," the comte said.

"Best not mention the arsenal to him, if he goes to Woolwich," Phoebe warned. "Or my uncle will be pestered to arrange a visit there as well."

"Perhaps you should accompany him to supervise, Miss Deane?" the admiral said.

"I'd love to, thank you," she said promptly.

He looked a little taken aback, and the comte laughed again. "I think she means it, Fenton."

Fenton nodded, a good-natured smile on his face. As he did so, Bella rose and announced that it was time the ladies retired. Bottles of port were brought in as the ladies left the room, but Phoebe was surprised when the menfolk entered the parlour only fifteen minutes later, glasses in hand.

"May I join you, Miss Deane?" It was the admiral again.

"Of course, my lord." Phoebe gestured to the empty seat next to her and he sat down.

"Were you serious about wishing to see a warship?"

"Yes, I think it would be interesting. And I enjoy sea journeys, although I have only ever crossed the Channel."

"I will arrange a visit. Could your brother come along? The ship's own officers may not have much time to show guests around."

"Thank you, my lord, I'm sure he'll be pleased to. Er... I think my cousin's governess would also be interested."

"And your maid? The footman? The housekeeper?"

Phoebe glanced at his face, wondering if she had offended him, but one corner of his mouth was turned up. She smiled. "No sir, I will not push my luck any further."

"Very well." The admiral smiled and moved off as Bella and her husband approached.

"I came to ask if you would like to go to Drury Lane tomorrow evening," Bella said. "It is *The Merchant of Venice*, I understand."

Phoebe shook her head. "I would have loved to go with you, but we are already invited by Lord Harlford." It was a pity, really—she would enjoy the play more in Bella's company. She suspected that a conversation with Lord Harlford about the play would be interesting, but that wasn't likely to be possible with her aunt and cousin present.

Bella turned the conversation to other forthcoming engagements, and the rest of the evening passed easily enough, with less talk of politics and more of concerts, theatres, and other entertainments.

Alex did not reach Grosvenor Square until late in the evening. He drew rein at the end of the square as he saw lights blazing from the lower windows of Marstone House and the line of carriages outside. Marstone did not entertain often and, from the small number of carriages, this looked like one of his informal discussion dinners.

The journey back from Devonshire had gone smoothly enough, but he'd spent four days on horseback. He wished for a moment that he'd headed straight for his own lodgings, but the thought of being looked after by the earl's staff while he was so exhausted had been far more appealing than his own cold and empty rooms. If he entered his usual way—via the mews and the servants' entrance—he wouldn't need to speak to anyone.

The doors opened and guests began to leave, most unidentifiable from this distance. A woman emerged, escorted by a much older man, the lights catching her bare head. Her hair flamed as red as Phoebe's, and his breath caught in his throat. But it couldn't be her—why would she be at one of Marstone's political dinners?

The carriages moved off and the door closed. He urged the horse onwards, past the entrance and round into the mews behind the house.

CHAPTER 36

*A*lex slept late the following morning, waking to Marstone's valet enquiring whether he required a bath. He stretched, then sat up and drank his coffee while his bathwater was brought in.

By the time he'd soaked the remaining aches out of his muscles and suffered Harrison's ministrations to make him look respectable again, it was almost noon. He ate a quick breakfast alone in the dining room.

"Is Lord Marstone at home?" he asked Brownlee, as the footman collected his empty plates.

"No, sir. He did, however, say that you need not restrict yourself to the house. He will expect a report later this afternoon."

"Thank you."

"Owen Jones is lodging at the Crown, sir, near Berkeley Square, if you want to talk to him. He accompanied Miss Deane up from Ashmouth, and stayed on."

Alex nearly asked why Owen was still here, but Brownlee wouldn't know. Seeing Owen would be a good excuse for a friendly chat over a tankard of ale.

· · ·

"Keeping an eye out for young Ellie, see," Owen explained, when Alex asked him.

"Ellie?"

"Denton's girl, from the inn in Ashmouth. Trasker took us in there —the wind was better. Miss Deane needed to have someone to look out for her inside the coach, he said. Then Ellie took it into her head to stay in Lunnon for a bit to see the sights. Miss Deane's abigail, she is now."

"And this robbery in the street—were you involved in that?" His voice came out rather more sharply than he'd intended.

"I did what Miss Deane said. Not my place, it wasn't, to tell her not to. She come to no harm."

"My apologies," Alex said. "I'm glad you were here to assist." There was no point reproaching Owen if both Marstone and Phoebe had determined on that course of action.

"I reckon I can get back to Devonshire now you're here. I'd like to make sure Gwen is settled, and Pierre isn't getting any bother from being a Frenchie."

"I've just returned from Ashton Tracey. I talked to Henri before I left—he seemed to think Pierre would find work easily enough, and Lady Marstone will make sure they have somewhere to live."

Owen nodded. "I'll be off soon, then."

"Have you got enough money?" Alex asked.

"Yes, Trasker gave me plenty."

"Very well. Thank you for being on hand, Owen. You'll be joining the *Lily* again?"

"Yes, sir. But I dunno what we'll be doing, now we're at war."

"I'll have to check on that, but I suspect that the usual activities will continue in some way. You're not out of a job yet, although I doubt we'll be using Granville again."

When they'd finished their ale, Alex set off for Berkeley Square, still debating what he should do. He wanted to hear from Phoebe herself that she was unharmed after taking part in Marstone's scheme, and to tell her what he had found out about Brevare's family. Phoebe had played a major part in the success of his mission—the fact that the decoy note had not yet flushed out the traitor was not her fault. He wasn't sure how much Marstone had told her, and she deserved to know that she'd been right about Brevare's motivation.

Alex hesitated at the entrance to Berkeley Square. He had no wish to encounter the comtesse or Hélène, and if Phoebe were enjoying a successful season, his paying a formal call might raise a few brows. Best to ask for her at the kitchen door rather than the front entrance. He would just have a few words with Phoebe, he told himself, then he would be on his way.

As he approached the house he heard shouts and laughter from the gardens in the centre of the square and stopped to look. A boy was making a creditable show of bowling to a man in footman's livery, a nearby servant girl being sent to retrieve the balls. She looked vaguely familiar.

Slipping through the gate, he stood watching for a few minutes. When a ball flew in his direction, the girl trotted over, pausing with widening eyes as she caught sight of him.

"Mr Westbrook?" She looked uncertain. "I be Ellie Denton, sir, from Ashmouth."

"So you are," he said with a smile, recognising her from her father's inn. "Owen said you were enjoying London. Is Miss Deane at home, do you know?"

"No, sir. She's gone for a drive with that marquess. Her ladyship is in, if you was wishing to see 'er?"

"I think that pleasure can wait," he said.

Ellie giggled.

"I'll try later. Do carry on," he added, seeing that they were attracting attention.

He walked slowly around the edge of the gardens, heading for the south end of the square and the street that led to Green Park. He'd intended to call on Bella next, but something had knotted in his stomach when Ellie mentioned Phoebe driving with a marquess.

It should not have been a surprise that Phoebe was being courted. Part of him was pleased for her but he realised, with some self-loathing, that another part of him wasn't pleased at all. As a poor relation, she had seemed almost within his reach. A woman being squired about by a marquess was well beyond him.

A high perch phaeton trundled into the square as he approached the corner. It was a dashing sporting carriage with black wheels picked out in gold, contrasting oddly with a pair of ordinary-looking, unmatched horses that could only be described as plodding along. The driver was a tall man dressed in black, sitting next to a lady in a beautifully tailored emerald green pelisse with matching bonnet ribbons.

He stopped abruptly, his heart racing—this fashionable woman was Phoebe. His mouth dried and his breath caught as he took in the red curls framing her face, the curve of her lips. She looked every inch the fine lady, stunning in her new clothing, but there was something missing. Her face didn't have the sparkle that made her truly beautiful, and there was none of the animation that he'd been picturing in his mind for the last few weeks. Her face was set, as if she were holding in irritation—an expression he'd often seen when she was with her aunt.

The phaeton drew up in front of the Calvac residence, and a tiger jumped from the back and ran to hold the horses. The marquess descended, then handed Phoebe down. Alex watched, clenching his jaw as she took the marquess' arm up the steps to the door, then turned to face him. Behind her the butler opened the door, but they made no immediate move to enter.

Alex scowled, looking at the stiff way she held herself, and wished he could hear what was being said as she took her leave of her escort and went into the house. High-ranking he may be, but Phoebe hadn't seemed too impressed by her escort.

The marquess turned abruptly and climbed back into his phaeton. As he drove past, Alex caught the crease between his brows—displeased, or perhaps confused.

His gloom lifted a little. He'd have to wait until he could talk to her, but it seemed that fine clothes and aristocratic suitors hadn't changed the Phoebe he knew.

He continued on his way. If he called now, he risked encountering the comtesse, and he wasn't in the mood to be polite to her. He'd have a walk, then deliver Lady Marstone's note to Bella.

Phoebe asked Cookson to send a tray of tea to her room and went upstairs, relieved that Lord Harlford had another engagement. It had been an enjoyable hour, on the whole, and she should not be so irritated because he hadn't wanted her to drive the phaeton through the streets. She hoped her farewell had not seemed rude.

Captain Synton had taken her driving twice, before he'd had to spend more time at the War Office. On those occasions she hadn't asked if she could drive beyond the park gates: Lord Carterton's blacks were expensive horses, and she didn't feel competent to control them amidst the noise and distractions of traffic. Today's horses would have been no problem, she thought, annoyed again as she recalled the way the marquess had taken the reins from her as they approached the gates on their way back without a word of explanation or apology.

On the other hand, the excursion had demonstrated that Lord Harlford wanted *her* company. If he were still trying to pay Hélène back for her continual lateness, he wouldn't have bothered with a driving lesson. A smile spread across her face as she recalled his surprise that she really could drive—although the animals he'd hired were not much of a challenge. She hadn't learned anything new today, but it had been useful practice and a chance to try her hand with unfamiliar horses.

She put her cup down and found an empty page in her sketchbook. Her pencil flew over the paper as she drew the phaeton in a busy street. She was in control, amidst a melee of carriages, carts, and street hawkers. Finally, with a smile, she added Harlford sitting beside her, cringing with a hand covering his eyes. She was probably being rather unfair to the man, but caricaturing him relieved the last of her irritation.

Alex would have let her drive in the streets, she was sure. No, he would have *encouraged* her. But he wasn't here. She hadn't heard from him since that brief note arrived—nearly a week ago now.

Shaking her head, she turned her thoughts back to Lord Harlford. He was one of the most eligible men on the marriage mart this season —good looking, wealthy, by all accounts, and only a few years older than she was. If she had any sense she would be encouraging him. Her aunt and cousin would never forgive her if she got an offer from Harlford, but that needn't bother her once she was married.

What would life be like, though, as a society wife—tedious, with a continual round of balls and other gatherings? It might not be too bad if he took an interest in politics and let her participate in discussions like the one last night at Marstone House, but his interests didn't appear to lie in that direction.

There was little point in such speculation, she told herself firmly. One driving lesson did not lead to an offer of marriage. Trying to change the direction of her thoughts, she picked up the copy of *Rights of Man* and began to read, noting down questions to ask her uncle later.

She gladly put the book to one side when Ellie returned to help her to change for the evening, hoping the visit to the theatre would lighten her mood.

Ellie laid out a pale blue gown with a deeper blue overskirt, trimmed with gold edging. As the maid put Phoebe's hair up, threading thin gold ribbon through and around the heap of curls, she chattered away, sharing the day's gossip and events.

"Mr Westbrook come round today, miss, did you know?"

"What? When?" Phoebe stared at Ellie in the mirror, her stomach giving a peculiar lurch.

"When you was out with the marquess. We was playing cricket in the square again with the young master. He asked if you was 'ome, and said 'e'd come back some other time."

"He didn't leave a card?"

"No, miss, he didn't go into the 'ouse. I think he didn't be wanting to see Madame."

"Ah. Yes."

Ellie chattered on, but Phoebe didn't pay attention. Although she had wanted to see Alex for weeks, the fluttering in her stomach and breathless feeling surprised her. But perhaps he'd only called to let her know what he'd found out about Brevare.

Conversation at dinner was limited. The comtesse managed to warn Phoebe not to monopolise Harlford's attention before the comte determinedly changed the subject to the play they were going to see.

"Oh, no-one goes to the theatre to watch the play, Edouard," the comtesse said dismissively. "We go to be seen!"

"You may find that Harlford does not share that view," the comte said mildly. "If you wish to give him a disgust of this family, by all means ignore the play and gossip instead."

The comtesse looked down at her plate, her mouth set in a hard line.

"Do you know who else is invited?" Hélène asked into the resulting silence.

"Lord Tresham, I think," the comtesse said. "But concentrate on the marquess, my dear, He'd be a much better match than a mere baron."

The comte shook his head, and tried once again to describe part of the plot to his family.

CHAPTER 37

*P*hoebe was pleased to find that her uncle had arranged for the hired carriage to drop them off some time after the doors to the auditorium opened, so the foyer was not as packed as it might have been. Nevertheless, there were still crowds of people waiting to enter the pit and the galleries, and the noise, heat, and mingled smells were almost overwhelming. She made her way behind her aunt and cousin as they kept close to the comte, the tall feathers on her aunt's headdress providing a beacon to follow.

She relaxed once they reached the staircase, where there were fewer people and movement was easier. A footman waiting near the private boxes showed them the way. Lord Harlford and Lord Tresham had already arrived, and bowed a greeting to them all.

Hélène scanned the box and looked out towards the stage, her lips curving in a happy smile. "This is a splendid position, my lord," she said, looking up at the marquess' face. "How lovely for you to have a box so close to the stage."

"It's actually Tresham's box, Lady Hélène," the marquess said. "Please, won't you be seated?"

Hélène's smile slipped—at the wasted compliment, Phoebe

guessed. But her cousin recovered quickly and took one of the seats at the front of the box.

"Miss Deane?" Lord Harlford said, indicating the seat next to Hélène. "You will get a much better view of the play from the front seats."

"Thank you, my lord." As she sat, she saw Lord Harlford's gaze turn to her aunt.

"I'll sit at the back," the comtesse said, before Lord Harlford could speak. "Why don't you sit next to Hélène, my lord?"

Lord Tresham, standing next to the marquess, bowed and moved to the empty chair next to Hélène. Phoebe suppressed a smile at the quick grimace that crossed her aunt's face. Lord Harlford's lips twitched as he took the seat next to Phoebe—far from resenting Tresham's usurpation of the place next to Hélène, he seemed amused by the manoeuvring.

Lord Tresham addressed several remarks to Hélène while they waited for the performance to start but received only perfunctory responses. Lord Harlford managed to carry on a conversation with Phoebe that also included her uncle, seated behind them. She listened with interest as they discussed the actors they were about to see.

Once Antonio came on stage with his lament, it was clear that the comte's opinion of Lord Harlford had been correct—he was at the theatre, so he would watch the play.

Phoebe was entranced by the performance. Portia, with her quick wits and intelligence, had always been one of her favourite Shakespearean characters when reading the plays, but it was much more enjoyable to listen to her words being spoken by a good actress.

She returned to the real world at the first interval when a footman entered bearing a laden tray. Phoebe gratefully accepted a glass of lemonade.

"How are you enjoying the play?" Lord Harlford asked. Phoebe was about to reply, but Hélène spoke first.

"Oh, it is wonderful, my lord. I'm so pleased you invited us."

Lord Harlford's brows rose. "Which character do you prefer, Lady Hélène?"

"Oh, the... um, Antonio is handsome, is he not? I mean..."

Rather than being irritated by Hélène monopolising the marquess, Phoebe observed him listen to her cousin's chatter. He didn't appear to be bored, but neither was he enthralled by her cousin's remarks.

"What is *he* doing here?" The comtesse's sharp question interrupted the conversation. Everyone looked at her.

"Who, my dear?" the comte said.

"*That man* is in the Cartertons' box! Why is Lord Carterton associating with someone like him?"

Phoebe's stomach performed the same somersaults as it had that afternoon—the only person she had heard her aunt refer to in those terms was Alex.

She followed her aunt's gaze, and saw Bella sitting in one of the boxes across the auditorium. The Carterton party must have arrived late, for she hadn't noticed them before the play began. Another woman sat next to Bella, and several men stood behind them—difficult to see in the dim light towards the back of the box. They moved forward again to take their seats as the performance restarted, and Phoebe's pulse accelerated as she saw that one of the men was, indeed, Alex.

"It is Mr Westbrook, sir," Phoebe said to her uncle in a low voice. "I believe he is an acquaintance of the Cartertons."

"The man who escorted you back from France?"

"Yes, sir."

"I think I should thank him for his help," the comte said. "Could you introduce me during the next interval?"

Phoebe nodded, trying to concentrate on the stage, but her glance kept sliding towards the Cartertons' box and she heard little of the dialogue. She hadn't thought their next meeting would be in so public a place—but an encounter in her aunt's parlour would have been no better, she told herself. Her stomach knotted as she wondered what she would say—and what *he* might say.

· · ·

Alex spotted the Calvac party during the first act, his attention initially drawn to the tall feathers on a woman's headdress. He recognised the comtesse, then turned his regard to the others in the box. Even from this distance, Phoebe looked wonderful in shades of rich blue. Hélène sat beside her, the two of them flanked by a couple of men.

Alex leaned forward and spoke to Bella. "May I borrow your opera glass?"

She looked at him with a raised brow, but handed over the jewelled tube. Moving back a few steps to make his actions less obvious, Alex put it to his eye and focused on the box opposite.

The man beside Phoebe was the marquess she'd been driving with this afternoon. The older man sitting next to the comtesse must be the comte; he didn't recognise the third man. Then he succumbed to temptation and turned the glass on Phoebe, even though it felt uncomfortably like spying on her. Her gaze was fixed on the stage, and she was absorbed in the play. *There* was the sparkle that had been missing that afternoon, a smile of pure enjoyment. If that smile could be directed at him—

Snapping the glass closed, he handed it back to Bella with quiet thanks. He tried to keep his attention on the play, uncomfortably aware of Bella's interested glances in his direction.

At the first interval, Lord Carterton and his friend left the box and Alex slid into a chair next to Bella.

"Who is that with the Calvacs?" he asked, trying for a note of nonchalance.

"Harlford," Bella said, without even looking. "The Marquess of Harlford, I should say." She picked up her glass and focused it. "And Lord Tresham—only a baron, that one. Tresham's courting Hélène—or trying to. Hélène has her sights on a higher rank."

Alex looked down at his hands, avoiding Bella's gaze. Hélène might have her sights on the marquess, but it was Phoebe who had gone driving with the man that afternoon.

"Harlford has only just been confirmed to his title," Bella went on.

"I imagine his mama is encouraging him to get married and secure the succession."

He caught a turn of her head from the corner of his eye.

"Good looking," she went on. "Wealthy, too, by all accounts, and not a womaniser."

"Hélène will be happy with him, then," Alex said.

"Mmm—if she can get him. It wasn't Hélène I was thinking of."

Bella had that quizzical look that usually preceded probing questions. He was tempted to leave, but excusing himself would only initiate the questions he was trying to avoid.

"The next act is beginning," he said with relief. Although he kept his eyes on the stage, he couldn't stop his thoughts wandering. The marquess would undoubtedly be a good catch for Phoebe, if that was what she wanted. And if it *was* what she wanted, then he should want it for her too.

The act stretched on interminably, as Alex made up his mind that he'd excuse himself for some refreshments at the next interval—he wasn't going to sit here and subject himself to Bella's teasing again. But before he left, he caught sight of movement in the box opposite. Both Phoebe and the comte looked directly at the Carterton box before disappearing through the door behind them.

Instead of making his way to the refreshment room, Alex waited in the corridor. If Phoebe was coming to see Bella, he'd rather not be there. If she was coming to see *him*, it was far better to meet her without Bella's curious eyes on him.

He felt his heart speed up as they came into sight along the corridor. Phoebe had one hand on her uncle's arm, and was looking at the doors of the boxes as she passed them, rather than ahead. Her hair was still a riot of red, but now she wore it looser, a few curls framing her face. The rich colours of her gown accentuated her clear complexion. He swallowed hard.

"Miss Deane," he said as they approached, surprised that his voice sounded almost normal. Phoebe's head turned quickly, eyes widening as she saw him. She smiled, and suddenly he couldn't breathe.

"Uncle, may I introduce Mr Westbrook?" she said, her tone formal but her smile still lighting up her face. "Mr Westbrook, my uncle, Monsieur le Comte de Calvac."

Alex bowed, forcing his mind to concentrate on what she was saying, and not on recalling that farewell on a Normandy beach.

"Westbrook, I had to come to thank—" The comte broke off as someone pushed past him, jostling his arm. "Shall we go to the refreshment room?"

Phoebe followed as Alex led the way, a curious combination of happiness and nerves knotting her insides. He looked well—the black eye had gone, and the lines of tiredness around his eyes were no longer in evidence. There had been a fleeting expression when she first saw him: admiration, she hoped, but she couldn't be sure. His face now was guarded, his smile appearing rather forced.

There wasn't space to sit down in the crowded room, and the babble of voices made conversation difficult. Alex steered them towards an alcove and, catching the eye of a passing waiter, procured three glasses of champagne. The two men stood with their backs to the crowd, giving them a little privacy.

Phoebe wanted to ask Alex if he was well, where he had been, but this was not the place.

"I must thank you, most sincerely, Mr Westbrook, for returning my family to England," the comte said.

"It was a pleasure, monsieur," Alex said, his tone formal. He smiled with his words, but it was a polite, society smile.

"It sounded most uncomfortable to me, from what Phoebe said."

She saw some of the tension in Alex's shoulders relax as he met the older man's gaze.

"It had its moments," he said.

That kiss? Phoebe felt heat rising to her cheeks.

"Nevertheless, I was pleased to be of service. And Miss Deane was of material help in my... in what I was trying to do."

Alex's eyes flicked briefly to her face—he must be wondering how much she'd told her uncle.

"I would ask you to call," the comte went on. "But I gather there is some…" He hesitated for the right word.

"Antipathy?" Phoebe suggested.

Alex's lips compressed, as if he were hiding a smile. Phoebe's nervousness began to fade. This was still the Alex she'd come to know in France.

"Unfortunately, yes," the comte said. "However, if there is any way I could be of service, Mr Westbrook, you have but to ask."

Alex glanced at Phoebe. "I… er, I would like to ask Miss Deane how her journey went after she left France."

"By all means." The comte gestured towards her. There was a moment of silence.

"Privately, if you don't mind, sir," Alex clarified.

The two men locked gazes, then the comte nodded.

"Very well. Perhaps you would care to take my niece for a drive in the park, Westbrook? If you have a steady nerve, that is. She appears to require her escorts to let her take the ribbons."

"Only in the park, though, uncle. Lord Harlford is so kind as to protect me from the dangers of driving in traffic, even with the gentle pair he borrowed for me this afternoon."

She could see that neither man was fooled by her demure tone.

"What else have you driven?" Alex asked.

"Lord Carterton's blacks," she said. "His cousin, Captain Synton, let me drive them in the park a few times."

Had she seen a frown when she mentioned the captain?

"But he's had to be at the War Office so I haven't seen those lovely animals for over a week," she added.

"Would a drive tomorrow morning be acceptable, Miss Deane?" Alex asked. "It is not the fashionable time, so it should be quiet."

And allow them to talk without interruptions. "Thank you, yes. Will ten o'clock suit?" That was before her aunt normally came downstairs.

Alex glanced at her uncle, and the comte inclined his head in agreement.

"Thank you, sir," Alex said. "Until the morning, Miss Deane." He gave a quick bow and an uncertain smile before joining the flow of people now returning to their boxes.

Phoebe let out a breath as she watched him go. She wasn't sure what to think, but at least they would have some privacy to talk tomorrow.

CHAPTER 38

The next morning, Phoebe was ready for her drive in plenty of time, dressed once again in her emerald green pelisse. Tired after a largely sleepless night, and unable to settle to read anything, she paced in the library while she waited for Alex to arrive.

Her stomach still had the fluttery feeling from yesterday as she anticipated their drive in the spring sunshine. Smoothing her skirts for the tenth time, she admitted to herself that the weather was irrelevant—it wasn't the prospect of drifts of daffodils in the park, or even the chance to drive again, that she was looking forward to. But there was also that niggling fear that perhaps Alex really did only want to learn about their journey home.

The clock on the mantelpiece began to chime ten, and she walked to the window, catching her breath as she saw Alex pull up outside, with the same black horses in the same phaeton that she had driven with Captain Synton. A groom in the seat beside him jumped down as the carriage came to a halt. Pulling on her gloves, she hastened down to the ground floor and slipped out into the square before Alex's groom had time to knock.

"Miss Deane," Alex said, as the groom handed her up and climbed onto the step behind. "You look well."

His smile looked less forced this morning, more genuine, with those crinkles beside his eyes that showed when he laughed.

"Thank you, sir," she replied, her tone less formal than her words. She studied his face with quick sideways glances as he drove out of the square. In daylight, she could see only a few faint and fading scars marking the cuts his face had taken during that fight. "I'm glad you got back safely."

He flicked a glance at her, then gave his attention back to the road. "Likewise."

Abruptly, the silence became awkward and she turned her gaze to the streets around them, not wanting to talk while the groom was present. She had many things she wanted to find out, but his opinion of the weather wasn't one of them.

Alex pulled up when they reached Piccadilly, and the groom got down from his perch behind them. Alex flicked him a coin. "Meet me at the end of Rotten Row in an hour or so."

"Very good, sir." The groom touched his hat and headed for the nearest inn, weaving his way between carts and hackney carriages.

"Appearances," Alex explained, when Phoebe looked at him with brows raised. "In case someone was watching."

"I cannot think who would be spying on me," Phoebe said, with exaggerated puzzlement, happy to see him relax into a laugh.

Alex held the reins towards her. "Do you wish to drive them to the park? It's less than a mile."

Surprised, then pleased, she smiled.

"You would let me?" Not only let her, but encourage her, as she'd thought yesterday. But these horses were far from the plodding hacks Lord Harlford had hired, and the street was busy.

"They look quite... lively," she added, suddenly doubting her ability to control them in this busy street. "You've only seen me driving that team in France, and they weren't the most difficult of animals."

"Some practice in the park first, then?"

She nodded, quelling her sense of relief. "That would be best. I don't want to get... I mean, Lord Carterton wouldn't like..."

Phoebe let the words trail off as she realised she had no idea what his relationship with Lord Carterton was. They must be friends, at least, otherwise he couldn't have borrowed the man's team and phaeton.

"As you wish." He set the horses going, and they continued on their way.

"Would you really have let me drive?" she asked again.

"If you thought you could handle them, yes." He glanced at her, smiling, before turning back to the road. "I wondered if you'd like to drive four, but the only thing Nick has rigged for that is a heavy travelling coach."

A warm glow started in her chest at his confidence in her ability— or at least, in her judgement of her own ability.

"Not too disappointed, I hope?"

"No, no, of course not. I... well, no-one else has even suggested I could try driving their horses in the street, let alone handle more than two."

"I pass the test then?"

Amused at the idea, she realised that it *was* a test, in a way. That kind of trust in her judgement was something she now knew she wanted in a husband. The thought brought heat to her cheeks, and she took a deep breath. He'd invited her for a drive to discuss what happened with his message—she should focus on that.

"A definite pass," she said. "Did you find... that is, did you get what you were looking for after you left us?"

"Very discreet," he said, a quick grin showing approval. He didn't talk as he negotiated the turn into the park, then glanced at her. "I don't think anyone can overhear us here."

As Alex described the last few weeks, Phoebe listened carefully, aware of the parts he glossed over as he explained what they'd done, the decisions they had made. She'd been expecting just a few words, and was flattered that he gave her so much detail.

"You were right about Brevare being blackmailed," he finished, with a smile in her direction that warmed her inside. He briefly outlined what Brevare's sister had told him, and that the two women were now safely hidden away in Devonshire.

"Should you be telling me all this?" she asked, concerned that Lord Marstone would not like it.

"Probably not, but you're involved. And you let Marstone persuade you into more danger, taking the decoy note."

"I volunteered," she corrected him, mindful of the faint disapproval in his tone. "It didn't feel nearly as frightening as that tavern in Granville."

"Why did you do it?"

She remembered that he had seemed almost angry as they were saying goodbye on the beach—with her or with himself, she wasn't sure. Fear for her safety, perhaps? Now, he sounded more resigned, but this time the potential danger was past, and she had not come to harm.

"Our plans didn't quite work," she said.

"Yes, Marstone told me what happened," Alex said. "I understand the idea behind allowing yourself to be robbed, but Marstone could have found some other way of delivering that decoy message. You needn't have put yourself in danger again, and he need not have accepted."

"The risk was mine to take," Phoebe said, her voice sharp. "I knew the possible consequences. Owen and two of Lord Marstone's men were nearby, if it had become anything more than a simple robbery."

Damn—he'd offended her, and he hadn't meant to. He pulled the horses to a halt, and turned to face her. "I'm sorry, Phoebe. I didn't mean to call your judgement into question. You clearly did think it through first."

"I didn't come to any harm," she reminded him, her face lightening.

He kept his gaze on her face for a moment, then set the horses into motion again. "None of that explains *why* you volunteered to do it," he said.

"I felt that I could be useful."

"Not a desire shared by many young ladies," he mused. "That was not a criticism," he added, with a sideways glance. "Not of you, at least. But I'm still sorry you had to be involved in this whole business." Except that he would never have met her if her aunt had been a sensible woman—he couldn't be sorry about that.

"I'm not," she stated.

"Really?" After all she'd been through?

"Everything was all right in the end, and if we hadn't got into trouble I'd probably still be the poor relation."

"How so?" Something good really had come out of it?

"It turns out that my uncle gave me an allowance when I first came to live with them, and my aunt had been spending it on herself and Hélène. If it hadn't been for her trying to prevent me going into society with Hélène, my uncle would never have found out."

"Bella said you're enjoying your season."

"Yes, thanks to her, for the most part. She introduced me to her mantua-maker, and that made a great difference."

He turned his head, glancing down at her pelisse then back at her face. She was beautiful, but her clothes were only the finishing touches. "Certainly an improvement on the orange dress," he said. He wasn't sure she'd want compliments from him—not on her appearance, at least.

Not trusting himself to say more, he looked around. The park was reasonably empty. "Time for you to drive." He handed her the reins, and watched as she drove along the carriageway. He tried to concentrate on the way she was handling the reins and not on the way her hair curled around her face or how well her pelisse fitted the curves of her body. Or how he'd missed talking to her, working with her.

Phoebe felt the thrill of the horses' power at her command as she varied their pace and steered them around bends in the track. Alex sat watching her hands, but said nothing; she didn't want to move her gaze from the road to see what he was thinking. Captain Synton and Lord Harlford had both provided a commentary while she was driving, telling her to pull or not to pull on the reins, or to steer in a different way. She found her awareness of Alex's closeness as unnerving as his silence, and eventually pulled up.

"Am I doing it correctly?"

"Yes—you've gained confidence since you drove in France, I think."

"You were very quiet." She looked at him, wondering if he'd meant what he said.

"I'd hate for you to look at me the way you looked at your marquess yesterday," he said with a grin.

"You saw me yesterday?"

"I was in the square when you got back. What did he do wrong?"

"He treated me as if I were still in the schoolroom." That might be a little unfair, but that was how he'd made her feel at the end of their drive.

"Do you want to practise, or to really have a lesson?"

Phoebe wanted to ask him what he would be doing next—would Marstone send him back to France? Would she see him again after this? She almost asked outright, but it wasn't her business, not really. And she was half afraid of getting an answer she didn't want to hear.

"A lesson, please," she said.

"What do you want to learn?"

"I'd like to be more confident driving them faster, but I'd also like to be good enough to drive in the streets. I suppose that means practising through narrow gaps?"

He nodded. "Let's try fast first, while the park is still fairly empty. How about if I take them for a while, explain what I am doing, and then you try?"

"That's a good idea."

She listened carefully as he drove as fast as was safe to the quieter side of the park, then took several corners at speed. He handed over the reins, and she did her best to emulate him. After half an hour she was taking sharp corners safely, and passing closer to obstacles than she would have dared the day before.

"Thank you—for showing me and for borrowing the phaeton," she said as she handed the reins back to him. She was uncomfortably aware that her pleasure in the exercise was due to his presence beside her rather than what she had learned.

"Had enough?" he asked. "Do you want to drive them back?"

"I'd like to try driving in the street. Could you... would you mind driving round the park for a while so I can rest my arms first?"

Alex was impressed at the progress she'd made in such a short time—teaching her had been both frustrating and a pleasure. She was a quick learner, and he'd spent most of the hour wishing they were back on that coach in France, with the cold giving him an excuse to sit closer.

They were nearing the gate where he'd arranged to pick up Lord Carterton's groom when there was a shout from behind. Phoebe twisted around to look, and raised a hand to wave. Alex pulled the phaeton over, and two men on horses came cantering up.

"Joe!" Phoebe said, a happy smile lighting her face. "Joe, this is Mr Westbrook, who helped us get out of France. Alex, this is my brother, and his friend, Lieutenant Marlow."

Sidling his mount close to the phaeton, Joe held out his hand. "My thanks, Westbrook. Did I see Phoebe taking the ribbons?"

"You did," Alex said.

"You took that corner pretty fast," Joe said to Phoebe, pointing back up the park to the last corner Phoebe had driven. "Brave man, Westbrook!" he added with a grin.

"Don't be horrid!" Phoebe said, with a laugh. "He didn't even close his eyes!"

Alex smiled, shaking his head at the idea that he'd need to.

"Can't linger," Joe went on. "We've an appointment at the Admiralty. Westbrook, could I stand you dinner by way of thanks? Tonight or tomorrow?"

"You're supposed to be going to the Stantons' ball with us tonight," Phoebe said, before Alex could speak. "*And* arriving in time for the supper dance!"

"Tomorrow will be fine, thank you," Alex said, amused at Joe's resigned smile. The banter between brother and sister was good to see —Phoebe would have a champion in her brother, he thought, should her uncle fail her.

Joe gave Alex his direction before the two men cantered off with a final wave goodbye.

"Do you still want to drive?" Alex asked, when they had collected the groom.

She nodded, biting her lip. "Yes, please, but not if it's too much bother to—"

"Don't worry about that." It was the least he could do.

"Talk me through it?" she requested, so he kept a lookout for possible hazards, quietly pointing out things she might not have spotted. She successfully negotiated hackney carriages and goods waggons in the stretch of Piccadilly before they reached the junction with Berkeley Street, so he suggested she keep going to give her more practice. They turned into Hay Market, then back along Pall Mall, and it wasn't until they had nearly reached Piccadilly again that a barking dog frightened the horses and he had to put a hand on the reins.

He remembered how she'd looked at the marquess, and apologised.

She shook her head, biting her lip. "No, you were right. I might have lost control. I think you'd better take them from here." She held out the reins.

"You did very well until the dog," he reassured her. "Really," he added, looking at her chagrined expression. "It's busy, and you're tired."

Phoebe sat rubbing her arms and flexing her hands as he drove back, trying to work out the aches in her muscles. He brought the horses to a stop when they reached Berkeley Square, and asked the groom to go to their heads.

"Thank you," Phoebe said, smiling at him. "You are a good teacher."

"You don't need much instruction," Alex said, warmed by her compliment and her smile. He jumped down, then helped her. They walked up the steps.

"I'd invite you in, but..."

"Your aunt?" Alex suggested as she hesitated.

"I'm afraid she wouldn't like it," Phoebe admitted, with a wry twist to her lips. Then she gave a proper smile, and he caught his breath. This was nothing like the farewell on the beach in France, but he felt the same urge to kiss her. It had been unwise then; it was impossible now.

Resolutely he turned away and plied the knocker, then bowed over her hand.

Alex climbed the flights of stairs to his rooms, breathing in the faint smell of polish. In his sitting room, it was immediately apparent that his cleaning woman

had been in while he'd been driving with Phoebe; the stack of newspapers he'd borrowed from Marstone was neatly aligned with the edge of the table and the fire had been laid.

He hung his hat and coat on the peg behind the bedroom door and lit the fire. The jacket and breeches he'd worn to the theatre last night hung from the curtain pole to air, no doubt carefully brushed. The sight reminded him of Phoebe's conversation with her brother in the park—for the first time, he regretted not having the entrée to fashionable events such as the ball she'd mentioned.

Would Phoebe be expecting him to go? She'd seen him with the Cartertons the previous night, and as she'd mentioned the ball in his presence, she might think he could get an invitation if he didn't already have one.

Would she even want him to? Selfishly, he hoped so, although it would be better if she didn't, he told himself, then she wouldn't see his non-appearance as a slight. Perhaps he should have made some excuse —a prior appointment—but that would imply he would be able to go to other such events.

For he did want to see her again. He'd occasionally wondered, during these last weeks, if his longing to be with her was only the product of unaccustomed loneliness, too many years of subterfuge, but today's encounter had finally dispelled that idea. Slumping into a chair by the fire, he gazed at the flames beginning to lick around the coals. A memory of Mary Helstone's father came into his mind—something he'd not thought about for years. Helstone had been furious, insulted that someone of Alex's birth had dared to look at his daughter, and wished out loud that the days of horsewhipping the lower orders were not past. And Mary, after all those professions of love, had not cared for him enough to defy her father and society. Or didn't have the courage to.

He rubbed a hand over his face. He couldn't even remember why he had thought he was so in love—other than possessing a china-doll, delicate prettiness and a sweet nature, Mary had little to recommend her. He could see now that he would have been bored within a few months. Phoebe, on the other hand...

Irritated at the way his mind would not leave it alone, he stood and reached for his coat. Nothing could come of it—his birth would be even less acceptable to her family than it had been to Helstone.

He must try to forget her. Some exercise might help him to think of something other than Phoebe—he'd try at the fencing salons. Failing that, he might just get drunk.

CHAPTER 39

*P*hoebe stood with her back to a pillar at the edge of Lady Stanton's ballroom, awaiting her partner for the next dance. The event was a definite squeeze, the room over-warm and packed with people. She couldn't help scanning the crowds, hoping to see Alex, and had to hide her disappointment each time a late arrival turned out to be a stranger. Hélène passed her with Lord Harlford, a happy smile on her face as she met Phoebe's eyes.

Her next partner arrived, a rather plump young man with a red, shiny face. He mopped his brow with a handkerchief, apologising profusely for being late. Phoebe did her best to concentrate and make conversation, all the while wishing she had Alex before her instead of this nervous young man.

Her cotillion with Lord Harlford was next, and they joined the same set as Hélène and Lord Tresham. Hélène's smile faded as she noted who Phoebe was dancing with. She might have had some sympathy with her cousin if she thought Hélène cared for anything other than his wealth and title.

Their conversation was rather disjointed because of the movements of the dance, but when they had exchanged the usual pleasantries, Lord Harlford mentioned seeing her in the park.

"It was a pleasant morning for a drive," Phoebe said. She thought it might be rude to say she hadn't noticed him—her attention had been on Alex or on her driving most of the time.

"Not many people go driving so early," he continued the next time the dance brought them together. His voice held a faint note of enquiry—was he trying to find out who she'd been with?

"It is often more enjoyable when it is quiet. You must find it so yourself, my lord?" she added.

"I was... well, yes."

She could see from his expression that he wasn't satisfied with her answer. "It is so much easier to enjoy being among trees and grass when there are no interruptions from other people," she went on, attempting to divert the conversation. She had no wish to discuss Alex with him. "It is the nearest I get to being in the country."

"You prefer the country to Town?" he asked.

"Oh, balls and so on are amusing for a while," she said, pleased her tactic had worked. "I enjoy visiting museums and attending the theatre, but I do miss being out of doors. The parks here are pleasant, but it is not the same."

"You have lived in the countryside, then?"

Phoebe studied his expression as the dance took them apart. This was the longest conversation they'd had about anything unconnected with balloons or horses, but he did seem to be genuinely interested in hearing her answer. When they paired up again, she described the Hampshire countryside where she had grown up.

Lord Harlford asked about her parents, and although one brow rose when she explained that her father had been a combined surgeon and apothecary, his interest in her descriptions did not wane. Then, the dance not yet being finished, she went on to talk about the countryside around Calvac. Was she chattering on as badly as Hélène usually did? She had no way of knowing—he was too polite to show any boredom he might be feeling.

"Thank you, Miss Deane," he said when the set ended. "Would you care to drive with me tomorrow?"

"Thank you, yes." She hoped he would not borrow those placid horses again, but before she could work out a diplomatic way of saying so, he raised her hand to his lips and took his leave.

Phoebe stared after him, surprised at his last action.

"My sister, a future marchioness!" Joe spoke behind her, a laugh in his voice. Thankfully Lord Harlford was well out of earshot.

"Nothing of the sort!"

"Does everyone kiss your hand, then, Fee?" he asked, more seriously.

"No, but he was just being polite, I should think."

"Pity," Joe said with a grin, then led her into the next set. He talked about his hopes for another posting soon, and Phoebe reminded him that he was supposed to accompany their party to see HMS *Antelope* at Greenwich the following day. During the set, she spotted Lord Hilvern dancing with a young matron, his florid face dewed with sweat. His eyes met Phoebe's as the pattern of the dance took him close to her, and he scowled and quickly looked away. She wondered if he still remembered their discussion about women learning languages.

Joe and Marlow left after supper, but Phoebe was not short of partners. She was just reflecting that she was enjoying herself despite Alex's absence when she saw a familiar figure at the far side of the ballroom. Brevare?

He appeared quite different in his elegant and colourful clothing, looking around him as he wandered between groups of people talking at the edge of the room. Phoebe's partner returned her to a chair near her aunt, and she opened her fan, waving it gently while keeping it between her face and Brevare. Her heart raced at the thought that he might recognise her and speak to her here, in full view of the highest sticklers in the *ton*. With such a potentially scandalous story to tell, he could get the whole family ostracised if he chose to.

Should she go to the ladies' retiring room? No, her movement might draw attention to herself. The fan still gently waving, she kept a stealthy eye on Brevare as he surveyed the room, breathing a sigh of relief when his gaze fixed on something and he began to push his way through the crowd. Phoebe tensed again as she realised he was making for Hélène. What did he want with her cousin?

"Miss Deane? This is our dance, I believe." Lord Tresham sounded impatient. Had he needed to speak a second time?

"I do beg your pardon, my lord," she said, rising. "I'm afraid my wits were wandering!"

"Are you feeling quite well?" he asked, his brow creased in concern.

"Yes, thank you. I was merely thinking on a puzzle. But a dance will clear my head."

"Very well." He offered his arm, and they moved over to where the set was forming. With any luck, Brevare would be taken up with Hélène and would not notice her. If he still thought her a servant, he wouldn't be expecting to see her here, which would help.

She managed to avoid Brevare for the rest for the rest of the evening, and not much was said in the carriage on the way home, although Hélène's expression could be described as smug. Phoebe wondered what Brevare had wanted, but managed to dismiss him from her mind for the moment. No doubt she would soon find out.

Phoebe didn't sleep well that night—it wasn't Brevare's appearance keeping her awake, but Joe's flippant comment about Lord Harlford's intentions. If Joe was right, she was on the point of making the catch of the season—with her red hair too!

Instead of excitement, she felt a knot of something more like doom in her stomach. The marquess was a decent man—polite and considerate—he danced well, and she couldn't ask for better in terms of wealth and rank. He was pleasant company, too, even if not very talkative.

But he wasn't the man she'd been thinking about every day for the last three weeks. She and Alex had slipped into their easy way of talking to each other today, almost as if no time had passed, but then they had parted with nothing more than a farewell she could have received from a mere acquaintance.

Alex had not come to the Stantons' ball, even though he had heard her mentioning it to Joe. Bella had been there, and if Alex had wanted to come, he could surely have asked Bella to bring him.

That kiss in France—she could still feel a faint echo of the way it had affected her. Had it meant more to her than to him? He must have kissed many women. If he had been prevented from attending the ball by another appointment, he could have said so.

It was unrealistic to expect Alex to feel the same way, she told herself. She had to marry someone; she could not expect her uncle to support her for ever. If Alex did not return her feelings, and if Joe was correct, could she put her own desires aside to marry the marquess? Did she owe it to her uncle to accept?

As Phoebe descended the stairs the next morning, heavy-eyed and tired, she could hear Georges' excited chatter from the dining room, and Miss Bryant's calm replies.

Green was on duty. "Monsieur le Comte wants to see you in his study, miss, before breakfast."

"Thank you, Green." It would be something about today's trip to see the frigate, no doubt.

Her uncle looked up as she entered. "Good morning, Phoebe."

"Good morning, sir."

"Lord Harlford is coming to speak to me this morning."

"Oh." Not the frigate, then. All her anxiety from the previous night came back to her.

"I suspect he is going to request my permission to pay his addresses to you," the comte went on.

She hadn't thought she'd need to make this decision so soon. "Are you sure it's me he wishes to ask about?"

"No, I'm not sure. His note only enquired if this morning would be convenient for him to call. If he *is* coming to ask about you, what do you wish me to say?"

Phoebe hesitated. She couldn't make this decision now, not without a chance to find out what Alex felt for her. The comte's words implied he would allow her to choose.

"Do you want me to accept, sir?" Best to be sure about that.

"It is a matter of what *you* wish, Phoebe," her uncle said, his expression concerned. "Do not accept him because you think I want you gone! You are family, and you may make your home with us for as long as you need to."

"I would like to marry someone who..." She took a deep breath. "My parents married for love, sir. I would like to do so too."

"Your parents were happy together? I did not see much of them after they were wed."

"Yes, very happy, sir."

"I'm happy to hear that." His gaze became unfocused, then he rubbed one hand across his forehead. "You do not wish to accept him, Phoebe?"

No, she did not. But nor did she want to explain her feelings for Alex.

"I feel I should, sir. I am not likely to get another offer from someone so... eligible. But..." She didn't have any real objections to Lord Harlford, other than not being the man she *did* want.

"You don't like him?"

"I don't dislike him. He isn't easy to talk to, but he is all a gentleman should be. I would like more than that in a marriage, though."

"I'm sure you will become more at ease with him when you know him better."

"I... yes, sir. I suppose so.

The comte's eyes narrowed as he studied her face. Phoebe glanced away, aware that her uncle was an astute observer.

"There is someone else?" he asked.

"Yes. I mean, no. There is someone I like better. A lot better, but I don't know if he... if he feels the same way about me." Saying it out loud brought a lump to her throat.

The comte's gaze briefly became unfocused again, and he did not press her to say who she meant. That was some relief.

"If this... this other man does not return your feelings, would you consider Harlford?"

"I… yes, I would give it serious consideration." Her heart sank—it felt so wrong to even think it.

"Very well. He may want to see me about something else altogether, of course. Now, you had best go to breakfast. I suspect you will need fortifying to cope with my son's enthusiasm."

"Yes, sir," Phoebe said, managing a smile, and headed for the sound of excited chatter.

Alex sat down in the chair indicated, wondering why he'd been summoned to the parlour to meet Admiral Fenton. He didn't think Fenton was involved in Marstone's operations, other than occasionally helping to organise transport of agents.

"Fenton was showing some people over a frigate today," Marstone said. "How did it go, Fenton?"

The admiral chuckled. "Most entertaining. I sent young Calvac off with some middies, and one of the lieutenants was free to show the ladies around."

Alex sat straighter in his chair at the mention of the Calvac name. Was Marstone trying to get Phoebe involved in something else?

"Ladies?" Marstone asked.

"Miss Deane asked if the boy's governess could come along. A Miss Bryant, I think it was." He laughed. "I'd have the pair of them on the board for lieutenants' examinations if I could—most amusing."

"How so?"

"I'd come across one of the lieutenants before," Fenton said. "Stanwick is an arrogant little lordling, thinks he knows it all. He began by trying to impress the young ladies with complicated explanations, but Miss Deane seemed to know a reasonable amount about rigging and such like already—"

Alex imagined her quizzing Trasker on the *Lily*, and smiled despite his growing concern.

"—and Miss Bryant has a technical mind. She kept asking him

why, and persisting until she got a sensible explanation. Never seen a chap so chastened!"

The earl gave a crack of laughter.

"Why are you interested, Marstone?" Fenton asked.

That was a good question.

"In fact, why was Miss Deane at your dinner? An unusual guest for you."

Alex frowned, recalling the night he returned from Devonshire, and the red-haired woman leaving the house. It had been Phoebe after all. His fingers gripped his brandy glass harder—Marstone was definitely planning something.

"Indeed," Marstone said. "She's an interesting young woman—got involved in a bit of trouble in France, but seemed to have handled herself well."

"Hmm." Fenton obviously thought this explanation was somewhat lacking, but didn't persist. "I had a talk with the brother while the women were being shown around. Competent chap, bit unfortunate in his last ship, but I think he'll go far."

"You'll sponsor him?"

"I think so, yes. From what he said, the second lieutenant on the *Galene* also seems worth a bit of attention. We're going to need all the good men we can get." The admiral glanced at the clock. "Was that all you wanted, Marstone?"

"Yes, thank you for coming."

The admiral stood and took his leave.

Alex could understand Marstone taking an interest in Phoebe, although he did not like it. The earl had always selected his agents based on their aptitude, ignoring rank, wealth, and gender. He could see why Marstone wanted to know how Phoebe had behaved on the frigate. What he didn't understand was why he'd been summoned to listen while the admiral was describing the visit. He set his glass on a side table and stood, avoiding clenching his fists only with an effort. It would not do to let his feelings show.

"What do you want with Miss Deane?" he asked.

Marstone leaned back in his chair. "Nothing," he said. "Not at present."

"Nor in the future," Alex stated. "Hasn't she been put in enough danger?"

"I will not force her to do anything." Marstone took a sip of his brandy. "I do not blackmail people. What is *your* interest in Miss Deane?"

He was *not* going to explain that. "A natural concern for the safety of anyone who gets involved in your… your plots."

"I'm sure Miss Deane can make her own decisions." Marstone stood, putting his own glass down. "It's time you and Kellet finished your notes. There's more work to be done over the next couple of days. I'll see you about that in the morning."

Alex went back to the library and the papers he had been working on with Kellet. He hadn't planned on staying in London, but perhaps he should. He didn't think Marstone would deliberately put Phoebe in danger, but he had to be certain.

CHAPTER 40

The day after the visit to HMS *Antelope*, Phoebe entered the library with some trepidation. Her uncle had been out when they returned from seeing the frigate, so she hadn't yet had a chance to find out what—or who—the marquess had wanted.

"Good morning, Phoebe," the comte said. "I'm not sure if you will think I have good or bad news for you."

"Lord Harlford?" At least he was getting straight to the point.

"Indeed. Do sit down."

Phoebe sat, trying not to clench her hands.

"As I suspected, he came to ask me about you. He said he wished to court you, with a view to asking for your hand if you continue to deal well together. I gave him my permission, Phoebe—"

How could he not?

"—but that does not mean I expect you to accept him if he does offer."

"Thank you, sir." Phoebe's hands released some of their tension. Not an immediate proposal, then, but she would still have to make a difficult decision fairly soon.

If only Alex had called again, or even made some arrangement for them to meet. She might have been able to work out whether he felt anything more than friendship for her.

"Phoebe..."

She brought her attention back to her uncle. "Sir?"

"This will not be a secret if Harlford does propose, but until then it might be better not to mention his visit. Luckily your aunt and Hélène were not at home when he called."

"I will say nothing, sir." Good lord, imagine the uproar if her aunt found out. She closed her eyes for a moment.

"Quite so," the comte said. "Now, before we start on our historical discussion, I wanted to ask you about the Vicomte de Brevare. He also called yesterday."

"What did he want?"

"He asked after Hélène and your aunt, paying his respects."

"Has he been away from London? It's nearly a month since we returned." She and Alex had speculated that Brevare would return to France to look for his family, but it would be useful to have that confirmed.

"He didn't say." The comte looked her in the eye. "He seemed surprised when I thanked him for helping to bring my wife, daughter, and niece home safely." He tilted his head slightly, clearly waiting for a comment from her.

"Surprised that you thanked him?" She didn't want to have to give further details of her subterfuge if she could avoid it.

"No." Her uncle shook his head. "After graciously accepting my thanks, as if he'd been the only one responsible for helping you, he expressed surprise that I mentioned you as my niece."

"He thought I was a maid," she explained.

The comte raised an eyebrow. "You didn't correct this misapprehension?"

"No, sir."

"This is connected with that business of Marstone's, I suppose," he said in resignation. "Never mind. Now, how is your reading coming along? What shall we discuss this morning?"

· · ·

An hour later, Phoebe went to her room—the day was fine and she felt like taking her sketchbook into the gardens in the square. A parcel wrapped in brown paper lay on top of the chest.

There was no name or direction on it, and it was heavy. Intrigued, she pulled the string undone. Inside the wrapping paper was a rectangular leather case. Lifting the lid, she saw two pistols, each sitting in its own compartment. The handles were of polished wood, with only a little ornamental engraving on the metal barrels.

Her heart racing, she looked through the box for a note or letter— she could think of only one person who might send her pistols. A sheaf of paper was tucked into a slot in the back of the case; amongst instructions for loading and cleaning the pistols she found a note written in Alex's hand.

I hope you never need these, but they are of no use kept unloaded in
their case. In an emergency there is rarely time to reload, so make
each shot count. Remember that a pistol will not fire instantly, so hold
it steady while you pull the trigger.
AW

She stared at the note, her conflicting feelings seeming to freeze her brain. He'd thought about her enough to make her a gift, but the note was impersonal. The action was that of a friend, no more.

Unwilling to admit what that could imply, she took one of the pistols out of the case, holding it as if about to fire. It was much smaller than the pistol that she'd almost used in France.

What else was in there? A stoppered flask must be for powder; the weight of it told her it was full. Another packet held a dozen balls and some leather patches, and there were a few strangely shaped tools and some spare flints.

She had thought the business with Lord Marstone was over—what did Alex know that she didn't? Was this gift linked to Brevare's return?

Lord Harlford would not be arriving for several hours, so she had time to familiarise herself with the pistols. Sketching could wait. She unfolded the instructions and read them carefully, then went to lock her door. She would tell Ellie she had them, as the maid was likely to come across them anyway, but it wouldn't do for anyone else in the house to see her trying to load them. Perhaps she could persuade Joe to take her somewhere quiet where she could practise firing them.

Handling the weapons felt like a link with Alex, but it was unwise to dwell on that. Time would tell, but despite her happiness in his company two days ago, and her impression that the feeling had been mutual, there was something very final about that impersonal note.

Phoebe hid the case of pistols at the back of a drawer when the time came for her drive with Lord Harlford. One would just fit in her pocket, but she could not imagine needing a pistol when with the marquess. The morning's drizzle had stopped and patches of blue sky were showing between the clouds.

In spite of the pleasant weather, the hollow feeling caused by Alex's note persisted. She hoped the marquess would not declare his intentions today—she needed more time to accept that a life with Alex might no longer be a possibility.

It's only two days since you saw him, she told herself, and he's likely to be occupied with Marstone's business. As Ellie dressed her hair, she determined to put such thoughts out of her mind and enjoy the afternoon.

Ellie laid out her pelisse and gloves, then cleared her throat. "May I be excused, miss? The young master wants someone to fetch 'is cricket balls."

"Yes, of course."

She was ready early so, rather than waiting in the parlour or library, she followed Ellie out into the square. Smiling, she recalled her first encounter with the marquess here—for someone who'd been so stiff and formal, he hadn't protested at nearly being hit with a cricket ball. She lifted her face up to the sun, enjoying its warmth on her skin.

Lord Harlford was on time, as usual, and bowed over her hand as he greeted her, then helped her into the carriage. As before, Phoebe sat in silence as he manoeuvred his greys through the busy streets, but this time the silence felt awkward.

"I accompanied my cousin—Georges, that is—to see HMS *Antelope* yesterday," she said, wanting to ensure the conversation kept to impersonal topics. "It was most interesting to see the kind of ship my brother has been serving on."

He looked surprised, but she was pleased that he made no comment about such a visit being unsuitable for women. They conversed readily enough, Phoebe drawing on things Joe had said as well as her own observations. As they turned in through the park gate, the marquess slowed to respond to greetings from acquaintances but didn't stop to talk. He pulled up when they were on a quieter part of the carriage drive, and turned to face Phoebe.

"Miss Deane, you said on our first drive together that you would like to drive my greys." Phoebe looked up at him, eyes widening in surprise, but he went on before she could speak. "It is relatively quiet now. Would you care to take the ribbons for a turn around the park?"

Was he really offering his greys?

"Miss Deane?"

"I… yes, thank you." She glanced at his face, still hesitant. "Are you sure, my lord?"

"You seemed to be handling the ribbons competently when I saw you here a few days ago."

Phoebe smiled, more pleased with that compliment from him than any she'd received about her appearance. She would take it much more slowly today—being given the chance to drive such a pair was honour enough.

Another carriage passed them as Lord Harlford handed over the reins. Phoebe, concentrating on grasping the reins properly, noticed only that it slowed down momentarily before the man in it flicked his whip to speed the horses up again.

"Some people cannot make up their minds," Lord Harlford muttered, looking after the carriage.

The greys were responsive to the slightest pull on the reins and moved with graceful ease. Phoebe kept them to a gentle trot, easing the pace well before they came up to other vehicles or corners, very conscious of the extra height of this vehicle. She tooled the pair around a complete circuit of the park before slowing to a stop. No-one in passing carriages addressed Lord Harlford, allowing her to concentrate on her driving.

"Thank you, my lord, they are truly a splendid pair." She'd love to see how fast they could go, but even if he allowed her to, Hyde Park in the afternoon was not the place to test them.

His smile answered her own as he took the reins. If he felt relief at getting his team through the experience unharmed, he didn't show it. "Would you like to drive them again? I could call in a few days' time."

"That would be lovely, thank you." And now she had some time to consider what she should say if he *did* ask her to marry him.

He turned the horses towards the park gates, slowing once more when Lord Tresham greeted him.

"Afternoon, Harlford. Miss Deane."

Lord Tresham did not return her smile. Although one of Hélène's admirers, he'd always been friendly towards her, albeit in a quiet way. Was something wrong?

"Can't stop, Harlford," Lord Tresham said. "Just wondered if you would be looking in at Brooks' later?"

"I was intending to, yes."

Tresham nodded briefly, then rode off without another word. Phoebe and the marquess looked after him, then at each other.

"I'll take you home, Miss Deane," the marquess said, puzzlement clear on his face. "The world seems somewhat out of sorts today."

They said little on the way back, and as Lord Harlford didn't like to keep his horses standing he didn't accompany Phoebe in for refreshments. He bowed over her hand again as they parted, repeating his promise to call again soon.

Cookson took Phoebe's pelisse and bonnet, and informed her that the rest of the family were out. She decided to read in the library, but once there, she stood by the window gazing out over the square.

How the marquess had changed from the man she'd first met: a man who didn't even see her when Hélène was present. Conversation with him was still often stilted, but he was definitely unbending. And today he'd trusted her with his greys—was that significant?

She had enjoyed her afternoon, but she hadn't felt the same thrill at handling the horses as she had when driving with Alex, the sense of shared enjoyment, or the feeling of closeness.

If Lord Harlford did offer for her, a marriage based on mutual respect and possibly friendship would work. But she had hoped for a loving marriage, like her parents had enjoyed. She could ask him for some time to think about it, and if Alex didn't call again, she would ask Bella where he was.

Hearing her aunt's voice, she wondered if she could cry off tonight's rout. An evening making polite conversation in a crowded and stuffy room did not hold much appeal at the best of times, even less so while her thoughts were on her future.

CHAPTER 41

*A*lex leaned back in his chair and stretched his arms. He'd spent most of the day cooped up in Kellet's office, going over the lists of contacts and discussing possibilities. Some of the people on the list might not be willing to help now that France was at war with Britain, and he'd been trying to recall their different motivations. The fact that his mind kept veering to an image of Phoebe had been no help at all.

"These lists are being kept here?" Alex asked, tapping his finger on the pile of notes.

"Yes. Lord Marstone has moved all the details of his own recruits here. Even if we find our traitor, I think he will not entrust such information to anyone outside his immediate control again."

Alex nodded—he'd expected no less, but still felt some degree of personal responsibility for the people he'd recruited. Unfortunately, that might include Phoebe. He could not shake off the feeling that Marstone had plans to use her in some way.

"Do you want to come out for an ale?" he asked, standing. The prospect of spending the evening alone in his lodgings was not attractive. He wouldn't be able to concentrate on a book, that was certain.

"Why not?"

Alex leaned on the wall in an upper room of the Queen's Head tavern, holding a half-empty mug of ale. A group of businessmen and drunken society men were gathered around a table, rolling dice in a loud game of hazard. He'd wandered in here with Kellet, curious what the noise was about, and they'd stayed to watch for a while. Large sums of money appeared to be changing hands, mainly being lost by the young sprigs of fashion, who were decidedly under the influence.

"Another?" Kellet asked, indicating Alex's mug.

"Why not? I'll get them." He stepped out onto the landing in search of a waiter. He had to go to the floor below, where he gave his order. Before he could return to the gaming room, he met Kellet coming down the stairs, his jaw set and brows creased.

"What...? Is something wrong?"

Kellet took his arm and turned him, pulling him down the flight of stairs. "Wait for me outside, will you?" he said. "I'll be five or ten minutes."

"What's going on, Kellet?"

"Tell you later. Just go."

"It's raining," Alex protested.

"Wait in the taproom, then," Kellet said.

"Oh, very well." Alex shook off the hand on his arm, and watched as Kellet hurried back up the stairs. The taproom was crowded, but he elbowed his way in. The waiter found him there and handed over two mugs of ale with a scowl at the bother he'd been put to.

Kellet *was* only ten minutes. He took both mugs from Alex and put them down on a nearby table. "Come outside."

Alex followed without a word. Kellet wasn't a man to dramatise things; there was clearly something wrong. Once on the street, Kellet pulled him into a shop doorway where they could stand out of the rain. "I was listening to gossip," he said. "About you."

"Me?"

"You and Miss Deane."

"What exactly was said?" Alex asked, feeling his heart accelerating. He'd been half expecting something like this since Phoebe had told him that Brevare was back in Town.

Kellet shook his head. "You can imagine. Behaviour unbecoming to a young lady, shall we say?"

"Who was it? I'll deal with—"

"No, you'll only draw more attention to the matter." Kellet's hand clutched his arm, and Alex drew a deep breath, his muscles rigid as he fought the need to answer the stories with his fists. Kellet was right, of course. And he'd been right to get Alex out of the room before he heard what they were saying for himself. His anger was likely to have overridden his judgement.

"Go home," Kellet said. "I'll find a few other places to listen, and come and tell you."

His hands still clenched into fists, Alex made himself do as Kellet recommended.

An hour later, Alex refilled his cup from the jug of coffee keeping warm by the fire, and poured one for Kellet. He doubted he could do anything tonight, but however attractive the idea of getting blind drunk was, it would not help anything.

"Well?"

"Same rumours in some other places, but only in taverns near the gentlemen's clubs," Kellet said, without preamble. Like himself, Kellet did not have the entrée to the higher class establishments. "Basically, you took advantage of Miss Deane—or she volunteered herself—in return for getting them all out of France."

Alex nodded, controlling his impulse to swear.

"The stories will have spread further by tomorrow," Kellet added. "I'll let Marstone know what I've heard."

"Is this Marstone's doing, Kellet?"

"Why would he spread such a story?" Kellet asked, genuine surprise in his face.

"Not spreading the story, but doing something that would make someone else do so?"

Kellet's brow creased as he thought. "The decoy note was delivered weeks ago," he pointed out. "It cannot be a result of that. However, Lord Marstone did mention that Brevare has been seen in London in the last couple of days."

Alex rubbed his face. He didn't know why Brevare would accuse Phoebe of wanton conduct, but the gossip was far more likely to be due to him, not Marstone.

There was nothing he could do tonight. He'd see Marstone in the morning, but Bella first—she'd be of more use supporting Phoebe if the rumours had spread further than the men's clubs.

Phoebe sighed as the hackney drew up outside the Brothertons' house on Hanover Square. The comtesse had insisted Phoebe accompany her on a social call, so she was resigned to half an hour of boredom. At least her aunt had agreed she could return home with Ellie afterwards, instead of sitting through their appointment with Mademoiselle Laurent.

The comtesse and Hélène alighted first, sending Ellie up the steps to knock on the door. Phoebe felt for her coin purse in her pocket and paid the hackney driver, hearing the Brothertons' butler say something but unable to make out the words. He stood in the middle of the open doorway instead of moving to one side to allow them in.

"Nonsense!" The comtesse's voice was loud, too loud for a public street. "Of course she is at home; we arranged to meet here today. Stand aside, man!"

The butler remained immobile, his face impassive. With a growing knot in her stomach, Phoebe recalled Lord Tresham's odd behaviour the day before.

"I should say, my lady, that Lady Brotherton is not at home *to you*. Good day." He stepped smartly backwards and closed the door in their faces.

"Well!" The comtesse's lips compressed. "You, girl," she said to Ellie. "Get another hackney. We'll go straight to Mademoiselle Laurent."

"Aunt, it might be wise to return home until you know why Lady Brotherton—"

"Nonsense, Phoebe," the comtesse said. "Just because of a misunderstanding? Lady Brotherton should not employ such insolent servants."

It didn't take long for Ellie to return with a hackney. Outside the mantua-maker's shop, Phoebe was once again left to pay. When she followed her aunt and cousin inside, she found them standing at the entrance to the main salon, their way blocked by one of Mademoiselle Laurent's assistants.

The leaden feeling in her stomach intensified. Something was definitely wrong.

"But we have an appointment in half an hour," the comtesse protested.

"I am sorry, my lady," the assistant said. "Mademoiselle Laurent has had to cancel your appointment today." Her eyes slid from the comtesse to Phoebe, one corner of her mouth turning up in a sneer.

"Does she wish me to take my custom elsewhere?"

Beyond the maid, several women sat on the sofas, drinking tea as they looked at pattern books and fashion plates. As the comtesse protested, books were set down and heads turned in their direction.

They should leave now, before the comtesse embarrassed herself any further, but Phoebe knew her aunt would reject any such suggestion from her. Hélène stood behind her mother, her gaze on the floor.

"We should go now," Phoebe said to her cousin, keeping her voice low. When Hélène looked at Phoebe, her eyes were glistening with unshed tears. Nodding mutely, she touched her mother's arm.

Phoebe went out with Ellie in search of yet another hackney, dreading the inevitable confrontation when they reached home.

. . .

Phoebe trailed behind as the comtesse swept into the house, almost running into Cookson as she pushed past him, demanding loudly to know where the comte was.

"In the library, my lady. Shall I tell him...?"

Cookson fell silent as the comtesse stalked towards the library and flung the door open so hard it slammed into the wall. The comte, startled, looked up from his armchair, then got to his feet as his wife came to a halt in front of him.

"I demand you send her away. Now."

"Come, sit down my dear and—"

"Now!" Her voice rose to a shriek. "I have been denied entry to the Brothertons' house and Mademoiselle Laurent's, and given the cut direct there."

"My dear—"

"It's all her fault!" The comtesse pointed a finger towards Phoebe, still standing near the door with Hélène, both shocked at the rage before them. "I heard her name mentioned several times in Mademoiselle Laurent's."

That must have been after she'd gone to find a hackney.

"I told you how it would be, Eduoard!"

"Lavinia—calm down, please." The comte looked helplessly past his wife, motioning to the girls to leave.

Phoebe turned and led Hélène out into the hall. The baize door to the servants' quarters was swinging gently, and Phoebe wondered how many of the staff had been listening. Her aunt's voice was still audible even though the library door was closed.

Hélène was in tears and well on the way to a fit of the vapours. "They'll take our Almack's vouchers away," she wailed. "I'll never make a brilliant match now!"

Phoebe herself felt slightly sick, and took a few deep breaths to calm her stomach.

"Get someone to bring a vinaigrette, Cookson, please," she said to the waiting butler. "We are not at home to visitors."

"Of course, miss."

The sounds from the library were becoming quieter. Phoebe could hear the low tones of her uncle's voice, although not his words. She ushered Hélène, now sobbing into a handkerchief, into the parlour on the first floor.

Waiting in tense silence to be summoned back, Phoebe tried not to think of the consequences. Whatever unhappiness she had been feeling yesterday, this was far worse. At least then she'd had the possibility of marriage. Now, with the family in disgrace, it seemed that even that could be denied her. If she *was* the subject of whatever gossip was circulating, she was fairly sure that her uncle would still support her, but living with the comtesse would be more unpleasant than ever. And what effect would a ruined sister have on Joe's career?

Finally, Cookson appeared in the doorway, asking them both to return to the library. The comtesse had obviously been pacified a little, and was sitting in one of the leather chairs, her face set in a scowl.

"Now, does either of you know what has happened?" the comte asked.

Phoebe shook her head.

"Hélène?"

Hélène looked way, and dabbed her eyes with her handkerchief.

"Come, Hélène," the comte said, his voice becoming sharp. "We need to find out what is happening."

"Last night, at the rout…"

"Go on."

"Sophia Brotherton asked if it was true that we were nearly taken prisoner in France, and that we were rescued by the Vicomte de Brevare."

Some version of events had been spread about then. From what Phoebe had seen yesterday and today, she had little doubt that her own actions would have been cast in the worst possible light.

"Is that all she said?" the comte asked.

"Yes." Hélène frowned in concentration. "That was all she said to *me*."

"What do you mean?"

"She seemed to be... pleased... when I said yes, then she went away and talked to her sister and to Maria and Susie. They were laughing at me!" Hélène started to sob again. "I thought they were my friends!"

"So, word of your escape from France has started to circulate," the comte said. "And an incorrect one, by the sound of it." He turned to his wife. "I did warn you, madame, that any slurs cast on Phoebe would reflect on the whole family. Now you see what has become of it."

"But I didn't!" the comtesse protested.

"Who else? You, Hélène?"

"No, Papa."

"Sir," Phoebe interrupted.

"Yes, Phoebe?"

"I think the story may have started with the Vicomte de Brevare." Who else but Brevare would have the knowledge of what had happened in France?

"Why do you say that?"

"It is possible the tale has spread through the men's clubs, not through drawing room gossip." Phoebe described the carriage that had almost stopped to talk to the marquess the day before, and Lord Tresham's odd behaviour. "Some people must have heard by last night's rout, but the story can't have spread widely until this morning."

"*That man!*"

Phoebe cringed at the venom in her aunt's voice.

"Mr Westbrook, do you mean?" the comte asked. He glanced at Phoebe.

"Not Mr Westbrook, sir." Whatever he felt—or did not feel—for Phoebe, he would not do such a thing. She was certain of that.

"Who knows *what* that man will do?" the comtesse said. "He isn't fit for—"

"Lavinia! *Please!*" His voice was loud enough to shock the comtesse. "Lavinia, you are tired," he stated firmly. "You should go to your room for a lie down. You, too, Hélène."

He stood, and offered his hand to his wife. She glared at him, then rose and allowed him to escort her out of the room. Hélène followed them.

CHAPTER 42

*W*hile her uncle was escorting her aunt upstairs, Phoebe thought back over the last few days. She'd seen Brevare at Lady Stanton's ball three nights ago. He'd called on her uncle yesterday and discovered she was no servant. He could have started to spread the gossip then—the timing fitted.

The comte returned, closing the door behind him.

"It *must* have been the Vicomte de Brevare who spread the story," Phoebe said, once her uncle had settled back into his chair.

"Your reasoning?"

"The only person who knows what happened in France, apart from Brevare, is Lord Marstone. I know Mr Westbrook is not responsible, and what reason would Lord Marstone have for spreading such lies, especially now?" She looked down at her hands, her fingers tightly interlaced, then back up at her uncle. "Does it matter who? The fact that there is scandal is bad enough, is it not?"

The comte regarded her, his brows drawn. "Phoebe, you do not seem *surprised* that scurrilous is spreading about your... adventures in France."

"I don't know what is being said. Madame was the one who said the gossip was about me."

"Very well. I assume, from what you *did* tell me, that it must be your behaviour that is being maligned?"

"Sir, I did not—"

"I'm not saying that, Phoebe," her uncle interrupted, his voice calm. "But you did say that some of the things you did could be misinterpreted."

Phoebe took a deep breath, and nodded. "Yes, sir. It seems likely that it is my behaviour that is under... attack." She recalled that scene on the beach, when Alex had nearly shot Brevare. He would not readily forgive someone who'd witnessed his fear.

"I suppose Westbrook or Marstone may know something about it." The comte looked thoughtful. "Phoebe, you said there was someone you liked better than Harlford. Would this man believe these rumours?"

Phoebe closed her eyes. She could not tell him that it was Alex himself she had meant. "No, sir, he would not believe them." That was certainly true. "But I am not sure that he returns my regard, sir."

The comte rubbed his hand over his face wearily. "I do sympathise, Phoebe. I will call on Marstone. I assume he can give me Westbrook's direction?"

"I do not know sir, but it is likely."

"Phoebe, thank you for not treating me to a third set of the vapours. Remember that you are family, and this unpleasant situation does not change that."

Phoebe felt a slight lessening of the tension within her. She had not expected him to cast her off, but it was good to hear him say so.

"Thank you, sir. You are very good." She took a deep breath. "Is there anything I can do in the meantime?"

"Make sure Miss Bryant keeps Georges out of the way of your aunt." He stood up, and rang for someone to get his coat and hat and to find a hackney.

Phoebe followed him out into the hall, on the way to her room. A note lay on the salver near the door.

"What is it?" Phoebe asked, seeing his expression change as he read it.

350

"Harlford sends his regrets, but is forced to cancel his arrangements with us this week."

"At least he let us know."

"Yes, I suppose that is something," the comte said sadly.

Phoebe went up the stairs. It appeared that Lord Harlford's regard for her was not so high that he would try to find out the truth of any rumours before believing them. It saved her having to think whether or not she should accept an offer from him, but that was small comfort.

Alex knocked on Bella's front door, for the second time that morning. This time Bella was at home, and Hobson showed him into her parlour.

"You've come about Phoebe," Bella said, as soon as the door closed behind the butler.

"Yes," he said, "but how did you—?"

Damn—the story had already spread.

"Sit down, Alex. I've been hearing several variations on an unbelievable story on my calls."

Some of Alex's tension left him, and he sat. He should have known Bella would not think ill of Phoebe.

"That is why I have been out so long, she went on. "I wanted to find out what was being said, and where."

"What have you heard?"

"Most of the stories say that you took advantage of—"

"Damn it." Alex jumped to his feet. It sounded worse coming from Bella than it had from Kellet the previous evening.

"Alex, that's not the worst, I'm afraid."

Alex clenched his fists, turning abruptly to look out of the window. He was angry not only with the gossips, but with himself for involving Phoebe in his business.

"There are other stories," Bella went on. "Most say that Phoebe...

351

well, offered herself first to Brevare, and then to you, if you would get them all home. Brevare, being the gentleman he is, refused."

"And I did not, I suppose." He made an effort to keep his anger in check.

That question needed no answer. He turned to find Bella regarding him closely.

"Alex, why has this started now? Phoebe has been in Town for weeks."

"Brevare has recently arrived in London. It is likely connected with him." He moved over to the fireplace, resting one arm on the mantelpiece and fixing his gaze on the fire. It was easier to hide the strength of his feelings from Bella that way.

"The Comtesse de Calvac..." Alex took a deep breath, trying to control the anger in his voice. "Did you know that Phoebe's aunt effectively tried to prostitute her when—"

"What?" Bella's eyes widened.

Alex described part of the evening when Phoebe had been made to wear the gold dress.

"Good God."

"The woman talked about, and to, Phoebe for the rest of the journey as if she really had thrown herself at me," Alex went on. "Including in front of Brevare. No doubt the comtesse said the same thing to her husband, but the comte seems to have supported Phoebe so far. But now? This will tarnish the whole family—will he still support her in such circumstances? Not to mention how distressed she must be at being the target of such slander."

"I doubt anyone will have repeated the slander to her face."

"Even so." He walked over to the window again, wanting to do something. Anything—but mostly to punch the men who were doubtless discussing such a juicy titbit in their clubs at this very moment.

"If she married, the stories would die down or be ignored," Bella said.

He turned to look at her, his breath catching at the knowing look —and sympathy—in her face.

"Not to me," he stated. "And to be forced into it by someone's slander? She would be little better off. Young ladies of the *ton* do not marry bastards in trade," he went on. "Not even the bastards of earls."

"You could let her decide that."

"No. If this scandal is averted, she'd still be cut off from society. She might think she won't mind, but she doesn't know what it's like. I can't do that to her—even assuming she'd have me." She'd only just escaped from being the despised poor relation in her aunt's family.

"Has it really been so bad, Alex?"

He sighed. "For me, not really—particularly given the alternative of being the illegitimate son of a village woman. But there was the time I tried to offer for Mary Helstone..."

"The outcome of that was just as well, from what I knew of her."

Alex shrugged. "As you say, it was for the best in the long run, but it wasn't... pleasant... at the time. I've always been between two worlds—I have friends in trade, some in the *ton*, and Marstone has kept me busy. But it's not the same for women, particularly if they are used to being in society."

"But if she loves—"

"Leave it, Bella." That came out too forcefully—none of this was Bella's fault, and she was only trying to help. He rubbed a hand over his face. "What can be—?"

A knock on the door interrupted him.

"Lady Jesson, my lady," Hobson announced.

A woman entered the room, a few years older than Bella, and tending to plumpness. Bella must have been expecting her, as the butler had knocked but entered without waiting for an acknowledgement.

What had Lady Jesson to do with this business?

"Maria, I don't think you've met Alex Westbrook. Alex, Lady Jesson."

"Lady Jesson," Alex said, his tone as polite as he could manage.

"Mr Westbrook."

Lady Jesson's gaze ran from his head to his feet and back again. "I've been hearing a lot about you this afternoon—"

"It's not—"

"—and I doubt any of it is true." Lady Jesson continued speaking over his words of protest.

"Do sit down again, Alex," Bella said. "I've asked Maria to assist us."

Alex stayed where he was, but didn't protest again. At least Phoebe had some allies, even if he couldn't think how they might help.

"I've only heard more of the same," Lady Jesson said to Bella, taking her seat. "As always, no-one seems to know where the story came from."

"I'm going to see Marstone," Bella said. "It's possible he may know something. But I'm worried how Phoebe is taking it. Could you...?"

"By all means," Lady Jesson said, getting to her feet again.

"If my brother isn't at Marstone House, I'll wait," Bella added. "Will you join us there after you've seen Phoebe?"

"Very well." Lady Jesson nodded to Bella and Alex, and left.

Alex turned to Bella.

"What the h—?" He stopped, and massaged one temple. "Bella, who is that woman?"

"One of the *ton*'s greatest gossips," Bella said, a mischievous smile on her face. "But she's on our side. Alex, did you tell Phoebe who you are?"

"No."

"That's good." She stood, and patted his arm. "I have the beginnings of an idea for mitigating some of the damage, but first we need to know what's happened in Berkeley Square. Maria will find out about that for us, so I don't want to get to Marstone House too long before she does. Ring for refreshments if you want something; I'm going to get changed. We'll leave in an hour."

Alex paced when she left, returning to the vague ideas he'd been toying with all morning. The timing, so soon after Brevare's return to London, left no doubt in his mind that Brevare was responsible. He'd contemplated using Brevare's sister and mother to force him to retract, but knew it wasn't possible. Brevare didn't know him well, but well enough to know he would not carry though a threat to harm them. And it was too late now for any retraction to stop the stories spreading.

CHAPTER 43

*P*hoebe had just reached her room when Green came upstairs to say there was another caller.

"Lady Jesson, miss. Cookson did tell her that no-one is at home to visitors, but she insisted."

"Madame is lying down, Green. She *cannot* receive visitors."

"No, miss, it was you her ladyship wanted. She's waiting in the parlour."

Was Lady Jesson such a gossip that she had to come and gloat so quickly? Phoebe took a deep breath—she was possibly being unfair. Bella had said the woman was not spiteful. She should see her now—if Bella was wrong, it was best to have the confrontation in private.

"Thank you, Green. Please tell her I will be down shortly, and get some tea sent in."

When Green had gone, Phoebe splashed her face with water from the pitcher on her dressing table and patted her face dry. She peered into the mirror, tidying a few loose strands of hair, then stood up straight. Shoulders back, she told herself, head high. You did none of the things they are saying.

Apart from returning his kiss.

Lady Jesson was wearing purple and grey again, cut in Miss

Fletcher's flattering style. She looked up as Phoebe entered the room, and Phoebe's apprehension diminished when she saw the woman's face—it was clear she had not come to gloat, but to sympathise.

"Oh, my dear," she said, before Phoebe had greeted her properly.

This unexpected kindness broke down Phoebe's defences at last and she started to cry, gulping into her handkerchief. The tears weren't only due to today's unpleasantness, but were a result of all the doubts she had felt the day before as well.

She was dimly aware of the tea being brought and the door closing again behind Green, then her back was being patted comfortingly.

Lady Jesson made no attempt to get her to stop weeping, but when her tears gradually began to dry up she handed her a clean handkerchief and then a cup of tea. Phoebe sipped it as Lady Jesson got up to ring the bell. She spoke to Green when he came, and the footman returned a few minutes later with more tea and a large plate of sandwiches and slices of cake.

"Have some cake," Lady Jesson said. "There's not much that cannot be made a tiny bit better by tea and cake." She held the plate towards Phoebe. "As you can see, it is a maxim I follow often."

Phoebe couldn't help a chuckle. Lady Jesson *was* a little on the plump side, and Phoebe was beginning to like her.

"That's better," Lady Jesson said.

The hot tea and sweet cake helped to revive her. "Why have you come, my lady?" she asked. She could recall talking to Lady Jesson on only a couple of occasions.

"You are afraid I have come to gather more gossip?"

"I was when you were announced."

"And now?"

Lady Jesson was smiling, but kindly.

"No, you're not here to gossip. But you hardly know me, yet you are the only person who seems to be willing to talk to me."

"There will be others, my dear. Not everyone will make judgements based only on rumours. Phoebe, have you heard what is being said?"

Phoebe flushed. "No, but I can guess."

"What I heard was that you all had some trouble during your return from France, that the Vicomte de Brevare and Westbrook were involved, and that you indulged in some extremely improper, not to mention wanton and immoral behaviour with the latter."

Phoebe opened her mouth to protest, but Lady Jesson held up a hand.

"I believe the first part to be true, and the second part to be a complete fabrication." Lady Jesson took another piece of cake while Phoebe was absorbing this statement.

"Why?" was all Phoebe could say.

"For the first part, I know that your aunt took you and her daughter to France recently—for what purpose I have no idea. A particularly stupid idea on Lavinia's part, given the situation over there, but then she always was a bit of a wigeon."

This agreed so well with her own opinion of their trip to France that Phoebe almost laughed. She liked Lady Jesson very much indeed.

"As for the second part," Lady Jesson went on. "You wouldn't do such a thing."

"How can you be sure of that, my lady?"

"I've been watching you."

Phoebe's eyebrows rose. A gossip must observe people, she supposed, to gather her information, but she couldn't believe that she was a sufficiently interesting target.

"That surprises you?" Lady Jesson said. "I watch everyone. You can hold your own in a sensible conversation, you've managed not to be rude to all those jackanapes who only danced with you to try to get closer to your cousin, and you are singular in your ability to be around Harlford without drooling over his wealth and title."

She leaned forward and picked up the plate with the remaining cake on it. "Do have some more."

Phoebe obediently took another piece.

"And I know Westbrook's... relatives, and know of Westbrook," Lady Jesson went on.

"You do?"

"I do. And the fact that these stories have Westbrook as the supposed villain of the piece make them impossible for me to believe. But I assume that your journey was not straightforward—do you feel like telling me what really happened?"

Phoebe hesitated—much of it was not her story to tell, and other parts might lead some people to believe that the rumours may be true. She didn't think Lady Jesson was one of those people, but she couldn't risk it.

"Obviously not," Lady Jesson said. "I can't say that I blame you. After all, you only know me as a gossip. I'm also a blackmailer," she added conversationally.

Phoebe choked on some cake crumbs. Coughing, she took a quick mouthful of tea. Was this some kind of test?

"Now, Phoebe, explain why you haven't summoned someone to show me out."

"It's not every day that someone announces that she is a blackmailer, my lady," Phoebe said, thinking it through as she spoke. "As I don't see how you can tell the *ton* anything that they don't already think they know about me, I assume you're not intending to blackmail me. So I'm interested to find out what else you have to say."

"Very good. Now, how can you turn blackmail into a good thing?"

"I presume you don't mean blackmail for money?"

Lady Jesson nodded.

This *was* a test. Phoebe's lips twitched as she wondered how well Lady Jesson and the Earl of Marstone knew each other.

"You could use… information… to persuade people to do… well, to do good things?"

Lady Jesson smiled approvingly. "As I said, I collect information. I pass along enough harmless gossip to maintain the impression people have of me, and to make sure I get invitations."

"Why do you need to do that?"

"A general lack of funds, and few high-born relatives," Lady Jesson said, without any sign of embarrassment. "I hear things, and I make connections. My staff are also good listeners. Often a surmise can be confirmed by a word or two—the unwary often give themselves away."

"So persuading people doesn't always require proof, just a good guess?"

"Precisely."

"But why do it?"

"You could say I'm a busybody, I suppose. I feel that I can occasionally influence things for the better."

Phoebe looked down at her hands. Lady Jesson had been very frank, and shared information that Phoebe didn't think she'd want repeating elsewhere. The woman had shown confidence in Phoebe's discretion; she should return the compliment. But first, perhaps Lady Jesson could tell her something.

"I think I saw my aunt with some letters when we were on the journey back," she said. "I wondered if they were what she went to Calvac to retrieve."

Lady Jesson's hand paused in mid-air, her tea cup half-way to her mouth. "Letters?" She put the cup down, her brow furrowed in thought. "Denville?"

Phoebe waited.

"Lavinia was being courted by Lord Denville's second son," Lady Jesson said at last. "I'm not sure what happened, but he went off to join the army and she married your uncle."

Love letters? And her aunt had not only kept them, but decided to accompany Anson on his journey to retrieve them. She wondered if her aunt had chosen Monsieur de Calvac only for his title, and regretted the loss of a former suitor.

She shook her head—it was none of her business. If her aunt regretted that long-ago decision, it was her uncle she felt sorry for.

But Lady Jesson had asked what had happened in France. "The trouble began when we were waiting to be served at an inn," Phoebe began. "My aunt didn't realise the dangerous situation we were in." She related the basics of the story, skating over the detail of the night the comtesse had made her wear the gold dress. She didn't mention the information Alex had been carrying. "And my uncle has gone to see if Lord Marstone or Mr Westbrook knows anything about these rumours."

"That is the complete story?" Lady Jesson asked, when she finished.

"No, my lady. It is all the information that is relevant, however."

"Well, that will have to do. I must say that I never thought Lavinia would be as spiteful as that."

"I don't know why she dislikes me so much. It isn't as if I can compete with Hélène for suitors."

"Apart from Harlford," Lady Jesson pointed out.

Phoebe shook her head. "That's over. He sent a note to my uncle." She felt a brief flash of regret—she did like the marquess, but he had shown he did not trust her.

"Hmm." Lady Jesson gazed at her, her head tilted a little to one side. "Did you know that your uncle made an offer for your mother?"

"No. Really? When?"

"A few years before he married Lavinia. Your mother declined, and married your father instead."

Phoebe knew that part of the reason her mother's family had objected to her marriage was because she'd turned down a high-born suitor to do so. She hadn't known it was her uncle. There hadn't been much contact between the sisters, and she'd always assumed it was because of her father's status as a surgeon and apothecary.

It sounded as if her aunt had been jealous of her mother, but why? The comtesse valued status and wealth, and she had those.

"You knew my mother?" Phoebe asked—that, too, was new information.

"Yes, quite well during my first season—she was only a few years older than me. She didn't come to Town again after her marriage and I lost touch with her, to my regret. I was still in Town when Calvac was courting Lavinia. Were your parents happy?"

"Yes," said Phoebe. And that brought her back to the current situation. "I do appreciate you calling, my lady. And for your candour. But I don't see what is to be done about these rumours."

"Marriage is the usual ending to such things."

Phoebe sighed. "To anyone who will have me? I had hoped to marry for love, as my parents did."

"You don't like Westbrook? He is the obvious candidate, after all."

Phoebe shuffled uncomfortably in her seat. "That is not the point."

"What do you know about him?" Lady Jesson raised one eyebrow. "Other than his spying activities, that is?"

Phoebe was about to reply, but hesitated. Did Lady Jesson *know*, or was she guessing? "Why do you say that?" she said carefully.

"Oh, very good indeed, Phoebe," Lady Jesson said, smiling.

"I beg your pardon?"

"A good, noncommittal answer." She nodded, the smile still curving her lips. "It gives no indication of whether or not you know he is a spy. I do not know myself, of course, but I surmise—why else would he be travelling in France at such a time? This Brevare fellow has more excuse, as he is actually French."

"He said little about himself, my lady."

"So you know nothing about his family or his background?"

Phoebe shook her head.

"Hmm." Lady Jesson stilled, her cup in mid-air, her eyes fixed on something across the room.

"Lady Jesson?"

"Oh, sorry. I must think about this." She put the cup down and stood up. "I will leave you now, but do not be too downhearted. *Something* can be done, I'm sure of it. It may take some time, though."

Phoebe rang the bell, and Lady Jesson asked Cookson to summon a hackney.

"Thank you for calling, my lady," Phoebe said sincerely.

"We are friends, are we not? Come now, no tears! I will not be the only one who does not think ill of you, you will see!"

CHAPTER 44

*A*lex followed Bella into the library at Marstone House. Lord Marstone was talking to the Comte de Calvac, but Lady Jesson had not yet arrived.

"Why are you here, Bella?" Marstone asked.

"To help decide what can be done about the gossip," Bella said, taking a seat. "Lady Jesson has gone to talk to Phoebe, and will join us shortly."

"I am quite capable of looking after my niece," the comte snapped.

"I only mean to help, monsieur," Bella said. "Phoebe is my friend, and Lady Jesson was one of Amelia's friends."

"Amelia?" Marstone asked.

"Phoebe's mother."

Lady Jesson really would be an ally, then.

"I don't see what there is to discuss," the comte said. "If the stories are about Phoebe, there is an obvious way to help—"

"Lady Jesson, my lord," Langton announced from the doorway.

The comte's jaw clenched at this second interruption. By now, Kellet or Marstone would have told him what people were saying, and Alex could guess what he was about to suggest.

"How is Phoebe?" Bella asked.

362

"Bearing up well." Lady Jesson took a seat next to Bella.

"You could have asked me that," the comte said, irritation clear in his voice. "Can we get on with this now?" He looked around, giving a little nod when no-one spoke.

"Thank you. As I have tried to say twice now, marriage is the obvious way to reduce—"

"Not necessarily," Bella interrupted.

She glanced at Alex as she spoke, her expression something between sympathy and amusement. Alex wondered if he was going to like her solution any more than the comte's.

"Do continue," Marstone said.

Bella glanced around at her audience. "At the moment, there are a number of scurrilous accusations flying about. What is needed is another story giving the opposite view. Perhaps that this Brevare character did not play a major part in the rescue of three ladies in distress and is ashamed of the fact, or that he propositioned Miss Deane—"

Alex's fists clenched as he recalled that Brevare had done so.

"—and was rejected, and he is spreading these stories to get his revenge."

"But we cannot put about such a story ourselves," Lady Jesson said. "It would seem too partisan. However, both Bella and I can arrange for the story to spread via servants—it may well be more effective that way, in any case."

Bella turned to the comte. "If anyone mentions any of it to your family, monsieur, it is essential that they all say the same—that Phoebe was never out of your wife's company."

"They will," the comte said.

"You will excuse me for saying so," Lady Jesson put in, "but your wife may need some encouragement to do so—over and above whatever you say to persuade her."

The comte's brows drew together, but finally he nodded. Alex felt sorry for him—it could not be easy being married to such a woman.

"How do you intend to...ah...encourage my wife?" the comte asked.

"Maria and I are working on the details," Bella said. "To start with, I think it will be best if your family is out of town for a little while, so I would like to invite your wife, daughter, and niece to Oakley Place for a week. Your son and his governess, too, if you wish. It's in Sussex, so only half a day's travel."

"Thank you. I will accept."

"It may be better for you not to accompany them," Lady Jesson added. "That might look too much like running away. I'll put it about that it's a long-standing invitation from Lady Carterton to your wife."

Bella spoke again. "Will, I'll need you and Alex there too."

So much for his resolution to stay away from Phoebe.

"I'm busy, Bella," Marstone objected.

"You can make time for this," Bella said firmly, fixing her gaze on him. "You need only stay for a day. Alex will need to stay longer, but I'm sure you can spare him."

"Oh, very well. Let Kellet know the details."

"Monsieur?"

The comte rubbed the back of his neck. "I will go along with this. Whatever else, you are right that my family would be better off away from London."

"Alex?"

Alex nodded. No doubt he'd find out soon enough what Bella had in mind. He listened as Bella and Lady Jesson settled the arrangements for the trip with the comte, then the three of them took their leave. Marstone moved over to his desk and sat, taking some papers from a drawer.

Ignoring these signs that the earl expected him to leave as well, Alex walked over to the desk.

Marstone looked up at him, then leaned back in his chair. "You think I had something to do with this?"

"I wondered, yes. You have some plans for Miss Deane, or why would you ask Admiral Fenton about her?"

The earl looked him in the eyes. "I give you my word that I have done nothing to prompt these rumours."

Alex let out a breath—he was glad to be reassured on that head. He contemplated persisting with his question about Fenton, but Marstone was unlikely to give him a satisfactory answer.

"Do feel free to stay here until you go down to Sussex," Marstone added. "I'd rather you didn't start a brawl with someone you might overhear slighting Miss Deane."

"Thank you. I will."

Phoebe retreated to the library when Lady Jesson left. Sitting at the table in the window with a book was preferable to moping in her room, even if her eyes did seem to be moving across the pages without really seeing the words. She tried to keep her mind from turning over possible futures; Lady Jesson had said something could be done, and Phoebe believed her. But what would be the result of her uncle's visit to Marstone House?

Determined not to waste her time, she eventually put aside the travel book she'd been attempting to read, and took out the books she had been discussing with her uncle. Going through them and making notes on significant points occupied her well enough, even if she was unlikely to remember any of the details later.

The comte returned around an hour after Lady Jesson had left. He nodded a greeting as he entered the library, but crossed the room to the tray of decanters and glasses and poured himself a drink.

Phoebe closed the book as he sat down by the fire, and moved to take the opposite chair.

The comte rubbed his forehead. "You are all invited to visit the Cartertons," he said. "In Sussex, travelling down the day after tomorrow. I will remain in Town for the moment."

Her uncle would know what the stories were now, and she'd expected him to say something about her marrying Alex. "It will be good to be in the country," she said, feeling some reply was needed.

The comte drained his glass. "Indeed. Lady Carterton and Lady Jesson seem to think that if they can get the true story of events circulated, the damage can be limited provided that everyone in this household keeps to the same story."

Phoebe wasn't sure how accurate the 'true' story would be, but anything was better than the horrible things they were saying about her now.

"Phoebe?"

"Is Georges to come too?" Phoebe asked, brought back to the present. "And Miss Bryant?"

"Yes. He will enjoy it, I think," the comte said.

"Lady Carterton has children of a similar age," Phoebe said. "I will let them know," she added, waiting for her uncle's agreement before going upstairs.

Georges was excited at the prospect of being able to ride in the countryside and make new friends.

"There's a boy and a girl nearest your age," Phoebe added, her lips pursed as she anticipated Georges' reply.

"Girls are no fun—" he started.

"Oh?" Phoebe said. "You won't want my company then. I hope you enjoy your stay there, Georges."

She walked towards the door, ignoring the whispering behind her, then Georges rushed over.

"I'm sorry Phoebe, I didn't mean you."

"I'm not a proper girl, then?"

"No. I mean, yes... Oh!"

"Why don't you go and choose some of your books to take with you?" Alice suggested, and Georges went over to the bookcase.

"Is this because of that gossip?" Alice asked, keeping her voice low.

Phoebe sighed. She didn't mind Alice knowing, but it was discouraging to find how far, and how fast, the rumours had spread.

"Lady Carterton has an idea of how to limit the damage," she explained. "I don't know the details yet."

"It will be a pleasant change of scenery," Alice said. "I've not been to Sussex before." She cast a sympathetic glance at Phoebe. "It's a shame it has to be in such circumstances."

. . .

Two days later, Phoebe leaned forward to peer out of the window as the coach turned between a pair of tall pillars. They passed through some woodland, then the house came into view. The pale stone of the square Palladian building was framed in green by the open lawn to its front and the woodland rising gently behind.

Bella and Lord Carterton came out onto the steps to meet their guests. After formal greetings had been exchanged they were shown to their rooms, the housekeeper informing them that the other guests were sitting in the south parlour. Phoebe went downstairs as soon as she'd tidied her hair.

The parlour was a pleasant room, decorated in pale yellows and greens. The windows framed a lovely prospect over the lawns and drive at the front of the house, currently basking in the afternoon sunshine. Phoebe was pleased to see Lady Jesson sitting by the window, next to a woman Phoebe did not recognise. She walked over and made her curtsey.

"Lady Lydenham, this is Miss Phoebe Deane," Lady Jesson said. "Phoebe, this is the Countess of Lydenham."

Lady Lydenham looked about the same age as Lady Jesson, Phoebe thought, although she was slender where Lady Jesson tended to plumpness.

"So this is Amelia's daughter," Lady Lydenham said, looking Phoebe up and down and then smiling.

"You knew my mother, my lady?" Was this another ally?

"Yes, we were all out at the same time. Your aunt as well."

A grimace passed over her face as she spoke, so brief that Phoebe wondered if she had imagined it.

"I corresponded with Amelia for many years," Lady Lydenham went on. "So I've read much about your childhood. And now Lavinia is giving you a season with Hélène. I didn't think she'd be so generous."

Phoebe opened her mouth to contradict this, but thought better of it.

"You can speak freely, Phoebe," Lady Jesson said. "Lady Lydenham is a good friend of mine, and was a good friend to your mother. Whatever we say here is said in confidence."

Lady Lydenham nodded encouragingly.

"My uncle was happy to take me in when my parents died, my lady." They could read into that what they pleased. Phoebe was fairly sure that Lady Jesson, at least, knew her aunt was not presenting her willingly.

"Now, Phoebe," Lady Jesson said. "I'd like you to tell Lady Lydenham what happened in France. Tell her what you told me."

Phoebe hesitated. She knew even less about Lady Lydenham than she did of Lady Jesson.

"It will go no further," Lady Lydenham promised. "Maria is assisting Lady Carterton with some kind of plan, I believe, although she has not told me what it is."

Hoping she was doing the right thing, Phoebe related the story she had told Lady Jesson two days before.

Lady Lydenham's eyebrows rose as she listened. "Maria told me Lavinia had behaved appallingly," she said, when Phoebe finished. "I didn't think she had that amount of spite in her!"

She reached over and patted Phoebe's hand. "And now these horrible stories—don't worry my dear, all will be well in the end."

Phoebe didn't quite believe that, but it felt good to have these allies. Perhaps there would be time later for her to ask them about her mother's season in London. Her mother hadn't spoken of it—mainly because it wasn't important to her, Phoebe guessed, and because Phoebe hadn't been interested in such things then.

What was their plan, though? She was about to ask Lady Jesson when Bella came into the room, followed by her husband.

"Ah, I see you have been introduced to our other guest, Phoebe," Bella said, sitting down. "Andrews," she addressed the butler, hovering in the doorway. "We will wait until the comtesse and her daughter come down before we have tea."

"Madame de Calvac has requested tea in her room, my lady."

Phoebe, relieved that she wouldn't have to be in her aunt's

company again for a while, saw that the others were not pleased. Was her aunt's presence necessary for the plan?

"You could tell her that the Earl of Marstone will be present," Lady Jesson suggested.

Lord Marstone? She hadn't expected him to be here. A fluttery feeling arose in her stomach. Did that mean Alex was here as well?

"No offence, Carterton," Lady Jesson went on, turning to Bella's husband, "but a mere baron cannot compete with an earl!"

Lord Carterton laughed. "None taken."

Bella turned to the butler. "Andrews, please ask Madame if she requires any food with her tea, and say what a pity it is that she is not feeling well enough to greet the earl, as he will not be staying long. Then serve tea here in half an hour, I think."

"Very good, my lady," Andrews bowed and departed, as if this kind of request were nothing out of the ordinary.

CHAPTER 45

*A*lex and Marstone handed their mounts over to a groom and, not standing on ceremony, made their way into the house through the back entrance. Andrews showed them up to their rooms.

The small trunk that Alex had sent on ahead had been unpacked for him, his coats brushed and hung to let the creases fall out. A jug of hot water arrived while he was still pulling his boots off, and he had a quick wash and changed into a clean set of clothing. When he had combed and retied his hair, he went to knock at the earl's door.

"All set?" Marstone asked.

"As ready as I'll ever be." Deceiving the comtesse and Hélène didn't worry him, but he'd be lying to Phoebe, too. "My part in this still seems pointless, and Bella's plan may not work. If the Calvac woman isn't stupid enough to believe you, and isn't ambitious enough…"

"You know her better than I do."

"Count yourself lucky, sir."

"Oh, I do! But does she really have the sense to see through it?"

"Probably not," Alex admitted. "Miss Deane will, though. She might give it away."

"Do you think so?"

Alex shrugged. He was certain that Phoebe would work out the truth, but whether or not she would tell her aunt, he didn't know. He just hoped that it would not distress her in any way.

"Bella should have told her the plan," he said, as Marstone stuck a diamond pin into his neckcloth and allowed his valet to help him into his coat.

"It was Bella's idea," the earl said. "I left her to it."

The parlour was cheerful, a blazing fire warming the room. Bella's guests were gathered near the tea table. Alex glanced around as they approached, feeling a little breathless at the sight of Phoebe, beautiful in a moss-green gown. Lady Jesson and another woman sat nearby with the comtesse and her daughter.

"Ah, Will, there you are," Bella said. "May I introduce the Comtesse de Calvac and her daughter, Lady Hélène? Madame de Calvac, my brother, the Earl of Marstone."

"Delighted to make your acquaintance, my lady." The earl bowed. The comtesse simpered, then Alex saw her expression sour as she noticed him standing behind the earl. Phoebe's lovely smile spread across her face, but there was also a trace of bemusement.

"I believe you have met each other before," Marstone said to the comtesse. "But may I formally introduce you to my eldest son?" He gestured towards Alex.

Alex gave the smallest bow he thought he could get away with. "My lady."

The comtesse's face was frozen, whether in shock or in horror he couldn't tell. Beside her, Hélène stood with her mouth open, and Bella turned away, biting her lips. Alex felt a flash of irritation—it was all very well for Bella to laugh—she wasn't the one carrying out this deception.

"Oh," the comtesse said at last, faintly. "I'm pleased to make your acquaintance properly, Lord..."

Alex guessed she was floundering for Marstone's secondary title.

"Just call me Westbrook, my lady," Alex said. If the comtesse knew anything at all about Marstone, she'd realise that Westbrook was not one of Marstone's secondary titles and he wasn't Marstone's heir.

371

Clearly, she didn't know. She simpered again, no doubt flattered by the invitation to use only his supposed title.

"Oh, Westbrook, it was so good of you to help us all in France. Dear Hélène and I are so..."

Alex stopped listening. Beyond her, Phoebe's brow creased in a frown, then her eyes widened and one hand went to her mouth.

"...heroic efforts. Such a pity you have not attended any balls this season..."

Phoebe's eyes met his, and he thought he detected amusement there, not distress.

"...chance for you to dance with Hélène. You would make such a..."

Phoebe's gaze shifted back to the comtesse, her lips pressed firmly together. Relief spread through him as he realised she was trying not to laugh.

"...think so, Westbrook?"

The silence in the room brought him back to the present. He wasn't going to agree to a statement he hadn't listened to, so he murmured something and inclined his head. Bella took mercy on him and started pouring tea, summoning the comtesse to the table to take her cup.

Phoebe went to sit beside Lady Lydenham, who must have seen something in her face, for she smiled but left Phoebe to her thoughts.

Alex was not Marstone's heir, so he must be an illegitimate son. But what was Bella hoping to achieve, apart from making her aunt look foolish in front of the other guests? She'd even persuaded the earl to lie—not directly, but he must have expected the comtesse to jump to the wrong conclusion. Few members of the *ton* recognised their bastards, let alone introduced them into society.

Was that why Alex had not attended the ball she'd mentioned— because he wouldn't be received? Lightness filled her at the idea that Alex might be avoiding her for her own good, however poor a reason that seemed to her.

"Is it well known that Mr Westbrook is Lord Marstone's son?" she asked Lady Lydenham.

"No—only among Bella's friends," Lady Lydenham said. "How are you enjoying your season?"

Lady Lydenham was easy to talk to, and they exchanged opinions of functions and people until Bella broke up the party, announcing that they kept country hours and it was time to change for dinner.

Phoebe hurried up the stairs after her. "Bella?"

"Come into my room," Bella offered. "I can see you have questions."

They sat together in chairs near the window, looking out over the darkening front lawn.

"You must be Alex's aunt," Phoebe said.

"Yes, although I'm not much older than he is. I was only four when it happened, but Will—Marstone, that is—told me the story later. Alex's mother was a girl in a nearby village. I'm sure it happens all the time, unfortunately, but my brother didn't abandon her. He gave the girl enough of a dowry to make a respectable marriage later, and found a couple who wanted a baby. Alex considers the Westbrooks his real parents, I think, although Will did see him now and then while he was growing up. Our father thought he was wasting his efforts and refused to give him any money—it used up most of Will's allowance for some time to sort it all out."

Phoebe absorbed this information, part of her wondering why Alex had never mentioned the relationship. Did he think she'd hold it against him?

Bella looked as if she were suppressing a smile. "Phoebe, did you see your aunt's face?"

"Not properly, but I can guess." Now was not the time to be thinking about Alex, not with Bella's too-perceptive eyes on her. "Was it very bad?"

"Oh, yes!" Bella's eyes crinkled up and her smile widened.

"She has spent so long insulting him, calling him *that man*, and now she's... she's..." Phoebe chuckled. "And she was correct before, really."

"When he said 'Just call me Westbrook'," Bella said. "She was so flattered—"

"And she has no idea!"

Phoebe stood while Ellie fastened her evening gown—this one in peacock blue fabric over a pale cream underskirt—then sat thinking while the maid brushed her hair. Alex's expression had been concerned while her aunt had been babbling, until he saw that she couldn't completely hide her amusement. Her doubts about his feelings had been too precipitate.

"Lady Carterton was lookin' for you, miss," Ellie said, breaking into Phoebe's thoughts. "Hold still, now, miss," she added, twisting a bandeau around Phoebe's hair.

"Did she say what she wanted?"

"Not exactly, miss. She said that if she didn't see you before dinner, remember that not everything is what it seems."

"That's all?"

"Yes, miss. Funny message if you ask me."

When Phoebe came downstairs, she was directed into a different parlour, this one decorated in shades of burgundy and gold. Taking a glass of wine from a footman, she went to sit on one of the sofas by the fire. Everyone except her aunt and Hélène was present. Alex stood talking to Lord Marstone and Lord Carterton, all three in well-cut but plain coats and breeches, their embroidered waistcoats their only ornaments.

"Miss Fletcher has done you proud," Lady Jesson said, coming to sit beside Phoebe.

"Thank you, my lady," Phoebe said, pleased. "She does everyone proud, I think."

Although the men appeared to be deep in a discussion, Alex looked over to where Phoebe sat, giving her a cool nod before resuming his discussion. But she had noticed the beginnings of a smile, hastily suppressed, and recalled the message that Bella had sent via Ellie.

He *was* happy to see her, she was sure, but was playing a part. She suspected that she had a part to play herself this evening, but she wished that someone had told her what it was to be.

Phoebe glanced at the clock on the mantelpiece; it was ten minutes past the hour that Bella had said dinner would be served.

"It seems their experience with Harlford has not cured them of making late entrances," Lady Jesson said in her ear.

The door opened. After a brief pause—enough time to ensure all attention was on the door, Phoebe suspected—the comtesse and Hélène swept in. Their embroidered gowns were trimmed with silver lace and bows of ribbon, and diamonds twinkled at the comtesse's neck and ears.

"More suited to a ball than a country dinner," Lady Jesson muttered. "All icing and no cake."

Phoebe suppressed a smile. She was perfectly happy with her own, far more restrained gown.

"So sorry we are late," the comtesse said, looking at Lord Marstone rather than her hostess. On cue, to her obvious delight, he crossed the room to greet her.

Lord Carterton and Alex exchanged a quick grimace, then Alex squared his shoulders and moved to stand before Hélène, bowing over her hand. "How beautiful you look this evening, Lady Hélène."

Hélène smiled, and fluttered her eyelashes. "Why, thank you, Westbrook."

Phoebe took a couple of deep breaths, determined not to laugh.

"May I have the pleasure of escorting you to dinner?" Alex held his arm out as if he were in no doubt of her reply. Hélène fluttered her fan, and laid her fingers on his arm. The earl similarly offered his arm to the comtesse and they led the way across the hall to the dining room.

"I'm afraid the seating will be informal," Bella apologised as her husband escorted her. "Having so many more ladies than gentlemen."

"It will be as good as a play," Lady Jesson said quietly, and Phoebe heard Lady Lydenham give a quiet chuckle.

In the dining room, Lord Carterton, as host, sat at one end of the table with the comtesse in the position of honour on his right. The

Earl of Marstone was next to her. Hélène was on Lord Carterton's left, with Alex on her other side. Bella, as hostess, took the foot of the table with the rest of the party. Phoebe was sure that several of the rules of precedence had been breached, for surely the earl, as the highest ranking man present, should have been next to Bella, where Phoebe herself was sitting.

During the meal, Phoebe enjoyed talking with Lady Jesson and Bella, and even Lady Lydenham across the table now and then. Odd snippets of Alex's remarks to Hélène reached them, and a few from Lord Marstone to the comtesse.

"...eyes like jewels," Alex said into an unexpected lull in the conversation.

Phoebe looked across the table as he glanced up, and bit her lips at his fleeting grimace.

"Such a pretty allusion," Hélène breathed, winding one curl around her finger.

"...as beautiful as your daughter..."

"...hair like spun gold..."

"Phoebe, tell me what young Georges will want to do while he's here," Bella said, her lips twitching. Phoebe kept her attention on her hostess—it would not do to laugh at the table.

Alex was not enjoying being forced to listen as Hélène described the balls she had been to, the gowns she had worn, and the titled gentlemen she had danced with.

"...three times would not be proper."

"No, indeed."

"But he asked me for a drive in the park the next..."

Glancing down the table, he was pleased to see Phoebe conversing with Bella and the other ladies.

"...only a viscount, but his father is..."

Bella glanced his way, a wry smile suggesting that he might be the cause of her amusement.

"...don't you think so, Westbrook?" Hélène fluttered her eyelashes at him again.

"Yes, indeed." He had no idea what he'd just agreed to, but her chatter did at least save him from the effort of trying to find a topic of conversation. Except that her silence was hinting that it was his turn to compliment her again.

"I regret that I have been unable to attend society events," he said. "It would have been a pleasure to dance with you."

"Oh, yes. I wonder if Lady Carterton could hold a—"

"Unfortunately there is no ballroom here, Lady Hélène." Best to nip that idea in the bud. What else could he say? He'd covered hair, eyes, skin, gown. Would she notice if he repeated himself? His only consolation was that Marstone, paying similar attention to the comtesse, must be equally bored.

He was relieved when Bella did not allow the company to linger over dessert, rising and announcing that it was time the gentlemen were left to their port. As the ladies left the room, Alex saw the comtesse sweep ahead, rudely assuming precedence over the other ladies, and audibly reminding Phoebe that she should be last.

Was that the way the woman always talked to Phoebe? He shook his head, hoping that Bella or one of the other women would step in if the comtesse became too obnoxious. His worry receded when Phoebe looked over her shoulder as she left the room; she caught his eye and smiled, amusement in her eyes, and he couldn't help smiling back.

CHAPTER 46

*P*hoebe followed Lady Jesson into the parlour, and they all settled themselves in the seats near the fire. Andrews supervised a footman bringing in the tea tray, and Bella waved a hand at Phoebe.

"Would you pour, Miss Deane? Lady Hélène can help you."

Thus dismissed, the younger women busied themselves pouring cups of tea and passing them round.

"So nice for Hélène, Westbrook paying her such compliments," the comtesse said, taking a sip of her tea.

"That's all very well," Bella said. "But it will come to nothing."

"Why?" the comtesse asked. "He was extremely attentive." She looked as smug as if the attention had been paid to her.

"He asked if he could escort me on a drive tomorrow, Mama," Hélène said, moving to sit beside the comtesse.

"There, you see?"

"But he is a man of honour, Lavinia," Lady Jesson said.

"Naturally. He is Marstone's son. What has that to do with anything?"

"Come, Lavinia," Lady Jesson said. "The reason you are here is because of the stories circulating about your time in France. All the stories say that Westbrook compromised Miss Deane's virtue." She leaned forward. "Any man of honour would do the right thing and make her an offer."

Phoebe was beginning to find this charade less amusing than she'd expected.

"In fact, I would expect him to make an offer while he's here," Lady Lydenham put in.

The comtesse looked horrified; Hélène's bottom lip began to stick out.

"I thought you intended Harlford for your daughter?" Lady Jesson said.

"Oh, I'd heard his attention was elsewhere now," Bella put in before the comtesse could reply.

"A bird in the hand…" Lady Jesson said. "At least, a bird in the hand would be better if Westbrook wasn't honour bound…"

"Nothing to be done, I'm afraid." Lady Lydenham shook her head. "It seems Miss Deane will be making an excellent match quite soon."

"But the rumours are untrue!" the comtesse said, her gaze flitting from one woman to the next. Under other circumstances, Phoebe thought she would have enjoyed seeing her aunt bested like this.

"When has that ever stopped people making a judgement?" Bella said. "I suppose the truth might also make the rounds if it were interesting enough. Unfortunately, stories where nothing apparently happened rarely get passed on. The story I heard was quite interesting—"

"What did you hear?" the comtesse asked. She glanced at Hélène, sitting in silence with her pout developing further. "Hélène, my dear, would you fetch my shawl from my room?"

Phoebe didn't want to listen to all this again, so as Hélène left the room she moved over to a table in the corner of the room where some books were laid out. Flicking through them, she chose one with illustrations of the Sussex and Kent coastline, and settled at the table to read it, trying hard to ignore the low-voiced discussion across the room.

She looked up when the men entered the parlour, her stomach fluttering as Alex and Lord Marstone came over to her.

"Miss Deane," the earl said. "Why are you sitting alone over here?"

"I did not wish to hear again my aunt's version of events in France, my lord."

"Hmm. Yes, I can see that might be... annoying."

"I trust you enjoyed your dinner, sir?" Phoebe said, knowing he had not.

Both men laughed at that. "As much as Westbrook enjoyed his, Miss Deane." The earl cast a wry glance at his son. "I have to leave for London in the morning, but it looks as if Bella has the plan well in hand."

Lord Marstone bowed and moved away, joining the group near the fire.

"Are you all right, Phoebe, really?" Alex asked, his voice quiet. "Some of the stories going round are—"

"They are not true, and everyone I care for or respect knows that." Looking into his face, any lingering doubts about his feelings disappeared. His worry was far more than concern for an acquaintance, or even a good friend.

"'Just call me Westbrook' indeed!" she went on. "You, sir, have no grounds to complain about the squire's horse!" She wanted to talk to him, but not here in front of all these people.

He laughed. "The truth, but not the whole truth?"

"Yes, but when you know very well that they will put the wrong interpretation on things."

Her aunt called from the other side of the parlour. Turning to look at the comtesse, Phoebe recognised the tight line of her mouth.

"Enjoy your *tête-à-tête*," she said to Alex as she got to her feet.

"What—?"

Phoebe smiled at Hélène as she passed the younger woman and approached the comtesse, sitting obediently when her aunt patted the empty place beside her on the sofa. From the corner of her eye she saw Hélène speaking to Alex, and his response—a smile that did not reach his eyes.

The comtesse wore a triumphant look. Phoebe was glad to find that the ladies had finished discussing France, and instead were talking about an expedition to the coast the following day.

"Weather permitting, of course," Bella said. "Nick can give us a guided tour of the castle at Pevensey, for those interested."

She would enjoy sketching the castle but there probably wouldn't be time for her to paint it as well. As the talk turned to other amusements, she wondered if she might paint in the grounds here one day. There would be spring flowers in bloom.

Bella broke the party up relatively early, saying they needed to be on their way well before noon the next day. Upstairs, Phoebe found Ellie waiting for her, but the girl made no move to help her to unpin her hair and undress.

"You be wanted in the library, miss," she said. "In a little while, when we're sure Madame has gone to bed."

Phoebe's eyebrows rose; this was no doubt part of Bella's plan.

"You'd better help me to decide what to wear tomorrow," she said.

Alex sipped a glass of port while he waited for the ladies to return. Marstone sat opposite, wearing one of his thoughtful looks. His occasional glances towards Alex sent a slight chill of unease through him— Marstone was plotting something, but he had no idea what.

Bella returned first with her husband, followed by Lady Jesson and Lady Lydenham, and their maids. Finally Phoebe arrived and sat next to Lady Jesson.

"It's time we explained properly, Phoebe," Bella said. "Simpson, here, is Lady Jesson's maid, and Matthews works for Lady Lydenham. They are to return to London tomorrow and start an alternative story circulating amongst the servants."

The two maids nodded; Alex guessed they had already been given their instructions.

"I have not been in society much recently," Lady Lydenham said. "But I think it's time I began to entertain again. I will be holding a rout next week."

"That is quite short notice," Bella pointed out. "But Simpson and Matthews will make sure that people know Lady Lydenham has been staying here and has more to tell on this latest supposed scandal."

"That, and curiosity, should persuade enough people to come," Lady Lydenham added.

"And I," said Lady Jesson, "can ensure that quite a few ladies, including some who like to think themselves very proper, will come and will acknowledge you and your aunt and cousin."

"It won't fix things right away," Bella said to Phoebe. "But in time people will forget. You, and Hélène, I suppose, might have to wait until next season to make a match, but that can't be helped."

"So what *is* supposed to have happened?" Phoebe asked.

"Roughly what really did happen, with a few revisions," Alex said, trying to put out of his mind the fact that reinstating Phoebe in society's good opinion only made his own prospects with her even more remote. "The trick is to give an alternative explanation for the main features of the story."

"My aunt has agreed to this?"

"She thinks she concocted it herself," Lady Lydenham said, a smile spreading across her face. "I haven't been so amused in an age!"

"Your party was unfortunately stopped by an over-zealous official," Alex went on. "Brevare and I came upon you and convinced the official that we were the proper people to take charge. Two of the Frenchmen detailed to accompany us fought each other over some money they had stolen out of your trunks."

"But what were you doing there?" Phoebe asked.

"Spying," Lord Marstone said. "I imagine most of you have worked out he must have been doing something of the sort." Marstone glanced around the room. "I'm afraid there is someone in the Foreign Office passing information to the French. They know Westbrook has been gathering information on troop numbers and so on in France, so it's not safe for him to go back now. Therefore it will do no harm if it comes out that he's been working over there."

Alex, watching Phoebe's face, noticed the faintest narrowing of her eyes before her expression returned to neutral. Marstone had taken a risk in not warning her of what he was about to say but, to anyone who didn't know her, she had not betrayed his lie.

"And Brevare?" Bella asked.

"He was looking for his mother and sister in France, and happened across me. He made advances to Phoebe and was rejected, and he is now spreading these stories out of spite, to make himself look better. Getting in his version first, before Phoebe realises he is in Town and might let drop what really happened."

Lady Jesson looked at her maid. "Have you got all that, Simpson?"

"Yes, my lady."

Matthews nodded, too.

Alex studied Phoebe's face as the maids left the room. What was she thinking? Hoping this would work, so she could continue to enjoy her season?

"My ladies, if you don't mind, I'd like a word with Miss Deane before I leave tomorrow," the earl said, glancing at each of the women. "Now is the best time."

Goodnights were brief, as they'd already been said once, and soon Alex was alone with Phoebe and Marstone.

"From what I have been able to gather of Brevare's movements," Marstone said, "he went back to France shortly after the decoy note was taken from you, Miss Deane. I suspect he went to look for his family."

"But by the time he tracked them down, I'd already removed them?" Alex asked.

"It seems likely. But I wanted to make it clear that he is not to be trusted, even if we are wrong about the source of these stories."

"Does that mean he really is working for France? If his family are safe now, he cannot still be blackmailed into—"

"*We* know they are safe," Marstone interrupted. "It is probable that our traitor knows it as well, but if Brevare hasn't found out, the traitor could still be blackmailing him."

"You still haven't told him? It's over a week since Alex brought them back!" Phoebe's eyes were wide.

"No," Marstone said. "Thank you, Miss Deane, that is all I wished to—"

"Why haven't you told him?" Phoebe persisted, her gaze fixed on the earl. "He must be very worried about them."

Alex suppressed a smile at Marstone's expression—he was not used to being questioned like that.

"Why are you concerned about him after the damage he is doing to you?"

"It doesn't seem right," Phoebe said. "Why not just tell him and ask him who he is working for?"

Her gaze was now a definite glare. Marstone sat impassively, his set mouth the only sign of his feelings.

"It's likely there is an intermediary between Brevare and the real traitor," Alex put in, ignoring the warning glance Marstone sent his way. Phoebe deserved an answer.

"That's enough, Westbrook."

"Certainly, sir. I'm sure Miss Deane can work out the rest for herself." He didn't wait for Marstone to respond, but turned to Phoebe.

"Miss Deane, may I escort you upstairs?"

Phoebe glanced from him to Marstone, then stood.

"I bid you good night, sir," she said. Turning, she took Alex's arm and they left the room.

Alex stopped on the upstairs landing and turned to face her. Lit only by their candles, it was difficult to make out her expression. Thoughtful?

"Phoebe, Bella's plan requires me to maintain the pretence of courting your cousin. She thinks your aunt may need some incentive to stick to the new story." He wanted to know she understood—that he was not slighting her.

"I gathered that." She smiled up at him.

There was so much more he could say, but now was not the time. Bella's plan, dubious as it was, would be spoiled if the comtesse or her daughter saw them together like this.

"I need to see if Marstone has any further instructions before he leaves for town," he said. "Sleep well."

"Good night, Alex."

He watched until she had entered her room and closed the door, wishing he was on the other side of it with her.

CHAPTER 47

hree mornings later, Phoebe awoke to see blue skies that promised another fine day and got up to have an early breakfast. The trip to Pevensey had been both enjoyable and frustrating—Lord Carterton had provided an interesting commentary on the ruins, but she'd had to watch Alex pretending to court her cousin. She smiled as she recalled Hélène's disappointment after dinner that night when, instead of joining them in the parlour, Alex and Lord Carterton had ensconced themselves in the billiards room.

Yesterday she'd taken her small easel and paints into the woods to the south of the house. She wasn't quite satisfied with her efforts, and Bella had told her about a pretty glade with a stream flowing through it that sounded an ideal spot for today's attempt.

After returning to her room to collect her pelisse and painting materials, she saw the comtesse and Hélène in the corridor. She stepped back, hoping to avoid their notice, but her aunt had already seen her.

"Good morning, Phoebe," the comtesse said. "Are you going painting again?"

"Yes." Did her aunt have other plans for her? "The day looks as if it will be fine."

386

"You must make the most of the grounds while you are here," the comtesse said. "Living in London doesn't give you much opportunity for painting scenery. And it is a lovely day for a walk."

Phoebe let out a breath of relief, surprised at her aunt's friendly attitude.

"Will you go back to where you were yesterday? The woods must be beautiful at this time of year."

"Near there, madame. Lady Carterton said there is a stream nearby with—"

"Perhaps you should take a walk, too, Hélène," the comtesse said. "After breakfast, naturally," she added.

"Phoebe!" Georges hurried down the stairs. "Can I come with you?"

Phoebe stopped to wait for him, letting her aunt carry on to the breakfast parlour. Miss Bryant was descending the stairs at a more sedate pace, clad in her pelisse and carrying Georges' outdoor coat.

"Are you not going riding again?"

"My behind is sore," he admitted ruefully.

"He's spent most of the last two days riding," Alice said. "We will find something else to do."

"Botany?" Phoebe suggested. "There are some lovely flowers in the woods."

"Flowers are for girls," Georges began, but stopped when he caught Phoebe's eye.

"Ask Miss Bryant to tell you about Sir Joseph Banks," Phoebe said. "He is famous for knowing all about plants. But yes, you are welcome to accompany me."

Phoebe arranged for a footman to show her the way to the stream, and to bring a picnic basket, and the four of them set off into the woods. The trees were still bare, allowing the sun to light up the clumps of wild daffodils and the primroses and celandines scattered amongst the grass. Phoebe breathed deeply, happy to be in the fresh air in such beautiful surroundings.

The glade was as pretty as Bella claimed, and Phoebe spent some time choosing her viewpoint before setting up her stool and easel.

Georges and Alice gathered handfuls of flowers and settled down on a rug to look at them in detail. Their voices were a gentle murmur in the background as Phoebe laid down her initial washes of colour. Birds chirped in the trees, and the sound of the bored footman whittling a stick merged with the slight breeze sighing in the branches.

Alex stood by his window, looking gloomily out at the sky. The overnight heavy rain had cleared, and the weather would provide no excuse for avoiding Hélène this morning. As he watched, he saw Phoebe set off with Georges, his governess and a footman.

He'd thought Bella's scheme idiotic from the first, and doubted the comtesse was silly enough to walk into Bella's trap, but she had. Now he was faced with another tedious day suffering Hélène's sycophantic prattling, when he'd much rather be spending his time with Phoebe.

He turned to the mirror, checking that his neckcloth was properly tied and his hair was neat. Then, taking a deep breath, he opened the door and headed down the stairs. He'd put off the evil hour as long as possible by being deliberately late to breakfast, but if he were any later Bella would come looking for him.

"What a lovely morning it is today, Westbrook," the comtesse said brightly when he entered the breakfast parlour. He made a noncommittal noise as he crossed the room and took a plate, filling it from the dishes set out on the sideboard.

"Just the day for a turn about the grounds," she added, raising her voice to be heard above the clatter he was making.

"The ground may still be rather wet," he said, adding another unwanted sausage to his plate. Turning back to the table, he saw Bella's gaze sharpen. He sat down at an empty place and began to eat.

"Nonsense, Westbrook," Bella said. "It will be dry in an hour. Particularly if you stick to the lawn and don't go into the woods. I'm sure Madame de Calvac would enjoy a stroll."

He almost choked on his bacon at the image this suggestion

planted in his mind. A quick glance at Bella's face—now suppressing amusement—showed him she'd done it on purpose.

"Oh, no, not me," the comtesse said, her gaze flicking between him and Bella. "I have... I have some urgent letters to write this morning. But Hélène would be glad of your escort."

He wasn't going to escape, so he should get on with it. He turned to Hélène. "Would you do me the honour of accompanying me on a turn around the grounds later this morning, Lady Hélène?"

"Why, thank you Westbrook," she smiled. "I'd be delighted."

"There's a summerhouse at the edge of the south lawn," Bella added, her expression guileless. "Just the place for a rest if the air is still chilly."

"That sounds lovely," Hélène said, a little breathlessly.

Alex saw her gaze slide towards her mother, and caught a movement of the comtesse's head from the corner of his eye. They intended to close their trap this morning.

"In half an hour, then?" he said, waving a fork at his plate.

Hélène fluttered, and then excused herself to go and change. The comtesse followed her.

"Wicked, Alex!" Bella said. "Only half an hour to change her dress?" Alex shrugged and concentrated on his breakfast. The dress she had on had looked perfectly acceptable to him. The comtesse's voice drifted in from the hall, the words barely distinguishable but the tone unmistakably demanding.

Bella rang the bell. When Andrews appeared, his face was carefully expressionless, but the tension in his jaw betrayed some irritation.

"My lady?"

"Please ensure there is a fire lit in the south parlour, and show Ladies Jesson and Lydenham there when they come down."

"Yes, my lady. Madame de Calvac has requested the same thing."

"They won't be here much longer, Andrews," Bella added.

"No, my lady," Andrews said, relaxing.

Watching the man turn and leave the room, Alex reminded himself that he wasn't the only one making sacrifices. Of course, he was the only one who would have his life ruined if this went wrong.

"How can you be sure they will attempt an entrapment?" Alex asked. "Hélène is a beautiful girl, if tedious, and should have little difficulty attracting a titled husband."

"Why else were they so interested in the summerhouse?" Bella asked. "They may not, of course, but there are several reasons why I think they will. There are not so many unmarried peers, or their heirs, as you might suppose, if you discount the ones twenty or more years older than Hélène."

"The comtesse wouldn't let an age difference bother her."

"No, but Hélène and her father are likely to want someone nearer her own age. Then there's Harlford—he was enamoured, but apparently no longer, so the most eligible prospect of the season has already escaped her. Our counter story may allay the gossip, but it is not guaranteed. And here you are, apparently the heir to an earldom, and a wealthy one at that. You are the next best thing on the market."

Alex sighed. "Don't let me down, Bella. If that annoying wigeon outmanoeuvres me, I'm not marrying her, whatever anyone says. I'd rather emigrate."

"Don't worry—remember what I said about the summerhouse, and wear a warm coat."

He grimaced as he swallowed his coffee.

"Oh, come, Alex, you've undertaken more dangerous deceptions, I'm sure."

Alex offered his arm to Hélène, and they set off along the path that skirted the lawn, shoes crunching on the gravel. This side of the lawn was edged with a deep border, at present graced only by a few evergreen shrubs and clumps of daffodils and backed with a tall yew hedge. Ahead, the summerhouse was positioned to give a good view of both flowerbeds and woods.

"...lovely garden, Westbrook," Hélène said.

What had he missed?

"Indeed," he said. "I do enjoy being out of doors; it's so peaceful."

"Yes, lovely," Hélène continued. "The sounds of the birds singing, so beautiful."

And completely inaudible with you chattering on, he thought, his irritation growing.

"May we sit and listen to them?" she added.

Alex glanced down at her face, tilted up towards his own with a hopeful smile. He had a brief flash of doubt—had Bella mistaken the intentions of the comtesse and her daughter?

"It will be lovely to sit there together," Hélène went on, pointing to the summerhouse.

No, she hadn't. He turned into the path leading to the small building and opened the door.

"If you wait one moment, Lady Hélène," he said, "I will ensure the bench is clean for you." He wiped it with his handkerchief and stepped back outside as Hélène entered. She sat and smoothed her skirts.

"Won't you join me, Westbrook?"

Alex leaned on the door frame, making no move to enter. A quick glance over his shoulder confirmed that he was in plain view of anyone looking out of the windows on the south side of the house.

"You will get cold standing there," Hélène said. "Do come inside and shelter from the breeze."

"I'm not cold, but thank you for your consideration."

"But I can't talk to you properly from here."

"Shall we walk on, then?"

Her face fell. Alex began to feel a little sorry for her—she couldn't know she was heading for a greater disappointment at the end of this farce. Then he recalled that she hadn't tried to help Phoebe while they were in France, and his sympathy vanished.

"Don't you *want* to sit with me, Westbrook? Don't you think I'm beautiful?" Hélène's brows had a small crease between them, as if she really couldn't understand why a man would not be attracted to her.

"Do you want my honest opinion, Lady Hélène?"

"Yes, of course." She shuffled along the bench, as if making space for him.

"I think you're one of the most beautiful women I've seen—"

A pleased smile spread across her face.

"—but your cousin is worth ten of you."

More than ten of her.

He felt that twinge of compunction again as her mouth fell open and tears glistened in her eyes.

"Phoebe stole Harlford from me," she said, her lips trembling. "And now you. At least the vicomte—"

"She didn't *steal* anything," Alex said. "And *she* is not the one desperate enough to attempt an entrapment." He noted her widening eyes with satisfaction. "You have nothing but your looks. Little honesty or intelligence."

Her bottom lip stuck out. "Mama says that ladies don't need those—"

"Your mother doesn't understand how decent men think." He tried to tamp down his anger. With a mother like hers, how could she have the same integrity as Phoebe?

"Do you know what you are attempting to do here, Lady Hélène?" he asked. "You want people to think we have had… relations. What if I wanted to—here, in this summerhouse?"

Hélène's face turned red, then pale, as he spoke.

"That is what you were going to say happened, is it not? What if I removed your clothing, whether you liked it or not? If I struck you?"

"You wouldn't!" Hélène's voice was now only a whisper.

"No, I would not." His hands clenched into fists. "But your mother didn't know that, did she, when she made Phoebe wear that gold dress?"

He stalked off, ignoring the sound of sobbing behind him.

After she'd painted for an hour, Phoebe went over to see how Georges' botany was progressing while she waited for a colour wash to dry.

"I know these." Georges indicted the gathered flowers. "And oak and holly and yew and beech," he added, pointing to a selection of fallen leaves he'd collected. "Can I build a dam in the stream now?"

Phoebe exchanged glances with Alice, who shrugged.

"All right," Phoebe said. "But down there," she pointed. "Not in the part I'm painting, if you please. And don't get too muddy."

There was little hope of that last instruction being heeded, she realised, smiling at his enthusiasm. The footman, glancing at her for approval first, followed him.

She turned back to the governess. "Alice, I can keep an eye on him if you wish to go back to the house. I'll need another hour, an hour and a half at the most."

Thanking her, the governess gathered up her books and the flowers and set off. Phoebe resumed painting, aware of Georges talking to the footman, and the occasional splash as he tipped stones into the stream. She lost track of time as her picture progressed, finally standing back to assess her achievement.

It was a pretty picture, but it didn't really capture the beauty of the spring day. She removed it from the easel and laid it to dry on top of her paint box. Georges must be enjoying himself—she would have expected him to start complaining about hunger by now. The dam-building activity produced a louder splash than usual and she smiled —he'd be quite wet and muddy by the time he'd finished.

"Oi, you can't—"

A man's voice. The footman?

Phoebe jumped to her feet, knocking against the easel in her haste, alarmed more by the sudden cessation of the shout than the words themselves. Had Georges fallen? Hurt himself?

She couldn't see anyone, but Georges had been playing just out of sight.

"Phoebe!" Georges' voice was shrill, panicked. "Phoe—"

Heart racing, Phoebe picked up her skirts and ran along the stream.

A strange man was holding a wriggling Georges, one hand clamped across his mouth. Another stood beside him, holding a stick. She skidded to a halt as both men looked in her direction.

She must help Georges... No, she could do nothing against two men—all she could do was go for help.

Her feet slipped in the mud as she spun around and started to run. The ground was uneven, and she tripped over a tree root and fell to her knees. Breath now coming in gasps, she scrambled up again. Two paces later, a hand grabbed her shoulder and swung her around.

She fell again, the man's unshaven face bending towards her.

"Help!" The scream was as loud as she could make it. "Hel—"

He slapped her face.

CHAPTER 48

"**Well**, Bella, did the plan work?" Alex asked as Bella entered the library.

"Success. Well done!" She smiled. "You should have seen the comtesse's face when she realised that she'd encouraged her daughter to entrap Marstone's illegitimate son. Then Lady Jesson pointed out what a juicy titbit that would be if the story spread."

"It doesn't feel well done to me," Alex said flatly. "I probably said more than I should have." He outlined what he'd said to Hélène, Bella's smile fading as he talked.

When he'd finished, she put out one hand to pat his arm. "Don't spend your time worrying about her," she said. "It was time someone made it clear that her mother's tactics do not work. If anyone's at fault, it's the comtesse."

Alex shrugged. "I suppose so."

"Well, it can't be undone," Bella said. "Phoebe's brother has arrived with Harlford."

"Are they part of your plot, too?"

"Good heavens, no. Deane has come to see how his sister does. As for Harlford, I imagine our counter story has spread far enough for him to have heard it and decide he might have been a bit hasty in cancelling his engagements with the Calvac family. Calvac would have told him we're all here."

Alex strode over to the window. "What does he want?" he asked, his throat tight. As if he needed to ask.

"He said he had come to see Phoebe."

"So the counter story has done its work." He addressed himself to the window, afraid that Bella would see too much in his face. "Was today's charade really necessary?"

"Yes, it was. As soon as she saw Harlford arrive, that woman started to say what a pity it was about Phoebe's reputation, and how much Harlford admires Hélène. Without the threat of Maria making her a laughing stock by spreading the tale of them trying to entrap you, she'd have gone back to town and said the original rumours were true after all, hoping that Harlford would switch his attentions back to Hélène. She fears the mockery her exposure would cause more than she wants Harlford for her daughter."

Alex shook his head.

"Ladies Jesson and Lydenham have just set out for London," Bella went on. "To make sure the correct stories are circulating, and organise a few engagements for Phoebe to attend."

"That's good," Alex said, wishing he meant it. "Excuse me, I need to get out of the house. I'm going for a ride."

An hour's ride couldn't clear Alex's head of images of Phoebe with the marquess. It's best for her, he told himself as he left his mount in the stables. Bella seemed to think Harlford was a decent man. Phoebe would be better off with Harlford than with him—safer, certainly.

Perhaps if he told himself that often enough, he'd come to believe it.

In search of Bella and something to eat, he paused in the doorway to the drawing room, his jaw tensing as he saw Bella talking to the marquess and Lieutenant Deane.

"Westbrook." Deane's smile was friendly as Alex entered.

"Alex," Bella said. "Harlford, have you met my nephew, Mr Westbrook?"

"We've not met," the marquess said. "I've heard much about you recently, Westbrook." He looked Alex in the eye. "Most of it untrue, I've no doubt."

"Probably, my lord," Alex said, relaxing a little. The man's tone was friendlier than mere politeness dictated.

"Would you all care for some refreshment?" Bella asked. "Food is laid out in the dining room." She caught Alex's eye. "Madame de Calvac and her daughter will be taking refreshment in their rooms."

"Will Miss Deane be joining us?" the marquess asked.

Bella's brows drew together as she glanced at the clock. "I thought she would be here by now," she said. "She knew what time we were eating."

"Where did she go?" Alex asked. "I saw her leave earlier with Calvac's son and his governess."

"Somewhere in the south woods," Bella said, and rang the bell.

Andrews appeared in the doorway. "My lady?"

"Has Miss Deane returned? Or Miss Bryant?"

"Miss Bryant has, my lady. I haven't seen Miss Deane or Master Calvac."

"Fetch Miss Bryant, please, Andrews."

Andrews nodded, returning a few minutes later with the governess.

"I left Miss Deane painting in the woods," she reported. "Georges was with her, and a footman. She said she might be another hour and a half, so she should have been back before now."

Could she have just lost track of time? Or sprained an ankle or had some other mishap? She should not come to much harm in the woods, but that didn't temper Alex's growing worry. A niggling memory of something Hélène had said that morning teased him—something he'd ignored at the time.

"Can you show me where you went, Miss Bryant?" he asked. "I'll check they are all right."

"Allow me to accompany you," the marquess said. "Deane?"

Miss Bryant led the three men across the lawn and into the woods. All Alex could hear, above their own footsteps, were birds and wind in the branches—no sound of Georges playing or anyone talking.

The path was narrow, and they had to walk in single file. He could see an open area ahead, then Miss Bryant ran on with a cry of dismay. An easel lay on the ground in the clearing by the stream, a few loose sheets of paper fluttering around in the gentle breeze. A weight settled in his chest as he quickly looked around—there was no sign of Phoebe or Georges.

"Good God, what has happened?" Harlford said.

"I don't know, but something is wrong." Could Brevare have something to do with this? Surely his spite would not extend to physically harming her?

"They've probably just gone for a walk and missed their way," the marquess said.

"Phoebe wouldn't discard her sketches like this." Deane swept a hand across the clearing.

Alex looked beneath the paints and drawing materials, but there was nothing more to be found. He wondered if she had a pistol with her—he hoped so, but he had no way of knowing.

"No, indeed," the governess said, moving over to pick up the easel. A large box lay beneath it, its open lid revealing paints and brushes. She looked at Alex, eyes wide, but with no sign of tears or panic.

"Miss Bryant, did the footman return to the house with you?"

"No."

"Over here!" Deane called, and Alex saw a recumbent shape half-hidden behind a bush. Deane knelt beside the body of a footman, his fingers feeling the man's neck then probing through his hair.

"Unconscious—he's been hit on the head," he said, showing Alex a hand sticky with blood. "Some time ago, I think. The bleeding has almost stopped."

If they're willing to do that, what might they have done to Phoebe?

"Do you have hartshorn?" Alex asked the governess, forcing his mind back to practicalities.

Miss Bryant shook her head.

Damn—he'd hoped the man might be able to tell him something.

"We need to get him to the house, sir," she said. "Shall I go to summon—?"

"No, you'd best stay and keep an eye on him, if you don't mind. Harlford, could you fetch help?"

The marquess set off briskly back the way they had come.

Miss Bryant pointed further down the stream. "Georges was building a dam over there."

Alex and Deane walked beside the stream, studying the banks. Beyond the part-built dam he spotted some footprints far too large to belong to Phoebe or Georges.

"Two sets," Deane said.

Walking on, Alex could still see the large footprints here and there, but found no sign of smaller ones. The tracks led to a patch of drier ground where all traces vanished.

"They must have been carried from here," Alex said. "We'd best get Carterton to search the estate."

"We've got to find her," Deane said, the suppressed fear in his voice matching Alex's own feelings.

Her head hurt. She was sitting, leaning in the corner of something, being rocked and jolted. Cloth sucked against her mouth when she breathed in; her heart beat uncomfortably fast, her pulse loud in her ears.

"Phoebe!"

Georges?

"Phoebe, *réveilles-toi!*" His voice was tearful, but persistent.

Her eyes flew open as she went to lift the cloth from her face and both hands moved together. She was tied up, in a carriage. How long had she been here?

Blinds across the windows shut out the view, bright strips of light along their edges showing it was still daylight. In the dim interior, she made out two men sitting opposite, one pointing a pistol at her. Moving her head, she winced at the stabbing pain in her skull.

Georges sat beside her, his face turned in her direction. "Phoebe!"

"Shut up, brat!" one of the men snarled.

"What d'you bring him for anyway?" the other asked, his voice higher than the first. "Should have knocked him on the head and left him like you did that footman."

"Didn't want to kill 'im," the first one said. "Anyways, 'is clothes are good—might be worth a bob or two to someone."

She tried to say something, but the gag reduced her voice to a muffled sound. She tried again, and rolled her head in frustration and the beginnings of panic.

"'Ere, can she breathe?" Low-voice said. "Better take that gag off. That Frenchie said the boss wanted to talk to 'er. No use if she kicks the bucket first!"

Frenchie? Brevare?

Phoebe gasped, wheezing loudly as if she were suffocating. She recoiled as an unshaven face was thrust into hers.

"You keep your trap shut, right?" It was High-voice, his hands fumbling behind her head. Eventually the cloth came free and she dragged in a lungful of air.

Harlford was with Bella in the drawing room when Alex and Deane returned. Bella's hands lay in her lap, knuckles white.

"Kidnapped," Alex confirmed. He would *not* consider that she might have been killed.

"It must have been young Calvac they were after," Harlford said. "Ransom the heir, perha—"

"That doesn't matter now," Deane cut off the marquess. "We need to find them first."

"Ransom is a possible motive," Alex admitted. It could be linked with Marstone's business, too, but he couldn't think how.

"Westbrook," Harlford said, "the... er... *revised* stories that were spreading around town yesterday had you as some kind of spy. Is there any truth in that?"

"Some." He was not going to go into details now. "That may have something to do with this, but we cannot know."

"You involved Miss Deane in *spying*?" Harlford asked, his face darkening.

"Spying?" Deane said at the same time.

"Now is *not* the time for recriminations," Bella interrupted. She glanced towards the doorway as her husband entered.

"I've sent men out to ride the estate," Nick said.

Alex nodded his thanks. "If it was a kidnap for ransom we could risk waiting until a demand for money arrived," he went on, trying to keep his mind on practicalities. "That might provide some clues about where they have been taken. However, we cannot afford to wait in case that is not the reason. They could be on their way to London or to France, or to anywhere else in the country."

"You brought Miss Deane into this," Harlford snapped. "You must have some idea who is responsible."

"No, although I do know of one person who may be involved—"

"This Brevare?"

"Yes. But that isn't much help. He doesn't have a home in England as far as I know."

"Might Marstone have an idea who has done this?" Bella asked.

"He might," Alex replied. "Nick, could we send someone to London right away? Calvac should be told, too."

"I'll see to it. You'll write a note?"

Alex nodded, and Nick left the room again.

"Someone should tell Madame her son is missing," Bella said. She looked at their faces, then stood. "I'll go, and I'll make sure she stays in her room."

"So they could be on their way to London," Deane said, getting back to details as Bella left the room. "Whoever takes the note to Lord Marstone could look out for them, if he knows what to look for."

"They could also be on their way to Dover—"

"Or Folkestone," Nick said from the doorway. "Or Hastings,

Newhaven, Rye, Hythe…" He walked over to a table and unrolled a map he'd brought with him.

"We are here," he said, placing a finger on the map. "There is the post road to London. To get to Dover or Folkestone is less direct, but they would be the best places to get a boat across the channel."

Alex looked at the map, tracing a finger along the towns Nick had mentioned. "Smugglers' coast." He was more familiar with the Devonshire coastline.

"Yes. If they have arranged their own boat, they could be headed anywhere here." Nick swept his hand along the map from Brighthelmstone to Folkestone.

"We can't stand here talking," Harlford said heatedly. "We must look for her… them!"

"Where do you suggest we look?" Alex asked, trying not to snap back at the marquess.

"The post roads?" Deane suggested. "Get to Folkestone or Dover before a coach could get there and make sure they aren't taken onto a boat?"

He had a point—Alex wasn't convinced the kidnappers would use the main roads, but they should check all possibilities. "Very well."

"I'll see the horses are prepared." Nick left the room again.

"Riding clothes?" Alex looked at Deane and Harlford, who nodded and left.

He looked up from the map as Bella came back into the room, one hand clasped firmly around Hélène's upper arm. Hélène's eyes were red and slightly puffy, and she was clutching a handkerchief in one hand.

"Where is everyone?" Bella asked.

"Getting ready to ride out," he said.

"This young woman has something to tell you," Bella said. "Hélène?"

Hélène sniffed. "I've done nothing wrong!" She buried her face in her handkerchief.

Bella rolled her eyes. "She met Brevare in the woods today, after she ran off from the summerhouse."

Alex's interest sharpened. "Brevare? You just happened to run into him?"

Hélène flushed. "He asked me to meet him. He talked to me at a rout last week. Then I received a note yesterday, saying he had to see me."

"Go on," Alex said, trying not to let his anger show. "We have to find your brother."

"He said... he said that Phoebe had stolen something from him in France and he needed to get it back."

"What exactly did you tell him?"

"Only that she was painting in the woods by the stream, but she'd be returning soon so he could call then. I didn't know Georges was with her, or that anyone would be harmed!"

Alex examined her face. Her bottom lip still stuck out, but she met his eyes without flinching.

"That's all you told him?" he asked.

She nodded.

"Was he alone?"

She nodded again.

"What time was this?"

Hélène glanced at the clock, lifting her shoulders. Alex's fists curled against the urge to shake her.

"How long after you ran off, Hélène?" Bella asked, clearly trying to control her own impatience. "Straight away? Or some time later?"

"Er... quite soon." Her eyes slid sideways, and Alex slammed a fist down on the table, making her jump and gasp.

"You have just helped get your cousin and your brother *kidnapped!*" He didn't shout, despite his frustration, but Hélène shrank from him. "Tell us *everything*, whether or not you think it is relevant."

"I... I was still cry—still distressed after you left the summerhouse..."

Alex waited.

"I remembered the assignation, and he was there. He... he... gave me a handkerchief—"

"And no doubt told you how beautiful you were, that Alex isn't worth bothering about, and he would never treat you that way?" Bella asked, her voice tart.

"Oh... Something like that. How did you know?"

Bella sighed, raised her eyes heavenward, and then turned back to Alex.

"Nothing else relevant then. I think it was getting on for half past eleven when Hélène ran off. I do think that's all she has to say. I'll take her back to her mother—they can comfort each other," she finished with a grimace. "I don't suppose it helps much?"

Alex shook his head. "It confirms my suspicions, but doesn't help us with when, or where they may be going."

He rubbed a hand across his face. There was still the footman. He would check, but Miss Bryant would have sent for him if the man had come round.

CHAPTER 49

*O*nce free of the gag, Phoebe sucked air into her lungs. Ignoring the pain in her head, she tried to think: two armed men, at least one more driving the coach—there was nothing she could do.

"Phoebe, *ou est-ce qu'on nous emmène?*" Where are they taking us? Georges had learnt to speak French before he learnt English.

"What's the brat saying?" High-voice asked.

"Dunno. It ain't English, that's for sure."

"Georges," Phoebe said, "*tu ne parles pas l'anglais, comprends-tu?*"

"*Mais...*"

"*Non—ne parle pas l'anglais!*" Phoebe insisted. She didn't know how, yet, but she might be able to make a plan with Georges if their kidnappers thought neither of them spoke English.

"What're you saying, then?" High-voice put his face into Phoebe's again, and she gagged at the smell of his breath. These two thugs did not understand the language.

She spoke in French again. "You haven't found the money in my pocket then?"

If they had the slightest idea what she had said, they would surely now be looking for the non-existent money.

"Georges," she said, facing the two men rather than the frightened boy. "Georges, *sois courageux*." Be brave. "Someone will come looking for us," she continued, in French.

She had no idea how long she'd been insensible. Her head hurt, yes, but she could see properly, and the slight nausea in her stomach was as much due to the foetid smell of her captors as to any head injury. It could not have been for long.

If she and Georges had not been missed yet, help could be some time coming. How could she delay their journey?

"Georges, you must remember to only speak in French. You must pretend that you do not understand English, so you must ignore anything they say in English."

She glanced at him briefly. His eyes were wide, and in the dim light inside the coach he looked pale, but he nodded slightly.

"Did they hurt you?" she asked.

"A bit," Georges said. "But I'll be all right." A slight wobble to his voice gave the lie to this statement, but at least he was holding up well enough to pretend.

"Thought it was some English mort we was supposed to be getting," High-voice said. "She don't sound English to me."

"The Frenchie said it was 'er in the woods," Low-voice answered, beginning to sound worried.

"There was two of 'em went out of the 'ouse with that brat this morning, when we was watching. Could be we got the wrong one?"

"You'd better check, hadn't you," Phoebe said hopefully, but still in French. "How about untying me as well?"

She held out her hands, but the men ignored her.

"Can't do nothing 'til we're at the inn," Low-voice said. "Stupid bugger should 'ave checked 'isself that we got the right one."

Phoebe had to be content with that. She raised her bound hands to rub her face, thankful they had at least tied them in front of her rather than behind her back. Pressing her hands down on her lap, she could just feel the pocket beneath her skirts, and the hard lump made by the pistol. With her hands tied together she couldn't reach it without the men seeing what she was doing, and in any case one bullet was of little use against two of them.

The jolting ride seemed to go on for hours, but it could not have been so long, for when Phoebe was finally dragged out of the coach the sun was still high in the sky, although a sheet of thin cloud was beginning to form. They were in front of a small inn, the paint peeling from its wooden-clad walls.

Ominous clouds loomed to the west, and the air was heavy with damp. In daylight her captors appeared no better than they had in the dark. High-voice was tall and lanky, with greasy hair and several days' growth of whiskers above a dirty shirt. Low-voice was stockier, with a broken nose and ragged ear.

High-voice draped a cloak around her, covering her bound hands. Phoebe's gaze swept her surroundings as High-voice took her firmly by the arm and led her towards the inn. There was no-one else around —no possible source of help. They had not tied Georges' hands, but the other man took his arm firmly enough for the boy to whimper, and dragged him along behind Phoebe.

Inside, they were taken into a side parlour. The room was shabby, the curtains faded and the tables and chairs worn, but it was spotless. Two men with tankards of ale sat by the fire. One was Brevare, looking far more strained and less confident than the last time she had seen him. She did not recognise the middle-aged man with thinning hair.

The pain in her head had changed to a throbbing ache but, despite that, she was feeling clear-minded and was beginning to turn over possibilities. There must be people in the kitchen or the taproom...

"Here she is," High-voice said.

"What is *he* doing here?" the older man asked, looking at Georges.

"These cowards kidnapped him as well." Phoebe spoke rapidly in French, pleased to see the man's brows draw together, no comprehension showing on his face.

"Speak English, girl," he said impatiently.

"Don't you understand what I am saying?" she asked again, in French.

"She ain't said nothin' in English," High-voice said, sounding nervous now. "We got the woman that was in the wood, like 'e said!" He jerked his head towards Brevare as he spoke.

"You've taken the wrong woman, Brevare?" The man's tone was sharp. "You know that milord wants to find out—"

"She's the one," Brevare said firmly as he walked towards Phoebe. Georges backed away and hid himself behind her.

"Come, Miss Deane, you *are* English. Try speaking it!"

"Your mother and sister are in England," she said, still in French. "Westbrook stayed in France to find them, and he brought them back. They are safe in Marstone's care."

She watched as colour drained from his face.

"Do you understand?" she asked, afraid he would give them away. "We thought you were being blackmailed into this—were we right?"

"How... how do I know you are not lying?" he asked.

"Do I know your family? Does Westbrook know them?"

He shook his head.

"Your sister is called Suzanne, and your mother is a dragon who hits her servants."

His eyes widened at the last part of this statement, but then his mouth relaxed.

"How would I know that unless Westbrook had told me?" She needed to convince him before the other man intervened.

"Well?" The sharp voice from the other man interrupted them.

Brevare turned towards him. "She's the right one," he stated, in English.

"*Sont-ils en bonne santé?*" he asked, turning back to Phoebe. Are they well?

"As far as I know." She continued speaking in French.

"Where are they?"

"If you get us out of this mess, you will be taken to them. If not—you have been spying against this country. You know how traitors are dealt with here?"

A pulse began to beat in his temple.

"Helping us would go a long way towards avoiding that," she said.

It sounded plausible, but she had no idea if it was true.

"I can't do anything," he said desperately. "There are two men with the coach as well as these two. And him as well." He jerked his head towards the other man.

"And this 'milord' he mentioned...?"

"I don't know who he is. I've only ever dealt with this one."

"Brevare!" the other man said impatiently. "Get on with it—it's time we were going."

"We need time," Phoebe hissed. "Help me to delay things."

Georges—he could be the excuse.

"Tell them Georges needs food, or he'll cry all the way to... to wherever you are taking us!"

High-voice started towards them, his expression menacing.

"And he is Calvac's son—the son of a peer—you don't want to risk harming him, and he might be useful as a hostage."

Brevare's gaze met hers, then he gave a quick nod, turning to speak to his companion. The older man rolled his eyes heavenwards, but walked over to the door and shouted. It appeared to Phoebe that he deliberately stood so as to prevent the girl who came from seeing into the room.

A few minutes later an older woman appeared, shorter and rounder, carrying a tray laden with plates of bread, cheese, and ham. A word from the older man sent High-voice hurrying across the room to take the tray from her, and Low-voice hustled her out. The woman cast a frowning glance at Phoebe and Georges as she left.

"Eat!" the older man ordered, and Phoebe and Georges moved over to the table. It was awkward with her hands bound, but she managed to eat a little.

Georges was eating as if he hadn't been fed for days; Phoebe's hands paused part-way to her mouth as an idea struck her.

"Well done, Georges," Phoebe said, as the woman from the inn sponged the vomit from his clothing. He'd managed to stick his fingers in his throat without any of their captors noticing, and the resulting mess was on her gown as well as his clothing. Although the smell was unpleasant, to say the least, it also meant delay.

She rubbed her wrists—Brevare had been told to untie her before sending them to be cleaned up. He was standing by the door, far enough away not to hear if she kept her voice low. He should be on their side now, but she didn't trust him.

"Something's wrong, miss?" The woman spoke quietly, shrewd intelligence in the eyes turned towards Phoebe's face.

"We've been kidnapped," Phoebe stated, fingers gently exploring the sore spot on her head.

The woman nodded, as if she had expected such an answer. "I'm Sal Robins." Her gaze slid towards Brevare. "There's six of them, and only three... only two men of any use here. I'm sorry."

She was an ally, though—that was a bonus she hadn't expected.

"Can you send a message?"

Sal nodded.

"Do you know of Oakley Place?"

Sal nodded again.

"Tell Mr Westbrook. Put where they're taking us, if you can find out, and write 'squire's horse' as well. It's a kind of code word," she explained as Sal frowned. The woman must have wondered if Phoebe had lost her wits.

What else could she do? If Alex could catch them up...

"Sal, please don't clean us up too well. If we still smell, some of them might stay outside the coach."

There wasn't time for more—a bang on the door made Brevare jump, and High-voice called that they had to get moving *now*.

Harlford and Deane arrived back in the parlour just as Nick returned to say that the grooms riding the estate had found nothing useful. A quick discussion concluded that Harlford should ride to London, and Nick and Deane would go to Rye, then along the coast in opposite directions.

"I'll ride south to Hastings, and turn west if there's no trace," Alex said. He didn't point out that all this would be useless if Phoebe and Georges were being taken on horseback; it would be easy for horses to avoid the main roads. In that case, they could be almost at the coast by now. Even in a coach, the searchers would be hard-pressed to reach the coast first, particularly if they enquired at inns on the way. Their only real hope was that the kidnappers might encounter some delay in their journey.

Grooms and saddled horses awaited them at the front of the house. Deane and Nick rode down the drive, two grooms accompanying them. Alex stood on the steps as Harlford swung onto his hunter.

"Why aren't you mounting?" Harlford asked as he settled himself into the saddle. "You won't find her by hanging around here."

"Nor will you by staying to berate me," Alex retorted. "Are you sure you don't want to take a groom?"

"I can find my way to the post road," the marquess snapped. He wheeled his horse around and spurred it to a fast trot, its hooves scattering gravel. Above, the gathering clouds promised rain to come.

Bella came out and stood next to Alex. "Do you think she will find a way to get word to us?"

"I'm hoping so." If anyone could, it would be Phoebe. He pushed aside the thought that she might be injured or dead.

Descending the steps, he checked that some food and a bottle of water had been put into the saddle bags. He looked at the remaining groom. "Stevens, isn't it?"

"Yes, sir."

"I'll head south," he said to Bella, preparing to mount. "If something *does* turn up, be sure to send someone after me."

"Wait!" Bella said, her gaze fixed on the drive.

He turned—hoofbeats were approaching, the horse at a gallop. Hope rose in his chest as the rider swung down, looking from him to Bella. He was young, not over twenty, in groom's clothing.

"Can I help?" Alex asked

Relief spread over the man's face. "I bin sent to Oakley Place with a message for..." The man hesitated, uncertainty crossing his features again.

"Lord Carterton?" Alex guessed. "Westbrook?"

His name seemed to register with the man, and a slow smile spread over his face.

"That's right."

"I'm Westbrook," Alex said.

"'Ere you are, sir," the man said, handing over a scruffy scrap of paper.

"What is it, Alex?" Bella asked.

He unfolded the paper.

Westbrook. Pett. Squires horse.

He let out a long breath of relief. The note wasn't in Phoebe's hand, but it was from her. Not only was this a clue, but it showed she was still alive.

"A message from Phoebe," he said abruptly, handing it to Bella. "Pett—it must be a place name." He looked at the messenger. "Do you know where it is?"

"No, sir," the messenger said, his face blank.

"Pett?" Bella turned. "Andrews?"

The butler appeared in the doorway.

"Fetch the map from the parlour table, please. Quickly!"

Andrews disappeared, and Bella turned back to Alex. "Squire's horse?"

"An old joke," Alex said, his attention on the man in front of him. "Where have you come from? What is your name?"

"I come from home, sir. My name's Ben Robins. Ma sent me."

"Where's 'home'?"

"Alex, don't bark at the man," Bella protested. "Ben, where is your home?"

"Black Bull Inn, my lady." Ben bobbed his head at her.

"I know where that is, sir," Stevens put in. "Half an hour's ride, if we don't spare the horses. Perhaps someone there will know more?"

"I hope so," Alex said. "Where the devil is that map?"

"Here, sir." Andrews ran up, holding the map out.

"Do you know where Pett is, Andrews?"

The butler's brow creased. "Somewhere east of Hastings, sir?"

Alex scanned the map. "Got it. Nearer to Winchelsea than Hastings." He looked from the map to the groom. "Stevens, where's this inn?"

"Not far from Dallington, I reckon."

Alex looked at the map again—Dallington wasn't on a direct route to Winchelsea, but it wasn't too much out of the way. "You can lead us there, Stevens?" He didn't know if he could rely on Ben to take them the fastest way.

"Yes, sir," the groom said confidently.

"Good man." He turned to Bella. "Do we have anyone left to ride?"

"A few, I think."

"Good. Send someone to get the marquess back, and tell him what you know when he arrives. Best to send him on to the Black Bull, I think. I'll leave a message there for him when I know what's happening. And send someone after Nick and Deane."

Bella gave Andrews the orders, and the butler disappeared towards the back of the house.

What if Pett were only a meeting place? Would Brevare still escape them?

"Bella, whoever goes after Deane and Nick can take the map. Can you write a note for them? Send them direct to Pett, if possible." He looked down at her, aware that he'd been overstepping his authority here. "I'm sorry—"

Bella smiled as she cut him off. "I understand. Go—you must be at least an hour behind them."

Alex strode over to the horse and mounted, trying to shut off the churning mess of questions in his mind. He set off down the drive at a gallop, Stevens and Ben following, but he quickly reined back to a canter. The chance of getting spare horses was slim, and there was no sense in tiring the animals too quickly.

CHAPTER 50

Stevens' estimate of half an hour to the Black Bull was a trifle optimistic, but not by too much. The building was small and shabby; more for local drinkers than travellers, Alex guessed. As they'd ridden, the high clouds approaching from the west began to thicken and block the sun. The smell of rain was in the air.

"Give them a drink, Stevens," Alex said as he dismounted in the stable yard. "Not too much; we should be off again soon."

"Right, sir."

"Ben, can you fetch your mother, please? Now."

His urgency must have got through to the man, as he disappeared into the inn at a run. Alex stood waiting, one foot tapping impatiently, hoping that the mother had more wits than the son.

Ben returned with a short, plump woman and another young man —a brother to Ben, from his looks. Mrs Robins' eyes sparked with intelligence as she looked Alex up and down, beckoning him to stand inside the doorway out of the cold wind.

"Who is the woman with red hair?" she asked. "And who is the boy?"

Alex let out a breath—she'd seen Phoebe, but she was suspicious. Honesty was the best approach.

"The woman is Miss Phoebe Deane," he said. "She's a niece of the Comte de Calvac. The boy is Calvac's son. Are they well? Hurt?" He would likely get better cooperation from her if he allowed her to make her own decision what to do. "They have been kidnapped by French agents."

Mrs Robins regarded him for a moment, then nodded. "They're well enough, considering. There were six men with them. Two nobs... er... gentlemen; one sounded like a Frenchie, one was older—he didn't say much. A rough-looking pair driving the coach, and another two the same inside, guarding them."

Six? He glanced at Stevens—would the man be any good in a fight? Would he even be willing?

He turned his attention back to the woman. "When did they leave?"

"Just over an hour ago. The nobs went ahead on horseback with one of the others. The woman and the boy went in the coach."

That was better—only three men to deal with.

"Did you write the note, Mrs Robins?"

An angry male voice called from within the inn. "Sal, get back in the kitchen. There's customers to be served!"

A grimace crossed her face, but she ignored the summons. "The young lady asked if I could find out where they were going, and send a note. She didn't have time to say much, just while we were cleaning them up."

"Do you know any more about where they were going?" Alex asked.

"Sam, my eldest," she indicated the second young man. "Sam got talking to the driver after we sent Ben off with the note. They had to get them all to an inn on the Pett levels by eight o'clock."

"Can someone guide me there?"

"SAL!"

"I can pay for his time," Alex added.

"Ignore him," she said. "That's my brother-in-law—owns the place now my John's gone. Bark's worse'n his bite." She glanced at her son.

"I reckon I'd send Sam with you anyway, pay or no. I don't like to see young ladies and boys treated like that."

"I need to write a note. There may be someone else coming after me."

"This way, sir." She led the way into a large steam-filled kitchen, leaving him while she fetched paper, pen, and ink.

Alex scribbled a brief summary of what he'd learned, and folded the note over.

"Who's it for?" Sal asked as he handed it to her.

"It could be one of several people," Alex said. It depended on what Bella said to whoever followed. "If anyone comes asking for me, or for Miss Deane, give it to them. Mrs Robins, I can't thank you enough for your help."

She nodded as she tucked the note into her apron. "God speed, sir."

Sam awaited him in the yard, already mounted, and Stevens was ready with their own horses.

"Are we going after them, sir?" Sam asked. "I mean, do you want to try to catch them, or get to the coast before them?"

"It's the same thing, isn't it?" Alex said.

"No, sir," Sam said. "I give the coach driver directions after the nobs rode off. If he done what I said they'll take a long time to get there."

"How's that?"

Sam gestured to the clouds. "There's been a fair bit of rain around here, sir. Most of the lanes will be deep with mud."

"He's right, sir," Stevens said.

"We try to catch the coach," Alex decided.

"Yes, sir!" Sam said with a grin.

The coach lurched sideways, throwing Phoebe against the wall and sending Georges tumbling onto her. Good, they were stuck in the mud again.

"Should of made 'em walk, like I told you," Low-voice said.

"Shut your face," High-voice snarled. "It wouldn't make no difference, and the brat might of run off. If I could get my hands on that bastard what give us directions at the inn..." He spat on the floor, barely missing Phoebe's feet, then thrust his face into hers.

"You sit still, you hear?"

Phoebe nodded without speaking. Even if they still thought she did not understand English, the menace in his voice and face was clear.

"You try to get out again, like last time, and I'll gag you and tie your feet. The boy, too."

A gust of cold air blew in a spatter of rain as the two men left the coach. The gloomy sky indicated that it was late afternoon.

Phoebe listened in satisfaction to the curses, and to the sound of the rain—that would make the muddy lanes even worse. This was the fourth time they'd got mired. Each time the two men had to get out to push, or try to turn the wheels by hand to get the coach moving again. The longer their journey took, the more likely it was that Alex would catch up with them.

The acrid smell of vomit from her clothing pleased her as well; Sal had left them smelling strong enough to make Brevare's companion decide he'd ride on with him and a groom rather than share the coach. Now, when Alex came—and he *would* come—there would be only three men to deal with.

Unfortunately it wasn't long before the men got the coach back onto firmer ground. This time only High-voice got in, after some muttered complaint from the other man about the smell. Phoebe kept her eyes on the window beside her as High-voice resumed his stare. He'd touched her breasts while manhandling her out of the inn, and his hand had lingered far too long on her bottom when pushing her into the coach.

The words of Brevare's companion went through her mind again. She was to remain unharmed until milord had spoken to her. He'd followed that up with a shrug. They weren't going to let her go afterwards, that was certain.

A shot?

The noise had come from behind the carriage. She sat up straighter, hope rising as her heart began to race. Rescue?

An answering shot came from above, then another. The coach tipped to one side and came to a sudden stop. From the roof, banging and swearing was followed by the crashing of breaking branches beside the coach.

"Another man inside," Phoebe shouted, as loudly as she could.

"Shut up, you!" High-voice said, and slapped her face.

Her stomach clenched as she saw High-voice drag his pistol from his pocket, drop the window and stick his head out. She couldn't see what was happening, could only hear the grunts and cursing of men fighting outside. As High-voice raised his pistol she felt for hers, twisting to fumble her bound hands through the slit in her skirts. There was no time to try to get the pistol out. It was pointing in the right direction—she needed only to cock it and pull the trigger.

Her ears rang with the noise, the smell of singed fabric filling the coach as High-voice jerked back and swore, his pistol falling from his hand into the lane as he clutched at one arm. She flinched, expecting him to hit her again, but he shoved the door open and disappeared into the pouring rain.

"His pistol," Georges said, slipping past her and jumping down before she could stop him. She clambered out and almost fell into the ditch beside the lane. A moaning heap in the ditch was Low-voice, clutching one leg.

"Georges?" She regained her balance as she looked about her, trying to make out details in the shadowed rough grass below the hedge.

"—pistol—dropped—find—" The barely audible response seemed to be coming from close by, Georges' voice drowned by grunts and muffled curses. Phoebe moved forwards, and the moving shapes turned into two men struggling near the horses' hooves, fighting for control of a knife.

It was Alex and High-voice, and High-voice's hand held the knife. Shouts and curses came from behind the coach; whoever had come with Alex couldn't help here.

Fumbling in her skirts again, she wrenched the pistol out to the sound of tearing fabric. She cocked it, the click sounding loud in her ears.

"Don't move."

Both men froze.

High-voice didn't turn his gaze from Alex or release his hold. "You've fired it."

"I had two," Phoebe lied.

Georges tugged on her skirts. "I found his gun."

Taking it from him, she cocked it and pointed it at High-voice. "This one *is* loaded," she said.

High-voice did look round this time. As he did so, Alex wrenched the knife from his hand and sent a fist into his face. The man went limp, and Phoebe felt weak with relief as Alex scrambled to his feet.

Alex ran his gaze over Phoebe, letting out a breath of relief as he saw that she was holding the gun steady in her bound hands, still pointing it at the man on the ground—she could not be injured badly. Staying out of her line of fire, he slid the knife carefully between her wrists and sawed at the rope.

"Sam?" he shouted, keeping his gaze on what he was doing with the knife.

"Shot one, got the driver covered," came a voice from the other side of the coach.

"There were only three of them," Phoebe said, before he could ask her.

"Are you all right?" he asked as the rope finally gave way.

She nodded, face pale.

"Can you hold the gun on him a little longer?"

"Yes."

He slipped the knife into his pocket, then removed his assailant's belt and used it to tie his hands behind his back, ignoring the man's moan of pain. He took the pistol from Phoebe, and she stretched her arms and rubbed her wrists.

"Not long now," he said, and went to help Sam tie up the driver. There had been a third man, as well as his own wounded groom.

"See what's happened to Stevens, can you?" Alex said, and Sam headed back along the road.

"There's one in the ditch here," a young voice called. Alex found Georges watching a man groaning and clutching one thigh. He couldn't make out much blood, so he dragged him over to the other two and tied him up.

"Phoebe, are you sure you're not harmed?"

"A headache," she admitted. "Nothing that a hot bath and a drink won't fix."

"Thank God." Then he did what he had been wanting to since he saw her. He pulled her into his arms, trembling from the emotions he'd been keeping under tight control for the last few hours. He felt her gradually relax against him, releasing her when she gave him a gentle push.

"Georges?" she called, looking around. "Are you hurt? Come here."

Georges moved over, and she crouched down and gave him a hug. Alex could see the tracks of tears running down the boy's face.

"You were very brave," she said. "You helped to save us all!" He sniffed and clung to her skirt, but stopped crying.

"You're not hurt?" Alex asked, bending so his face was level with the boy's. Georges shook his head. "Thank you for helping," Alex said, seeing a faint smile.

He felt a hand on his shoulder, and stood.

"Are *you* hurt?" Phoebe asked.

"Nothing that a hot bath won't fix," he said. He heard her little snort of laughter—slightly shaky, but definitely laughter. Awed at her courage, he noticed a brief shudder in her shoulders.

"You two get back in the coach out of the rain," he ordered. "One of Nick's grooms was with us; I need to see what happened to him."

He watched Phoebe help Georges into the coach, and then walked back down the lane. He found Sam bending over a prostrate figure.

"Silly bugger got himself shot and then fell off his horse," Sam said.

Easing Stevens into a sitting position, Alex opened his coat. A bright patch of red stained his shirt, low down under his ribs.

"Just a graze, sir," Stevens said, gritting his teeth. "But I put my shoulder out when I fell."

"No more riding for you then. Come, we'll get you in the coach. We'll soon have you back at the Black Bull."

Sam helped Stevens to get up, lifting the groom's good arm over one shoulder, and they walked slowly back up the lane. Alex hurried ahead when he saw Phoebe still standing beside the coach.

"Do you know where they were taking us?" she asked.

"You should be in the coach," he said.

"Did you know Brevare was with them?" she asked, ignoring his comment. "At the inn. He was with another man, but they were taking me to see someone they called 'milord'. This milord must be the man Marstone is after. He's waiting for them—us—at the coast, but I don't know where."

"Pett, near Winchelsea," Alex told her, turning as Sam and Stevens reached them. "This is Sam, from the inn. He found out from the driver where they were going. Your brother and Nick should be on their way there by now." He opened the door and helped Stevens to get inside.

"They'll only be looking for me and Georges," Phoebe continued, one hand grasping his arm. "They won't be looking for Brevare and the man with him."

"I can't leave you here," Alex objected, knowing what she was hinting at. "I've got to take you back."

"You've got to catch this man!" she insisted.

His head agreed with her; his heart did not. This was the best chance they were likely to get to identify the chief traitor. But to leave a woman and a young boy alone? It was a long way back to the inn, it was still raining, and it would be dark soon.

"It's going to be difficult getting back through all this mud," Alex said.

Sam snorted. "Not if you go the sensible way, sir. It's not far to the post road. Easy after that."

421

"Stevens?" Phoebe put her head into the coach and addressed the groom. "Do you know the way back to the inn from here?"

"I reckon I could find it from the post road," he said. "But I can't drive the coach, miss!"

"I'll be driving," Phoebe said. "You'll only need to show me the way." She looked at Sam and Alex. "If you can get us to the post road before you leave?"

"It's cold," Alex pointed out. He knew she was right, but he didn't want her to be. "You'll catch your death!"

"Give me one of their coats," she said. "Or give me yours and you take one of theirs. It might help you to get closer to milord when you find him—he might think you're one of his men."

"I can't risk leaving you alone with those men," Alex said.

"Leave them here. You can come back for them later."

"It's cold," Alex said again.

"So?"

Her meaning sunk in and he gave a brief crack of laughter. "Quite right. You're sure you can do this, Phoebe?"

"You have to go," Phoebe said. Her lips were turned down, but her voice was determined.

He capitulated. If this 'milord' wasn't caught, he might make another attempt to harm Phoebe.

"Sam, are you willing for more?" Alex asked.

"Yes, sir!"

Ten minutes later, with the prisoners bound to a nearby tree, Alex helped Sam push the coach out of the ditch while Phoebe led the horses. Stevens was perched on the box, his arm in a sling fashioned from his neckcloth, with Georges beside him.

How far was it from here to Pett? If Sam knew the way, they might just reach the levels before the coach was late and the men meeting them on their guard. Phoebe was right—he had to try.

"Best lead them to the road, sir," Sam said. "It's not far, and the walk'll warm Miss a bit."

Alex saw the sense in that, and joined Phoebe, grasping the harness and helping her to lead. When they came to a wider road, Sam turned the horses. He lit one of the lanterns fastened to the front of the coach. "It'll be dark before you get back," he said, then gave Phoebe directions for reaching the inn.

"Tell Stevens as well," Alex said, and Sam clambered onto the box.

"Phoebe?"

She moved closer, looking up into his face. His arms went around her before his head told him he shouldn't.

"Phoebe, you're feeling good now you're safe?"

She pulled back slightly, nodding. "Apart from the headache," she said.

"I know the feeling," he said seriously. "It feels good—but it will wear off and you'll feel bad—frightened."

"I'd better get us back to the inn before that happens, then."

"Phoebe—"

"I *do* understand what you're telling me, Alex. We'll manage."

She would, this woman he wished were his. He pulled her closer, and her turned-up face was too much of a temptation.

Phoebe came to him without prompting, reaching to cup his face with one hand, curling the other around his neck. Their lips met gently at first, but then the pent up emotions of the last few days went into the kiss: all the longing for her he'd felt while making up to her cousin, the fear for her safety, the relief at finding her largely unharmed.

The feel of her mouth, her hand on his face and her body pressed against his own—those things would keep him warm for some miles on his way.

On that thought he lifted his head, ignoring a faint sound of protest from her, even though it almost killed him to do so. He—they —had tasks to complete.

"Be careful," he said. "If anything goes wrong, just stay in the coach. I'll check on my way back."

He felt, rather than saw, her nod of agreement.

"There are two loaded pistols inside," he added. "Stevens—"

She put a finger on his lips. "We'll manage. Come back... come back to me?"

"You ready, sir?"

Sam's voice interrupted them before he could answer, and he dropped his arms.

She touched his cheek again, then moved away, waiting by the box of the coach for him to help her up. There was no time to say more.

"Go carefully," he said again, as Phoebe set the horses into motion.

"And you." Her words were almost lost in the clatter of hooves.

Mounting up, Alex followed the coach until it rounded a bend, almost wanting an excuse to go with her. But although she was driving slowly, she was in control.

He turned his horse and spurred back down the road to rejoin Sam.

CHAPTER 51

*P*hoebe shivered. It had stopped raining, but the chill wind still carried moisture with it. She had a thin pair of gloves, but they were intended for a walk on a spring day, and the cold bit through them, numbing her fingers. The sun had set some time ago, but the clouds were beginning to clear.

That last embrace, the kiss, had warmed her through, adding to the lightheaded feeling of relief that she was out of milord's clutches. But, as Alex had warned, that sense of relief was ebbing, the responsibility for Georges and Stevens looming larger in her mind. Had sending Alex off to the coast been a mistake?

"There's another signpost," Georges said from beyond the injured groom. Screwing up her eyes, she could just make out a fingerpost showing pale against the trees behind it. She slowed to a stop.

"Stevens?"

The groom was a heavy weight against her shoulder, but he roused enough to look around. "Left here, miss. Not too far now."

Thank goodness. Another gap in the clouds allowed moonlight through, and she could see the road more clearly. She took the corner slowly—if she steered into a ditch their only option would be to wait or walk. Stay in the coach, Alex had said—the idea was tempting.

No, she had to get Georges and Stevens somewhere warm. There was no saying how long Alex would be away. She put from her mind the idea that he might not return at all.

Concentrate.

She could do this.

The trees beside the road gave way to fields, then Georges spoke.

"Look, Phoebe, lights!"

"It's the inn, miss," Stevens confirmed, sitting up straighter.

Someone must have been watching, for two shadowy figures came out into the road as Phoebe slowed the horses to a final stop.

"Sam? Mr Westbrook? Best if you drive them straight round the back."

It was Sal Robins.

"No, they went on."

"Bless me, Miss Phoebe driving?" The woman came right up to the coach, the surprise on her face showing in the light from the inn's windows. "Ben, you lead these horses round."

The second figure went to the horses' heads, and Phoebe gratefully relinquished control.

"We'll get you inside through the back, miss. No need for the folks in the taproom to gawk at you. Who else you got there?"

"My cousin, and one of the Oakley Place grooms. He's injured."

"Ben, help them get down, then see to them horses."

Ten minutes later Phoebe and Georges had been taken into Mrs Robins' private sitting room, stripped of their damp outer clothing, and wrapped in blankets. The mug of hot soup warmed her hands and insides, and the heat from the fire was beginning to thaw the rest of her.

Georges huddled closer, and she put an arm around him. He'd been incredibly brave.

"I've got Stevens in bed, miss, and the doctor sent for," Mrs Robins announced, a hubbub of talk from the taproom drifting in through the open door.

"Thank you, Mrs Robins. Make sure he sends the bill to Oakley Place."

The woman dismissed the offer with the wave of a hand. "I'll sort all that out tomorrow. D'you want him to take a look at you as well, when he comes?"

"No, thank you. He'll only tell us to keep warm and rest," she said. "If we could have something more to eat, though?"

"Right, miss." She eyed Phoebe critically. "You'd best borrow a gown of mine, miss. It won't do to be sitting around like that." A broad smile crossed her face. "It'll only fit where it touches, like, but at least you'll be decent."

Taking Phoebe into what was clearly her bedroom, she pulled out a gown and laid it on the bed. Phoebe changed, using a sash to pull the gown in at the waist and grimacing at the way her legs stuck out at the bottom.

When she returned to the parlour, her mouth watered at the savoury aroma of stewed mutton. Mrs Robins had left a tray for her, and Phoebe ate eagerly, mopping up the gravy with a thick slice of bread, then tucking into a solid slab of fruit cake. Georges, too, made short work of his meal. He seemed to have recovered from the experience—temporarily, at least.

What to do now? She should see if someone could drive them back to Oakley Place—Bella would be worried. But she was warm here, and increasingly drowsy. Mrs Robins could send a message, and then find them a bed for the night.

She shook her head—Alex was probably still on his way to Pett, riding into danger while she was wondering if she could go to sleep.

A raised voice—a man's voice—in the passageway outside roused her from a doze. A lower murmur must be Mrs Robins answering, then the parlour door opened.

"There's a Lord—"

Mrs Robins broke off as Lord Harlford pushed past her. What was he doing in Sussex?

His gaze flicked around the room and settled on Phoebe. "Miss Deane!"

"My lord," she acknowledged.

"You are well?"

"Yes, thank you."

"Where's Westbrook?"

She couldn't tell if his tone was concern or irritation. "He went on to—"

"He left you here alone?"

Why was he so concerned? He was not responsible for her in any way, and was presuming too much.

"You should not jump to conclusions, my lord," she said. He was a marquess—if he'd shown any confidence in her back in London that would have gone some way to counter the scandal, and they wouldn't have needed to come to Sussex in the first place. "I can make my own decisions," she added.

Mrs Robins spoke. "My lord, I have a—"

"Not now!" His brows drew together. "I need a carriage putting to, right away. I must get Miss Deane back to Oakley Place."

She had no say in the matter, of course.

"This inn don't own a carriage for hire," Mrs Robins said.

"What? What about the one that brought Miss Deane here?"

"If you want to take the Frenchie's carriage, that's none of my business. But I haven't got anyone to drive it for you."

"There must be someone!"

"You calling me a liar, my lord?" Mrs Robins had her hands on her hips now.

Phoebe suppressed a smile—it was clearly some time since anyone had said no to Harlford.

"My groom—he's in the taproom. Go and..."

His voice tailed off at Mrs Robins' belligerent glare. With a final glance at Phoebe, he muttered a curse and left the room.

"He means well, Mrs Robins," Phoebe said, in spite of her irritation at his manner.

"Hmph. You sure you want to go off with him?"

"Yes, it would be best to get back." She had been thinking that herself, after all. "I can't thank you enough for your assistance."

"Think nothing of it, miss." Mrs Robins glanced at Georges. "You'd best take some blankets with you. Keep warm." She gave a brisk nod. "I'll make sure Ben's putting the horses to again."

Twenty minutes later Harlford handed Phoebe into the carriage, a sleepy Georges climbing in after her. Once again she suppressed a smile as the marquess muttered about damned grooms who didn't know how to drive, and climbed onto the box. Glad not to have to talk to him on the journey, she settled herself in one corner of the coach. Georges huddled up next to her with a blanket tucked around him.

Sam reined his horse in and peered at a fingerpost, the fitful moonlight just bright enough to show the lettering.

"Have we taken the wrong road?" Alex asked. If they didn't catch up with Brevare and the other man, his abandonment of Phoebe would have been in vain. He should trust her judgement, he knew, but it still felt wrong.

"No, sir. Just checking."

They rode on, Alex finally smelling salt in the air as they came to a row of cottages beside the road. Light spilled from a building ahead. A few men entered as he watched, then he made out a sign swinging above the door. The King's Head.

"Reckon this is Pett, sir," Sam said. "The inn we want'll be further on, between here and Winchelsea. Their driver was complaining about how they might get bogged down in the marshes."

"D'you know where that inn is?"

"No, but I reckon we could ask in here."

If Bella's note had reached Deane and Nick, this inn was the most likely place they'd be, too. He put out a hand to stop Sam moving on. This was a smugglers' coast; the people here would not be forthcoming with information.

"You'll have more luck asking than me, Sam." He felt in a pocket and handed over all the coins he had. "Use what you need—but we must be as quick as we can."

"Right, sir."

Inside, the smoke-filled air made Alex's eyes water. Blinking, he spied Nick sitting by the fire, a mug of ale on the table before him. He sprang to his feet as Alex approached.

"There's been no sign of a coach here," he said, keeping his voice low. "I *think* the locals would have said—"

"She's safe," Alex said, hoping it was true.

"Thank God." Nick rubbed a hand across his face.

"She's on her way back to Oakley Place," Alex went on. "But the men responsible don't know that. We need to catch them, if possible— Phoebe is still in danger if they remain at large. They were aiming for an inn down on the levels."

"Right, yes. Deane persuaded an excise man in Winchelsea to tell us where smugglers might rendezvous—could be the inn you're talking about. Deane and two of the grooms are watching the road out of Winchelsea in case the kidnappers arrive that way." He stood and drained his mug of ale.

"Well, they won't be arriving now," Alex said. "But Deane could be useful there if anyone tries to escape in that direction."

Another man stood as they walked towards the door; Alex recognised Charlie from the stables at Oakley Place. Sam joined them as Nick and the groom tightened the girths on their horses and mounted up.

"Did you find where the inn is?" Alex asked Sam.

"Yes, sir. Down this lane for a mile or so, then look for a track off to the left. It's about a mile on into the marshes."

"That sounds like the place Deane's excise man described," Nick added, as they all spurred their horses into motion.

The smell of salt became stronger as they rode, and eventually Alex thought he could hear the roar of waves breaking on shingle. They slowed before they reached the shore, turning onto a muddy track with pools of water gleaming faintly on either side.

The going was slower here, but Alex finally made out a building, a solid shadow against the marshy land. As he looked, a brief gleam of light showed, as if a door had been opened and then closed again.

"We might have been spotted," he said, urging his horse onwards. As they neared the inn, a sharp sound made him rein in, and he glanced at Nick.

"A shot." Nick confirmed Alex's conclusion.

Two more reports sounded, and Alex spurred his horse on. There was no point in stealth now. As they approached the building, a horse and rider galloped away, soon becoming lost in the darkness.

"Sam, Nick! Catch him!" Alex shouted, and they set off in pursuit. Only one horseman had left—there should still be two of the men he wanted inside. He checked that Charlie had a gun, and sent him to the back of the building. After giving him time to get in position, Alex kicked the door open and stepped inside, pistols at the ready.

A terrified serving girl cowered in one corner. A man lay on the floor, face up—the dark pool spreading beneath him and his open, staring eyes told their own story. Brevare sat against a wall, hunched over, one hand holding his side where blood was spreading through his coat.

"Westbrook," he said faintly. Banging noises beyond the room drew Alex's attention, then Charlie entered, pushing a man before him, one arm twisted up behind his back.

"No-one else," Charlie stated. "This one says he owns the place and he doesn't know anything."

"Is that true?" Alex asked Brevare, receiving only a nod in reply. "Who rode off?"

"Milord," Brevare gasped. "His fault, he ordered..." His words faded and he closed his eyes.

Alex swore, and put a hand to the side of Brevare's neck. His pulse was strong—he had probably just swooned. Trying to revive him now would waste too much time.

"You, girl, stop this man's bleeding." He indicated Brevare, then turned to the man Charlie was still holding and pointed in the general direction the rider had taken. "Where does that track go?"

"Winchelsea."

"Anywhere else?"

The man shook his head.

"There'll be a reward if you and the girl are still here when I get back, and if he's still alive," Alex said, pointing to Brevare. "This is nothing to do with the excise men. Understand?" The man nodded. Alex stooped to search Brevare's pockets and found another pistol, still loaded.

"All right Charlie, you can let go of him. Take this pistol as well, and keep these three here until I get back." He wasn't sure the mere promise of a reward would stop the man running off.

Alex rode as fast as he dared—an injured horse would be no use to him. The track was indistinct in the fitful moonlight: glittering reflections could be puddles across the track or deeper pools. There was no sign of anyone ahead of him—the sound of the sea obliterated any hoofbeats, and riders would be merely black shapes against shadowed land.

Ten minutes later, a flurry of shots sounded somewhere in front of him. Alex resisted the impulse to speed up, praying that Deane and Nick weren't injured. It was another frustrating five minutes before a shout sounded ahead and he pulled up.

"Who's there?" the voice called again.

"Westbrook."

"Come on, sir."

As he made his way further, the outlines of riderless horses and the glimmer of a lantern became visible, then he was close enough to recognise the voices.

"Alex? Over here."

Nick was kneeling on the ground next to a prostrate body. "I hope this is who you're after," he said, "because I've just killed a peer of the realm."

Alex slid off his horse and knelt next to him. "Who is he? Are you sure he's dead?"

"Afraid so. He's the Earl of Hilvern. I didn't know he had anything to do with the Foreign Office."

"Neither did I." Damn—with the man dead, it would be difficult for Marstone to find out who else was involved. "Better dead than at large," he muttered.

"What now?" Nick asked.

"Back to Oakley Place—Marstone's been summoned there, and he needs to know this as soon as possible." He stood up, thinking what needed to be done. Get Hilvern's body taken back, swear the grooms to silence, see if Brevare was still alive, and question him if possible.

It was going to be a long night.

CHAPTER 52

*P*hoebe stared at the ceiling, which was lit only by the dying fire. When they'd arrived back here, Bella had ordered hot baths, fires in bedrooms, and hot bricks in beds for both her and Georges. She turned over, trying to empty her mind of worry, but although her head ached and her body was tired, her mind was turning over too many possibilities to allow her to go back to sleep.

Alex—was he still out in the cold night? Had he found Brevare and the others?

Those men were ruthless. They wouldn't hesitate to kill—

No!

She pulled on a robe and crossed to the fireplace. The clock on the mantel said three o'clock. A hot drink might help her to fall asleep again, or at least occupy her until the men returned.

Andrews was dozing in a porter's chair by the front door. Phoebe hesitated, reluctant to wake him, but he must have sensed her presence.

"Miss?"

"Is no-one else back yet?"

"No, miss. But I don't reckon they're late yet, if you know what I mean."

She worked out how long it would have taken Alex to get to the coast, and then to return here. With that, and the time he'd need to look for Brevare and the other man, he couldn't have been back much before now even if everything had gone well. She shouldn't worry yet, but that was easier said than done.

"I was going to get a hot drink, Andrews."

He heaved himself up out of the chair. "I'll come and make sure the range is still alight, miss."

Phoebe made tea, and sat at the kitchen table cupping the warm mug in her hands. At her nod, the butler sat nearby with his own drink. She didn't want to wait alone.

She was pouring herself another cup of tea when she noticed Andrews' head tilt to one side. Then she heard hooves and voices.

"I reckon they'll be going straight round to the back, miss," Andrews said, getting to his feet. Phoebe pulled her robe about her more tightly and followed him out of the back of the house.

The stable yard was a milling mass of horses and men, lit only by a few lanterns, but she gradually made some sense out of the confusion. That was Lord Carterton giving orders; those grooms were unloading two long packages that had been draped across the back of a horse. They looked like...

Phoebe's head swam and she gripped the door post against a sudden dizziness. They *were* dead bodies. Alex? Joe?

Across the yard, someone called an order, and her knees almost gave way in relief as she recognised Alex's voice. What about Joe?

The bodies were heaved unceremoniously into the stables. Not Joe, then—they would have treated him with more respect.

Grooms started removing saddles and leading horses away as Phoebe crossed the yard, stepping warily in the dark. The first person to recognise her was Lord Carterton.

"Miss Deane! Westbrook said you were safe—are you unharmed?"

"Yes, thank you. Where is my brother?" She was still anxious.

"He's well. He stayed behind with Brevare, but should be back tomorrow—later today, I should say."

Phoebe felt the last knot of worry disappear.

. . .

Half an hour later Phoebe was finally alone with Alex, sitting in the kitchen and watching him eat. There'd been no opportunity to speak to him alone until now. Just the sight of him brought back the memory—and the feelings—of that kiss in the dark. She inspected him as he ate, able to detect nothing wrong beyond tiredness; the eagerness with which he addressed the food before him was reassuring.

Alex polished off a slice of cold pie quickly, and drank from his mug of ale, before meeting Phoebe's gaze.

"My apologies, I was rather hungry!"

Phoebe grinned. "Really?"

At that, his face relaxed and he almost laughed. "Yes, really!" He kept his gaze on her face for what seemed like a long time. The look in his eyes sent a familiar warmth spreading down Phoebe's body, but then he looked back down at his plate with a shake of his head. He was right—this was not the time.

Unfortunately.

"Who were the... bodies? And what happened to Brevare?"

"Brevare was wounded, but not critically, I think. Deane will bring him back here in the morning. One of the bodies is the man you saw with Brevare. The other one is, according to Nick, the Earl of Hilvern."

"Hilvern?" The fat earl was a spy?

"You know him?" Alex's attention had sharpened.

"I met him at Lord Marstone's dinner. I was... not rude, exactly. I suppose you could say I outwitted him in conversation, and in front of Lord Marstone's other guests. But that cannot be why he kidnapped me."

"No. I'll go through it in detail tomorrow when Marstone gets here, but from what I managed to get out of Brevare before we left him in Pett with your brother, Hilvern was the man who'd been blackmailing him, although today was the first time he'd seen him in person and Brevare didn't know his name. And Brevare had never mentioned *your* name to Hilvern's man until he returned to London recently and discovered that you were Calvac's niece."

"That still doesn't explain why he would kidnap me."

"We'll never know for sure, but I suspect that once he found out that the dim maidservant Brevare had described was actually you— not only astute and observant but in a position to be listened to if you had obtained any information from Brevare—he must have wondered if Brevare had let anything drop that might give him away. The replacement for my decoy note said I had information about the traitor, and Brevare will have told him that you and I spent a lot of time together, so Hilvern may have thought that you already knew about him. So I imagine he wanted to find out how likely he was to be exposed, and to remove one possible source of information. Your... encounter... with him probably only made him more ruthless in attempting to find out."

"You can tell me the rest in the morning," Phoebe said, seeing him eyeing his plate again. "Eat. Can I get you something hot? Coffee?"

"Tea, if you can manage it. Thank you." Alex took another mouthful of pie while Phoebe put the kettle on the range. He finished his meal while the tea was brewing and leaned back in his chair.

"You obviously got back all right," he said. "You didn't have any trouble?"

"I took it slowly. Harlford arrived at the inn not long after we did, and drove us back here."

"He decided it was too late to come after us then?"

Her puzzlement must have showed on her face.

"I left a note in case anyone arrived later," Alex said.

"I don't remember a note—" She broke off, remembering the scene in the inn parlour. "Mrs Robins tried to give him something, I think, but he was too busy giving orders about the coach. Did it matter?"

"As it happened, not really, but he wasn't to know that."

Phoebe could see that Alex wasn't pleased. She poured the tea into mugs, handing one to him.

"I'll take this up with me," he said, standing.

"Alex, thank you." Phoebe said. "I don't know what... I mean..."

"No," he said, with a shake of his head. "It was a joint effort—I wouldn't have found you in time if you hadn't managed to delay the coach and get Mrs Robins to send a message."

He looked into her eyes for a few moments, and Phoebe thought... hoped... he was going to kiss her again. But he didn't. He kissed her hand instead, releasing it with a gentle squeeze that left her wanting more.

"Sleep well," he said. He held the door open for her, letting her precede him up the stairs.

Damn the man. Why does he have to be so honourable?

Phoebe's head still ached in the morning, but not enough to keep her in bed. The comte and Lord Marstone were already in the breakfast room when she entered, both still in mud-splashed riding dress.

"Phoebe!" Her uncle came towards her, putting his hands on her shoulders and looking her over carefully with a worried frown. "The butler told us you had both been returned to us as soon as we arrived. You are well? The message we received was rather alarming. Georges?"

"We are both well, uncle."

"And Joseph?"

"I believe he is merely delayed for some reason."

"That's good." His face lightened a little. "What happened?"

"Calvac," Lord Marstone broke in. "Can I suggest that you let Miss Deane have some breakfast?"

"*Quoi?* Oh, yes. Please sit, Phoebe. Coffee?" The comte signalled to a waiting footman and Phoebe was presented with coffee and toast.

"I understand that Westbrook and Carterton are being woken," the earl went on. "Much as it pains me to wait, it might be best if we keep our questions until everyone is present. It will save Phoebe having to repeat herself."

"Yes, quite right."

Bella and Lord Carterton came in soon afterwards, with Lord Harlford. Alex followed behind, not as pale as he'd been last night, but still looking tired and strained. Phoebe's heart warmed on seeing him, but she looked away, not wanting to give away her feelings to the rest of the company. Lord Carterton looked equally tired. Lord Harlford was almost glaring at Alex, but Alex either hadn't noticed or was managing to ignore him.

Bella sat down next to Phoebe and examined her face. "Nick told me you were well," she said. "I can't say that you look it."

"My head aches," Phoebe admitted. She lowered her voice to a whisper. "Why is Lord Harlford here?"

"He didn't say," Bella replied. "I assume the counter story spread by Lady Jesson and Lady Lyndenham's maids reached him somehow. I've more to tell you, but this isn't the place."

Phoebe nodded, and returned her attention to her toast.

When breakfast had been cleared and the door closed behind the last footman, the comte addressed Alex. "My thanks, Westbrook, for returning my son and niece. And to Harlford and Carterton for assisting."

"My pleasure, sir," Alex said.

"What exactly happened, Westbrook?" Lord Harlford asked. "How did Miss Deane come to be at that dilapidated inn on her own?"

He could have asked *her*, Phoebe thought, wondering if it was only her headache making her feel irritable.

"The details are a matter of national security," Lord Marstone said, before Alex could reply. "The fewer people who know about it, the better." He glanced at Bella as he spoke.

She stood. "I'll leave you to it then, Will," she said. "Nick? Harlford?"

Lord Carterton joined her, but the marquess did not move. The earl raised an eyebrow, but it seemed the marquess was not to be cowed as lesser mortals might be.

"I'm sorry, Harlford, but this is confidential business," Marstone said. "I wish to speak privately to Westbrook and Miss Deane."

The two men's gazes locked, Marstone's calm, Harlford's displaying rising anger.

"Oh, very well," the marquess said finally. He stood and followed Lord Carterton out of the room.

"Marstone," the comte said, when the others had left the room. "National security or not, I require an explanation for the kidnapping of my son and my niece."

"Westbrook hasn't told me yet, Calvac," Lord Marstone said. "Whatever he says, it must go no further than this room."

"Naturally," the comte said stiffly.

"Perhaps Miss Deane should begin?"

Alex watched Phoebe's face with concern as she spoke—she did look pale. Had Bella summoned a doctor? As she told of the two men in the coach his hands clenched into fists and he wished he'd done worse to them than leave them tied to a tree for hours. From the frown gathering on the comte's face, her uncle's feelings were similar.

"Westbrook?" Marstone prompted, when Phoebe had finished.

He kept it brief. Marstone listened with his usual concentration, then sat in silence, seemingly deep in thought.

"Westbrook, Miss Deane, you both did very well," Marstone said at last. "Westbrook, you and I will return to London, and we will ask Carterton to have Brevare escorted to Marstone House when Deane brings him here."

"Brevare has been communicating with your daughter, my lord," Alex said to the comte. Bella could tell him later about the attempted entrapment, but the man did need to be warned about keeping Brevare away from Hélène, if Marstone did not have him arrested for kidnapping.

The comte sighed. "It seems that Sussex isn't far enough from London to avoid trouble."

"I have an estate in Scotland that you are welcome to use for as long as you wish, Calvac," Marstone said. "My man Kellet can make the arrangements."

Alex watched Phoebe as the comte thanked Marstone for his offer, relieved to see that she didn't seem particularly distressed by her cousin's betrayal. She rubbed her head again, her eyes closing in a long blink. Alex stood and rounded the table, annoyed with himself, and with Marstone, for keeping her here when she should be resting.

"Phoebe, you look like you should be back in bed."

She looked up at him, her face pale. "Yes, sorry. I feel rather... lightheaded. Dizzy."

"You've nothing to be sorry for." He held her chair as she stood. "I'll get Bella to send for the doctor."

"Thank you."

He walked to the door with her. "I don't know when I'll... this business of Marstone's..." He was babbling. "We need to find the people Hilvern was working with, or blackmailing, as soon as possible."

"Be careful," she said, putting one hand on his arm.

"I will," he said, knowing it was most likely a lie.

She smiled, and he stood watching as she climbed the stairs.

"Westbrook?"

Marstone still sat at the table, drinking coffee.

"We're for London?" Alex asked. Whether he should return here afterwards was a question for later.

"The sooner the better." Marstone stood, some sympathy in his gaze. "I'll borrow Carterton's carriage. You can get some sleep on the way."

"Phoebe?"

Phoebe opened her eyes to see Bella sitting on the end of her bed, the room filled with light.

"I thought you might like some tea." Bella gestured to the table by the window, set with tea and a plate of sandwiches. "Doctor Morrison will be here to see you in an hour."

"Oh." She sat up cautiously and took a deep breath. "How long was I asleep?"

"Several hours."

It wouldn't do to sleep all day—she'd spend the night awake if she did. She stood, cautious in case the dizziness returned but, although she felt rather wobbly, her head *was* feeling much better. She smoothed her gown and tidied her hair as best she could, then sat at the table with Bella.

"Your brother is back. He wants to see you, if you're feeling up to it, before he goes back to London with Brevare. Marstone and Westbrook went back—"

"He's gone already?" A silly comment—she'd known he had to go, and the matter was urgent.

"Marstone said he needed him to help sort out unfinished business. You *did* mean Alex?"

Phoebe nodded, not yet awake enough to decide whether she wanted other people to know of her feelings.

"I thought so," said Bella with satisfaction. "He sent his... best wishes. He's not the only one absent, though. You may be pleased to learn that your aunt and cousin—Hélène, that is—have both decided they are feeling unwell and will spend the day resting in their rooms."

"They are ill?" Phoebe asked, concerned. She didn't like her aunt, but she didn't wish her ill.

"Embarrassed, more likely," Bella said with a laugh. "Madame, in particular. I wish you'd been there yesterday."

"Yesterday?"

"When Hélène and Alex were walking in the garden, she encouraged us all to admire the view of the south lawn from the parlour window—wanting us as witnesses to Alex and Hélène spending far too long alone together in the summerhouse. That was until it became apparent that Alex wasn't going to go in and compromise the little widgeon, at which point she tried to distract our attention."

"So *she* could say she'd seen them?" Phoebe didn't find that surprising.

"Yes. Then Harlford arrived, and she seems to have decided that an actual marquess was a better proposition than the heir to an earl, and she started talking about how Alex had compromised you after all—"

"Leaving Harlford for Hélène?"

Bella nodded. "Maria gave her a copy of a peerage and told her to look up Marstone's entry."

"No Westbrook mentioned there?" Phoebe felt a bit guilty at the amusement she felt. "And there's a significant difference between 'eldest son' and 'heir'?"

"Exactly. Oh, you should have seen her face when she worked it out, and realised what a laughing stock she'd be if it ever got out that she'd attempted to entrap Marstone's natural son."

Rather than laugh, Phoebe was surprised to find herself actually feeling a little sorry for her aunt.

"Now, Phoebe, don't think ill of me for enjoying her confusion. My father was a tyrant—worse than your aunt, because he had all the power. It still encourages me to see people like that bested. And it was necessary—now Maria Jesson has something to hold over her, to make her stick to the story we agreed a few days ago. I don't think you'll have to put up with her for much longer."

"Oh?"

"You are welcome to stay with me for as long as you wish—here, and when we return to London. That's one possibility. The other is Harlford. He is still here, and wants to speak to you as well."

Phoebe sighed. "He did help last night. I suppose I should see him."

"I suspect you are about to get a proposal of marriage." Bella raised an eyebrow at Phoebe's grimace. "You're going to say no?"

Phoebe rubbed her face, then nodded. She hadn't thought about it recently, but there was no question of accepting. Not after that... not now.

"Harlford is the catch of the season," Bella went on. "Why are you going to turn him down?"

Phoebe regarded her warily. "Does it matter?"

"I'm interested!" One corner of her mouth turned up. "I suppose saying that I'm prying would be more accurate."

Phoebe couldn't help a snort of laughter escaping.

"We would not suit," she said. That wasn't quite true—she had been increasingly enjoying his company over their last few outings, but friendship was not enough.

"I think you would, in time. He's intelligent, means well, and you couldn't do better for rank, money, or looks."

"I know," Phoebe admitted. "I did wonder if I was being foolish. But those aren't the most important things to me."

"And you care more for someone else. Love someone else, even?"

Of course Bella knows.

"Will Alex come back?" Phoebe asked.

"Not of his own volition, I think. Or at least, not yet."

"Why not?" she asked, even though she suspected she knew the answer.

"In his own words, young ladies of the *ton* do not marry bastards, even the bastards of earls."

Phoebe shook her head. "Are all men such fools?" This one was a fool that she loved, though. She would just have to convince him that she cared nothing for what the *ton* thought.

"Most of them are, in one way or another," Bella said. "Some more than others. He'll come round to the idea that you don't care about his birth or the effect it might have on you, but it may take some time. However, my brother may take a hand."

"Lord Marstone? Why?"

"I don't know what he will do, but I suspect he would like to see you and Alex together."

Phoebe's doubt must have been evident in her face.

"Partly to make the pair of you happy," Bella said. "He may also see some advantage to himself in the match. He can be a master manipulator at times, but he does mean well. I think you don't need to worry about chasing Alex down."

"You make me sound like Hélène, or my aunt."

"No, no." Bella said, "not the same at all. Now, shall I tell your brother he can come in?"

CHAPTER 53

*P*hoebe drew her pelisse about her tightly. The air still had a nip to it, but this seat in the corner of the formal garden was sheltered from the breeze. Turning her face up to the warmth of the afternoon sun, seeing its glow through her eyelids, she breathed the scent of damp earth as the sound of birds twittering filled her ears.

Joe hadn't stayed with her long—he'd wanted to check for himself that she was well before taking Brevare back to London. The doctor's visit, too, had been brief; his verdict was that no permanent damage had been done but she should rest for a few days and send for him if she felt dizzy again.

She'd go up to the nursery later, to see how Georges was getting on, but Alice would be looking after him well. For now, she was enjoying the fresh air—and the peace that came from the knowledge that her aunt and Hélène were still keeping to their rooms.

The world went dark. She opened her eyes to see Lord Harlford standing in front of her, blocking the sunlight.

"May we talk, Miss Deane?" he asked, stepping to one side. With his back to the sun, she couldn't make out his expression.

She had to have this conversation at some point, so it may as well be now. And it would be less awkward out here than closeted in a private parlour.

"Shall we walk, my lord?" She stood as she spoke, and took the arm he offered.

"Are you well, Miss Deane, after your ordeal yesterday?"

"Yes, thank you. A little tired, still, but that will pass."

"Good."

They walked on a few paces, then he stopped and turned to face her, his gaze fixed on her eyes.

"Miss Deane, I have come to admire you greatly over the last few weeks, and enjoyed our time spent together. Will you do me the honour of accepting my hand in marriage?"

Although Bella had suggested that Lord Harlford was going propose, Phoebe hadn't expected him to come out with it so quickly. But she knew what she had to say.

"Thank you for your kind offer, sir. I am truly honoured, but we would not suit."

A small crease formed between his brows. "I think we would suit very well, Miss Deane. You are intelligent, and capable of conversing on matters beyond gowns and balls. Would you not enjoy the benefits that would come from being my marchioness?"

Phoebe looked up at him, her head tilted to one side. "You wish me to wed you for your rank and wealth? My lord, there are any number of women who would marry you for those reasons."

"They would bore me to tears within a se'nnight."

She looked away, not wanting him to see her expression. It was not terribly flattering to be admired only because she could make sensible conversation. However, she was glad his affections were not truly engaged—she did enjoy his company, and would have regretted hurting his feelings.

He offered his arm again, and they walked on. She thought that was the end of it, but he stopped again when they came to an ornamental fountain.

"Miss Deane, as my wife, you would want for nothing. I would look after you, not expose you to the perils that have come your way through your association with Westbrook. You will not be put in such danger again, or expected to take such risks."

He was in earnest, offering what he thought she wanted. There was no point arguing, but she had to convince him that she was not going to change her mind.

"I would wish to marry for love, my lord. I hold you in great esteem, but I do not love you, and you have said nothing about loving me. I realise that such sentiments are not common in people of your station, but *I* do not need to be ruled by those conventions."

"Affection can develop, can it not?" he asked, the crease forming between his brows again.

"It can, sir. But my affections are already engaged elsewhere."

"I see."

She turned, and started to walk back to the house. After a few steps, he caught up and walked beside her, the silence between them tense.

"It is Westbrook, I suppose?" he said, when they were half-way back.

He was looking straight ahead, his posture rather stiff. Was he offended?

"Does it matter who it is?" she asked.

He glanced down at her with a wry smile. "It should not, Miss Deane. I'm afraid that my male pride is suffering from having been of so little practical use when you were abducted, that is all."

That was surprisingly honest, and she liked him better for it. "Only due to circumstances, my lord. You didn't know who had taken me, or why. Mr Westbrook suspected I might be taken to France, and planned accordingly."

"Thank you for that."

They walked on for a while in silence, but now it did not feel quite so awkward.

"May we remain friends?" he asked.

"Thank you, I would be honoured." It *was* an honour for him to say such a thing. "May I ask you a favour?"

He looked wary, and she chuckled.

"Do not be alarmed, sir. It is only to escort me to the Black Bull. The woman there played an important part in rescuing me—I wish to thank her. But I don't think it advisable to travel around the countryside with only a groom in the light of what happened two days ago."

"It will be my pleasure, Miss Deane. Will tomorrow suit? Then I must return to Town."

They strolled on in companionable silence.

Phoebe found her uncle waiting for her when she returned from the Black Bull the following afternoon.

"Phoebe, could you come in here, please?"

She followed him into the room and, at his gesture, took a seat by the fire. He sat without speaking, head slightly bowed, one hand pinching the bridge of his nose.

"Is something wrong, sir?" Phoebe asked, concerned.

"Nothing on the scale of recent events, no." He drew in a breath. "Let us deal with the more pleasant item first. Harlford asked to speak to me yesterday while you were asleep. He asked permission to ask for your hand."

Phoebe nodded.

"You don't appear surprised. Has he already spoken to you?"

"Yes, sir. I declined."

"I thought you might. He is a good man, Phoebe."

"Yes, sir, but I do not love him." Was he going to ask her to change her decision? No, there was no hint of disapproval in his face or voice.

The comte nodded. "When we discussed this earlier, you said there was someone else you preferred. This person is Westbrook, I assume."

Phoebe felt heat rise in her face. "Yes, sir." Did everyone know her business?

"Yet he has gone off with no plans to return, as I understand it."

"Indeed, sir." She looked down at her hands, thankful now for Bella's earlier frankness. "He thinks his... his birth would be too much of a stigma. According to Lady Carterton, at least."

"In addition to his way of life being wholly unsuited to taking a wife."

She had been thinking about whether Alex returned her feelings, not considering any practical aspects of a possible future. It was only in the last few days that she'd thought there might be a real chance of some kind of life together.

Looking up, she met her uncle's eye. "His way of life is little different from that of an officer in the army, or the navy."

He leaned back in his chair, his gaze making her shift uncomfortably in her seat.

"Phoebe, you will be of age at the end of the year, and I suspect that if I were to forbid any union with Mr Westbrook, you would just wait until your next birthday."

"I... He..." She raised her chin. "Yes, sir."

To her surprise, he smiled. A small smile, but he appeared to be amused more than anything else. Then his face sobered again.

"You are old enough, Phoebe, and sensible enough, to consider carefully before you take any irrevocable step. I think that Westbrook has not yet said anything to you, but if he does, and you have given the matter proper thought, you will have my blessing."

Whatever she had expected him to say, it wasn't that. He didn't wait for her response, but carried on.

"The other matter concerns Marstone's offer to use his Scottish estate. I intend to accept this offer, and I have already written to tell him so. We will be leaving in a couple of days."

"For Scotland, sir? So soon?" The comtesse would not be pleased at missing most of the season. Nor would Hélène.

"I had a talk with Hélène earlier, and your aunt. They inadvertently let slip their attempt to entrap Westbrook." He pinched the bridge of his nose again. "I do not wish Hélène to marry anyone who has to be forced to the altar in such a way, and the fact that Lady Carterton thought it necessary to set up—"

He broke off, shaking his head. "Suffice it to say, I think it best to make a fresh start next season."

"Very well, sir."

449

"Lady Carterton has invited you to stay here at Oakley Place, and go with her when she returns to London."

Spending the season with Bella would be more enjoyable than it had been so far, but the prospect of a continuing round of balls and other social activities was not enticing.

"On the other hand," the comte continued, "I would enjoy your company in Scotland, as would Georges and Miss Bryant. I do not require your decision on this matter now, but please give it some thought and let me know tomorrow."

"I will, thank you, sir."

"Yes, well. Family, Phoebe, family."

Phoebe slept late the following morning, but Bella was still at the breakfast table when she went downstairs.

"A letter for you," Bella said as Phoebe sat down. "It is from my brother."

Phoebe broke the seal and scanned the page, then read it again carefully.

"Lord Marstone has offered me, and the rest of the family, passage to Scotland by ship," she said. "As a safer means of travel, given that he has not yet traced all the traitors within his department. If the rest of my family decline, he recommends that I still accept his offer. Joe will come with me, to keep to the proprieties."

Bella's eyebrows rose as Phoebe spoke. "Do you think your aunt and uncle will accept?"

Phoebe laughed. "No, certainly not. He says the *Lily* will take us—the vessel that brought us back from France. It only has two small cabins, and my aunt was sick all the way across the Channel."

"You'd be perfectly safe on the road," Bella said sceptically. "Unless you're being watched here, but in that case you'd be in just as much danger getting to Dover as you would be setting out for Scotland."

"No watchers would expect me to be going by sea, though, or to be heading south."

"They would watch the house," Bella said, shaking her head. "No, I think there is a different motive entirely here."

"Oh?" Phoebe had her own idea, but perhaps she was being too fanciful.

"Lieutenant Deane may not be your only escort," Bella said. "And it is rather difficult to run away when you are at sea."

"You think so?" she asked, hope rising in her.

"It's a definite possibility," Bella said. "Knowing my brother."

"It would seem a bit like trapping Alex," Phoebe said, thinking of Hélène's recent behaviour.

"Not in the slightest," Bella said, her tone brisk. "It will give you a chance to explain your side of things. Alex will come to his senses eventually; this will just expedite matters."

Phoebe wasn't sure she believed her, but she wasn't going to turn down an opportunity of talking to Alex—assuming Bella's supposition was correct.

∼

Alex sat in Marstone's library, wanting a brandy but knowing the coffee steaming gently in front of him would be far more useful. Next to him, Kellet summarised the results of a frantic twenty-four hours of enquiries. Across the desk, Marstone listened carefully, his fingers steepled and resting on his lips.

"...Chambers has checked, too, and both can account for all the critical documents we had not already brought here. There is only Fanshawe's office to..."

Brevare was upstairs in bed, his minor wound having turned him feverish. The doctor said he would recover, but in the meantime an armed footman was guarding his door. When questioned, Brevare had readily confirmed that the dead man Alex had found at the inn was the one who'd met Phoebe at the Black Bull, but that was the only useful information they had obtained. Brevare didn't even know the dead man's name, although Alex suspected that Marstone did.

By the time Marstone had finally given up, Alex was fairly sure that Brevare really didn't know more. He was beginning to have some sympathy for Brevare—Hilvern had proven himself to be both ruthless and dangerous. Marstone—or his wife—would make sure the vicomtesse and Suzanne were taken care of, and probably wouldn't deal too harshly with Brevare who had, when it came down to it, acted in a way that he thought would protect his family. His treatment of Phoebe wasn't very different from the behaviour of most men of his class towards what he considered the lower orders.

"...bankers at Hoares and Coutts will need persuasion from someone higher than me to check for suspicious transactions..."

Alex had never seen the London side of Marstone's operation in action. Within half an hour of their arrival the day before, the house was almost empty of staff as Kellet dispatched them to call on friends in the households of people on a list Marstone had written in the coach. Hilvern did not work in the Foreign Office, therefore he must have collaborators, willing or unwilling, who did. And once news of Hilvern's death got about, some might flee with information to buy themselves sanctuary in France.

"...rely on gossip or hearsay if the people involved are merely clerks..."

Kellet finally wound down, and Alex asked the question he'd been wondering about for the last couple of days. "Didn't you have any suspicion of Hilvern, sir? Phoebe met him at one of your dinners, I understand."

"No, to my shame," Marstone said. "I invited him for his political views—almost guaranteed to be the opposite to most of the men I call friends. But I've never considered him much more than a pompous windbag."

"And therein lay his advantage."

"Indeed. And we have yet to find out how far his activities spread. Now, I've another task for you, unless you would like a few days to recover?"

Some time off would be good.

"You could go back to Oakley Place," Marstone continued, without waiting for a reply. "Much more relaxing than hanging around here."

Phoebe would still be there. He wanted to see her again, but not if she'd accepted an offer of marriage from Lord Harlford. He did his best to banish that idea from his mind.

"No?" Marstone said. "Well, the other will let you get some rest as well. There's a packet I need to be delivered in person to the governor of Gibraltar—the *Lily*'s ready for you at Dover. I've a few things for you to do tomorrow, but you can be on your way in the afternoon."

CHAPTER 54

"$\mathcal{W}$elcome back, Miss Deane," Trasker said, appearing at Phoebe's side as she stepped onto the deck of the *Lily*. His cheery grin faded as he greeted Joe.

"This way, miss." Owen picked up her trunk and led the way down into the narrow corridor. "Nice to have you on board again. Can I get you some refreshment?"

"Tea, if you please," Phoebe said. She'd eaten her fill only an hour before when they'd stopped at an inn.

Although she had been sitting for most of the day, the captain's cabin was far more restful than the jolting coach, and Phoebe took her time drinking her tea. Joe joined her, holding a sealed packet and a roll of charts, and sat down across the table from her.

"A letter?" Phoebe asked.

"Sealed orders," Joe said. "Not to be opened until I was on board." He broke the seal, revealing another sealed packet and a note.

Leaning across the table, Phoebe saw that the second packet had 'Only to be opened at sea' written on it. "What does the letter say?"

"We are to await another passenger." He looked up at Phoebe, frowning. "The passenger is not to know you are on board until we have cleared the harbour."

Phoebe smiled, a strange mix of happiness and apprehension rising in her. She'd resolved to enjoy this voyage with Joe even if Alex did not come, but she was very pleased to find that Bella's guess had been correct.

"Are you going to tell me what's going on, Fee? There's a locked box as well, not to be opened until my other sealed orders permit."

"I don't *know* any more than you told me," Phoebe said. "Anything else would just be supposition. Will Trasker know when the extra passenger is due? Do you think you need to warn him not to say anything about me?"

"I suppose so," Joe said. He gulped the rest of his tea and left again.

Back in their cabin, Ellie had finished unpacking the few things they would need that night. There was no room to unpack more—she would have to live out of her trunk while they were on board.

"Come on deck and look around," Phoebe said, picking up the boat cloak that Joe had lent her. Ellie put her coat on and followed her up the steps. The wind felt even stronger than it had on the quay, blowing spumes of foam from the tops of waves beyond the breakwater. Beneath a thin sheet of cloud, the setting sun gave a warm glow to the castle walls above the harbour. Phoebe walked to the rail and looked over, glancing back when she realised that Ellie had not joined her but was standing with her back to the mast, the corners of her mouth turned down.

"Looks a bit rough, don't it, miss?"

"I'm sure they won't set off if it's dangerous," Phoebe said encouragingly. "You grew up by the sea, didn't you?"

"Yes, miss, but looking at it from the shore baint the same as looking at it from 'ere."

"You've never been out on a boat?"

"No, miss."

"Well, this will be a good experience for you, like visiting London!" Phoebe said bracingly, feeling a little guilty that she hadn't asked Ellie if she minded accompanying her.

Ellie looked unconvinced, and soon went below to get out of the wind. Phoebe rather liked it, as long as Joe's boat cloak kept her warm.

The wind was from the north-east, bringing a distinct chill with it, although Joe had been pleased as it would speed their voyage along the Channel.

Half an hour later she was almost cold enough to go below, the little warmth from the sun gone as it neared the horizon. She crossed to the rail nearest the shore for a last look at the town. Carriages and carts had been moving on the quay all the time she had been on deck, loading and unloading crates and barrels; now her eyes fixed on a man carrying a small trunk along to one of the waiting boatmen. The light was too dim, and the man too far away, for Phoebe to see his features, but she recognised him even so, and felt suddenly breathless.

Remembering Joe's instructions, she walked over to the companionway, standing to one side as crewmen swarmed up from below, some going to the halyards at the foot of the mast and some preparing to weigh the anchor. Trasker must have recognised him too, and would be wasting no time getting under way.

It was far too early to go to bed, so she took a book from her trunk and lay on the top bunk. She didn't read, but wondered what exactly she would say to Alex when she saw him. Finally she told herself sternly not to worry about it. The words would come.

Alex breathed in the salt air, and the smell of seaweed and fish. It made a nice change to be boarding the *Lily* for a voyage without the prospect of danger. Perhaps Marstone was right, and it would be a chance to relax. At this time of year, the Mediterranean warmth would also be welcome.

How much more pleasant it would be, though, to have a companion. Watching the activity on the *Lily* as the boatman rowed them closer, the things he'd been contemplating in the coach came to mind again.

He didn't want to spend the rest of his life running around Europe at Marstone's behest. The novelty had worn off years ago, but it wasn't until those few days with Phoebe in France that he'd realised how different such a life—or any life—could be with a trusted partner. One particular trusted partner.

Phoebe would be a companion and friend as well as a lover and a wife; after that kiss in the rain, he was in little doubt that she wanted him too. The kiss could have been merely the reaction to another terrifying day, but he didn't think so. Deciding that he should stay away from her for her own good went against one of the many things that he admired about her—her ability to make her own decisions.

The boat bumped into the *Lily*'s hull, and he hoisted his trunk up and scrambled aboard. Trasker greeted him briefly as he reached the deck, and led the way below.

"The lieutenant's in here," he said pushing open the door to the main cabin. Phoebe's brother was examining a chart spread out on the table.

"Deane?" I didn't expect to see you here."

Deane glanced up, then stood up straight. "Westbrook?"

"The lieutenant's been sent to check up on me," Trasker said, his voice flat.

"Well, you've never taken the *Lily* as far as Gibraltar before," Alex said.

Trasker grunted, slamming the door behind him as he left the cabin.

"Gibraltar?" Deane said. "We're—" He closed his mouth with a snap.

"I've a packet to take to the governor," Alex explained.

"Oh. Yes… well, Trasker's about to get under way, so I'm needed on deck. Owen will get you some food." He ran a hand through his hair and reached for his hat. "We can sort it out in the morning. It's the same course for a while, whoever is right about our destination."

Deane left, and by the time Alex had taken his coat off, Owen had arrived with a plate of his usual stew and a bottle of wine. Alex ate, wondering why Deane didn't know their destination. Never mind— he'd find out soon enough. He poured another glass of wine and sat with it, swaying gently with the familiar motion of the ship.

Phoebe.

When he got back to England, he'd go to Oakley Place, or follow her to London, or Scotland if Calvac had taken up Marstone's offer. They should at least discuss the possibilities.

If she hadn't already accepted Harlford, that was. But if he was right about her feelings for him, she would not accept the marquess. His Phoebe would not be dazzled by title and wealth.

He might be laying himself open to a rejection, but it would be cowardly to not even ask. If he didn't ask, he definitely wouldn't get what he wanted. And he'd been certain for some time that Phoebe was the one woman he *did* want, and love.

On that thought, he took himself to bed.

Alex slept soundly and, for the first time in a week, awoke feeling well rested. He lay staring up at the base of the top bunk, listening to the creaks and groans of the *Lily* in motion, and the rush of water past the hull.

Last night he'd noticed another trunk next to his own on the floor of the tiny cabin, but had thought no more about it. The trunk was still there, and now he could see 'Lt Deane' stencilled on it—he must have slept through both Deane retiring to his bunk and getting up this morning.

More importantly, there was a perfectly good cabin across the narrow corridor, so there must be another passenger besides himself and Deane. As Deane was here, could that passenger be…?

No—he could see no reason why Phoebe would be sent to Gibraltar.

Ready for some breakfast, he shaved, peering awkwardly into the tiny mirror fastened to the bulkhead, and changed into a fresh shirt.

He pushed open the door to the day cabin and froze.

Phoebe was eating breakfast with her brother, and looked up with a smile, as if nothing were out of the ordinary. He clamped down on the sudden rush of happiness. What he wanted to say, he wasn't going to say in front of her brother.

"Good morning," she said cheerily.

She looked wonderful.

"I'm sure Owen will be bringing some more coffee," she said. "You slept well?"

"I... er... good morning." He cleared his throat. "Very well... I mean, yes, I slept well, thank you." He'd wanted to talk to her, although he hadn't expected it to be so soon. But the sight of her firmed his resolve—the sooner the better. "Why are you here, Phoebe?"

"Joe is escorting me to Scotland," she said. "Or Gibraltar."

"How did you know about Gibraltar?" Deane asked.

"The cabin walls are thin," Phoebe said. "I heard you last night." She lowered her voice. "Ellie is still in bed next door, not feeling well."

Alex shook his head, and sat down where a third place was set across from Phoebe. Owen came to fill his cup and put a bowl of porridge in front of him so he began to eat—he needed something in his stomach before he could work out what was going on here. While he was eating, Deane reached into an inner pocket and took out a sealed packet.

"The next set of orders?" Phoebe asked with interest.

"Next set?" Alex asked, content to deal with this minor mystery first.

"Joe opened his sealed orders last night," she said. "This next packet was with them, not to be opened until we were on our way."

"From Marstone?"

Deane said nothing, breaking the seal and unfolding the paper. A small key fell out onto the table.

"He's very good," Phoebe said approvingly. "I would have opened all of them straight away."

"That's why women aren't in the navy," Deane muttered.

"Well, what does it say?" Phoebe asked, ignoring this comment. "Are we going to Gibraltar or Scotland?"

Deane looked at his orders again, scratching his head.

"Well?" Phoebe asked.

"It says that you and Westbrook will tell me where we're going," he said, more quietly than before. "And there's a letter for each of you in the trunk." He shook his head. "What the hell is going on here?"

"Who gave you the orders?" Alex repeated. "Marstone?"

"Yes—I thought I was supposed to be taking Phoebe to Oban, and also assessing how well the *Lily* and her crew are suited to longer voyages. No-one said anything about Gibraltar. Why did you think—?"

"Marstone gave me a packet for the governor there, to be delivered in person. Perhaps those letters you have will clarify things?"

Deane grunted, and squeezed around the end of the table to go to his cabin. He brought the little trunk back with him and set it on the table. Alex and Phoebe peered in with interest when Joe unlocked it and lifted the lid. There were several more sealed letters inside, on top of a dozen books.

Deane handed one letter to Phoebe, and passed him the second, sitting down to open a third. Watching, Alex left his own letter on the table, noting with some amusement that Phoebe had done the same. Deane's brows rose as he read, his expression smoothing when he finished. He folded the letter and tucked it into a pocket. "Aren't you going to open yours?" he asked, looking at Phoebe, who was calmly sipping her coffee.

"No. What did yours say?"

"I'm not supposed... I can't tell you. Just read yours, Fee," Deane pleaded.

Phoebe shook her head.

"Westbrook, what does yours say?"

Alex, with porridge and several cups of coffee inside him, was beginning to think more clearly. "I think I'll leave mine sealed for a while too," he said. If Marstone was making this kind of mystery of Deane's orders, he was up to something. He wanted to talk to Phoebe without Marstone's plans getting in the way.

"They're orders—" Deane protested.

"We're not in the navy, Joe," Phoebe said.

Deane turned to Alex. "You work for Marstone."

"Not in the way you work for the Admiralty," Alex said.

"But we need to know where we're going."

"How soon do you really need to know?" Alex asked. "Last night, you said the course would be the same for a while."

Deane thought for a moment. "Not until we near Start Point, I suppose. This evening, if this wind holds; tomorrow if it drops."

"I'll open my letter before you need to change course," Phoebe promised. "Will that do? I want to talk to Alex first," she said. "Without that," she poked the letter disdainfully, "without whatever *that* says interfering."

She really *was* a mind-reader at times.

"So talk."

"Alone."

"I can't leave you… I mean, your maid…" As if on cue, there was a retching sound loud enough to be heard through the cabin wall.

"I don't think Ellie's a good sailor," Phoebe said.

Alex caught Joe's eye. "We could go on deck, Deane," he offered, as a spatter of rain dashed against the window.

"Oh, very well, stay in here." Deane gave in with poor grace. He drained the last of his coffee and got to his feet. "I'll make sure Owen keeps you supplied with coffee," he said. "At frequent intervals!"

CHAPTER 55

*P*hoebe gazed at Alex as the door closed behind Joe. She'd been encouraged by the mixture of pleasure and surprise on Alex's face when he first walked into the cabin; now she felt butterflies in her stomach. There was a lot at stake.

"Do you really have a message for Gibraltar?" she asked, starting with an easy question.

"Yes." He leaned back against the bulkhead. "Why did you think you were here?"

"Marstone said I needed to be protected, and it would be safest if I went to his estate in Scotland by sea. But Bella thought there might be another reason." Phoebe stopped, wondering if she was about to make a complete fool of herself. "She… she said that it was difficult to run away when you were on a ship."

"I wasn't running away. Marstone needed me in London."

"You weren't going to come back, though, were you?"

"Not if you were…" His words faltered. He fiddled with his coffee cup before looking back up at her, his face set. "Phoebe, did Harlford ask you to marry him when he was at Oakley Place?"

"Yes, but I turned him down." She could see some of the tension leave his face as she spoke.

462

"It would have been a good match for you."

"Except for the fact that he thinks he knows what is best for me, like most men—even Joe. No, I want more from life than financial security. When it came down to it, that was all I would have gained from Harlford."

"Have I been deciding what is best for you?"

"No." She bit her lip—that wasn't quite true, and this discussion needed honesty. "Mostly not," she amended.

"I realised that," he said, his face still serious.

"You stayed away because 'young ladies of the *ton*—'"

"—do not marry bastards," he finished for her, with a shake of his head. "Not only was I deciding for you, I was letting other people's opinions make the decision."

"You were going to come to talk to me, though?" she asked.

"Yes, as soon as I was back in England."

Phoebe couldn't help chuckling. "Marstone," she explained, not wanting Alex to think she was laughing at him. "He went to all this trouble to get us together, and you were going to see me again anyway."

"Ha, yes." Finally, he smiled. He looked at the sealed letters, still lying on the table. "I suspect there's more to it than just ensuring I can't run away," he added.

"That can wait," Phoebe said, pushing them to one side. "What were you going to talk about when you caught up with me?" He hadn't actually asked her to marry him, but she was now sure he wanted to. Why else would he have avoided her earlier for the reasons he gave?

He leaned back again, a wry smile on his face. "I hadn't got as far as working out exactly what to say," he admitted. "Apart from asking you what *you* want. Did you enjoy your season?"

"What there was of it, yes." She looked him in the eye. "It's not enough, though, and the thought of doing the same things, with mostly the same people, year after year..." She shook her head. "Alex, my parents were happy without all that. They loved each other, they worked together, and they used their skills to help people. I want a life like that, where I can learn things, and use what I know."

Aware that her voice had risen while she talked, Phoebe took a deep breath and sat back in her seat. Was he worried that she would grow tired of a life with him—a life beyond the society her uncle frequented? "You like being useful?" she asked.

Alex nodded.

"I do, too. Ever since my parents died I've not been useful. I've been tolerated, at best, by my aunt. My uncle was... distant until we were back in London. Harlford is a good man, I think, and pleasant enough, but he only asked me because he needs an heir. That's not what I want."

"You wouldn't be received," Alex said, the words coming out before he realised the implication. "I mean," he added hurriedly, "if—"

"I'd be received by the people I like," Phoebe interrupted. "And the people who won't want to know me—I think I'd be quite happy not to know them."

He owed it to her to point out all the pitfalls of a possible life together, although he was happy to have his points dismissed so easily.

"I spend a lot of time—" He broke off as boots clattered along the corridor outside, and the door opened.

"Well?" Deane asked. "Have you decided to open your letters yet?" He glanced at them, his brows drawing together. "It's stopped raining," he went on. "If you haven't finished talking yet, you can do it on deck."

Alex hadn't noticed the lightening sky outside—there were even a few patches of blue. Deane's gaze was almost a glare.

He suppressed a smile as Phoebe glared back. "Joe, what exactly do you think we are going to do in a tiny cabin like this with no lock on the door? Besides, we can't open the letters on deck—spray would make the ink run."

Deane glared at them, but finally gave in. "Oh, very well." He turned on his heel and left, pointedly leaving the door open.

Alex went to close the door, but instead of resuming his seat, he went to stand before the stern window. His pulse accelerated as

Phoebe came to stand close to him, her shoulders almost touching his. He caught the faint scent of her hair.

"Phoebe..." Reaching out, he captured a few stray strands and tucked them behind her ear. The smile she gave him as he did so took his breath away.

"I love you, Phoebe, you must know that."

Her nod and smile were clear, and she briefly put her hand to his cheek. She said nothing—she could hear the 'but' coming, no doubt.

"Why do you want... why me?" he asked. "Most people would say I'm a bad bargain, especially for someone like you."

She didn't answer him immediately, her gaze sliding away and becoming unfocussed. "You... you were kind when you gave me back my sketchbook. You rescued us from Perrault and me from Sarchet—"

"I don't want your gratitude," he interrupted harshly.

"More importantly, though," she went on, meeting his eyes, "you treated me like a person, you let me help, you didn't assume I couldn't do things because I am a woman, you let me judge for myself what I thought I could or couldn't do."

He saw the shine in her eyes as she looked aside again. "No-one has done that since my father. I felt as if we were working *together* to do something important." Her eyes met his. "I don't think feelings—love—can be explained, really. But as far as they can, that's why."

He swallowed a sudden lump in his throat. She *did* love him then. He'd thought—hoped—she did, but hearing her say so affected him more than he'd expected.

There were still the disadvantages of his situation to point out. He'd seen enough other marriages descend into indifference or outright hostility—he didn't want that to happen to them. Love was not always enough.

"I'd be away on Marstone's business a lot—"

"So are army officers, and naval officers. Other women put up—"

"I don't want you to have to 'put up' with anything." It wasn't much of a life for the women left at home, although the idea that she was willing to do so warmed him. But that wasn't what he wanted, either.

"Are you going to carry on doing the same kind of thing?" she asked. "I thought you couldn't go back to France for a while?"

"I don't know what Marstone wants." He'd said nothing about what Alex was to do after this trip to Gibraltar. "I suppose I could go back to work at Pendrick's."

She must have seen something in his expression, his doubts about such a boring life. That had as little appeal for him as the social season did for her.

"You'd do that?" she asked, then shook her head. "Shall we see what Marstone's letters say?"

He turned and leaned on the table. Picking up his letter, he broke the seal and unfolded the single sheet. When he looked up again Phoebe had finished reading her own letter.

"Marstone wants to thank me for helping get your list back to him," she said. "He'll give me a good dowry if my uncle won't, and make sure we can afford a nice house."

He didn't need her dowry—and Marstone knew that. From her expression, Marstone's offer was as unattractive to her as it was to him.

She looked at his letter. "What bribe is he offering you?"

He smiled—the offer did sound like a bribe. "He seems to think that I didn't like working at Pendrick's because I wasn't in charge. So he's going to set me up with my own import business. It will be a safe place for agents to take refuge, and he's offered me the *Lily* so I can organise transport as well." He refolded the letter and tossed it onto the table.

"That would be a useful job," she said. "It is also a job that almost anyone could do."

Her words mirrored his thoughts so exactly that she surprised a crack of laughter out of him. "You know, your habit of mind-reading can be rather disconcerting at times!"

"You don't want that, do you?" She looked straight into his eyes. "Alex, what *do* you want?"

You—in my life, in my arms...

"When I was trying to find Brevare's family in France," he said, "I wanted you." He put one hand behind her head, his thumb stroking gentle circles in her hair.

"I wanted you as a partner, to talk things through with you, to work things out together. As well as this…" He leaned towards her, and she turned her face up to his, her lips parting slightly. That was enough encouragement, and he bent his head towards hers.

"Westbrook!" Deane's voice made them both jump.

"Go away, Joe," Phoebe said crossly, but she pulled away from him all the same. "And yes, we've opened our letters, and no, they do not say where we are to go."

"But do you agree to the proposition in the letter?" Deane asked.

Alex caught her quick glance his way, and shook his head. Marstone would not have gone to the trouble of organising this trip on the *Lily* merely to get someone to co-ordinate agents. Her quick smile showed she'd worked that out as quickly as he had.

"No, we don't," Phoebe said. She peered into the little trunk as Joe unlocked it, recalling the books she'd seen earlier. Joe removed a bundle of papers, handing another letter to Alex.

"What are those books?" Phoebe asked.

Joe didn't reply, his eyes on Alex as he read the letter.

"Did your orders tell you not to let me see them?" she persisted, irritated.

"No." Joe waved a hand towards the box. She lifted out the volumes to read their spines. There were several dictionaries and books of grammar—Portuguese, Spanish, and Italian. That promised a more interesting offer in the latest letter.

Alex's brows rose as he read, then he handed the letter to her without comment. She read it through twice, keeping her expression bland in spite of the excitement building inside her.

"Well, what does this one say?" Joe asked impatiently.

"It says that it is not unknown for merchants' wives to accompany them on trading voyages," Phoebe said. "And that a ship fitted out as a fast privateer could safely investigate trading options in the Mediterranean while also being useful in other ways."

Joe looked from her to Alex as he worked out the implications. "But you're not a merchant's wife."

"I will be if a merchant asks me."

"What merchant?" He glanced at Alex, who was regarding him patiently. "Oh. Good grief—give me a hurricane or a ship of the line to fight off—it would be far simpler!"

Alex looked at Phoebe, a smile beginning on his face. "Are you sure?"

"Yes—if you are." She could restrain her own smile no longer.

"We accept this offer, Deane," Alex said, putting the letter back on the table. "Now what?"

"Thank God for that!" Joe pushed a final packet of papers over. "Does that tell us our destination?"

Alex opened the packet, and handed back a single sheet that was addressed to Joe.

"Ashmouth," Joe said, shaking his head. "For a few days only, then on to Gibraltar."

"You'd better go and let Trasker know," Phoebe suggested. There were things they had to say, but not in front of her brother.

Joe hesitated, then flushed slightly. "Oh, yes. Sorry." He turned back as he left the cabin, about to say something.

"Let me propose in peace, will you, Deane?" Alex said impatiently.

Joe shrugged and left.

"Why all that rigmarole with the letters?" Phoebe asked, when Joe left. Does Marstone usually complicate things like that?"

Alex shook his head. "Not for operational matters—the more complex something is, the more there is to go wrong." He read through the letter again, then laid it on the table. "This isn't a safe option, in spite of what this letter says."

"You're not going to tell me it's too dangerous for me, are you?"

He gave a wry smile. "I'm trying hard not to," he admitted. "I suspect it was so he could say he hadn't forced you... us... into this option."

"He could have given us both options at once."

"Forget about Marstone." He stood up and pulled her towards him. "Phoebe, I love you. Will you be my wife and my partner?"

"Yes, please!"

She moved into his arms, tilting her face up, but just holding him close at first. She felt the same warmth flood through her as their lips met, travelling right down to her toes, but this kiss was better than the others, and with the promise of more to come. One of his hands tangled in her hair, the other pressed on the small of her back, pulling them together. She curled her arms around him, pulling him closer still, feeling the play of his muscles as he moved.

Alex finally moved back, taking her shoulders and gently pushing her back a step.

"Phoebe, stop," he pleaded, his breath coming hard. "We can't do this now."

She sighed, her heart gradually slowing. "I suppose not," she said regretfully, but didn't let him go. "We might get interrupted."

"Interruptions or not, I'm not going to risk…"

He looked down at her, drawing in a breath. "I suspect there is a special licence in Marstone's packet. I know it's only a few days, but if something were to happen in the meantime… I could fall overboard. I'm not risking leaving you with—"

Phoebe silenced him with a kiss, then stepped back, releasing him with reluctance

"Shall we see what else Marstone sent us then? To help pass the time?"

When Joe came back into the cabin half an hour later, with much clearing of his throat in the corridor, they were sitting side by side at the table, a map of the Mediterranean spread out before them. And if there were not quite enough hands visible above the table, he very sensibly did not say anything.

EPILOGUE

Northern Mediterranean, September 1793

The dusk air was still pleasantly warm as the *Hermès* sailed into Ajaccio, on the western coast of Corsica. A tricolour flag flapped lazily in the breeze as men swarmed up the rigging to take in the sails, and it dropped anchor beneath the citadel. The captain appeared to be in no hurry, and it was not until the following morning that boats were sent ashore for water and supplies.

Unusually, most of the crew stayed on board. The owners, a Monsieur and Madame Blanchet, explained to the port authorities that the sailing master was going to take their vessel to a suitable beach so her hull could be scraped.

If the harbour master thought it odd that such a new-looking vessel should need weeds removing already, he was soon distracted by Madame Blanchet's pretty smile, her wonderful red hair, and her enquiries about accommodation. He managed to pay attention to Monsieur for long enough to give him the requested list of the local wine merchants and vineyards.

Over the following weeks, the Blanchets could be found touring the island. The vineyard owners plied them with their best wines, and

Monsieur made some of them happy by buying a lot of their stock and promising to return the following year.

Madame enjoyed tasting the wines too, and was so friendly with the wives, and interested in their lives and their children, that many of them found themselves confiding in her far more than they meant to. Madame and Monsieur were obviously loyal subjects of France, but they did have some sympathy for the Corsicans whose country had been occupied by the Genoese for centuries, before being sold to the *ancien régime* and conquered by French armies less than thirty years before. When they were less than discreet about their distaste for their French masters, Madame promised to say nothing with such a friendly smile that they believed her—and heeded her warnings that it would be better to say nothing at all about this conversation to anyone, not even their closest friends and neighbours.

The Blanchets returned to Ajaccio in mid-October, and the *Hermès* sailed out of the harbour, its small cargo hold loaded with wine and cases of local cheeses and cured meats.

Gibraltar, October 1793

Alex walked up the street, the wooded slopes of the rock towering above him on the right, finally reaching the old monastery that was now the governor's residence.

Merchants were not often granted direct access to the governor's home, but the butler recognised him from earlier in the year and showed him into Sir Robert's office. The men following with a cartload of wine were helped to unload their burden, and provided with refreshment before returning to their ship.

Sir Robert asked Alex to sit, and a footman brought over a tray with decanter and glasses before bowing himself out of the room.

"Success, Westbrook?" Sir Robert asked, pouring a glass for each of them.

"I think so, sir," Alex said, taking a sealed report out of his pocket and laying it on the table. "There is a general feeling that a change would be welcome amongst the merchants and minor landowners.

Paoli's assertions to Admiral Hood that the populace support him do not appear to be exaggerated." Taking a sip of brandy, he rolled the fiery liquid around his mouth in appreciation. "We don't mix in the highest levels, you understand?"

"At least, not in your current role," Sir Robert gave a short laugh. "Details in that, I suppose?" he went on, indicating the letter.

"Yes—some useful contacts, too. Marstone hasn't authorised me to tell you any more than the gist."

The governor nodded. Alex guessed from his demeanour that such confidentiality was usual.

"And the *Hermès*? No problems with her?"

"No. The crew is settling in well. Some aren't too happy with not being allowed their normal runs ashore, but if we supply enough casks of ale and rum they don't seem to mind too much."

"Good, good." Sir Robert settled back in his chair. "Denning's made a list for you," he went on. "General stuff, shipping, privateers about, and all that. Make sure you pick it up before you go. And let him know anything else you've spotted."

"Thank you, I will."

Sir Robert handed Alex a letter. "Orders."

Turning it over, Alex noted Marstone's crest in the seal before putting it into his pocket.

"There's a soirée tomorrow evening," Sir Robert went on. "Bring Mrs Westbrook. In fact, why don't you both stay here while you're in Gibraltar? It must be more comfortable than a ship's cabin."

Alex glanced around the room, taking in the luxurious furniture and thick carpets. It would make a nice change from the *Hermès*. On the other hand, they could take a room in a hotel for a few days, which would allow them have time to themselves without having to be sociable and spend time with their host.

"The soirée, yes, with thanks. We'll still be resupplying tomorrow, even if my orders send us on our way again soon." He rose to his feet. "As for staying here, it would attract too much attention—you don't invite other merchants to stay. I do thank you for the offer, though."

The governor poured himself another drink. "Yes, well. Good luck with whatever… I suppose I should say 'good trading'—ha!"

They shook hands and Alex left, heading back to the harbour via several hotels.

The *Hermès* looked like a laundry when Alex returned. Clearly, Sal Robins had managed to acquire enough fresh water to wash clothing properly; everything from undergarments to dresses hung from lines strung across the waist of the vessel. He pushed his way through the wet fabric and down into the stern cabin, where he was rewarded with the sight of his wife's bottom in the air as she knelt over a bucket, a towel on the floor beside her.

"Phoebe?" he asked in sudden anxiety. Was she ill?

The worry vanished as she lifted her head, dripping water onto the floor. Of course, fresh water also meant a proper hair wash after weeks at sea.

He turned and locked the door, removing his coat and waistcoat and hanging them on the back of a chair. Phoebe sat back on her heels and watched him approach, a knowing smile curving her lips. His pulse accelerated as he took the rinsing cup from her hand. Running his fingers through her hair, he finished pouring the clean water through her curls until all the soap was out. Then he sat on the floor behind her and pulled her into his lap, drips of water soaking cold into his shirt. He picked up the towel and worked it through her hair, rubbing until it was only damp.

"New orders?" Phoebe asked, leaning back against him.

"Hmm." Reaching around her, his fingers toyed with the fastenings down the front of her gown. "You seem to have got your dress wet—can't have you sitting around in wet clothing."

He began to unfasten the buttons, his cheek close to hers as he leaned over her shoulder to see what he was doing, his breath warm on her skin.

"Where are we going next, then?" she asked.

She shifted slightly, making it easier for him to reach the tapes beneath the buttons, that familiar ache starting deep inside her before he'd even got down to skin. She could feel his interest through all the layers of her skirts.

"Marstone seems to think the Knights may be in need of Corsican wine, and Miss Fletcher could use some Maltese lace," he said. "But we've plenty of time to restock and give the crew some time ashore."

Moving his hands up to her shoulders, he began to push the tops of her sleeves down. "I've taken rooms for us in the Hotel George for a few nights," he added.

Her breath came faster as the gown slid off her shoulders and he started to unlace her stays.

"You think the hotel might be a bit more comfortable than here?" she asked, twisting round to face him.

He leaned down, his face very close to hers. "Possibly, but we are here now," he whispered against her lips, and she laughed.

"I think you're a bit over-dressed for that..." she said, pulling his shirt out of his breeches.

HISTORICAL NOTE

The French Revolution is familiar to many romance readers due to the *Scarlet Pimpernel* and other tales involving the rescue of aristocrats from what is called the Reign of Terror.

Although some historians consider the Reign of Terror as beginning in late 1792 with the September Massacres, the victims then were almost all common criminals. The wholesale arrest and execution of those who opposed the interests of the poor—including the nobility—did not start until the autumn of 1793, which is months later than the setting of this story.

Readers may also have heard of the Committee of Public Safety. This body was formed in April 1793, and became the effective government for some years. The Committee of General Surveillance, which Alex claims to be working for when he first confronts Perrault, was a similar body that later worked alongside the Committee of Public Safety.

AFTERWORD

Thank you for reading *Playing with Fire*; I hope you enjoyed it. If you can spare a few minutes, I'd be very grateful if you could review this book on Amazon or Goodreads.

Playing with Fire is Book 3 in the Marstone Series. Each novel is a complete story with no cliffhangers.

Find out more about the Marstone Series, as well as my other books, on the following pages or on my website.

www.jaynedavisromance.co.uk

If you want news of special offers or new releases, join my mailing list via the contact page on my website. I won't bombard you with emails, I promise! Alternatively, follow me on Facebook - links are on my website.

ABOUT THE AUTHOR

I wanted to be a writer when I was in my teens, hooked on Jane Austen and Georgette Heyer (and lots of other authors). Real life intervened, and I had several careers, including as a non-fiction author under another name. That wasn't *quite* the writing career I had in mind!

Now I am lucky enough to be able to spend most of my time writing, when I'm not out walking, cycling, or enjoying my garden.

THE MARSTONE SERIES

A duelling viscount, a courageous poor relation and an overbearing lord—just a few of the characters you will meet in The Marstone Series. From windswept Devonshire, to Georgian London and revolutionary France, true love is always on the horizon and shady dealings often afoot.

The series is named after Will, who becomes the 9th Earl of Marstone. He appears in all the stories, although often in a minor role.

Each book can be read as a standalone story, but readers of the series will enjoy meeting characters from previous books.

SAUCE FOR THE GANDER

Book 1 in the Marstone Series

A duel. An ultimatum. An arranged marriage.

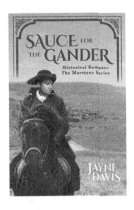

England, 1777

Will, Viscount Wingrave, whiles away his time gambling and bedding married women, thwarted in his wish to serve his country by his controlling father.

News that his errant son has fought a duel with a jealous husband is the last straw for the Earl of Marstone. He decrees that Will must marry. The earl's eye lights upon Connie Charters, whose position as unpaid housekeeper for a poor but socially ambitious father hides her true intelligence.

Connie wants a husband who will love and respect her, not a womaniser and a gambler. When her conniving father forces the match, she has no choice but to agree.

Will and Connie meet for the first time at the altar. As they settle into their new home on the wild coast of Devonshire, the young couple find they have more in common than they thought. But there are dangerous secrets that threaten both them and the nation.

Can Will and Connie overcome the dark forces that conspire against them and find happiness together?

Available from Amazon on Kindle and in paperback. Read free in Kindle Unlimited. Listen via Audible, audiobooks.com, or other retailers.

A WINNING TRICK

A Winning Trick is a short novella, an extended epilogue for *Sauce for the Gander*.

What happens three years later when Will has to confront his father again?

It is available FREE (on Kindle only), exclusively for members of my mailing list. Sign up via the contact page on my website:

www.jaynedavisromance.co.uk

If you don't want to sign up, a paperback is available on Amazon.

A SUITABLE MATCH

Book 2 in the Marstone Series

Both are seeking a suitable match. Just not with each other.

England 1782

Lady Isabella is bound for London, in search of a husband. While excited at being free of her father's ruthless control, her joy is overshadowed by knowing her aunt will arrange a match that will benefit her father. His requirements are for a title and influence—not the things a young girl dreams of.

All is not lost. Bella is no stranger to subterfuge, and she knows her brother will help her avoid an unwelcome union. But when he is called away on urgent business he asks Nick Carterton to stand in for him.

Nick, a reserved scholar who relishes the quiet life, has avoided marriage for years but is finally giving in to his father's request he seek out a bride. Keeping a headstrong miss in check is not the way he'd choose to spend his time. Instead of looking for a wife, he finds himself accompanying Bella on a series of escapades around the city. Meanwhile, Bella's eye lights on a totally unsuitable young man. It seems neither is set for matrimony any time soon.

A more than suitable match is right in front of them... if only they could see it.

Available from Amazon on Kindle and in paperback. Read free in Kindle Unlimited.

PLAYING WITH FIRE

Book 3 in the Marstone Series.

Phoebe yearns for a love match like her parents'. Revolutionary France is not where she expected to find it.

France 1793

Phoebe's future holds little more than the prospect of a tedious season of balls and routs, forever in the shadow of her glamorous cousin and under the critical eye of her shrewish aunt. She yearns for a useful life, and a love match like her parents'.

But first she has to endure the hazards of a return home through revolutionary France. Her aunt's imperious manner soon puts them into mortal danger.

Alex uses many names, and is used to working alone. A small act of kindness leads him to assist Phoebe's party, even though it might come at the expense of his own, vital mission in France.

Unexpectedly, as he and Phoebe face many dangers together, his affections grow for the resourceful and quick-witted red-head, despite their hopeless social differences. Alex dismisses the possibility of a match between them, not realizing that she feels the same way about him.

Before they can admit to their affection for each other, they must face the many difficulties that lie ahead.

Available from Amazon on Kindle and in paperback. Read free in Kindle Unlimited.

THE FOURTH MARCHIONESS

Book 4 in the Marstone Series

He's looking for a suitable wife. She's looking for a traitor. It could be a most unusual courtship.

England, 1794

James, Marquess of Harlford, wants nothing more than to be left alone with his scientific research. Unfortunately his mother is determined to see him married and with an heir to secure the succession. Faced with a house party of her selected candidates, he finds himself drawn towards the least likely—and most thoroughly unsuitable—of the guests.

While the other ladies are fluttering their eyelashes, Alice Bryant is sensible, kind and intelligent. Although he knows little else about her, James decides that Alice would do nicely as his wife.

For Alice, an out-of-work governess, taking up a position as a lady's companion would be ideal—if that was all the post entailed. Espionage, no matter how righteous the cause, sits ill on her conscience.

Alice does not wish to believe that the seemingly honourable and increasingly attentive Lord Harlford is capable of treason, but it's her duty to find out if he really is selling secrets to the enemy.

They could make an ideal match… if not for the espionage. Can love prosper, or will deceit and subterfuge carry the day?

Available from Amazon on Kindle and in paperback. Read free in Kindle Unlimited.

THE MRS MACKINNONS

England, 1799

Major Matthew Southam returns from India, hoping to put the trauma of war behind him and forget his past. Instead, he finds a derelict estate and a family who wish he'd died abroad.

Charlotte MacKinnon married without love to avoid her father's unpleasant choice of husband. Now a widow with a young son, she lives in a small Cotswold village with only the money she earns by her writing.

Matthew is haunted by his past, and Charlotte is fearful of her father's renewed meddling in her future. After a disastrous first meeting, can they help each other find happiness?

Available on Kindle and in paperback. Listen via Audible or AudioBooks.com.

AN EMBROIDERED SPOON

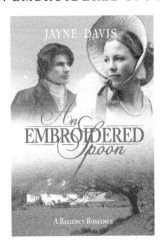

Wales 1817

After refusing every offer of marriage that comes her way, Isolde Farrington is packed off to a spinster aunt in Wales until she comes to her senses.

Rhys Williams, there on business, is turning over his uncle's choice of bride for him, and the last thing he needs is to fall for an impertinent miss like Izzy – who takes Rhys for a yokel.

Izzy's new surroundings make her look at life, and Rhys, afresh. But when her father, Lord Bedley, discovers that the situation in Wales is not what he thought, and that Rhys is in trade, a gulf opens for a pair who've come to love each other. Will a difference in class keep them apart?

Available on Kindle and in paperback. Listen via most retailers of audio books.

CAPTAIN KEMPTON'S CHRISTMAS

A sweet, second-chance novella.

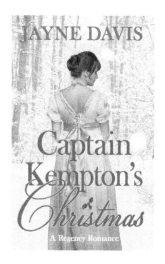

Lieutenant Philip Kempton and Anna Tremayne fall in love during one idyllic summer fortnight. When he's summoned to rejoin his ship, Anna promises to wait for him.

While he's at sea, she marries someone else.

Now she's widowed and he's Captain Kempton. When they meet again, can they put aside betrayal and rekindle their love?

Available on Kindle and in paperback.

Made in the USA
Coppell, TX
30 May 2021